Master of Hells

"Twice now I have been denied the realm that is mine to rule—once in ancient Siluvanede, and a second time at Myth Glaurach. This city is the seat of my third realm, Malkizid, and here I will raise a mighty kingdom indeed. All I need is time, time to master more of your mythal lore, time to build my armies again."

"You need not fear that possibility, Sarya," said the devil-prince. "With the right mythal spells, you could stand a siege of centuries within Myth Drannor's ruins."

"I have spent ages uncounted buried in traps and prisons! I am not going to simply sit within these crumbling ruins and allow my enemies to contain me here forever."

"Then you must destroy Evermeet's army. Since you cannot reach them where they are now, perhaps matters will turn to your advantage if they place themselves within your reach."

Seemingly defeated on the battlefields of the
High Forest and Evereska, Sarya Dlardrageth's
daemonfey legion has gone to ground.
As some among the elf defenders ponder a peaceful return
to Evermeet, others realize that the war for the souls of
all elvenkind is far from over.
Sarya hasn't been defeated, she's gone to the one place
she'll feel most at home, a ruined city that holds
the secret to true power.

Myth Drannor.

FORGOTTEN REALMS®

THE LAST MYTHAL
Forsaken House
Farthest Reach
Final Gate

Realms of the Elves
Edited by Philip Athans

Also by Richard Baker

R.A. Salvatore's War of the Spider Queen, Book III
Condemnation

The City of Ravens
The Shadow Stone
Easy Betrayals

STAR·DRIVE
Zero Point

From Wiley Publishing
Dungeons & Dragons for Dummies
(with Bill Slavicsek)

FORGOTTEN REALMS®

FARTHEST REACH

THE LAST MYTHAL
BOOK II

RICHARD BAKER

FARTHEST REACH
The Last Mythal, Book II

©2005 Wizards of the Coast, Inc.

All characters in this book are fictitious. Any resemblance to actual persons, living or dead, is purely coincidental.

This book is protected under the copyright laws of the United States of America. Any reproduction or unauthorized use of the material or artwork contained herein is prohibited without the express written permission of Wizards of the Coast, Inc.

Published by Wizards of the Coast, Inc. FORGOTTEN REALMS, WIZARDS OF THE COAST, and their respective logos are trademarks of Wizards of the Coast, Inc., in the U.S.A. and other countries.

All Wizards of the Coast characters, character names, and the distinctive likenesses thereof are property of Wizards of the Coast, Inc.

Printed in the U.S.A.

The sale of this book without its cover has not been authorized by the publisher. If you purchased this book without a cover, you should be aware that neither the author nor the publisher has received payment for this "stripped book."

Cover art by Adam Rex
Map by Dennis Kauth
First Printing: July 2005
Library of Congress Catalog Card Number: 2004116904

9 8 7 6 5 4

ISBN: 978-0-7869-3756-1
620-96706000-001-EN

U.S., CANADA,	EUROPEAN HEADQUARTERS
ASIA, PACIFIC, & LATIN AMERICA	Hasbro UK Ltd
Wizards of the Coast, Inc.	Caswell Way
P.O. Box 707	Newport, Gwent NP9 0YH
Renton, WA 98057-0707	GREAT BRITAIN
+1-800-324-6496	Save this address for your records.

Visit our web site at **www.wizards.com**

For Alex and Hannah

I didn't know anything until you came along

Acknowledgements

My thanks to Phil Athans for his trust and
encouragement in tackling this ambitious story,
and to Steven Schend and Eric L. Boyd for the
great pieces of this tale they left buried in half a dozen
Realms books going back almost ten years now.
Thanks to my good friend Warren Wyman, a first-class
sounding board for just about every problem I've run
into for the last couple of years, as well as fine company
on many long, steep walks around Mount Rainier.
Finally, a special thanks to Ed Greenwood
for his generosity with his valuable time and his
beloved world. We've all had it backward for years;
Elminster's privileged to know Ed,
not the other way around.

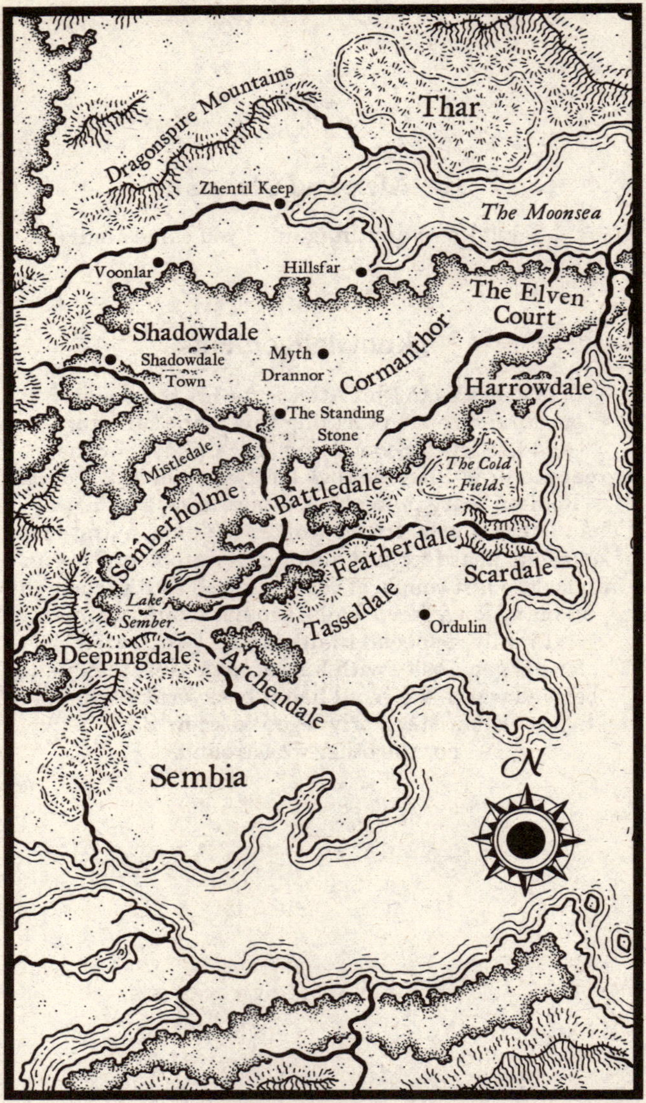

Dragonspire Mountains
Thar
Zhentil Keep
The Moonsea
Voonlar
Hillsfar
The Elven Court
Shadowdale
Shadowdale Town
Myth Drannor
Cormanthor
Harrowdale
The Standing Stone
The Cold Fields
Mistledale
Semberholme
Battledale
Featherdale
Scardale
Lake Sember
Tasseldale
Ordulin
Deepingdale
Archendale
Sembia
N

PROLOGUE

26 Kythorn, the Year of Doom (714 DR)

In a gentle summer rain shower, Fflar Starbrow Melruth and his company fought for their lives on the outskirts of Myth Drannor. The streets of the Sheshyrinnam—the Temple Ward—were choked with blood-maddened throngs of gnolls whose battle cries sounded like the barking and snarling of hyenas. Towering mezzoloths, insectoid fiends armed with heavy iron tridents or simply their own sickle-like claws, waded through the feral gnoll warriors to reach the elven ranks.

"There are too many, Fflar! We cannot reach the tower!" cried Elkhazel.

The sun elf swordsman was not generally given to despair, but Fflar could hear the hopelessness in his voice. All morning long the armsmen in Fflar's command, a sturdy company of Akh Velar infantry, had fought alongside many others to repel the assault on the Temple Ward. But the evil warriors came on without a break, heedless of their own lives.

"We cannot abandon Crownfrost!" Fflar replied. "The arms-major is still fighting inside!"

He turned away from Elkhazel to meet the attack of a pair of axe-wielding gnolls. He cut one down with a quick drop and thrust into the warrior's midsection, deflecting the blow with an expert turn of his left-hand dagger. The other simply disappeared into the confused melee. Unfortunately, Elkhazel was right—there *were* too many foes, more savage warriors and hellspawned fiends than Fflar could have imagined in the whole world. So many gnolls lay dead or dying in the street surrounding Fflar's company that the elves could not form ranks or fight the battle of maneuver that might have favored their quickness and skill over the gnolls' brute strength.

Only forty yards ahead of Fflar's embattled company, the pale walls of Crownfrost Tower rose over the streets. Home to one of the city's wizard schools, it held no great secrets that Fflar knew of—but it happened to be a strongly built building on the city's outskirts. As such, the fiendlord commanding the enemy horde had chosen to launch his assault on that part of the elven city by seizing Crownfrost. Arms-Major Olortynnal had had no choice but to deny it to him. Somewhere in the tower Olortynnal and a small company of elite bladesingers and champions fought to repel the horde's attack, but the press of gnolls, mezzoloths, and other foul warriors had surrounded Crownfrost, keeping the elf armsmen outside from going to the aid of their commander.

We need a better plan, Fflar thought.

He stepped back from the front ranks, searching for some alternative, some order he could give that would change the character of the fight. As long as his soldiers were under assault from nearly all sides at once, there was little he could do.

He glared at Crownfrost, so near, and yet so unattainable, and to his surprise he spotted a pair of elves fighting desperately on the broken battlements—Arms-Major

Olortynnal himself, commander of Cormanthyr's army, and his second, Arms-Captain Selorn. Mezzoloths attacked the two recklessly, coming on despite horrible wounds, and nycaloths flapped ponderously in the air above the tower, closing in for the kill.

"Fflar! The arms-major!" Elkhazel called.

"I see him," Fflar answered. He didn't know how he could help the beleaguered champions, but he had to do something. Shouting a war cry in Elvish, he dashed forward into the line again, and hurled himself against the press, slashing and cutting on all sides as he struggled step by step for Crownfrost.

By the random opportunities of battle, or by the fury of his own counterattack, Fflar found a narrow space around himself.

"Follow me!" he called, and pressed ahead.

When next he found the chance to look up to Crownfrost, he saw a nycaloth alight behind Selorn and cleave the arms-captain to the breastbone with its heavy axe. The blow crumpled the warrior to the ground at one stroke. Olortynnal half turned to meet the new threat. With his back unguarded, the mezzoloth that had been in front of him stepped close and jammed the points of its trident between the elflord's shoulders. More weapons flashed, and blood splattered the wet stone of the tower's top. The arms-major sagged, only to be seized by the nycaloth and hurled down from the battlements with a shout of infernal triumph.

"Arms-Major!" Fflar cried.

Olortynnal struck the white flagstones of the street only a few feet from Fflar and lay still, his sword Keryvian clattering from his loose fingers. The gnolls all around Fflar hooted and yipped, shaking their weapons in delight, while the young captain stared in dismay at the broken body of Cormanthyr's great champion.

"Olortynnal. . . ." he said.

A gnoll standing near the fallen elflord stooped and split the dead arms-major's skull with its battle-axe. It howled in delight and shook its gory weapon in the air. Fflar's momentary horror vanished in an instant, replaced by a white-hot fury. Without even knowing how he did it, he hurled himself through the remaining gnolls and rammed the point of his long sword through the breastbone of the gnoll that had struck the fallen Olortynnal. The creature spun away, Fflar's blade lodged in its heart, and wrenched Fflar's sword from his hand.

Gnolls all around the young captain snarled with hate and moved in, axes and maces raised. Fflar found himself standing astride Olortynnal's body, wielding only a dagger in his left hand.

At least I will die defending a great champion, he told himself.

Then his eye fell on Keryvian, the arms-major's sword.

Quick as a fox, Fflar discarded his dagger and stooped to pick up Keryvian. It was a heavy hand-and-a-half sword of arcane blue steel, its edges slightly wavy, its hilt worked in the shape of a blue dragon's head and wings. Whether it was meant for him or not, he was in need of a sword, and better that he should take it than leave it to be stolen by gnolls or broken by demons.

A brilliant azure gleam sprung from the blade as his hand touched the hilt, and a cold steel voice seemed to whisper in his mind. *I am Keryvian, last of Demron's blades. I will not fail in my strike, warrior.*

Fflar nearly dropped the weapon in astonishment, but he was already in mid-swing, a wicked uppercut that sliced through the throat of the nearest gnoll and ended by cleaving the snoutlike face of a second one standing nearby. Keryvian burned with holy fire, and Fflar wheeled to face any other gnolls nearby.

They were backing away from him, yellow eyes fixed on the mighty sword. Fflar's soldiers cried out in acclaim, and surged forward to drive off the savage warriors, cutting down any who did not run. A great shadow fell over Fflar, and he looked up to see the nycaloth who had slain Selorn spiraling down toward him, great black wings spread wide, axe dripping in its claws.

"Get away from my prize, fool!" the monster bellowed. "I slew him. I claim his arms!"

Keryvian burned bright in Fflar's hands, and the captain raised the sword above his head in a high guard. The big warblade felt as light as a willow switch in his hands, and he could feel it burning with holy wrath against the infernal creature approaching. Fflar met the master with a grim smile.

"There is no prize for you here, hellspawn!" he called to the nycaloth. "Come any closer, and I will send you back to the foul pits from which you crawled!"

The nycaloth roared in wrath and plummeted down on Fflar. Despite his defiant words, terror knotted his chest—but then Keryvian spoke again in his mind.

I will not fail in my strike, the sword promised.

CHAPTER ONE

*30 Tarsakh, the Year of Lightning Storms
(1374 DR)*

The high mage's summons found Araevin Teshurr in his workroom, quietly making ready to leave Tower Reilloch. He was just finishing with the last of his spellbooks, efficiently stowing them in a well-warded magical trunk, when the lilting voice of Kileontheal, last surviving High Mage of Reilloch Domayr, whispered in his mind.

Mage Teshurr, please join us in the great hall, she said. *We would speak with you.*

Araevin looked up at the interruption, and a flicker of impatience tightened his brow. He had frankly hoped to avoid this leave-taking, when it came down to it. But no elf wizard declined a summons from a high mage, let alone a roomful of them, and he knew that Kileontheal was not alone. He sketched a graceful bow to the empty air. "I will come," he replied.

That is the second time this year I have been called to the great hall by the high mages, he observed. They are beginning to make a habit of it.

He shook his head and placed the last spellbook in the trunk, closing and locking it with a whisper of powerful magic. Then he straightened and surveyed the workroom with a long, slow gaze. For better than eighty years Araevin had belonged to the Circle of Tower Reilloch, earning the right to call himself Mage, as well as the respect of his fellows. But the time had come for him to leave his studies there.

He caught a glance of his visage in a mirror hanging by the door, and smiled without humor. He looked the same as he had the day he first set foot in the tower, a tall sun elf with a long, sparely built frame, and an intelligent, inquisitive expression to his bronzed face. But his eyes were colder than they used to be, and there was a hardness to his demeanor that hadn't been there only a few months ago. After arduous travel, great battles, and deadly peril in the wildernesses of Faerûn over the past four months, Araevin had become as sharp and unyielding as a blade of fine elven steel, as if fate had conspired to hammer out of him the ease of his former life.

He did not like the way that felt.

"Enough delay," he told the face in the mirror. "I am not so important that I can expect high mages to wait on me."

But Araevin took one more moment to touch his hand to his chest, running his fingers across the smooth purple gemstone that lay embedded there. The *selukiira* of Saelethil Dlardrageth was invisible to any but a wizard's eyes, and it lay concealed beneath his clothing, but Araevin found that he was hesitant to appear before Kileontheal and the others with the stone on his person.

They will notice if I do not bring it, he decided.

He frowned into the mirror again then slipped out the door, locking it behind him with another word of power. Even though Tower Reilloch was arguably one of the best-defended places on Evermeet, Araevin had acquired a very active sense of caution of late. Only a few months before, the daemonfey had proved that even a wizards' tower in Evermeet was not beyond attack.

Araevin strode easily through the familiar halls, strangely ill at ease on the day of departure. But the Queen's Guards who stood watch before the hall's doors of blueleaf and mithral greeted him amiably enough, and admitted him to the high mages without hesitation.

Bright sunlight filled the great hall, streaming in through the simple glass panes of the dome overhead. The high hall had been virtually demolished during the daemonfey raid against Tower Reilloch, but in the hundred days since the battle, artificers had worked long and skillfully to repair the battered chamber. The dome was not yet set with magic theurglass—that was the work of years, not months—but for the time being mundane glass served well, filling the elegant hall with slanting rays of warm spring daylight.

"Ah. Welcome, Araevin. Thank you for joining us." High Mage Kileontheal stood amid a half-circle of five high mages, the most Araevin had ever seen together in one place. She was a slender sun elf woman who might have been a girl of thirty, but she was in fact a full five centuries in age. Like all high mages, Kileontheal embodied a spirit of tremendous power in the frail envelope of a mortal, the potency of her Art almost shining from her wise face and slender form. She had been gravely injured by a madness spell during the daemonfey attack on the tower, but she had since been restored to her power and sanity by subtle songs of healing. Kileontheal had been fortunate; the High Mages Philaerin and Aeramma Durothil, the other two high mages of Reilloch Domayr, had not survived the attack.

"I am at your service," Araevin replied, bowing.

He stole a quick glance at the other high mages who stood with Kileontheal. To his surprise, he recognized the Grand Mage of Evermeet, Breithel Olithir himself. Next to him stood the wry and good-humored moon elf Anfalen, then a cold and distant moon elf diviner named Isilfarrel, and finally a stern old sun elf whom Araevin guessed to be the lorekeeper Haldreithen.

"Are you well?" Kileontheal asked. "How is Ilsevele?"

"I am well enough. Ilsevele is in Silverymoon, visiting the court of Alustriel on behalf of her father. I have not seen her in a couple of tendays now, but we have spoken in sendings." In truth, Araevin had found that he had become accustomed to being apart from his betrothed. Despite the months they'd traveled together earlier in the year, they had spent years away from each other during their two decades of engagement. "How may I help you, High Mage?"

"I have heard that you intend to leave Tower Reilloch," Kileontheal said.

"Yes, High Mage. I feel that my studies here are concluded, at least for now. It's time for me to follow my own road."

"Where will you go?"

Araevin glanced at the others, who stood watching with impassive faces. High mages did not assemble for small talk, and he could not believe that they were all so interested in his comings or goings.

"The House of Cedars, Lady Kileontheal. I have not kept it up as I should have. And its solitude will suit my researches well."

"I am sorry to see you depart Reilloch, Araevin. So many of our comrades were lost in the daemonfey raid. Tower Reilloch is not the place it used to be." Kileontheal studied his face for a moment then added, "But perhaps you are not the mage you used to be, either."

He looked up sharply at that. Kileontheal did not miss much, did she? He met her gaze levelly.

"No, High Mage. I am not. The trials of the last few months have hardened me, and Saelethil's *selukiira* has provided me with whole new fields of lore to decipher, things I could not have imagined before." He indicated the great hall with a turn of his hand. "I have done everything that I can here at Reilloch."

"The study of high magic awaits you here if you stay, Araevin."

Araevin smiled and said, "While I have changed much in the last few months, I have not grown fifty years older."

"It is not an unreasonable wait," the moon elf Anfalen said. "You would be taking up high magic at less than three hundred years of age. Very few of us do that, Araevin."

"I know. When the time comes, I will be honored to begin my studies." He looked at the high mages facing him and frowned. "Is there some reason I should not leave Reilloch?"

Kileontheal inclined her head. Without meaning to, she seemed to be looking down at him from a great height indeed, though she was barely five feet tall. "We have been discussing your recovery of the *selukiira,* and your subsequent reweaving of Myth Glaurach's mythal. Lord Seiveril reports that your efforts resulted in the dismissal of a small army of summoned fiends, and led directly to his victory on the Lonely Moor, as well as the flight of the fey'ri legion and their daemonfey lords. You have accomplished great things since you left Evermeet a few short months ago."

"Thank you, High Mage."

"However," Kileontheal said, not quite interrupting him, "We are . . . concerned about the nature of the high loregem you have found, this Nightstar." She glanced at the others, and back to Araevin. "May we see it again?"

"It is deadly perilous to touch, High Mage. I have escaped harm only because of an accident of genealogy. The Nightstar of Saelethil will not spare you if you are careless."

"We will be careful, Araevin. None of us will try our strength against Saelethil's today," Breithel Olithir answered. The grand mage was new in his post, having ascended to his duties only a year ago. He too was a sun elf, dignified and stolid, but Araevin still sensed uncertainty about him. So many of Evermeet's mages had perished in the past few years, killed in Kymil Nimesin's rebellion of six years past, or lost in the expeditions to defend Evereska against the monstrous phaerimm only four years later. Olithir would have been the fifth or sixth choice for the title he held had other high mages lived, and most knew it.

The grand mage offered a small nod, and Araevin acquiesced with a flickering frown. He reached his right hand into his shirt and closed his fingers around the cold facets of the *selukiira*. The gemstone slipped painlessly from the flesh over his breastbone, leaving not a mark on him to show where it had been anchored to his very bones a moment before. Araevin willed it to become fully visible, and it appeared in his hand, a fine crystal of deep violet about the size of a woman's thumb, etched meticulously with tiny lavender runes.

He whispered a word and left it suspended head-high in the air, floating in place under the power of its ancient enchantments.

He withdrew three steps and said, "I remind you again, the Nightstar is very dangerous."

The high mages moved closer, though none approached closer than a full arm's length. Kileontheal pursed her lips thoughtfully as she studied the dark facets. Breithel Olithir whispered the words of seeing spells and stared intensely at the flickering spell-auras he read in the gemstone. The loremaster Haldreithen simply frowned, saying nothing.

Finally Breithel sighed and turned away from the Nightstar. "It is an old stone, of that I am certain—old, and strong."

"That is what I told you," Araevin said.

"Yes, but I wanted to see for myself. The *selukiira* might have instructed you to lie about its origins."

"Grand Mage, I am not under the stone's control. Examine me, if you are not sure."

"We have already," Haldreithen said. The scholar measured Araevin with a long look. "Just because no sign of the stone's dominion is obvious does not mean that you are not under its influence. After all, through this thing you wielded spells of mythalcraft we did not even suspect were possible. Who is to say that this Saelethil Dlardrageth didn't possess enchantments that we cannot detect?"

"If the Nightstar had overthrown my mind, Loremaster, why did it then permit me to strike against Sarya Dlardrageth and bar her from the mythal of Myth Glaurach?"

Araevin demanded. "For that matter, why did it not hide its identity, and invent a more innocuous origin? It could have used me to subvert one of you if it had concealed its true origin."

"Sometimes half a truth is the best way to cover a lie," the moon elf Anfalen said. "Still, I agree that your Nightstar would probably not have allowed you to tell us so much about it, if it really controlled your mind."

"Even if you are not shackled to the stone's will, you may be under a more subtle influence," Kileontheal said. "If you are right, the Nightstar is the handiwork of a monster. *Selukiira* hold much of their maker in them, and it seems to me that you might be wise to put it away somewhere for safekeeping and never handle it again."

"Better to destroy the thing outright," Haldreithen added.

"I understand your concerns," Araevin replied. "But consider this: The Nightstar holds spells of mythalcraft that no elf has known for five thousand years. Secrets as old as ancient Aryvandaar remain inside the *selukiira*. I do not understand all of them now, but in time I will."

Kileontheal gazed on the stone for a long time, then looked up at Araevin and asked, "Is the *selukiira* capable of instructing you in high magic?"

Araevin hesitated. He felt the other high mages awaiting his answer. He did not want to speak the truth, but he dared not attempt to deceive them.

"Yes," he said at last. He heard soft intakes of breath and sensed widened eyes and sharp sidelong glances around him. It was not often that high mages were surprised. "The spell I used to sever Sarya Dlardrageth from the mythal of Myth Glaurach was a spell of high magic. There are a number of even more powerful high magic spells in the Nightstar, as well as a great store of lore on mythalcraft and similar works. I have only scratched the surface of the *selukiira*'s contents."

"Have you embarked on the study of the other high magic spells contained in the lorestone?" the diviner Isilfarrel asked.

"Not yet, High Mage, but it is my intent to do so." Araevin felt the consternation of the others, but he did not look away. "Sarya Dlardrageth did terrible things with the mythal of Myth Glaurach. What else might she do, given the chance? Who else might be able to do such things, now that the daemonfey have demonstrated that they are possible? Faerûn is littered with the remnants of elven wards, vaults, and gates." He paused, allowing the high mages to consider his words. "I fear that things are stirring in Faerûn, things that our forefathers buried and forgot long ago. Our ignorance may prove deadly."

"The impudence!" growled Haldreithen. "Kileontheal, you erred gravely with this one."

Kileontheal's eyes flashed, but she kept her voice calm. "Araevin, you have no way of knowing what perils might sleep in that ancient lorestone. Even if you succeed in your efforts, we may all have cause to regret it later. If nothing else, your defiance of our will in this matter speaks poorly of your readiness to become a high mage."

"I understand, High Mage. I have weighed all these factors in my decision. Whether you believe it or not, I am the best judge of the perils of the Nightstar."

"You will not study that lorestone here," Kileontheal replied.

"I know," Araevin said. He offered a deep bow. "That is why I have chosen to depart the tower. As I said, the time has come for me to follow another path."

Deliberately, he stepped forward and closed his hand around the *selukiira* as the high mages watched. He slipped the lambent gemstone beneath his tunic, and pressed it to his breastbone again. Then he turned his back on Kileontheal and the others, and strode out of the great hall.

☙ ☙ ☙ ☙ ☙

Patches of snow still lingered beneath the green branches of the evergreens that mantled Myth Glaurach's rocky shoulders. Despite the bright sunshine that had lingered all day, spring did not come early to the Delimbiyr

Farthest Reach • 13

Vale. The air was damp and cold with the snowmelt, and not far from the ruined walls and broken domes of the ancient elven city, the Starstream—second of the four Talons that fed the mighty Delimbiyr—roared and rushed with white, cold floodwaters, so loud that its roar filled the air miles from the river's course.

Fflar Starbrow Melruth pulled his cloak closer around his broad shoulders, and gazed over the jagged stumps of a long-abandoned colonnade on the city's southern heights, watching the last embers of daylight painting the snow-covered mountaintops and high, wooded hills with soft splashes of gold and orange. He was a moon elf, tall and strongly built, with the strong hands and long arms of a born swordsman.

"A clear night coming," he remarked. "The stars will be out, but I think it will be cold."

Lord Seiveril Miritar looked up from the large map he was studying on a table nearby. He was a noble sun elf with red hair showing silver streaks at his temple, a high cleric of Corellon Larethian who wore a surcoat emblazoned with the star and sword of the elven god he served.

"I think I've come to like the spring here," said Seiveril. "I find it . . . bracing."

As High Captain of the Crusade—even Seiveril had come to think of Evermeet's expedition as "the Crusade," despite the fact that he'd resisted the appellation for some time—he had chosen the ruins of Myth Glaurach's library for his headquarters. Though the empty shell of white stone was mostly open to the sky, the building still possessed strong walls that were easily enclosed with light screens and rugged canopies. Nearly six thousand elf warriors were encamped in the city's ruins or in the forest nearby. An elite guard of twenty Knights of the Golden Star stood watch within a stone's throw of the old library, along with dozens of officers and aides who helped Seiveril and Fflar to keep order in the elven army.

"A couple of months ago you might have thought differently," Fflar said. "The wood elves of Rheitheillaethor told me how bitter the winters are in these lands. Do you know the ice broke on the Delimbiyr only a tenday ago?"

Fflar was more than he seemed, an ancient hero of fallen Myth Drannor whom Seiveril had called back into life with a powerful spell of resurrection. Together the sun elf cleric and the moon elf champion had led Evermeet's Crusade in a fiercely fought campaign to defend Evereska and the High Forest from the daemonfey legions of Sarya Dlardrageth.

"Will we still be here in midsummer? Or the fall, perhaps?" he continued.

Seiveril straightened up from his map table and looked at Fflar. "There's more on your mind than the weather, my friend. What is it?"

"How much longer can you keep this army together, Seiveril? Araevin banished Sarya's demons, we destroyed her orcs and giants, and her fey'ri have fled the field. It seems to me that you have accomplished your goal: Evereska has been preserved, the folk of the High Forest are safe. Your army has no enemy to fight." Fflar turned from the open colonnade and climbed a couple of weathered stone steps to the empty shell of the library, lowering his voice. "For that matter, have I now accomplished the purpose for which you summoned me from Arvandor? What am I supposed to do now?"

Seiveril frowned. "I do not know that I have an answer to your second question, Fflar. What are any of us supposed to do?"

"You called me back from Arvandor to beat an army of demons. Now that Sarya's demons have been defeated—through no doing of my own, I'll add—I find myself wondering whether I am supposed to, well, go back." Fflar looked at Seiveril and shrugged. "Do I just discorporate when I'm ready to go this time, or do I have to go throw myself off a precipice or something?"

"Is that what you want to do?"

Fflar looked at his hands for a long time. "I don't think so. I feel alive enough right now. I miss Sorenna, I miss her terribly. But I know she is waiting in Arvandor for me, and time does not mean much there, Seiveril. In the

Farthest Reach • 15

meantime, there seems to be more of the world for me to see and more things for me to do. I just don't know if it is wrong for me to linger now."

Seiveril stepped close and set a hand on Fflar's shoulder. "I think I know Corellon's will in this," he said. "You were not called back to live one hour, or one day, or one battle. You were called back to *live*, for as long as fate, chance, and your own heart allow. There is nothing wrong in tarrying here. It is nothing more or less than any of us do."

Fflar looked up, a crooked smile on his face. "Well, good. I would hate to leave again without finding out where in Faerûn the fey'ri legion has gone to ground."

"You and I both," Seiveril murmured. He returned his attention to the map spread out on the table. "You asked me a moment ago how long I intend to keep the army here. My answer is this: I will stay here until I am convinced that Sarya's legion won't return, and cannot be found. I don't expect all of our warriors to stay that long, but I certainly hope that some number of them do. We have unfinished business with her."

Fflar joined him at the map. "We fought her at the Lonely Moor eighteen days ago. As recently as ten days ago, she and her fey'ri were here at Myth Glaurach." He tapped on finger on the Delimbiyr Vale, thinking. "Some of her fey'ri can teleport, but not many. They would have used that tactic in combat, if it was available to them. But they do fly. How fast could a flying army travel? Fifty miles a day? Sixty?"

"They didn't seem to be tremendously strong or fast flyers, not like an adult dragon or a giant eagle. And they must carry some equipment with them. I expect they've abandoned anything like a supply train. Sixty miles a day, ten days . . . that would be six hundred miles from here." He looked more closely at the mountains and forests depicted before him, and frowned. Within that distance lay tremendous swaths of the great desert Anauroch, most of the wild backcountry of the Nether Mountains, the Graypeaks, the southern High Forest, the High Moor and the Evermoor, as well as the forbidding Ice Mountains north of Silverymoon, and even the Spine of the World and the High Ice. "She could be anywhere."

"Have you been able to divine any clues?"

"I have been casting divinations every day, with little luck. I suppose I must redouble my efforts, and ask Vesilde Gaerth and Jorildyn to have their own clerics and mages begin the search, too. Perhaps if enough of our spellcasters search at once . . ."

"I suppose it's the best chance we have. But Seiveril—if we do not find some sign of the fey'ri soon, you will have to give thought to how much of this army you can send home."

"Excuse me, Lord Seiveril?" Both elves turned as the priestess Thilesil entered the hall. She was also a cleric of Corellon, junior to Seiveril, who had joined Lord Miritar on his quest and served as his adjutant and chief assistant. "Lord Keryth Blackhelm of the High Council is here to see you."

"Keryth, here?" Seiveril frowned. Keryth was the High Marshal of Evermeet, leader of the island's armies, and one of Queen Amlaruil's most valuable advisors. "Show him in."

Thilesil nodded, and beckoned their guest in. "This way, sir."

She stood aside to permit Keryth to enter, and followed him in, anticipating decisions to record or orders to issue.

Keryth Blackhelm was a moon elf of middle years, perhaps a little past his prime as a swordsman, but still hale and fit. He was not as tall as Fflar, but he was a commanding presence anyway, with a fierce determination burning in his eyes and a gruff, confident manner.

"Lord Miritar," he said. "Thank you for receiving me."

"Of course, Keryth." Seiveril took Keryth's hand in a firm clasp. They'd served together on Evermeet's High Council for many years, and even if they did not always agree with each other, they shared a mutual respect. "Have you traveled long? I can ask for refreshments to be brought."

"No, the trip was quick. The grand mage loaned me the services of a sorcerer who knows the spell of teleportation. We left Evermeet not more than half an hour ago." Keryth looked about the ruined building. "How is Ilsevele?"

"She is well. I spoke to her just this morning. She is visiting Silverymoon with her companions, though I believe Araevin is attending to some business at Tower Reilloch."

"I have not seen Silverymoon," Keryth replied. He wandered into the old library and through to the ruined colonnade outside, taking in the view. "This was Glaurachyndaar?"

"Yes. It was called the City of Scrolls in its day." Seiveril gestured at the ruins beyond the library. "The daemonfey used the grand mage's palace as their lair. While I have seen no sign of them since I have been here, I decided it was not prudent to take up residence in their quarters. There are deep vaults and armories hidden in the heart of the hill beneath the palace, and I am not sure that we have found all of their secrets yet."

"It seems that you have matters well in hand otherwise," Keryth said. He faced Seiveril. "Speaking of which, I have been sent here to ask if you would consent to attend the High Council's meeting in seven days and provide the queen and her advisors with a firsthand account of your campaign. We have heard many stories, and we want to get the most accurate report we can."

"You may have forgotten, Lord Blackhelm, but I am no longer a Councilor of the Realm."

Keryth shook his head. "No, the queen is not summoning you as such. Nor is she summoning you at all, to be honest. She only requests that you come to speak before the council, my friend. She will send a mage to teleport you, if you like, so it should not take you long at all. And to be honest, you will save us a lot of pointless debate in which Veldann or Durothil question the veracity of every report we have received."

Seiveril considered the request for a moment. He was certain that Selsharra Durothil and Ammisyll Veldann would question him harshly on any account he cared to provide. On the other hand, he could think of nothing he cared to hide, and he no longer needed to be particularly polite to the conservatives and antimonarchists on the council, did he?

He looked over to Fflar and asked, "Lord Starbrow, can you keep things in order here for a time?"

Fflar shrugged. "I'll know where to find you if I need you."

Seiveril turned back to Keryth. "All right, then. If the queen requests my presence, I will not tell her no. I will be there."

☙ ☙ ☙ ☙ ☙

The House of Cedars stood on a rocky headland on Evermeet's rugged northern shore, hidden within a sparse forest of wind-shaped cedars and hemlocks. It was a rambling old elven lodge of open verandas and promenades anchored into the very rock of the headland. Araevin's ancestors had built themselves a home in which they remained a part of the world outside, instead of a burrow from which they could shut things out. Light screens of wooden paneling and large windows of strong glass in clever wooden frames allowed him to close or open most of the rooms as he saw fit.

Early in the winter Araevin had spent a tenday there, repairing the damage of many long years of weathering. As the spring turned toward summer and the days grew bright and windy along Evermeet's shores, he was pleased to see that his repairs were keeping well. He had lived in the house as a child, more than two hundred years past, but no one had lived there for a century or more. When he'd finally gotten around to visiting the place a few months before it had been in poor shape.

On his arrival Araevin spent three days arranging the personal effects and arcane tomes he'd had sent from his chambers in the Tower Reilloch. The house featured a handsome library on its eastward face, which Araevin filled with the collection of grimoires, spellbooks, journals, treatises, and scrolls he had accumulated over eight decades of residence at Reilloch. Next to the library stood an empty hall that Araevin converted into his workroom, installing at one end the cabinet of theurglass in which he stored his collection of magic wands and other such devices. He also wove a potent fence of abjurations and magical defenses around the entire house, since he could no longer count on the wards of Tower Reilloch. He wove careful illusions to hide the books and artifacts he was most concerned about, and summoned magical guardians to defend the house if necessary.

As the sun set on the sixth day since he'd stood before the high mages, he removed the Nightstar from its hiding place over his heart and set the purple gemstone in a small stand before him.

"I think the time has come for you and I to speak at length," he told the *selukiira*.

The Nightstar made no answer, but Araevin thought he saw a lambent flash in its depths. The high loregem was a living artifact. It held dozens upon dozens of spells, much as Araevin's own spellbooks did. But beyond that useful function, the Nightstar protected the deeper secrets of mythalcraft and high magic. Already it had shown him spells for examining and shaping mythals, but the secrets of even greater power still awaited within the stone.

He drew a deep breath, and focused his attention on the flicker of light that lived in the heart of the gem, allowing his perception, his consciousness, to sink deeper and deeper into shining purple facets. The stone grew brighter, and distant voices whispered in his mind—and with an abrupt plunge he felt himself drawn into the gemstone, falling into a vast and illimitable expanse of towering amethyst ramparts.

He opened his eyes, and found himself in the poisoned garden of the Nightstar's soul. It was a magnificent place, a palace of gold colonnades and elegant arcades that existed nowhere except in the gem's own intellect. Lovely vines and flowers filled the open courtyard, but they were malicious and alive, things that slowly coiled and hunted with thorn and venom. In an old house on Evermeet's shore, his body stood locked and immobile, facing a shining purple gemstone, but as far as Araevin's senses could discern, he was physically *here,* a visitor in the infernal grandeur that lay at the heart of the gemstone.

"Saelethil!" Araevin called. "Come forth! I wish to speak to you."

The hungry flowers rustled and groped at the sound of his voice, but Araevin did not fear them. They were not real, and had no power to hurt him. He simply exerted his will and made a small brushing gesture with his mind, and the sinister things recoiled from him, leaving a clear circle around his feet.

"Saelethil! Come forth!"

Araevin frowned and glanced around, wondering if perhaps he had erred in some way, but when he looked back Saelethil Dlardrageth was standing silently only an arm's reach from him, regarding him with bright green eyes that held all the malice and venom of an asp. Despite himself, Araevin took a step back.

The ancient sorcerer smiled at the motion. In life Saelethil Dlardrageth had been a tall and regal sun elf, with handsome if cruel features, and the figment of his consciousness and personality that was embodied in the Nightstar chose to manifest itself in his living appearance.

"The measure of an undisciplined mind," Saelethil rasped, "is that the intellect allows emotion to challenge the observed truth. You know that I am not permitted to harm you, and yet you quail like a child at the mere sight of me, Araevin Teshurr."

Araevin did not refute the accusation. Saelethil would have excoriated him for denying it, in any case. The shade of the long-dead intellect that had crafted the Nightstar despised self-deceit more than anything. Instead, he decided to take the offensive.

"I spoke with the high mages about you recently," he said. "They wish you destroyed, and I am not altogether certain I disagree with them."

"Your high mages are fumbling incompetents, Araevin. They have no idea what it means to be worthy of that title." Saelethil sneered in contempt, but he turned away to inspect the garden, folding his arms imperiously across his chest. "Bring one here, and I will demonstrate the extent of their ignorance for you."

"Tell me of the high magic spells you hold, and I will judge the question of their ignorance for myself," Araevin replied. "You have shown me only one high magic spell so far, even though you claim to know a dozen more."

Saelethil glanced back at Araevin and grinned without humor. "Ah, perhaps there is some Dlardrageth in you after all, my boy. You've tasted true power, and now you thirst for more."

"What I thirst for is not your concern, Saelethil. Now, are you able to make good on your claims or not?"

The Dlardrageth archmage studied Araevin for a moment, his eyes cold and measuring. "I could, but you are not yet suited for the spells I haven't taught you."

"Not yet suited? In what way?"

"The highest and most dangerous art of high magic is the manipulation of magic more powerful than the mortal frame can bear. Your so-called masters in Evermeet accomplish this by forging a circle of mages to wield high magic. They cooperate with a number of other high mages to collectively shape a magic that would destroy any single one of them who attempted it."

"I know that much," Araevin said.

"Indeed. Well, there is another tradition for wielding high magic, Araevin Teshurr. Those of us who did not care to shackle our power to the weakest of our fellows wielded solitary high magic, free and unfettered by the prejudices of our peers. In order to wield power that otherwise would destroy us, we devised the *telmiirkara neshyrr,* the rite of transformation. We sculpted our very natures to suit ourselves for the power we intended to wield. With such preparation, a single high mage could transcend mortal limits and manipulate powers that otherwise might require a whole circle of high mages to manage."

"I did nothing of the sort when I severed Sarya from the mythal."

"You did not need to. Many spells of high magic can be cast without the aid of a circle or a transformation. The *mythaalniir darach,* the spell of mythal-shaping you wielded against my kinswoman Sarya, does not conjure into existence the awesome power of a high mythal. It simply allows manipulation of an existing font of power." Saelethil shrugged. "However, I did not see fit to preserve many spells of that sort in my Nightstar. The rest of the high magic spells I recorded require the *telmiirkara neshyrr.*"

Araevin frowned, considering the notion. He did not think that Saelethil was permitted to deceive him, but he was certain that the Nightstar's persona was capable of choosing not to tell him something he didn't ask about.

"So you can teach me the rest of the high magic spells you hold if I perform this *telmiirkara neshyrr*?"

Saelethil nodded.

"What sort of transformation is involved?"

"You exchange a large portion of your mortal soul for demonic essence. Demons are magical beings by their very nature; a demonic nature serves to shield one from power of untrammeled high magic." The Dlardrageth smiled cruelly. "It is not very difficult."

Araevin blanched in horror. He understood the bargain the Dlardrageths had made so long ago.

"I will not do that!"

"Then you will find most of my high magic spells inaccessible," Saelethil said with open contempt. "I expected no better of you."

Araevin glanced down, thinking hard. He noticed that the poisonous creepers squirmed closer to him, and he brushed them aside again. If Sarya had access to the sort of mythalcraft he did in the form of the Nightstar, she would be able to wield those spells as if she were born to them . . . which, in fact, she was. He found himself thinking of the melodious voice of Malkizid, the sinister presence he had felt in Myth Glaurach's mythal when that device had been under Sarya's control. What had Malkizid told Sarya about him? What did Malkizid know about mythals and their uses?

A thought occurred to him, and he said to Saelethil, "Demons are not the only creatures of supernatural power in the multiverse. Can your *telmiirkara neshyrr* bind other essences to a high mage, essences not steeped in evil?"

Saelethil hesitated, but said, "Possibly. You must transcend your mortality to wield these spells safely, but there may be more than one way to do that. Chaos, order, the elements, the concept you term 'good' . . . all these principles give rise to supernatural forces, and might prove suitable."

"What other transformations do you know, then?"

"I do not know any other than the one I used."

"Do you know of anyone else who would know?"

The Dlardrageth archmage frowned. "Yes," he said finally. "Ithraides and his students wielded high magic without the benefit of a circle."

"Ithraides?" Araevin said in surprise. He knew that name. Ithraides was the grand mage of fallen Arcorar, the ancient archmage who had driven the Dlardrageths out of Cormanthyr thousands of years in the past. From there Sarya Dlardrageth had gone on to subvert the realm of Siluvanede and breed her legions of fey'ri warriors . . . but before all that House Dlardrageth had been defeated by Ithraides and his allies, more than five thousand years ago. "Was he also bound to a demonic essence?"

"No. He shared your useless scruples. He discovered another soulbinding, something that allowed him to match my mastery. I sincerely doubt he would have had the stomach to follow the path I chose."

Araevin offered a grim smile and said, "No, I suppose he wouldn't have."

He took a step back, and willed himself up and out of Saelethil's poisoned garden. There was a dizzying moment of soaring recklessly upward into a world of great purple planes and dancing storms of lambent fire, and he opened his eyes with a sudden gasp of breath.

He sat in his library in the House of Cedars, the Nightstar gleaming on the table before him. The sea wind rattled the windows of his study, and the ocean was dark and wild beyond.

Ithraides knew how to wield high magic without a circle, just like Saelethil, he reflected. And he did it without transforming himself into a demon. That knowledge might still exist, if he looked in the right place.

"Arcorar," Araevin breathed, his eyes distant. Arcorar had become the realm of Cormanthyr, and Cormanthyr's capital was the city of Myth Drannor, which had fallen only six hundred years ago. Much lore of ancient Arcorar had been carried out of Myth Drannor in its final years to Evermeet and places such as Evereska and Silverymoon. Evermeet's hoard of Cormanthyran lore had been largely destroyed when Kymil Nimesin destroyed the Towers of the Sun and Moon five years ago, but what of Silverymoon? Araevin had heard that many Cormanthyran mages and scholars fled there when Myth Drannor fell.

It seemed as good a place to start as any, and Araevin had other reasons to visit the city in any event.

He reached out for the Nightstar and slipped the gemstone inside his shirt again, pressing it to his breastbone. He had a journey to make ready for.

CHAPTER TWO

6 Mirtul, the Year of Lightning Storms

Sarya Dlardrageth stood on the broken battlements of Castle Cormanthor beneath a warm, steady spring rain, and surveyed her new realm. The daemonfey queen was strikingly beautiful, with the arresting features and enticing curves of a noble sun elf woman, but her skin was a deep, perfect crimson, and she possessed a powerful pair of batlike wings she kept folded behind her like a great dark cape.

Her domain was quite small, really, not more than a couple of miles from one end to the other, for she could not claim to reign over the great forest that surrounded Myth Drannor's ancient buildings and walls. But it is a start, she told herself. Her eye fell on the rose-tinted tower the human clerics had raised within the very walls of Cormanthor's ancient capital, and she bared her slender fangs in a vicious smile.

The shrine stood blackened and burnt, scorched by fey'ri spells and ancient Vyshaanti weapons. Its smoke was sweet in the air. Her fey'ri legion—a thousand swordsmen-sorcerers, the pride of ancient Siluvanede—had made themselves masters of the ancient city.

Sarya was not defeated yet, not by a wide margin.

"Lady Sarya, a handful of the Lathanderians escaped," said the fey'ri lord Mardeiym Reithel as he approached carefully, offering a bow as he addressed her. "They used a hidden portal to flee our last assault. We could not follow."

Mardeiym, and the rest of the fey'ri for that matter, were much like Sarya, sun elves of high and ancient lineage who had been imprisoned thousands of years ago. Like her, they were winged demonspawn, with skin in fine hues of red and great dark wings. But they were still more mortal than not, elves with a demonic taint. Sarya and her son Xhalph were true daemonfey, with much stronger demonic bloodlines.

"The portal refused you?" Sarya asked.

"Yes, my lady. The Lathanderians possessed some key or password that we lacked. Since we cannot use the device, I ordered it sealed with stone."

"Good," Sarya replied. "I am not concerned with the escape of a handful of human priests. We are the masters of this city now. But I would not want spies to slip back through the portal and learn more about us."

Her army of fey'ri had easily overwhelmed the small companies of human adventurers and hidden nests of cultists and necromancers formerly encamped within Myth Drannor. The temple to Lathander had been the last bastion of explorers and adventurers remaining within the walls. Of course, monsters of all descriptions still lurked within their lairs and catacombs. But Sarya had no real need to eliminate such guardians, and most of the fearsome beholders, nagas, liches, dragons, and other such denizens of the ruins recognized that Sarya's legion of well-armed fey'ri was a foe beyond their ability to drive off. The fey'ri did not go out of their way to trouble such creatures in their lairs, and for their part, the intelligent ones did not emerge to challenge Sarya's warriors.

"There are still the devils to contend with," Mardeiym said. "If we leave them alone, I promise you they will turn on us." Hundreds of the supernatural fiends were bound to the ruined city. Before the arrival of Sarya and her legion, they had formerly ruled as masters over Myth Drannor. "We outnumber the filthy hellspawn. Our fey'ri warriors can defeat them now, before they have the opportunity to betray us."

Sarya regarded her chief captain with a cold glare. Mardeiym sensed danger and dropped his gaze to her feet. Under most circumstances, Sarya—a princess of the demon-ruled Abyss by birth—would have regarded any spawn of the Nine Hells as a hated enemy. Demons and devils had fought each other throughout eternity, the unbridled destruction of demonic evil battling for supremacy against cruel, infernal tyranny.

"Do not question my judgment," she said. "I have uses for the devils of this city."

"I apologize, Lady Sarya. I do not mean to question your decisions, but it is important that you know when the fey'ri are troubled." Mardeiym waited on her, his head still bowed in respect.

"Troubled?" Sarya said.

She turned away, pacing along the battlements. Flexing her wings, she luxuriated in the sheer pleasure of freedom. She would have liked to lash out at Mardeiym, remind him of the fearsome power she commanded and reinforce the ancient pacts by which she ruled absolutely over the fey'ri Houses. But the war captain was loyal to her, and spoke nothing more or less than the truth. She would do well to avoid teaching her subjects that bringing her bad news always led to punishment.

"Very well, Lord Reithel. Summon the House lords to my audience chamber, and I will explain more."

"As you command, my lady," the war captain said.

He bowed again, and vaulted over the battlement and took wing. Sarya watched him glide away into the ruins, then descended from the battlements into the spacious royal chambers she had claimed in the castle.

She allowed Mardeiym half an hour to gather the leaders of the other fey'ri Houses, busying herself with renewing the powerful abjurations and contingency spells with which she normally guarded herself, and she went down into the grand hall of Castle Cormanthor. Centuries ago, the coronals of the elven kingdom of Cormanthyr had presided over revels and banquets in the grand hall. Its walls were still painted with magical murals of woodland scenes that slowly changed from season to season, and the great columns that lined the walls were carved in the shape of tall, strong trees so realistic that stone blossoms and fruit could be glimpsed in the branches.

The leaders of her fey'ri legion awaited her in the hall. Each of the dozen demon-elves was the leader of one of the fey'ri Houses. Some, like Reithel, were ancient Houses from Siluvanede that were strong and numerous, having been imprisoned in the Nameless Dungeon for fifty centuries. Others, like Aelorothi, were survivor Houses, families of daemonfey who had passed their demonic heritage down through twenty generations from the time of Sarya's ancient realm to her revival only five years ago. The descendant houses were smaller and less numerous than ancient houses such as Reithel, but they were made up of fey'ri who had grown up in the world Sarya and her ancient legion had suddenly found themselves in. They were comfortable with the new world in a way that Sarya and the other ancient prisoners could never be.

Not for the first time, Sarya found herself wondering what had become of Nurthel Floshin. He was from one of the descendant Houses, and had served as an able spymaster and lieutenant. But he had not returned from the expedition she had dispatched to recover the Nightstar, and she could only assume that he was dead.

She turned her attention to the proud, cruel lords and ladies gathered before her. "Look around you," she began. "This will be our home, the founding-stone on which we will build our new realm. Before I and my family came to

Siluvanede, we dwelled here in Cormanthyr. It is only fitting that this is the place where we begin to rebuild."

Sarya leaped down from the steps on which she stood, flaring her wings to alight in front of the fey'ri lords. She did not look forward to what must be said next.

"You all know that this is not what I planned when I broke open Nar Kerymhoarth three months ago," she began. "I intended to erase the realms of the High Forest and Evereska from the map, and claim vengeance for the destruction of Siluvanede five thousand years ago."

She paused, holding the eyes of her minions, and said, "That, however, was a mistake.

"Perhaps events might have fallen out differently if Evermeet had not responded with so much force, or if Nurthel Floshin had not failed to recover the Nightstar, or even if the fortunes of battle had favored us against Evermeet's army. But these things did not happen. I underestimated our enemies' strength and resolve, or overestimated our own strength, or did not plan to overcome ill fortune—it does not really matter. The consequence of my mistake was that we had to abandon our stronghold at Myth Glaurach and leave our work in Evereska and the High Forest undone."

The daemonfey queen turned away from her fey'ri, deliberately putting her back to them as she paced. She hated the idea of introducing her own fallibility into her follower's minds, but it had to be there already, didn't it? Still, she did not want to let the fey'ri lords consider that last thought for long. She looked back over her shoulder at her captains and lords.

"It would be foolish of me to pretend that I am incapable of making mistakes," she said. "What I intend to do now is to *learn* from our mistakes. Before we take the field again or challenge the usurpers who have stolen our lands and treasures, we must grow much stronger. We will hide here in Myth Drannor, protected by the ancient power of its mythal. Within these ruined walls our enemies cannot divine our existence or scry out our strength. We will grow strong in secret, until the time is right for us to return."

"What of the baatezu?" Alysir Ursequarra asked. "When do we destroy them?"

"They are not our enemies," Sarya said firmly. "You are to strike no blow against the devils in this city unless I tell you to." The fey'ri lords shifted uneasily, some risking quick glances at their fellows. Sarya turned back to face her followers. "The devils that were summoned here decades ago were outcasts from the Nine Hells, mercenaries and marauders who have no loyalty to the rest of their kind."

"So they would have us believe," Alysir volunteered boldly. "How can we know they are speaking the truth?"

Sarya stalked close to Alysir, and lowered her voice to a menacing hiss. "I have investigated the matter, Lady Alysir. Do you think I have allowed myself to be deceived?"

Alysir Ursequarra paled slightly, but held her ground. "No, Lady Sarya."

Were her fey'ri not irreplaceably rare, Sarya would have killed Alysir Ursequarra on the spot. But each fey'ri warrior was worth twenty orcs or five ogres. She could not be careless of their lives. Sarya smiled coldly. "You forget, Alysir, that the devils are bound to this city, and we are not. Spells anchored to the mythal by human wizards twenty years ago trap the devils within Myth Drannor. I can alter the mythal to allow some, all, or none of them to escape from this place, or call them back and confine them any time I wish—but I will exact fealty from each devil I allow to leave. The devils cannot escape unless I help them, and I will not help them unless I am certain of their loyalty. They will serve in our armies alongside the demons and yugoloths we summon to serve us. Does that meet with your approval, Lady Ursequarra?"

Alysir Ursequarra offered a deep bow. "I am sworn to serve you, my lady. I do not question your commands."

"Good. It would go poorly for you if I thought you did." Sarya wheeled away, her tail lashing like a whip. "We hide, we wait, we grow strong, and we marshal the devils of this city to our service," she said. "Does anyone disagree?" None of the fey'ri spoke. Sarya nodded, and looked to a gaunt fey'ri sorcerer who stood a little apart from the other House lords. "Very well. In that case . . . Lord Aelorothi, please describe for your peers the shape of the human lands that have grown up around Myth Drannor. These will be our foes someday, but not until we are ready for them."

The captains and lords turned their eyes on the sorcerer-lord. Aelorothi was a descendant House, and Vesryn Aelorothi had traveled widely all across Faerûn for many years. He affected a gracious and courteous manner, but Sarya knew him to be capable of exquisite cruelties. A tenday ago she had named the gaunt fey'ri sorcerer her new spymaster, and set him to the task of insinuating daemonfey gold, assassins, and sorcery into the halls of power in every nearby land.

"It would be my pleasure, Lady Sarya," he purred.

"Listen carefully to Vesryn, my children," she told the fey'ri lords. "Many of you will be traveling these lands in the coming months, spying out their strengths and their weaknesses."

She motioned for the sorcerer to continue, and left her assembled captains behind her.

Vesryn stepped forward as she left, and moving very deliberately—Vesryn was nothing if not cautious—he wove his hands together and muttered the words of a spell of illusion, conjuring in midair the image of a great map.

"This," he began, "is the forest of Cormanthor . . ."

☙ ☙ ☙ ☙ ☙

Araevin left the House of Cedars in the morning after his conversation with the Nightstar. He followed rarely traveled paths into the wild pine forests and hills overlooking the sea, drinking deeply of the scent of the trees and the cool spring rain. Early in the afternoon he reached a worn old portal glade, a small clearing around a weathered stone marker that had stood in that spot for thousands of years.

Most of Evermeet's portals were closed forever, deliberately sealed in the past few decades to guard the island from any possible attack through the magical gateways, but a few still existed—some well guarded, others only one-way portals that allowed travelers to depart from Evermeet but not return, some so old or uncertain in their working that they were risky to use. Araevin had always been fascinated by portals, and he had spent many decades exploring them in both Evermeet and Faerûn. He thought he might be the only person alive who knew how to wake the one in the glade.

He spoke the spells needed to activate the portal, and passed through. With a single step Evermeet's misty forests vanished, only to be replaced by the high, windswept downs of the Evermoors. Dusk was falling, the end of a bright and cold spring day; the Evermoors were far to the east of Evermeet.

"What becomes of the hours I missed?" Araevin wondered aloud.

He studied the featureless moorland, speckled with the first small blooms of spring despite the lingering patches of snow that still lurked in the shadowed places. It was important to be sure of his exact location in case the portal had somehow malfunctioned.

Satisfied, he closed his eyes, envisioning a small hilltop shrine he knew well, and uttered a spell of teleportation.

There was a moment of darkness, a vertiginous sense of falling without motion, and Araevin stood in the small wooded bower of a shrine to Labelas Enoreth, a mile beyond the walls of Silverymoon, another hundred miles from the portal-stone in the Evermoors. Two large blueleaf trees had long ago taken root in the veranda, shouldering aside the shrine's flagstones and forming a living roof over the elf deity's altar. A small balustrade of old white stone, overgrown with green vines, offered a view of the swift river Rauvin and the city of Silverymoon, cupped around both the river's banks.

"Well, there you are. I have been waiting for you."

Araevin turned at the words, and found himself looking on the face of his betrothed, the beautiful Lady Ilsevele Miritar. She was a sun elf like he, but she was much fairer than he was—in both senses of the word—with a radiant mane of copper-red hair and green eyes. She wore a tunic of green suede over cream-colored trousers, bloused into high leather boots decorated with tiny gold thread patterns. A slender long sword was sheathed at her hip.

"Ilsevele," he said, and he took three steps and caught her up in his arms.

"It's only been a couple of tendays," she said with a laugh, finally pushing him away. "You've gone years at a time without thinking to look in on me."

"I have spent too much time around humans lately," he answered. "After two hundred and fifty years, I believe I am losing the habit of patience."

"Well, you must wait a little longer. Our wedding is still two years away, in case you have forgotten." Ilsevele looked out over the human city nearby. Hundreds of lanterns were flickering to life in its tree-shadowed streets and graceful buildings, reflections glimmering in the dark waters of the Rauvin, and the stars were coming out in the darkening skies. "I am glad that you told me of this shrine. The view is lovely. And I've had several hours to admire it."

"I am sorry. I had a later start than I'd anticipated."

"No matter. I enjoyed a couple of hours to myself." She took his hand. "Come on, Maresa and Filsaelene are waiting in the city. They're anxious to see you, too."

The two sun elves followed an old path leading down from the shrine to the human city below. This close to Silverymoon, there was little danger even as darkness fell, but Araevin noted that Ilsevele wore her sword, and he approved.

"Where are you staying?" he asked. When he'd sent word to Ilsevele that he was coming, he had used a sending spell, and didn't know where it might have found her.

"An inn called the Golden Oak. It's quite nice, really. I like it much better than that Dragonback in Daggerford."

"I know the Oak. You have expensive tastes," he said with a smile.

Ilsevele drew closer under his arm. "I decided that I owed Maresa and Filsaelene some comfort, after what we've all been through over the last few months."

"I certainly don't begrudge you that."

They'd crisscrossed the Sword Coast and the North in search of the *telkiiras* containing the clues that would lead him to the Nightstar, facing brigands, trolls, wars, demons, imprisonment, and worse. And not all of their companions had survived their adventure.

Araevin's old comrade Grayth Holmfast had been murdered by the daemonfey, and Grayth's armsman Brant torn apart by demons in the fight to find the *telkiira* stones before the daemonfey did. Thinking of his lost companions, Araevin lapsed into a long silence as they neared Silverymoon's gates.

After a time, Ilsevele glanced at him and said, "You seem troubled."

"I was thinking of Grayth and Brant. They deserved better."

"I know." Ilsevele leaned her head on his shoulder for a moment. "He did not want to return, Araevin. We brought him to Rhymester's Matins, the temple of Lathander in this city, and the human clerics cast divinations to determine whether his spirit would return willingly if they chose to raise him. Grayth is content with his life, and his death. All you can do is honor his sacrifice, and carry him with you in your memory."

"Grayth is wiser than I, for I am not content." Araevin said. He knew he was responsible for his friend's death. The daemonfey had killed Grayth to compel Araevin to lead them to the Nightstar. If he had yielded earlier, the cleric might still be alive. Araevin had destroyed Nurthel, the fey'ri who had actually killed Grayth . . . but Sarya Dlardrageth, the author of his death, had so far escaped justice. "We still have business with the daemonfey."

"I have not forgotten," she replied, with an edge of cold steel in her voice. Ilsevele was a warrior as well as a highborn lady; she believed that some things could only be set right with steel and courage, and she knew her own measure better than most.

They passed the guards at the city gates, and walked Silverymoon's broad boulevards until they reached the

Farthest Reach • 35

Golden Oak—a large, comfortable inn whose common room was an open atrium beneath the spreading branches of a great oak tree, from which dozens of small lanterns hung. A bard strummed a lute, and many of the inn's guests sat drinking wine or ale beneath the oak tree, quietly conversing.

"Araevin!" called a loud voice. More than a few heads turned as Maresa Rost leaped to her feet, calling to the two elves. Maresa was an individual of striking appearance, a young woman whose skin was literally as white as snow. Her hair was long and silver-white as well, and it drifted gently around her head as if stirred by breezes unfelt by anyone else. She was a genasi, a human whose ancestry included beings of the elemental planes—in Maresa's case, air elementals of some kind. She wore crimson-dyed leather and carried a rapier at her hip. "You were supposed to be here hours ago!"

Araevin started to bow and apologize, but Maresa surprised him, throwing her arms around him and offering a fierce hug. "I-it is good to see you, too, Maresa," he stammered. He looked over Maresa's shoulder to the genasi's companion, a rather slight and young-looking sun elf woman who wore the emblem of Corellon Larethian's clerics on her tunic. "And you, too, Filsaelene."

Filsaelene offered a shy smile, and raised a goblet of wine. "Join us, please. I am afraid we are a little ahead of you already."

Freed from the daemonfey stronghold only a few tendays ago, none of her former comrades had survived their battle against the demonic invaders. Filsaelene still struck Araevin as timid and retiring, but she seemed to be recovering well under Maresa's care.

Maresa finally released him, and Araevin glanced over at Ilsevele. His betrothed shrugged.

"I could stand some song and wine," she said. "Why not?"

They spent the evening drinking good wine, enjoying the music of the bard, and trading stories of old adventures. After a time, the lutenist was joined by a flutist and a drummer, and the three struck up a lively dance, in which Araevin was kept quite busy by dancing with all three of his companions in turn. Finally, tired and pleasantly aglow with the warm wine, he and Ilsevele said their goodnights to the others, and retired to Ilsevele's comfortable room.

Whether it was the wine, the dancing, or simply the hidden relief of having survived their trials of the past few months, they made love for a time. Then they spent the hours after midnight lying together, content to be near each other without speaking. Such moments had become rare in the past few years, it seemed.

Ilsevele's fingers glided over the cold, hard gemstone sealed to Araevin's chest, and he felt her frown.

"You brought the *selukiira* with you?" she asked.

"I still have more to learn from it," he told her. Then he reached up to mesh his fingers with hers, and brought her hand to his face, holding her close as they drifted off into Reverie together.

"I thought you said it was dangerous—an artifact of the daemonfey of old."

"It is," he said, and said no more about it.

The next morning, Araevin stirred from his Reverie and dressed himself in the dark hour before dawn. Ilsevele roused herself as he rose, drawing a deep breath as she called herself back to the inn room from whatever far memory or dream she had wandered in her own Reverie.

"Where are you going?" she asked.

"The Vault of the Sages," Araevin replied. He looked over at her. "It is the best library in the city, perhaps all of the North, and I have some research to do."

"The Nightstar?"

"Yes. I have not yet solved all of its mysteries." Araevin drew his cloak over his shoulders, and picked up the worn rucksack in which he carried many of his notes and journals. "I must learn more about the magic of ancient Arcorar, or at least some specific spells and rites from that era, if I am to unlock the deeper secrets Saelethil concealed in this lorestone."

Farthest Reach • 37

Ilsevele sat up sharply. "Is it a good idea to do that? You were lucky once with the Nightstar. Perhaps you shouldn't delve any further into it unless you have to."

"Last night we spoke of our unfinished business with the daemonfey. If I ever mean to finish it, I think I will need to know what other secrets the Nightstar holds."

Ilsevele stood too, and said, "I will come with you, then."

"There is no need. I'm not sure how much you could help, to be honest. I'm not entirely sure what I'm looking for."

Ilsevele's eyes narrowed. "I remind you, my betrothed, that I know a little bit about magic too. Besides, I have nothing else in particular to do today, and I might like a chance to look around a fine library for my own account, not yours."

He winced. "I did not mean to imply that you were unable to help me," he managed. "I would enjoy your company, if you wanted to come along."

Ilsevele crossed her arms. "I find that less than convincing."

They ate a quick breakfast of warm bread and apple butter in the inn's common room, and set out across Silverymoon as the human town slowly woke. The Vault of the Sages was a tall horseshoe-shaped building of stone, sturdy and strong. Araevin and Ilsevele entered only moments after the priests of Denier, who kept the Vault, opened the doors for the day.

An old human cleric with a fringe of snow-white hair around his bald pate looked up from a desk to greet them.

"Ah, good morning! It is not often we are visited by two of the *ar Tel'Quessir*. I am Brother Calwern. How might we help you today?"

"I am Araevin Teshurr, and this is my betrothed, Lady Ilsevele Miritar," Araevin replied. "I am interested in making use of your library."

"Of course. What topics interest you, sir?"

"I am looking for books or treatises on the magical lore of ancient Arcorar, from the early days of Cormanthyr—the centuries following the Twelve Nights of Fire, or perhaps the Fifth Rysar of Jhyrennstar. You may also have writings by the wizards Ithraides, Kaeledhin, Morthil, or Sanathar."

Araevin did not mention Saelethil Dlardrageth. Saelethil would never have shared any of his writings with other mages, or left a record of his studies other than the Nightstar intended for members of his own House.

Brother Calwern raised a bushy eyebrow, and leaned back in his seat. "We have few works of such antiquity here. The wizards you named, are they from the same era?" Araevin nodded, and the Deneirrath priest continued. "I will have to examine our indices and catalogs to see if we have anything that might help you. It might take a little time. In the meantime, I can certainly recommend a likely tome or two for you to begin with. I presume you read Loross and Thorass?"

"Among others, yes."

"Excellent!" The Deneirrath priest stood up, and gestured toward an archway leading deeper into the great building. "If you please, then—this way."

Araevin glanced at Ilsevele and offered a small smile. When it came down to it, he couldn't resist a scholarly mystery, and there was not a better place in Faerûn to solve one than the libraries of Silverymoon. Together they followed Brother Calwern into the Vault of the Sages.

۞ ۞ ۞ ۞ ۞

"High Lords and Ladies of the Council, the Lord Seiveril Miritar of Elion!"

Seiveril faltered on the threshold of the Dome of Stars, surprised to hear his own name announced. He glanced at the herald-captain, a young sun elf who stared straight ahead, giving no further sign that he recognized Seiveril's presence.

Eighty years on the Royal Council and never once have I been announced, Seiveril wondered. Instead, he had always been a member of the body that guests were announced *to*.

He felt the eyes of the minor lords and functionaries in attendance fall on him, as he stood unmoving in the chamber door. Then Seiveril recovered, and he strode with growing confidence into the Dome of Stars.

The high council chamber of Evermeet, the Dome was part of the sprawling palace compound in Leuthilspar. A striking chamber with a dark, star-flecked marble floor and a great clear ceiling of magic theurglass, the Dome was illuminated by the warm yellow light of late afternoon, striking bright gleams from the glossy stone underfoot. It was a magnificent chamber, and in its center stood the glassteel council table, a delicate ornament of frosted-white glass magically hardened to the toughness of steel. It had always struck Seiveril as a good metaphor for the elf race—beautiful to look upon, yet stronger than the eye could believe.

Six of Evermeet's councilors waited on Seiveril's approach. Closest to him, at the left-hand foot of the horseshoe-shaped table, sat the old scribe Zaltarish, one of the queen's most valued advisors. Beside Zaltarish sat the High Admiral Emardin Elsydar, master of Evermeet's navy, and on the other side of the admiral—past Seiveril's own former seat, apparently still vacant—was the High Marshal Keryth Blackhelm, leader of Evermeet's army.

On the right-hand wing of the table sat two of Seiveril's most determined opponents: Lady Selsharra Durothil, matron of the powerful sun elf Durothil clan, and Lady Ammisyll Veldann, another sun elf noble who governed the southern city of Nimlith. Both highborn sun elves stared daggers at him as he came near. To Veldann's left sat Grand Mage Breithel Olithir, another sun elf. Seiveril had always thought well of Olithir, even if the fellow did not trust his own wisdom.

At the head of the table sat Queen Amlaruil herself, dressed in a resplendent gown of pearl-white that was set with countless gleaming diadems. Her raven-dark hair was bound by a simple silver fillet, and she held a thin scepter of shining mithral across her lap.

"You are welcome here, Seiveril Miritar," Amlaruil

said in a warm voice, and she smiled graciously. "So little time has passed since you left, and yet we have so much to speak of."

Seiveril looked up into Amlaruil's eyes, and felt his heart flutter at the sad wisdom and perfect beauty of her face. To look on Amlaruil as she sat in state was to catch a glimpse of Sehanine Moonbow's throne in Arvandor, or so it was said. For his own part, Seiveril knew of no son or daughter of Evermeet who could stand before Amlaruil unmoved.

"I thank you, Queen Amlaruil," he replied, and he bowed deeply.

When he straightened again, Amlaruil looked left and right to her advisors. "I asked Lord Seiveril here today, in the hope that we might hear from his own mouth the tale of his battles to defend Evereska and the High Forest from the daemonfey army. Few events in Faerûn within the last few years have portended so much for the People, and we would only be wise to inform ourselves as best we can about Lord Seiveril's campaigns." Amlaruil looked back to Seiveril, and said, "Will you speak, old friend?"

"Of course, Your Highness. Where should I begin?"

"Begin with your mustering at Elion," Keryth Blackhelm said. "We were all here for your call to arms when you spoke of returning to Faerûn, and we remember the arguments that led to your oratory. Tell us what happened after you left this chamber."

"Very well," Seiveril agreed, and he began his tale.

He recounted the gathering of companies and volunteers in Elion, and the efforts to organize useful military units from the horde of individuals who had answered his call. He described their quick transit to Evereska by means of the ancient elfgates when it became clear that the city was in imminent peril, and the victory of the Battle of the Cwm, in which Seiveril's Crusade had stopped the daemonfey horde from laying siege to Evereska. Then he went on to the pursuit of Sarya Dlardrageth's army through the wild lands north of Evereska, to the climactic battle at the Lonely Moor.

"That was a terrible fight," Seiveril said. He could see it before his eyes even then, remembering the onslaught of demons and the furious battle as the Crusade found itself surrounded on all sides by Sarya's forces. "We fell on the ranks of orcs, ogres, and such, and decimated them. But Sarya and her demons teleported to our flank, and attacked fiercely, while her fey'ri took to the air and fell on our rearmost ranks. It seemed desperate indeed, but then Sarya's demons all vanished at once—each one of them banished back to its native hell as the spells holding the demons in our world failed. That turned the tide. The fey'ri warriors abandoned their orcs and ogres and fled the field soon thereafter."

"The demons vanished—that was Araevin Teshurr's work at Myth Glaurach?" asked the grand mage.

"It was."

"What has happened since?" Zaltarish the scribe asked.

"Well, we have searched all of the North, or so it seems, for any sign of where Sarya and her surviving fey'ri warriors might be hiding. The spellcasters among our army have cast divination after divination, hoping to uncover some sign that our scouts might have missed. We have also helped the wood elves to hunt down the last of the orc warbands and ogre gangs that accompanied the fey'ri in their assault against the High Forest."

"You have won a great victory," Selsharra Durothil said. Seiveril fixed his eyes on her, instantly suspicious. Lady Durothil had not spared many kind words for him over the past few months. Selsharra ignored his dark look and continued, "The daemonfey attack against Evereska and the High Forest has failed. Events have vindicated you, Lord Miritar. I do not think I was wrong to argue for caution when we debated this question a few short months ago, but I certainly cannot argue today that your impetuousness did not accomplish a great good."

Seiveril carefully kept his face neutral, merely inclining his head in response to Durothil's concession.

What is she up to? he wondered.

"So," Keryth Blackhelm said, "When can we expect the return of your army?"

"When I am certain that the threat of the daemonfey has truly passed, and that no other enemies will try Evereska's strength as soon as I leave. Some companies I could send home within a month or two, I think. Others I may ask to remain longer."

"How will you judge when the daemonfey have been finally defeated?" the high admiral asked. "What if you simply cannot find them again?"

"I am prepared to wait."

"A few months is one thing," Ammisyll Veldann observed. "What if you find no sign of the daemonfey for a year? Two years? They are evidently well hidden, after all. Is Evermeet to be left shorn of its defenders for as long as you see fit to be stubborn?"

"The daemonfey are not the sole standard by which I shall judge my errand in Faerûn completed," Seiveril replied. "The daemonfey were tempted to strike against Evereska because the People withdrew so much of their power from Faerûn. I mean to find a way to set that right before I say I am done."

"That will be hard on your warriors, will it not?" Veldann asked. "They joined you to defend Evereska, and Evereska has been defended. They did not answer your call in order to garrison gloomy old ruins in the middle of the wilderness for years."

"I require none to remain who are not willing," Seiveril said.

Ammisyll Veldann threw up her hands, and leaned back in her seat. "Nothing has changed," she muttered.

Selsharra Durothil looked around the Council table, and let her gaze linger on Amlaruil. "I would like to put forward a proposal," she said.

If Queen Amlaruil anticipated more argument from the conservative sun elf, her face did not show it. She graciously nodded. "Of course, Lady Durothil."

"While I do not necessarily agree that Lord Seiveril requires an army quite as large as he now has at his command," Selsharra Durothil began, "I think we have all seen the wisdom of his arguments about maintaining a presence in Faerûn. In fact, it seems to me that this task may be important enough to justify a lasting amendment to Evermeet's defenses. Instead of relying on the zeal and good intentions of those who happen to take interest in affairs in Faerûn, we should shoulder this responsibility ourselves, and formally recognize and support Lord Seiveril's actions so far. Let us name him the East Marshal of the Realm, admit him again to the High Council, and designate his standing army in Faerûn as the East Guard.

"We can incorporate the East Guard into the armies of Evermeet, and thereby ensure that our brave soldiers need not abandon their oaths to the Crown in order to take service in Lord Miritar's army. In fact, we can assess both Evermeet's current defenses and the forces Miritar will need to continue his watch overseas, and divide our forces with more deliberation than before. Both the defenses of Evermeet herself and the strength of our East Guard should be improved with some careful planning."

Seiveril stared at Selsharra Durothil, not bothering to hide his amazement. He noticed that most of her fellow councilors were staring, too.

She can't have decided that I was right! he told himself.

Almost grudgingly, Keryth Blackhelm nodded in agreement. He looked to Queen Amlaruil. "There is a great deal of sense in that idea, my queen," he murmured. "We could station the forces best suited for each job in the right place. Evermeet would be safer, and we would be better situated to intervene in Faerûn when the need arises."

Grand Mage Olithir also nodded and said, "The same is true for our mages, spellblades, and bladesingers. And I for one would welcome Lord Seiveril's voice at this table again."

Ammisyll Veldann turned a furious look on Selsharra Durothil. "You are not seriously suggesting that we *reward* Miritar's disobedience by returning him the seat that he surrendered in this council!" she snapped.

"I do not condone the manner in which Lord Miritar assembled his expedition and decided for himself what was right for all of us," Selsharra answered, "but I cannot deny that his vision and foresight secured Evereska, and perhaps saved thousands of our kindred from destruction and slaughter."

"The constituency of the High Council is the queen's prerogative," Zaltarish observed. "It is for her to decide such matters."

"I must consider the suggestion for a time before I know my answer," Amlaruil said. She looked at Seiveril. "And I suspect that Lord Miritar will wish to consider the question, too. You are asking him to take up a heavy burden, Lady Durothil."

"A burden that he sought out, Your Highness," Selsharra replied.

Amlaruil rapped her scepter on the glassteel table. "We will reconvene in a few days to deliberate the question at length. Until then, Lord Miritar, I would be delighted if you could tarry a few days here in Leuthilspar."

Seiveril bowed again. "Of course, Your Highness," he said.

Farthest Reach • 45

CHAPTER THREE

10 Mirtul, the Year of Lightning Storms

For three days, Araevin explored the depths of Silverymoon's Vault of the Sages. He passed long hours poring over ancient yellow parchments and carefully thumbing through heavy tomes of thick linen paper. He wandered from chamber to chamber, examining the orderly stacks kept by the priests of Denier, or he waited in reading rooms while the helpful clerics brought him books and scrolls they thought might interest him. It was not inexpensive, of course—to make use of the library cost him hundreds of pieces of gold—but Araevin did not begrudge the cost. The clerics of Denier used the fees to acquire and copy rare texts from other libraries all across Faerûn.

Ilsevele helped him in his search, screening works of potential interest to determine whether or not Araevin needed to see a particular reference. She saved him countless hours of reading through dead ends, or wasting time on old works that simply had no bearing on the subject matter he was after. The two sun elves arrived at the library an hour after dawn every morning, and remained until after dark each night before heading back to the Golden Oak and joining Maresa and Filsaelene for the evening meal, wine, and dancing.

They had little luck at first, spending the first day looking at old records and accounts of Arcorar that had nothing to do with magic or mythals. On the next day they successfully narrowed their search by reviewing a list of potentially relevant tomes assembled by the Deneirraths; less than sixty books or documents in the Vault possessed the right combination of antiquity and subject matter to warrant close inspection. A dozen titles into the list, on the morning of the third day of their search, they stumbled across what they were looking for.

"Araevin, I think I've found something," said Ilsevele. She straightened up from the desk where she sat, reading through a set of ancient scrolls. "This scroll describes a judgment by the Coronal of Arcorar against House Dlardrageth, and records how the House was expunged from the realm."

Araevin looked up from the window bench where he was sitting, consulting his journals, and asked, "Who is the author?"

"A court mage named Sanathar."

"I know that name," he said. He set down his journal and joined Ilsevele at her table. He found the passage she indicated, and murmured aloud as he read: "Yes, I see it . . . the high mage Ithraides gathered a company of wizards, and they used their spells to destroy or drive off the Dlardrageths, finally walling off the Dlardrageth tower in Cormanthor—that was the old name for Myth Drannor, of course . . ." He skimmed the old manuscript, careful not to handle the ancient parchment more than was absolutely necessary. "Look, here. More passages were added later. The spell-prison raised around House Dlardrageth

Farthest Reach • 47

was finally removed almost five hundred years after the coronal's mages moved against the Dlardrageths."

"I saw that. They found that they had missed several of the daemonfey."

"Sarya and her sons, and a few others. Yes, that makes sense. We know that the daemonfey escaped from Arcorar and insinuated themselves into several powerful Houses in Siluvanede, creating the fey'ri." Araevin read farther, and his eyes widened. "Interesting," he breathed. "This may be what I was looking for. Near the end of this account Sanathar tells us that the Nightstar was interred in a secure vault—that we know, of course, since I eventually found it there—but he also says that Ithraides departed for Arvandor soon after the creation of the vault. The star elf Morthil took many of Ithraides's tomes and treasures into his keeping."

"Star elf? An unusual turn of phrase. Do you think he meant sun or moon elf?"

"No, it's quite clear. Look, other sun elves and moon elves are named here, and here. I think the text implies a separate race or nationality."

"I've never heard of star elves before," Ilsevele said. "A kindred of the People who died out long ago? Or maybe he is referring to elves who came to this world from another world? Some of Evermeet's folk are descended from elves who sailed the Sea of Night in flying ships."

Araevin studied the ancient yellow parchment for a long moment, eyes narrowed in thought.

"Just because we haven't heard the term 'star elf' before doesn't mean that no one else has," he finally replied. "My friend Quastarte has spent years studying the realms and races of elvenkind in this world. He knows far more about the topic than I do. Perhaps he could tell us more about who these people were, or where and when they lived. For that matter, there might be information close at hand here in the Vault."

He began reading the passage more carefully, studying the exact nuances of the text.

Ilsevele set aside the pages of the manuscript that

Araevin was interested in, and continued to read ahead while he pored over the older pages. The two of them read together in silence for a short time, until Ilsevele stiffened and drew back from the old parchment in front of her.

"There is something else, Araevin."

Araevin glanced up from the scroll. "What?"

"There's a passage by Ithraides. He's writing about the Nightstar here." Her brow furrowed. "Ithraides records that the *selukiira* killed two mages of Arcorar. The *selukiira* was protected by fearsome wards, spells designed to make sure that only daemonfey wizards would be able to use the stone. In fact, Ithraides writes here that he did not dare touch it himself." Ilsevele glanced down at Araevin's chest, even though the lorestone was hidden beneath his shirt. "If the Nightstar is that dangerous, why didn't it destroy you, as well? Did the deadly spells fail with time?"

"No, they're still there." Araevin looked down at the tabletop before him. "The Nightstar spared me because it recognized me."

"Recognized you? What do you mean by that?"

He could not bear to look up to her face. "I mean that it found Dlardrageth blood in me. The Nightstar is not permitted to destroy a Dlardrageth—at least, not one who knows enough about magic to make use of its powers. I am related to Saelethil Dlardrageth, at least distantly."

Ilsevele drew in a soft breath. "Araevin, I didn't—why didn't you tell me?"

"I did not know for certain myself until I attempted the *selukiira*. Oh, I suspected that I might have a distant kinship to one or the other of the fey'ri houses—a very long time ago, my family dwelled in Siluvanede, in the years before the Seven Citadels' War. And when I spoke with Elorfindar in the House of Long Silences, he reminded me of our relationship. But I never dreamed that I could be a Dlardrageth."

He made himself meet her gaze, and said, "I understand that you will break off our engagement, of course. I can't blame you."

"Break off the engagement?" Ilsevele stared at him. "Because twenty or thirty generations ago a Dlardrageth or a fey'ri married into your family? If you go back that far, we all have hundreds—thousands—of ancestors, don't we? Who can say whether we would be proud to be descended from each of them?" She shook her head. "Why, I've touched the lorestone myself, and it hasn't harmed me. I might have a Dlardrageth ancestor, too."

"You've never touched it except when I was holding it. If I ever set it down, don't lay a finger on it, Ilsevele. It will gladly destroy you. It would *enjoy* destroying you."

Ilsevele shuddered. "You keep it next to your heart. How can you abide that?"

"It's harmless to me. As long as it is bound to me, it cannot harm anyone else, not without a great deal of carelessness. And I don't have any intention of being careless with this device."

"Still . . . if it's dangerous, and you know it's dangerous, why wear it at all? Maybe you should return the Nightstar to that vault Ithraides built for it."

Araevin reached inside his tunic and curled his fingers around the Nightstar. He brought out the lambent gemstone, holding it in his thumb and forefinger. The purple facets glimmered with an eldritch light.

"I can't do that yet," he said. "The Nightstar has taught me much already, but there is more to learn. When I master the secrets of this stone, there is nothing Sarya Dlardrageth can do that I won't be able to undo."

"What secrets?" Ilsevele asked. "You already learned enough mythalcraft to sever her from the mythal of Myth Glaurach. There is more?"

He hesitated, and said, "Yes."

Ilsevele studied him for a moment, and her eyes hardened. "High magic?"

Araevin nodded. "Yes. High magic. The Nightstar can give me Saelethil's knowledge of high magic. The high magic spells and high mythalcraft in this stone will let me defend or reweave any mythal Sarya attempts to subvert. Or any other enemy, for that matter."

"I thought Philaerin and the other high mages directed you to wait fifty years before taking up the study of high magic."

"I don't think they appreciate the dangers of waiting, Ilsevele. I have spent decades roaming the human lands of the North, and I've seen the works of Aryvandaar and Illefarn that sleep in the wilds of the Sword Coast. They are dangerous things, and they are growing more perilous every year."

"So you have decided that you know better than a circle of high mages?" Ilsevele was incredulous. "Araevin, did it ever occur to you that they wanted you to wait for your own good? How can you so lightly disregard their advice?"

"Because I know what this lorestone is, and what it can teach me. If I waited fifty years to study it, I would be no more ready than I am now." Araevin gazed into the Nightstar, then sighed and slipped it back inside his shirt. "You saw what I was able to accomplish with only a portion of the Nightstar's lore. I banished hundreds of Sarya Dlardrageth's demons at one stroke! Your father might have won the battle at the Lonely Moor without my help, but even if he did, how many elves would have died to destroy those monsters?"

"Yes, you made good use of what you learned from the lorestone," Ilsevele said. "But you can't seriously be arguing that the end justifies the means! That is a very slippery slope, and you know it. What if you could have won the battle by casting some terrible spell of necromancy, animating the bodies of our own fallen warriors so that they would continue fighting? Yes, the battle would have been won, and yes, no more of our own would have died who hadn't been killed already—but would it have been worth the price?"

"Banishing demons is hardly comparable to defiling our own dead! You know I would never do something like that."

"Using an evil weapon to accomplish a good end is dangerous ground, regardless of the exact nature of the weapon or the end in question."

"Of course. But the spells and the knowledge contained in this *selukiira* are only tools, Ilsevele. The device can't harm anyone as long as I do not permit it to do so, and it offers me invaluable insights into spells and lore lost to the People for ages." Araevin threw his hands wide in an angry shrug. "*Someone* has to study the arts our enemies might turn against us, simply to understand how we might defend ourselves when they are used against us. At the moment, I seem to be the only one who can dare this high loregem to do that."

"But the daemonfey don't have access to Saelethil's lore now," Ilsevele protested. "Why else would they have been looking for the Nightstar before? I don't understand why you shouldn't just put it back where you found it, Araevin. Ithraides's defenses kept the Nightstar out of evil hands for five thousand years, after all."

"Sarya Dlardrageth was entombed for almost all that time, so it's not at all clear to me that Ithraides's defenses were in fact sufficient to the task."

Ilsevele stood, seizing her cloak from the chair back she had draped it over and throwing it around her shoulders.

"I'm not sure you understand as much about the Dlardrageths or the Nightstar as you think you do," she said. "An ancient marriage and a glimmer of kinship don't stain you with evil, Araevin. Flirting with dangerous and hateful powers because you think the end justifies the means—that is what you should worry about."

She gave him one final sharp glance, and strode stiffly out of the reading room. Araevin watched her leave.

Is she right? he wondered. Maybe I should simply bury the Nightstar again, until I know for certain that I need it.

He rubbed his fingers over the small, cold facets above his heart, and sat down to read more about Morthil, Sanathar, and Ithraides, and their accounts of the device from fifty centuries ago.

Scyllua Darkhope, Castellan and High Captain of Zhentil Keep, stared intently at the stronghold rising on the green verge of the forest that lay, low and distant, beyond the ruined walls of Yûlash. Here on the outskirts of the abandoned city a new Zhentish watchtower was being raised, and the heavy wooden scaffolds and booms surrounding the shell of cold gray stone seemed as light and fragile as a birdcage.

It struck her as incongruous that a work of enduring strength could be born within such a light and impermanent cocoon. A bad windstorm could blow down the scaffolding in an hour, but once its work was done, why, her new tower might stand for a thousand years.

She studied the work a little longer, not really watching the indentured masons and stonecutters at their tasks, simply lost in the metaphor. Her own life could be described in a similar way, she decided. Out of the fragility and impermanence of the flesh, a stone-hard spirit took shape. Out of the weakness of her heart and her foolish early hopes, the foundations of true purpose and real clarity had been laid. When her true self had finally taken form, well, it was of no account that the scaffolding of her ideals and her former dreams had been discarded, was it?

"High Captain?"

Scyllua pulled her gaze from the ongoing construction, and turned to her lieutenant. The Zhentish officer visibly steeled himself when she glanced at him. She was not a tall woman, but she was broad-shouldered and athletic, and the black plate armor she wore with the ease of long experience only contributed to her formidable presence.

"Yes, lieutenant?"

"The wizard Perestrom is here. You asked for him after reading his report."

"Have him brought up," Scyllua commanded without looking at the lesser officer. She rarely bothered to look anyone else in the eyes, and had the habit of staring off over a shoulder or fixing her blank gaze on someone's breastbone as if she might bore a hole through his heart with simple concentration. She didn't realize that she had that habit, and certainly didn't do it deliberately; she simply found face-to-face conversations distracting, and did not like to break the chain of her thoughts.

The lieutenant struck his fist to his chest in the Zhentish salute—not that Scyllua noticed—and withdrew briefly, before returning with a tall, vulture-faced wizard in black robes, the Zhentarim mage Perestrom.

"High Captain Darkhope," the wizard said, offering a shallow bow as an insincere smile creased his sharp features. He looked up at the tower under construction. "That is something of a vanity, you know. The Art offers many ways to render such an expensive defense useless."

"A tower built with care and foresight may not be impervious to a skilled wizard, Perestrom, but at least it will discourage the less competent ones." Scyllua smiled thinly to herself, even though she faced away from the others. "And we can take steps to discourage attacking wizards, of course. For example, I have heard that our clerics have mastered a rite that would reave the life from a wizard, transforming him into a ghost, and bind him to a specific task for all eternity—for instance, the defense of this tower against enemy sorcerers. I shall have to give some thought to where I might find a wizard of suitable skill for such a task."

"I will be happy to provide several recommendations," Perestrom replied. If his arrogant smile faltered just a hint, Scyllua did not see it.

"Of course. Now, about your report . . . What were you doing in Myth Drannor, exactly?"

"I am the master of a small adventuring company, the Lords of the Ebon Wyrm. I have led several expeditions into various ruins around the Moonsea and old Cormanthyr, in search of various glimpses of arcane lore and magical treasures. A tenday ago we arrived in the ruins of Myth Drannor, intent on retrieving whatever artifacts we could find from the old city. We explored the ruins for several days, with a little success. But five days ago, late in the afternoon, we were attacked by a large company of flying, demonic sorcerers. I lost several of my fellow Ebon Wyrms before we managed to escape into the ruins."

"Demons and devils of all sorts are known to plague Myth Drannor," Scyllua observed. "And they often slay adventurers there. I see nothing remarkable about your tale so far, Perestrom."

"As you say, High Captain," Perestrom said, again offering a small, insincere bow. "However, I found it noteworthy that these demonic sorcerers had the features of elves, and spoke Elvish to one another."

"Elves?" Scyllua glanced over her shoulder at the tall mage. "Unusual, I admit, but why does it merit Zhentarim attention?"

"Because I think there are a thousand or more of these fellows in Myth Drannor now, a whole army of them." Perestrom's smirk faded a bit. "They attacked several other adventuring companies in and around the city over the next day or so, and we were attacked by several different demon-elf bands during this time. We eluded most of these attacks through my spells—illusions to hide our presence, summonings to conjure up monsters that could cover our withdrawal—and I kept careful notations on the arms and devices of each such band we encountered.

"When we finally abandoned the ruins, I spent another two days spying out as much as I could about these new foes, using various spells and devices. I will be happy to share my notes, if you would care to examine my evidence in detail."

Scyllua faced Perestrom. He had managed to seize her attention, all right.

"A thousand?" she asked. "All of them spellcasters?"

"Better than half, I would say. Few as accomplished as I am, of course."

"Of course." Scyllua considered that for a time. "What about the baatezu? Did they destroy many of these newcomers?" That would be a good measure of their strength, anyway.

"As far as I could tell, the devils did not contest their presence. I saw no fighting between the demon-winged sorcerers and the devils of Myth Drannor. In fact, on a few occasions I saw devils in the company of the newcomers."

Farthest Reach • 55

Despite herself, Scyllua felt her clarity slip just a fraction. What could Perestrom's report signify? she thought. A new army in Myth Drannor? One that could rally the devils of the city to their banner? At the very least, it meant that further Zhentarim expeditions to the ruined elven city must be undertaken with even more care and preparation than usual. Could it pose a threat to Zhentil Keep itself? That many spellcasters and devils would be a formidable force, if they found a way to escape the wards imprisoning them within Myth Drannor's walls. But there were lesser states between Myth Drannor and Zhentil Keep—the Dales, for instance, or Moonsea cities such as Hillsfar.

Threat, or opportunity?

"Very well, Perestrom. I agree that this merits more investigation." Scyllua lifted her unfocused gaze to the wizard's eyes until Perestrom looked away, his self-assurance not quite up to the intensity of her attention. "I will speak to Lord Fzoul about this, and we will consider how our ignorance might be amended."

☙ ☙ ☙ ☙ ☙

Ilsevele left Araevin to continue his researches by himself, spending her time in the company of Maresa and Filsaelene. She said that she simply wanted more time to wander Silverymoon's tree-shaded streets and explore its odd shops, quaint markets, and famed universities, but Araevin could read her silent disapproval well enough. He promised himself that he would set aside his work for a time and join her in taking in Silverymoon's sights, but first he wanted to see what he could find out about star elves and the long-dead mage named Morthil, who had helped Ithraides destroy the Dlardrageths in Arcorar five thousand years ago.

On the morning of his fifth day in the Vault, and his second alone, Araevin found himself striding from reading room to reading room in search of Calwern, anxious to locate the next manuscript on his ever-growing list. He glanced out the leaded glass windows that marched along the hall, noting the bright spring sunshine outside and the soft and distant sound of the breeze caressing the branches of the stately old shadowtops sheltering the Vault's windows, when he felt the cold, tingling presence of strange magic arise within his mind.

Araevin recoiled, dropping the sheaf of paper he carried and whirling to search the empty halls around him. Faint whispers of distant magic coiled in his mind, and he felt a presence forming, a sense of grim competence behind it.

He started to speak the words of an arcane defense, but then he felt a familiar visage behind the magic, a stern face with a thin beard of black and gray, features somewhere between an elf's and a human's.

"A sending," he murmured, feeling more than a little foolish. He relaxed and focused his attention on the message.

Araevin, this is Jorildyn, spoke the distant voice in his mind. *We have found portals under Myth Glaurach. Starbrow suspects the daemonfey built them. Can you come and investigate?*

The magic of the sending lingered, awaiting his response. Araevin frowned, considering Jorildyn's message.

I will be there in a few days, he replied. *Contact me again if you need me to be there any sooner.*

Then Jorildyn's sending faded, its magic expended by Araevin's response.

He glanced up at the bright spring sunshine filling the old library, and fought off a shudder. Portals . . . of course, he thought. But where do they lead? Sarya and her followers might easily have made their escape through the magical doorways. A portal might lead anywhere—a forgotten dungeon, an undead-haunted tomb, the sunless depths of the Underdark, even a network of other portals—*anywhere*. And without the proper key, it might prove impossible to pursue Sarya and her followers at all. Araevin had certainly studied enough of the magical gateways to know that.

"Master Teshurr, are you well?" Calwern asked. The Deneirrath cleric hurried into the hallway, his kind old face anxious with concern.

"Yes. Forgive me—I just received a sending," Araevin said, coming back to the library with a start. "I am afraid I must go."

"Is there anything we can do for you?"

"No, my friend, I think I must leave Silverymoon."

"I see. Do you know when you will return?" Calwern asked.

"A couple of tendays, I hope?" Araevin stooped and picked up the lists he had dropped, quickly setting them back in order again. "While I am gone, will you have your sages look into these sources for me? I will come back soon and see what you and your colleagues have learned."

"Of course." Calwern took the papers, bowed, and touched his brow and heart in the elven manner. In Elvish he said, *"Sweet water and light laughter until we meet again, then."*

"And to you," Araevin replied.

He returned the cleric's parting, then hurried out of the Vault of the Sages, making his way to the Golden Oak.

In the middle of the day, the inn yard was almost empty, the tables beneath the great oak tree deserted and silent. He found his way to the room Ilsevele and he shared. She was not there, nor were Maresa and Filsaelene in their own rooms, so Araevin began to pack up his belongings, making ready to leave. He settled the account with the innkeeper for all of them, and he waited for his companions.

Not long before dusk, Ilsevele, Maresa, and Filsaelene returned to the inn, tired but in good spirits after another day of wandering Silverymoon's streets and markets. Araevin stirred himself from a shallow Reverie as they bustled into the room, laughing at some jest or another.

"Good evening," he said. "I've been waiting for you."

"You're an elf, you're good at it," Maresa observed. She grinned at her own wit. "In fact, we can go back out again for a while, if you'd like."

Ilsevele glanced at his pack and staff by the door, and the soft smile faded from her perfect features. She looked back to Araevin, her expression guarded.

"What's happened?" she asked.

"I've heard news of the daemonfey, I think." Araevin stood. "Starbrow had Jorildyn speak to me in a sending. Your father's warriors have found some portals hidden beneath Myth Glaurach, and Starbrow suspects that the daemonfey might have built them or used them for their own purposes. He asked me to examine the portals. I told him I would come within a few days."

"Portals? Leading where?" Maresa demanded. "More troll-haunted forests, or monster-plagued caves? I've had enough of portals, thank you."

"I won't know where they lead until I see them for myself," Araevin said. He looked at his companions, and gestured at the inn room. "Starbrow asked for me, and I intend to go. But there's no need for you to leave Silverymoon, if you would prefer to stay."

"I'll come," Ilsevele said at once. "My father's fight against the daemonfey is my fight, too, and my place is with you."

Araevin nodded. He hadn't really expected anything other than that from her, even after their argument in the Vault.

"It may be nothing," he said. "But, if Starbrow has stumbled onto the trail of the daemonfey, it might be more than a little dangerous to follow them. I might stumble into the middle of Sarya's audience chamber again. Or they may set magical traps or monstrous guardians to discourage pursuit."

"You are going to attempt those portals, regardless of the danger," Ilsevele observed. "I will, too."

"Why do they need you for this task, Araevin?" Filsaelene asked. "Aren't there dozens of skilled mages with Seiveril and Starbrow at Myth Glaurach?"

"Yes, there are, but Araevin's made a special study of portal magic over the last few years," Ilsevele answered for him. "He knows as much about portals as any mage in Faerûn by now."

"When are you leaving?" Filsaelene asked.

"Tonight or tomorrow morning," Araevin said. "I can make arrangements for you to remain here as long as you

Farthest Reach • 59

like, Filsaelene. I don't want to turn you out in the street. You too, Maresa."

Filsaelene frowned, her eyes dark and thoughtful. "No, I think I would like to come with you. If your business with the daemonfey isn't finished yet, the least I can do is help you finish it. If you hadn't found me when you did, I doubt that Sarya would have left me alive in that dungeon when she abandoned Myth Glaurach."

"You don't owe us any debt, Filsaelene," Ilsevele said. "We would have aided anybody in your circumstances."

"I know," the young sun elf said. "But . . . even if I owe you nothing for saving me from the daemonfey dungeons, I owe something to my friends who died fighting the daemonfey. If I can help to make the daemonfey answer for the evil they have caused, I will."

"Well, I'm certainly not going to stay here by myself," Maresa muttered. She crossed her arms and glared at Araevin. "Next time, let's find something that needs doing in a city like Calimshan or Waterdeep, instead of some musty old ruins in the middle of the wilderness."

"It's our task, not yours," Araevin said. "You don't have to—"

"Oh, yes I do," Maresa said. "I didn't know him as long as you did, Araevin, but Grayth was my friend, too. And Brant, as well. If you have any chance of finding where that demonspawned bitch Sarya is hiding, I want to be a part of it. I'm in the habit of killing people who murder my friends."

Araevin grimaced. Maresa had struck straight at a point he had half-forgotten. Caught up in the mystery of Saelethil's lore, it had somehow slipped from the forefront of his mind that his oldest and truest human friend had not survived their battles against the daemonfey.

"I will be glad for your company, then," he told Maresa.

Ilsevele looked down at the pack by the door. "So we are leaving now?" she said.

"Soon," Araevin replied. "I just wanted to be ready. But if we all are going . . . it's dusk, and the daemonfey already have a twenty-day head start. Tomorrow morning is good enough."

Maresa brightened. "Well, good, then. I was afraid I wouldn't have one more chance to drink and dance all night long before we set out."

"It'll be a hard day of travel tomorrow, if you overdo it this evening," Filsaelene warned.

"That," said Maresa, "will be tomorrow's problem."

CHAPTER FOUR

13 Mirtul, the Year of Lightning Storms

Seiveril Miritar spent much of his time in Leuthilspar closeted with Keryth Blackhelm and other captains of Evermeet's armies and knighthoods, describing in exacting detail the course of the campaign his Crusade had fought across the wilderlands of the North. As best he could, he told them how he had confronted the daemonfey army and their demonic allies—which tactics worked against an army of winged sorcerers, which weapons and spells served to defeat demons and which did not.

When he finished with that task, he steeled himself for a duty he had no heart for, but that he had to do. After he tarried in Leuthilspar for a day more, he outfitted a riding horse in the stables of his family's villa in the capital and left the city. He rode north into the green meadows and airy forests of the western hills, to the small forest estate of Elvath Muirreste. There he visited with Nera Muirreste, Elvath's wife, and as best he could he told her how Elvath had died. She had heard of Elvath's fall already, and greeted him wearing the gray veil of mourning.

"I am so sorry for your loss," Seiveril said to her. "Elvath was more than my captain-at-arms and adviser. He was my friend. I cannot tell you how much I regret his death."

Lady Muirreste sighed. "I know, Seiveril. Elvath thought the world of you, and he answered your call to arms with a willing heart. His death is almost more than I can bear, but it gives me comfort to know that he died fighting for a good and true cause." Nera sat in silence for a time then she set her hand on his and asked, "How did it happen? I only heard that he fell fighting outside Evereska."

"Elvath had command of our right flank," Seiveril said. He found that he was glad of the opportunity to simply recount the tale, rather than search for comforting words. "Our cavalry was there. They fought valiantly and well all morning. Elvath's forces were outnumbered, but he commanded some of our best companies, and they used their speed and courage to great effect.

"After an hour of fighting, we repelled the daemonfey attack, and their lines broke. Their army fell back in retreat. I sent our cavalry in pursuit, and Elvath and his Silver Guard drove the orcs and ogres and the rest out of the West Cwm, sealing our victory. But near the top of the Sentinel Pass on the far side of the Cwm, Elvath was killed by a boulder thrown by a giant. He was simply looking the wrong way and had no chance to dodge it." Seiveril paused then added, "He was killed at once."

"Were you there?"

"No, I was tending to wounded on the far side of the vale when he fell. I might have been able to save him, had I been closer. But so many of our warriors were injured in the early fighting . . ." He made himself look into Nera's eyes. "I left the pursuit in Elvath's hands, because my healing was needed so badly where I was. I should have led the pursuit myself."

Nera squeezed his hand. "Did others live because you chose as you did?"

Seiveril considered the question. "Yes. The healing spells I cast that day likely saved a number of people who otherwise would have died."

"Then I am certain that I do not regret your decision, Seiveril. And I know that Elvath would not, either." Nera Muirreste released his hand, and smiled sadly behind her veil.

Seiveril took his leave an hour later, and rode back to Leuthilspar in the afternoon, taking his time. Hundreds of elves who had followed him to Faerûn had fallen in battle, and he owed visits to many more people, a burden that should have broken his heart. Yet Nera's question kept him from drowning in the grief he felt.

Did others live because I chose as I did? he asked himself. And the answer was an unequivocal yes. Elf warriors who fell in battle against the daemonfey had undoubtedly spared many more lives, the lives of many others who had no skill for battle and otherwise might have died terrible deaths. He grieved for each son or daughter of Evermeet who died following his banner, but he could not bring himself to believe that he had been wrong to take up arms against the daemonfey threat.

He returned to Leuthilspar late in the afternoon, following the familiar boulevards and winding ways that led to the Miritar villa. He tended to his horse himself, dismissing the groom as he unsaddled the animal, rubbed it down, brushed its coat, watered it, and put away the tack and harness. He had just filled the feed bag and was finishing his work, when he became aware of someone watching him from the stable door.

"Yes?" he said without turning.

"I'm glad you haven't lost the habit of doing such work for yourself," Queen Amlaruil replied. She glided into the stable and paused to pat the horse's neck. "I see you have been out riding."

Seiveril recovered from his surprise, and bowed. "Yes, my lady. I have just returned from Elvath Muirreste's home."

"He fell near Evereska, didn't he?"

"Yes, he did. Calling on Nera was the least I could do."

Amlaruil looked over the horse's shoulders at him. "That was good of you, Seiveril."

Seiveril brushed off his hands and said, "If you like, we can go inside. For some reason I feel uncomfortable entertaining the monarch of Evermeet while standing in my stable."

"It has the virtue of being a place where we are unlikely to be listened to," Amlaruil said. "I can think of a few people who might be tempted to scry on you. Or me, for that matter."

"In that case, I suggest the garden." Seiveril led Amlaruil through another door to a small bower between the stable and the manor itself. A simple stone bench overlooked a small, natural waterfall that trickled through the grounds. It was nothing compared to the expansive gardens ringing Amlaruil's palace, but it was quiet and private. And just to ensure their privacy, Seiveril spoke a prayer to Corellon and wove a spell designed to obscure any efforts to spy on them.

When he was done, he turned to Amlaruil and asked, "What brings you to my house, my lady?"

"I wanted to know what you thought of Selsharra Durothil's suggestion. Are you willing to resume a Council seat and hold an office such as she describes?" Amlaruil sat down on the bench and arranged her silver-hued gown.

"The East Marshal?" Seiveril frowned, thinking carefully. "Are you asking me to accept this duty?"

Amlaruil smiled. "Answer my question first, and I'll answer yours."

"Well . . . no, I do not think I want to hold such a title."

"Is it because Selsharra suggested it, or do you have some other objection?"

"I am certainly suspicious of Selsharra's motives," Seiveril admitted. "After all, she reversed her position with the skill of a pirouetting dancer, didn't she? But even assuming that she was completely honest and forthcoming, I still am not sure that what she suggests will work."

Farthest Reach • 65

The queen tilted her head. "Go on."

"If I swore myself to your service again, and accepted a titled office that made me a high captain of your army, I would naturally be subject to your commands. I would arrange my forces as you asked, I would march when you ordered me to march, and I would not march against an enemy unless I asked you first." Seiveril shrugged. "That also means answering to the council for everything I do or don't do."

"The council does not have the authority to tell me what to do," Amlaruil said. "It is true that I think twice before I disregard their suggestions, but the responsibility for Evermeet's governance and safety are mine, not theirs. I will not allow the Durothils and Veldanns of the council to question my decisions beyond a reasonable point."

"I am not certain that is as true as you would like it to be," Seiveril said. Amlaruil's eyes flashed, and he quickly hurried on. "You will not be on the throne forever, Amlaruil, and I will not be your general in Faerûn for long. An arrangement we make now, because it suits both our talents and our interests, may not survive our successors."

"Even I do not know when that day will come, Seiveril. We can hardly allow ourselves to refrain from making good and sound judgments now because we think those who follow us may overturn them."

"Nevertheless. The next monarch to sit on Evermeet's throne may not possess the mandate of the Seldarine, as Zaor did and you do. Even if a Moonflower heir succeeds you, the succession may entail compromises, limits on the monarch's power. In that scenario, your heir may not be able to refuse a council demand to recall any standing army you leave in Faerûn." Seiveril looked down at his feet. "I do not want to see my work in Faerûn reversed, because Evermeet's monarch or council—or the next holder of my prospective title, for that matter—change their minds about engaging Faerûn in a decade or two."

"Seiveril, I have no intention of departing for Arvandor any time soon."

"That's not always left to our choosing, is it?" he countered.

"You truly believe that you will have an easier time maintaining a presence in Faerûn through your voluntary call to arms, when the council and the crown are willing to consider formalizing what you have done?" Amlaruil shook her head in disbelief. "Seiveril, I have been won over by the persuasiveness of your arguments so far, but I simply don't see how this can be true."

"I know," Seiveril said, "but I have given it a great deal of thought over the last few days."

The queen rose, and regarded him for a long moment. "The council meets again in a little less than a tenday, my friend. I am inclined to lend my support to Selsharra's suggestion. It would place you in an awkward position if the council appointed a different lord to go to Faerûn and assume command of those in your army who would prefer to serve under the Crown."

"I will have an answer for you and the council," Seiveril said.

Amlaruil nodded. She took his hand, and smiled. "Then I suppose I will go. Thank you for hearing me out."

"You are welcome in my stable any time you care to visit it, Your Majesty," Seiveril replied.

Amlaruil laughed, and turned to go. Her gown glittered like starlight in the gathering dusk. But at the moonstone archway marking the garden's entrance, she paused and looked back at him.

"One other matter I meant to mention," she said. "I have heard that one of your captains wields Keryvian, the last of Demron's baneblades. I knew the sword was in your possession, but I thought that it had answered to no hand since the fall of Myth Drannor."

"Yes. I gave Keryvian into the keeping of my captain, Starbrow."

"I do not know him," Amlaruil said with a frown. Seiveril could understand her confusion. Any champion with skill and experience enough to merit such trust would have been known to her in Evermeet. "You must hold him in high regard indeed."

"He is not who he seems to be."

Farthest Reach • 67

Amlaruil studied him for a moment, and her eyes widened.

"It can't be Fflar," she whispered. "Not after so many years."

"Please, do not speak of this," Seiveril asked. "He prefers to remain just Starbrow for now."

"Seiveril, you can't simply resurrect dead heroes when you need them! And he died so long ago."

Seiveril glanced up at the darkening skies. "It wasn't entirely my own idea."

Amlaruil measured him, her expression stern. "You spoke of my mandate earlier. I sincerely hope you have the mandate you think you do. If you are wrong about what you're doing, the consequences would be disastrous."

She swept away into the dusk, leaving Seiveril alone in his garden.

The cleric sat down on the bench again, and watched the first dim stars emerging overhead.

"I hope I do, too," he murmured.

◈ ◈ ◈ ◈ ◈

Five days of hard travel brought Araevin, Ilsevele, Maresa, and Filsaelene from Silverymoon to the ruins of Myth Glaurach. Spring rains drenched them for several days, until Araevin began to wonder whether it would be better to seek some form of magical travel to speed their journey. But he disliked teleporting unless he felt that he absolutely had to do so—sometimes teleportation magic went awry, after all.

Fortunately, they found villages and inns for much of their journey—first along the road from Silverymoon to Everlund, then at Lhuvenhead and Jalanthar. From Jalanthar, at the east end of the Rauvin vale, they struck out south and east through Turnstone Pass, and arrived at the ruins of Myth Glaurach an hour after sunset. As before, the ancient city was ringed with the lanterns and modest campfires of the elven army, a cheerful sight after days of riding.

Araevin and his companions left their horses at a large camp corral where the cavalry companies of the Crusade housed their steeds, and climbed up Myth Glaurach's winding old footpaths, which circled steadily as they ascended the forest-covered hilltop on which the city stood. Small encampments of elf warriors and patrols of vigilant guards filled the old city, calling out friendly greetings as they passed by. With a few questions Araevin and his companions learned that Starbrow and Vesilde Gaerth were currently in charge of the army, since Seiveril Miritar was away on Evermeet, and that the commanders were headquartered in the city's old library.

They found Starbrow and Gaerth poring over supply and equipment records, wrestling with the question of how to feed and arm not only the warriors of the army—elf warriors in a forest could get along for quite some time with few stores, and most had brought their own weapons and armor—but also the thousands of horses and the more exotic creatures that accompanied the army.

The two commanders made an odd pair. Starbrow was nearly six and a half feet tall and about as burly as a moon elf ever got, while the sun elf Vesilde Gaerth was a full foot shorter and slight of build. Starbrow looked up as they entered, and grinned.

"I was wondering where you were," he said. "I was about to have Jorildyn cast another sending for you."

"It's a long ride from Silverymoon," Ilsevele replied. She wrung out the hem of her cloak, leaving a puddle of cold water on the floor, and glared at Starbrow. "You had better have a good reason for sending for us."

Vesilde Gaerth raised his hand in greeting. "Mage Teshurr, Lady Ilsevele, welcome back! I am glad to see you. Not to speak for Captain Starbrow, but I think we have a sound reason for seeking Araevin's expertise. Our mages have had no luck with opening the portals the daemonfey left behind."

"I'll have a look first thing in the morning," Araevin promised. "Right now we're all tired, cold, and wet, and I wouldn't say no to a hot meal and a mug of mulled wine, if anything like that can be found around here."

"That's the best idea I've heard in a tenday," Maresa added.

"Of course. I'll see if our quartermasters can find something for you."

Vesilde called for an aide, who then headed off in search of some food and good accommodations for Araevin and his companions.

"We heard that my father went to Evermeet," Ilsevele asked Starbrow. "Do you know when he will return?"

"Three or four days, most likely. He said there was one more council meeting he wanted to attend before he came back—but if you find something in the portals, he'll return at once."

Araevin and his friends dined with Vesilde and Starbrow, listening to the commanders' accounts of the Crusade's fruitless search for any sign of the daemonfey and the discovery of the hidden portals in Sarya's buried vaults. Then they were shown to an old ruined chapel, its long-vanished roof replaced by well-secured canvas to make a reasonably warm and dry room in which to camp.

In the dark hours before dawn, Araevin roused himself from Reverie, found his spellbooks, and chose a small alcove of the old temple to illuminate with a pale light spell while he studied his spells of portal lore. When the sun came up, he joined the others for a breakfast of dried fruit and porridge provided by the quartermasters of the army.

"Arm yourselves for battle," Araevin told them after they ate. "If we try our luck with an unknown portal, we might step through into the fight of our lives."

While they were arming themselves, Starbrow appeared in the chapel's old doorway. He wore a long green cloak over his shoulders with Keryvian belted to his waist, and he carried a large rucksack. The moon elf looked them over, and grinned.

"You certainly *look* ready," he said.

Araevin looked at Starbrow in surprise. "You're coming with us?"

"Unless you tell me not to."

"Aren't you needed here?" Ilsevele asked. "My father left the army in your hands, after all."

"Actually, he left Lord Gaerth in command. I'm just his second. Besides, we've been sitting here for days. If there's even the slightest chance that we might sniff out the daemonfey, I want to be a part of it."

"I've seen his work with that sword of his," Maresa observed to Filsaelene. The genasi set her hands on her hips, her crimson leather armor gleaming darkly. "I'm not going to tell him we don't need him."

"Very well," Araevin answered. "Let's have a look at these portals you found. It may be a short trip if I can't open them."

Starbrow laughed out loud, then he led the small company into the streets of Myth Glaurach. A short walk brought them to the onetime palace of the city's rulers. It was an impressive ruin, with great gaping arches and broken towers reaching to the gray skies.

"The grand mage's palace," Starbrow said. "The daemonfey used it as their stronghold."

They climbed up the shattered steps to the open foyer, passed through into a courtyard within the overgrown walls, and there found a stone stairway deep in the palace, descending into the darkness below. Araevin frowned, and steeled himself. He knew all too well the vaults and passages beneath the palace, as did his companions.

Starbrow's soldiers had illuminated the dark passageway with small lanterns, and they followed the string of lanternlit hallways and stairs as they descended deeper and deeper into the cold rock of the hillside. They passed several contingents of guards, vigilant elves who stood watch in case some undetected evil emerged from a hidden depth of Sarya's dungeons.

"Have you had any trouble down here?" Araevin asked.

"We've found a couple of magical traps—spell glyphs, symbols, things like that," Starbrow replied. "But we haven't found any fey'ri assassins lurking in the cellars, or demongates to the Abyss, or dragon lairs, or anything truly dangerous. I think Sarya simply didn't have the time to cover her tracks as well as she might have liked."

The moon elf turned aside into a long, narrow gallery that Araevin recognized from his cursory exploration of the place a few tendays ago. Statues of grim-looking gargoyles crouched near the ceiling, leering down at them. The gallery ended in a blank stone wall, a single featureless block contained within a stone lintel carved in the shape of a winding vine climbing a trellis.

"Here it is," Starbrow said.

"That's not daemonfey work," Araevin said at once. He pointed at the decorative stonework. "They have no use for carvings like that."

Starbrow looked sharply at him. "You mean this is a dead end?"

"No, I didn't say that. There's no reason that Sarya and her vultures couldn't have used a portal like this."

Araevin studied it, searching for any markings or lettering to read.

"Can you open it?" Filsaelene asked.

"Possibly," Araevin replied. "Let me try a spell first."

He whispered the words of a simple detection spell, and carefully examined the flickering auras that glimmered around the ancient doorway.

"It has the right sort of magic," he decided. "And it's certainly strong and well-woven enough to have lasted for quite a long time."

He spoke another spell, one that would divine many of the secrets of the portal. In his eyes the magical Weave ghosted into existence, bright and many-colored, each strand hinting at work done well and carefully long ago.

"It's a keyed portal," he said.

"Which means?" Starbrow asked.

"It won't open unless we take the right action or present the right device—a token of some kind, a password, some specific thing that would keep just anybody from opening the doorway."

Araevin examined the blank gateway for a few minutes longer, and he began to chant the words of a longer and more difficult spell, seeking to wrest from the portal itself the knowledge of what key would activate it.

He finished the spell, and in his mind's eye he caught a glimpse of a small white flower, a tiny bell only the size of a thumbnail, really.

"That makes sense," Araevin said with a soft laugh.

"What? Have you figured it out already?" Starbrow said.

"It's only a matter of knowing the right spells. They're somewhat rare, and I suppose not all that many wizards have studied them." Araevin straightened, and reached out to tap the carving of the vine surrounding the doorway. "This vine—it is rellana, isn't it?"

Starbrow and the others exchanged blank looks, but Ilsevele nodded.

"Yes," she said. "I think it is."

"That's all we need. Each of us must carry a petal of a rellana blossom and speak a short password—*nesyie alleisendilie*—and the portal will activate."

"I'll send for some," Starbrow said at once. He quickly trotted out of sight and called out to the nearby guards. In a few minutes, he returned with a handful of tiny white blossoms. "Here you go," he said. "What would they do if they needed to use the portal and these weren't in bloom?"

"The builders probably kept a small jar of old petals somewhere near this place," Araevin said. He helped himself to a small petal, and held it pinched between his thumb and forefinger. "Now, how do we want to do this? It might be best if I went ahead alone, in case there's some trap I didn't expect—"

"Nesyie alleisendilie!" Maresa said.

She touched the blank stone of the archway, and disappeared in the blink of an eye, leaving nothing but a small white petal drifting down to the floor.

"Maresa!" Ilsevele snapped, but the genasi was nowhere in sight. The noblewoman snarled. "Now what do we do?"

Farthest Reach • 73

"She doesn't like to waste time, does she?" Starbrow observed. "Well, let's hope that Araevin can get us out of wherever we wind up."

He plucked a single petal out of the handful he held, dropped the rest into Araevin's hand, and followed Maresa into the portal. With a sigh, Ilsevele snatched up a petal and hurried after him, followed by Filsaelene a moment later.

Araevin took a moment to scoop up the whole handful of rellana flowers, just in case there were multiple portals on the far side that made use of the same key. Then he followed his comrades into the unknown.

☉ ☉ ☉ ☉ ☉

Sarya Dlardrageth studied the founding-stone of Myth Drannor's mythal, dreaming of the things she could do with its power. Unlike the stone in Myth Glaurach, which was a massive natural boulder, Myth Drannor's was a well-shaped obelisk of deep rose-colored stone on a plinth of granite. Golden light seemed to glimmer in the translucent stone, hinting at power waiting to be harnessed.

The daemonfey queen carefully swept the rest of the chamber with the most acute detection spells she could manage, making absolutely sure that she knew precisely what was or wasn't enclosed in the mythal chamber. It was a relatively large and airy room, a spacious vault with a high, graceful arch to the ceiling. By some ancient artifice six bright columns of sunlight shone down into the room, relayed through Castle Cormanthor's upper floors by hidden shafts. The floor was a complex design of intersecting circles rendered in several different varieties of marble, covered in a thick coat of dust from centuries of disuse.

Satisfied that no scryings or magical traps awaited her, Sarya returned her attention to the mythal stone. "I am ready," she announced.

"Excellent," replied someone from within the mythal's living fountain of magic. Melodious, even beautiful, the voice was masculine and perfect. "Open your gate, then, I will join you there."

Sarya raised her hands and began to declaim the words of a very powerful spell, one of the most dangerous she knew, a spell designed to breach the barriers between the planes and create a magical bridge into another realm of existence. The mythal thrummed in response, the intangible pulse of the old device taking on a new and different note. Sarya ignored the mythal stone's change and pressed on, finishing her gate spell with skill and confidence.

"The gate is open!" she cried. "Malkizid, come forth!"

Before Sarya a great ring or hoop of golden magic coalesced from the air. Through it she glimpsed the realm of Malkizid, an infernal wasteland of parched desert, windswept rifts, and black, angry skies torn by crimson lightning. Then, through the gate, the archdevil Malkizid appeared. With one smooth step he crossed from his infernal plane into the mythal chamber.

He was tall, well over six feet, and sturdy of build. His skin was marble-white, even paler and more colorless than that of a fair-complexioned moon elf. His hair was long, black, and straight, and his eyes were large and absolutely black, with no hint of pupil, iris, or white. He wore a long crimson robe embroidered with gold designs, and he carried a large silver sword point-down in one hand, keeping it close by his side. A small trickle of dark blood ran down his face from some unseen injury in the center of his forehead, but Malkizid paid it no mind.

"I am here," he said.

"So I see," Sarya replied.

She let her gate lapse, and immediately spoke the words of a second spell. Beneath Malkizid's feet a complex summoning diagram flared into existence, encircling the powerful devil with a barrier of impenetrable magic.

Malkizid glanced down, and his mouth twisted in a cold imitation of a smile.

"What is this, Sarya?" he asked.

"A binding diagram that should hold even you, Malkizid. Simply a precaution in case you were not forthright about aiding me once summoned."

"It is hardly necessary, I assure you. I have come to help you, after all. What could I possibly gain by betraying you now?"

"I have no idea, but I see no reason to invite treachery." Sarya watched Malkizid carefully, a spell of dismissal only an instant from her lips.

Malkizid shrugged. Blood dripped from his wounded forehead.

"As you wish, then," said the devil. "I can instruct you just as well from within this diagram. Now, will you speak the spell of mythal reading? You will need to make visible the threads that bind this artifice together."

Sarya hesitated. "Is there any chance of warning the mythal's creators by casting that spell here? Several of those who raised this mythal are still alive. I can think of at least one who wields Mystra's silver fire."

"I know of whom you speak," Malkizid replied. He did not name the wizard Sarya was thinking of, for it was well known that Mystra's Chosen could hear their names spoken anywhere in the world, and any words that the speaker uttered after the name. "I do not fear him, but then again, I am protected inside this exceedingly thorough summoning circle. However, the first thing we will do is silence the mythal's alarms and prevent it from sending out any kind of warning to its creators. I will show you how."

"Can you be certain that it will work?"

Malkizid's dark eyes flashed, and a frown creased his noble countenance.

"Sarya Dlardrageth, I forgot more about mythalcraft ten thousand years ago than those who raised this stone managed to accumulate in all the time since. This mythal was raised by mere novices. Long ago I taught the Vyshaanti how to build wonders you could not conceive of! In the days of Aryvandaar's glory mythals were weapons of war, and mythalcraft was the grandest and most terrible of the martial skills. Of course I know how to conceal my presence from such a device!"

Despite herself, Sarya took half a step back. For just a moment she glimpsed the ancient anger that Malkizid hoarded beneath his calm demeanor, and demon queen that she was, she still took note.

"You have had access to this mythal for nearly twenty years," she observed. "If you are so knowledgeable, why haven't you subverted it already?"

Malkizid grounded the point of his silver sword in the smooth stone floor and glowered at her. "First, I am not an elf, nor the recipient of any special blessing of Mystra's. You still possess enough elf blood in your veins to deceive some of this mythal's defenses, Sarya, while I do not. Second, I dare not set foot in the bounds of this mythal through any use of my own power. The wards raised by the Zhents two decades ago trap devils within the mythal's bounds. I will show you how to modify that stricture soon, but until I found you, I had no one to bring me to this place who would not instantly trap me here."

"You could be trapped here now," Sarya said, nodding at her binding circle.

"Only if you wished to betray me," Malkizid replied, "and I would advise you to carefully consider any such course of action, for the consequences would be severe. If nothing else, you would find me much less forthcoming with my secrets of mythalcraft if you thought to coerce me."

Sarya weighed the devil's words, comparing them with what she thought she knew.

"I will not betray you, Malkizid. I only seek to protect myself." She indicated the mythal stone with a flick of her wing and asked, "Now, how do we proceed?"

"First," said Malkizid, "I will show you how to inspect the mythal's very structure and identify the properties that are useful, those that are dangerous, and those that you can modify with some work. Then, we will make you the mistress of this mythal, so that no one else can contest your mastery of the device or sever you from it in the way Myth Glaurach's mythal was taken from you. Now that we have learned that your enemies can do such a thing, I see no reason to allow it to happen again."

CHAPTER FIVE

19 Mirtul, the Year of Lightning Storms

The first portal led to a ruined chamber high on the shoulders of an icy, windswept mountain. The bitter cold struck Araevin the instant he stepped through the magical gate, and the sting of wind-driven snow and the roar of the storm left him barely able to see or hear at all in the first moments after he arrived. He threw up one arm to shield his eyes, and peered at the old stonework around him.

"Araevin!" Ilsevele shouted to make herself heard above the wind. "Where are we?"

"I don't know!" he called back.

Araevin finally blinked his eyes clear. The others stood around him, backs to the wind, holding cloaks close around their throats as the garments flapped and fluttered. Narrow window slits looked out over a scene of magnificent desolation, a cloud-wracked sea of black peaks and deep valleys. The chamber—and presumably, whatever structure it was a part of—actually stood well above the cloud layer. Sunlight streamed into the room, painfully bright.

About the same time of day as before, Araevin noted. *We haven't moved terribly far to the east or the west. What mountains of such size stand near Myth Glaurach? The Nether Mountains, but they are not so tall. The Spine of the World, or maybe . . . ?*

"I think these are the Ice Mountains," he told his companions. "Two hundred miles north of Myth Glaurach, perhaps? It's only a guess, though."

"We can't stay here long," Starbrow replied. "Can we return through the portal?"

Araevin turned to examine the blank stone face of a gateway, framed by a similar rellana vine device.

"Yes," he replied, "but we'll need rellana again. I've got the rest of the blossoms if we need to go back."

"It's not so bad here," Maresa observed. The genasi seemed more at home in the frigid air and howling wind than Araevin could believe. Her cloak hung from her shoulders, ruffling gently in the wind that streamed the others' cloaks like pennants behind them, and her long white hair drifted gently. She was a creature of the elemental air, and she was well suited for high places and strong winds. "So what do we do now?"

"Explore," said Araevin. "See if we can find any other portals the daemonfey might have used, or a trail or path leading away from this place."

Starbrow shifted Keryvian so that the heavy sword's hilt was close to his hand. He looked out the window slit at the steep slopes beyond.

"There might not be a road, Araevin. All the daemonfey have wings—maybe they just flew off from here."

"We'll consider that possibility when we have to." Araevin looked around the tower. The row of windows overlooking the mountain slope below stood to his left. To his right a broad swath of the chamber's wall was simply gone, as if something had cleaved the old building with a titanic axe stroke. The stonework had an elven look to it—somewhat heavier than elves might normally build, but given the evident remoteness and difficulty of the location, he could hardly blame the builders for using whatever materials were close at hand.

Was the place a watchpost of some kind? he wondered.

They made their way through an empty archway in the intact wall to another room, this one a large rectangular hall or banquet room, also brightly lit by the dazzling sunlight on the snow. Most of the roof was absent, lying in piles of rubble and debris on the floor of the chamber. Deep snowdrifts clung to the corners of the room.

It could have been a watchtower, Araevin decided. The elves of ancient Eaerlann would have wanted to keep an eye on the Spine of the World for dragon flights or armies of orcs and giants.

"What a miserable post this must have been," he muttered.

"Yes, but the view would have been worth it," Ilsevele replied. A gust of wind slammed into the stonework hall, kicking up high plumes of blowing ice and snow. She shivered and pulled her cloak as tight as she could. "For an hour, anyway."

At the far end of the hall, they found a stairway leading down into a dim chamber below. Filsaelene spoke a brief prayer to Corellon and imbued a slender wooden rod with magical light, and they followed her down into the rooms below. There they found a set of chambers with thicker, sturdier walls, broken only by a couple of thin arrow slits less than a handspan wide. The roar of the ever-present wind diminished to an eerie moaning as they descended into the shelter of the lower floor.

Filsaelene raised her light rod higher then took a step back.

"There's a body," she said.

"Undead?" Starbrow demanded, unsheathing Keryvian.

The sun elf cleric hesitated then replied, "No, simply dead."

Araevin and Ilsevele moved up to stand on either side of Filsaelene, looking down on the corpse. The fellow had died sitting with his back to the wall, and had remained more or less in that position, his chin slumped down to his chest as if he had dozed off. The cold or the dry air had preserved him remarkably. He was human, dressed in the robes of a wizard, with a wooden staff clasped in his icy fingers. His eyes, dark and half-lidded, stared blankly into his lap.

"He just froze like that?" Ilsevele asked. "Who was he? How did he get here? Did the daemonfey kill him?"

Starbrow glanced at the dead mage and said, "Look at him. He might have been here for a hundred years, just like that. I doubt the daemonfey had much to do with it."

"I can try to question his spirit," Filsaelene said. "But I must prepare the proper invocations to Corellon Larethian first, and that I cannot do until moonrise tonight." The sun elf girl frowned then added, "On the other hand, if he's been here for a long time, this husk will hold no memory of the spirit. He might have been dead too long for my spell to work."

"We'll try to question him if we find nothing else here," Araevin decided. "He isn't going anywhere for now."

From the chamber at the bottom of the stairs, an archway led into a long, barrel-vaulted gallery or redoubt of some kind that was illuminated by a row of shuttered arrow slits looking out over the steep mountainside. Araevin wondered who the builders regarded as enemies. The place was in such a lofty locale that it seemed hard to believe that any conventional army, the sort of enemy who might be stopped by stonework and arrow slits, would be able to reach the watchpost, let alone attack it. Then, along the back wall of the room, they discovered no less than five portals, each framed in its own stone archway, the lintels worked in the designs of various flowering plants and vines. Araevin recognized felsul and holly; the others he could not name.

"What is this place?" Ilsevele asked as the wind moaned eerily in the ruins above them.

Farthest Reach • 81

"A portal nexus," Araevin said. "Many portals are simple two-way devices, but sometimes portal builders wanted to link several destinations together in a network of portals. This is clearly such a place. You could step through one of those portals, and in a few moments use any of the others, choosing from a number of destinations."

"In other words, the daemonfey could be behind any of those doors," Starbrow said. He frowned. "Damnation. What if they lead us into a whole daisy-chain of magical doorways? We might be at this for days."

"Or longer," Araevin answered. "This explains the dead mage outside the room. He was probably a portal explorer, who used one of the doors leading into the nexus but then lacked the key to open another door to leave by. Without the right key, any or all of these doors would be nothing more than empty stone arches."

Maresa shuddered. "Gods, what a lonely way to die. It just goes to show you that you should never break into a place you can't break out of."

"Well, I anticipated that I might have to decipher several portals today, so I have prepared a few of the right sort of spells," Araevin said. "Give me a few moments, and I'll see what I can divine about these doorways."

The rest of the company stood watch, while Araevin chose the first portal on his left and spoke the words of his seeing spell. He realized at once that at least that one was damaged beyond repair. Only a fraying remnant of its magic remained, not even enough to guess at where it might have once led. He suspected that simple time and decay had been enough to ruin it. The second portal was still working and he divined its key—a small token of wood, marked with a few Elvish letters. Anyone who carried or wore such a token could use the portal, but no one else could.

I'll wait on that one, he decided. If he needed to, he could attempt to manufacture a proper token to awake it, but first he wanted to examine the other possibilities.

The third portal was functional. Its key was a simple spell—inscribing an arcane mark on the door would open it for a short time. Many, if not most sorcerers or wizards knew that particular spell. But perhaps the dead mage in the other room hadn't known it, or had been caught without the right spell ready. Araevin moved on to the fourth portal, and he found that this one had something close to the same key that the portal beneath Myth Glaurach had used, a rellana-blossom and a short phrase in Elvish.

He turned his attention to the last of the portals in the gallery, and he recoiled at once. It was an insidious trap. It was keyed to a simple pass phrase that was actually carved in the stone lintel above the arch, but Araevin observed that its magical strands were designed to unravel after conveying the user to some unknown destination.

"Stay away from the portal on the right," he warned his companions. "Don't say the word that's carved there, and don't touch the stone. I don't know where it leads, but it is designed to strand you there for a tenday or more."

Maresa happened to be nearest the trapped portal. She glanced at it suspiciously, and carefully stepped away from the device.

"Not that one, then," she said. "Which door did the daemonfey use?"

"The third or the fourth, I think—maybe the second, but I doubt it," Araevin answered. "Take your pick."

"One moment, then," Filsaelene said. She pressed her hands together before her chest, and looked up at the blank stone overhead, murmuring the words of a prayer to Corellon Larethian. "Which door did the daemonfey use?" she asked.

The others watched as the slender sun elf waited for a long moment, eyes closed. Then Filsaelene shook herself with a small start.

"Go left," she said. "The third door is the one the daemonfey passed through."

"Very well," Araevin said. "Everybody, be ready to pass through the portal quickly after I activate it. Portals opened by spells normally remain open for only a few moments, so you will have to hurry after me."

His companions gathered close around the portal.

Araevin checked to make sure they were ready, and he whispered the word to the spell and traced on the stone surface the mark he used as his own sigil. Blue fire awoke in the ancient gate, rippling around its perimeter, and Araevin was snatched away to somewhere else.

He found himself in deep, near-total darkness, with only a faint glimmer of light spilling down from somewhere overhead. Despite the lack of illumination, Araevin took three quick steps away from where he had arrived, knowing that his friends would be arriving right on his heels. He barked his shin hard on something, stumbled and caught himself on a stone pedestal in front of him. Muttering a human curse—and any human tongue was much more suited to profanity than Elvish, after all—he managed to call a light spell from his staff and see where he was.

The room was a vault or cellar below a large stone building, evidently in ruins. A stairwell leading up stood across the room to his right. The soft glow of daylight filtered down, the glimmer he had seen when he first entered. He looked down, and discovered that he had very nearly tumbled headlong into a deep stone well in the center of the room. The knee-high lip surrounding the shaft was what he had walked into in the darkness.

"Damn," Araevin breathed. He might have managed a quick spell of flying while falling in darkness—or he might not have.

Blue light crackled behind him, and Araevin turned to guide Starbrow away from the doorway. The moon elf had Keryvian out, and looked around, anxious for any sign of a foe.

"Are they here?" he hissed.

"I don't know. Now, step aside, the rest are coming," Araevin said. One by one Ilsevele, Maresa, and Filsaelene arrived in the same manner, simply appearing in the air next to the blank stone archway marking that end of the portal.

Araevin carefully studied the chamber of the well. It was another heavy stone room, built in the form of two intersecting barrel-vaults made of large stone blocks. At the end of three vaults stood empty stone slabs, perhaps meant to hold sarcophagi, but no such crypts were in evidence. The stairs climbed up at the end of the room's fourth arm. The vault opened out in the center, providing a little space around the well. The portal was set in one curving wall ringing the well, with another old portal opposite. He couldn't begin to guess what the place might once have been.

"Another portal," Ilsevele observed.

"Let's check the stairs and see what's above before we try the next portal," Araevin said. "Or for that matter, the well shaft. It might lead somewhere, too."

Maresa leaned over to look into the dark well. A cold breeze faintly sighed up from below, musty and damp.

"There's some light down there," she said in surprise.

Araevin frowned. He didn't remember seeing any such thing before. He leaned over to look, and he saw it too, a faint silver phosphorescence that danced far below them. It glimmered and swirled for a moment—then it started to rise, climbing swiftly toward them. For a moment, he continued to peer at it, trying to figure out what he was looking at, but then he decided that anything in such a place that was moving toward him and moving fast was not likely to be friendly.

He recoiled from the well, and called out a warning to his comrades. "Watch out, it's coming up!"

Maresa retreated from the edge, too, just before a swirling stream of spectral silver light exploded up out of the well. In the baleful glow Araevin could see the misshapen form of a person, a human face with an oddly dark and downcast gaze, the suggestion of regal robes hanging in tatters, and a shining silver staff clutched in ghostly fingers.

"It's the wizard!" Filsaelene gasped. "The one from the mountainside!"

The apparition hovered in the air above the well, its features cruel and proud. It fixed its empty gaze on Maresa and snarled out something in a tongue Araevin did not recognize.

Farthest Reach • 85

"Hai zurgal memet erithalchol na!" it said, its voice imperious and demanding. *"Memet na irixalnos nairhaug!"*

"Araevin, what's it saying?" Starbrow asked in a low voice. He kept his sword raised before him in a guard position.

"I can't even begin to guess," Araevin replied. The elves exchanged looks with each other. "I have heard stories of travelers dying in portal networks, which their ghosts then haunt. Let's just leave it alone, and try the stairs. Move away slowly."

Maresa carefully backed away, feeling her way along the wall toward the stairs leading up out of the vault. Filsaelene followed close behind her. But before the two had moved more than ten feet toward the door, the ghostly wizard muttered something else in its incomprehensible tongue, and attacked. It flung out one spectral arm, blasting at Maresa with a sickly purple-white bolt of crackling lightning.

The genasi cried out and dived away from the bolt, which gouged a fist-deep scar across the stone wall behind her. Smaller side-bolts stabbed out at Filsaelene and Araevin. Araevin managed to parry the lightning bolt before it struck him, grounding it with his staff and a quick defensive spell, but Filsaelene was spun around and knocked off her feet.

"That was a stupid idea!" Maresa shouted.

The genasi scrambled to her feet and snapped off a quick shot from her crossbow, which passed clean through the center of the ghost's chest without leaving the faintest mark—though it made Starbrow curse and duck on the other side of the well.

Ilsevele whispered a spell as she put an arrow on the string of her bow. The arrowhead burst into cold silver flame as she loosed it. The missile tore a dark hole in the ghost's torso. The ghost howled in its forgotten tongue, but it did not recoil or crumple as a living person might have done. It simply ignored the wound, even as streamers of mist blossomed from the ragged hole and faded into nothingness.

The ghost seemed to gather itself for a moment, glaring at Ilsevele, and its eyes flashed with a pale and terrible light. Ilsevele screamed and raised her arms to shield her face, but her hands and arms turned dead white and smoked under the ghost's awful gaze. Her bow clattered to the floor.

"Ilsevele!" Araevin shouted as he wheeled on the ghost.

He hurled a spell of his own, riddling the spectral figure with a barrage of glowing blue darts. Like Ilsevele's arrow, the magic punched black holes in the silver image. More missiles followed an instant later, repeating the attack as Araevin threw his best effort at the specter. But the ghost, though hurt, kept its baleful eyes fixed on Ilsevele, searing her with its chill gaze.

"I can't reach it!" Starbrow snarled.

Keryvian glowed in his hand, a shining blade of holy fire, but the ghost hovered over the center of the well, outside any conceivable sword-reach. The moon elf reversed the enchanted sword in his hand, cocking his arm as if to throw the blade, but he hesitated. Ilsevele wailed again, writhing under the ghost's cold-burning stare, and Starbrow muttered a curse and straightened up.

With calm deliberation, he walked over and interposed himself between the ghost and Ilsevele, turning his back on the apparition and shielding his face.

The pale glow surrounding Ilsevele faded at once, only to spring into existence on Starbrow's back. He groaned, but keeping his back to the monster, he seemed to avoid the worst of it.

"Araevin . . . somebody . . . kill this damned thing!" he gasped.

"Maresa!" Araevin cried. "Use your wand!"

Then he seized one of the wands at his own belt and snatched it out, blasting the ghost with dart after dart of glowing energy. Maresa dropped her useless crossbow and did the same, pelting the ghost from the other side.

The ghost howled again, and wrenched its gaze away from Starbrow and Ilsevele. The moon elf crumpled to his knees, collapsing on top of her. Then the specter intoned another spell, and blasted Araevin into senselessness with a mighty word of power. Araevin staggered back and tumbled to the hard stone floor, eyes seared white, ears ringing, blood streaming from his nose. He could see nothing, hear nothing, could scarcely even move as his thoughts reeled drunkenly.

His vision cleared a little, and he looked up through unfocused eyes as Filsaelene picked herself up off the floor. She steadied herself with one hand on the wall, and presented the star-shaped holy symbol of Corellon Larethian, shouting out a prayer that Araevin couldn't hear through the ringing in his ears. A great ring of golden light burst from her raised hand, racing through the chamber. When it touched the ghost, the apparition's substance simply boiled away into nothing. The same golden glow washed over Araevin and the others, bringing vigor, strength, and renewal.

Buoyed by the cleric's spell of healing, Araevin climbed to his feet as his eyes focused again and his ears stopped ringing. He groped for the magic wand he had dropped, closed his fingers around it, and hammered the ghost again with more of the magical darts. The spirit's whole form flickered and danced uncertainly, as if it was having trouble keeping itself together.

"Keep after it!" Araevin cried. "We can destroy this thing!"

The ghost drifted down toward the floor of the chamber, reaching out with one spectral claw for Filsaelene. The cleric quickly recoiled, backing up as the apparition drew closer.

"Shield me, Corellon!" she cried, and she spoke a prayer, guarding herself with a shining golden radiance that the ghost could not seem to reach past.

She whirled her long sword in front of her, but the weapon simply passed harmlessly through the ghost.

Araevin tried another spell—a bolt of fire—but the ghost's otherworldly body simply wasn't affected.

Think, he told himself. What other spells do I have that might destroy a ghost?

Before he could determine the next attack to try,

Starbrow scrambled to his feet and charged at the ghost's back, Keryvian in his hands. The ancient sword burst into brilliant white flame as he slashed at the specter. Unlike Filsaelene's sword or Maresa's crossbow bolts, Keryvian proved quite capable of damaging the spirit. One slash dragged Keryvian through its torso from shoulder to hip, and Starbrow's spinning follow-up drove the point of Demron's last and greatest blade through the center of the ghost's forehead.

The ghost groaned horribly, a sound that chilled Araevin to the bone, and it slowly dissolved into nothingness. Starbrow held his sword ready, in case it re-formed, but the phosphorescent mist simply dimmed and vanished.

"Thank the Seldarine that's over," the moon elf breathed. He looked around. "Is everybody all right?"

"Thanks to Filsaelene's spell, I am unhurt," Araevin replied. He hurried over and knelt by Ilsevele, who still crouched by the floor, broad swaths of her flesh dead-white and ice-cold to the touch. "Ilsevele is injured!"

"S-so c-cold," Ilsevele gasped.

She locked one of her hands around Araevin's forearm, pulling herself close. Araevin hissed with the cold of her touch. Then Filsaelene hurried over and knelt beside them. The cleric spoke the words of a healing prayer and set her own hand over Ilsevele's injuries. Beneath the warm golden glow of her touch, the pallor of Ilsevele's wounds faded, and her shivering stopped.

Ilsevele shook herself and stood up slowly.

"Thank you, Filsaelene," she said. She rubbed her arms vigorously, and the color returned to her face. She retrieved her bow, and looked over at Starbrow. "And thank you, too, Starbrow. You risked your life to shield me from the ghost. I don't know what to say."

Starbrow said with an awkward smile, "It just seemed like the best thing I could do, since I couldn't reach the ghost as long as it hovered up there. I couldn't stand there and do nothing."

Ilsevele stepped over and reached up to kiss him on the cheek. "Thank you, again."

Araevin couldn't help but smile at the sheepish look that came over Starbrow's face.

"Well, come on, then," the wizard said. "Let's see where we are and where the daemonfey went from here."

☙ ☙ ☙ ☙ ☙

Curnil Thordrim stalked something terrible through the forest gloom a few miles from the old Standing Stone. He didn't know for certain what it was, but it had killed two of his fellow Riders of Mistledale in their simple camp a few hours before, and they had died badly indeed: bodies marked by odd punctures surrounded by swollen, blue-black flesh, limbs broken and twisted, and awful bites gouged out of faces and skulls. He knew all the dangerous animals and most of the deadly monsters that haunted the depths of old Cormanthor, but he had never in his thirty-five years seen anything in the woodland that killed in that manner.

Curnil was a burly man with thick black hair on his forearms and a heavy black beard. Despite his size, he glided through the underbrush without sound, his dark eyes flicking from sign to sign as he followed the trail of something that stood as tall as an ogre and had long, narrow feet with small claws at the toe. He was not entirely sure he wanted to catch up to it, if he was to be honest with himself.

He came to a small stream trickling through the woods, and looked and listened for a long time before breaking out of the ground cover. Curnil had learned his woodcraft from some of the best, the moon and wood elves of Elventree, a hundred miles to the north. Nothing but the burbling of the stream greeted his ears. Curnil drew a deep breath, and slipped out of the bushes to the stream bank, looking for a print that might show whether his quarry had continued on or turned aside there.

It only took a moment for him to find the end of the track. The creature's footprints simply ended in the wet sand, as if it had taken to the air or just vanished outright.

"That's impossible," he muttered, brow furrowed in confusion. "What in the Nine Hells vanishes into thin air?"

He grimaced—the Nine Hells indeed. The pieces fit together all too well. Something wicked, something strong, something that disappeared without a trace. Myth Drannor was not far off, and he'd heard plenty of stories about the horrible devils that haunted the ruins. But they were supposed to be trapped within the old elven mythal, weren't they?

"Some idiot set one of those things loose," he decided.

Some cruel new plot on the part of the drow who lived in the shadows of the forest? Or a stupid blunder by some glory-hunting adventurers in Myth Drannor. Who would set such a creature free?

For that matter, why assume that only one was loose in the forest?

Curnil looked around at the silent woods, and shuddered. He was sure that he had not seen the last of the monster he'd just tracked to the empty streambed, and he didn't look forward to finally meeting it. He didn't look forward to that at all.

❖ ❖ ❖ ❖ ❖

The structure above the chamber in which they fought the ghost turned out to be a mausoleum of some kind, buried deep in a forest unfamiliar to Araevin. Starbrow believed it might be one of the woodlands near old Myth Drannor, possibly the old realm of Semberholme in western Cormanthor. Araevin had never visited the eastern forest, but the fact that it was near dusk when they emerged gave him reason to believe that the portal had carried them a fair distance to the east of the mountaintop stronghold.

"Why would the folk of Myth Glaurach or Semberholme have built that mountain stronghold we first explored?" Ilsevele asked Araevin. "Are you certain the portal-builders were elves?"

He nodded. "All the portals we've seen so far have shown the same workmanship and design. I suppose it's possible that someone carved newer portals and attempted to match the workmanship of the older ones, but the spells that bind the portals together all seem to be about the same age, too. I favor the simpler explanation that the whole network was constructed at one time—most likely by mages of Myth Glaurach who wanted to join their city to several distant destinations."

Starbrow studied the forests, rubbed at his jaw, and said, "You know, it might have been mages of Myth Drannor who built this portal network. They were masters of such magic, and created portals to many distant places. Myth Glaurach might have been a destination, not an origin."

Eventually they all decided that it didn't matter very much, since Filsaelene's divinations revealed that the daemonfey had not emerged from the portal network there. Instead, their adversaries had fled through the second of the two portals in the chamber below. They rested for the night in the forest above the mausoleum, and returned to the vaulted chamber beneath the empty tomb.

Araevin cast his spells of portal sensing again, and studied the doorway they had passed by before. As he suspected, it was another keyed portal, requiring nothing more than a simple phrase in Elvish. However, the magic guarding it was intermittent. Once opened, the portal would not work again for hours.

"All right, I am opening the portal," he told the others. "The portal will remain open for a short time, just a few moments likely, and it won't open again for hours. You must follow me quickly."

He spoke the pass phrase, and watched the old lichen-covered lintel glow brightly. He reached out and tapped the blank stone of the door, and felt the familiar dizzying sense of moving without moving. All went dark for an instant, and Araevin found himself looking on a small forest glade. One side of the glade ended in a stone wall, in which the portal's archway stood. The morning was young there as well, the sky pale gray and streaked with high, rose-colored clouds.

"Neither east nor west this time," Araevin observed.

He stepped away from the doorway, and studied the dark forest looming around him. The broken fingers of slender stone towers rose a short distance away, glimmering softly in the coming dawn over the treetops.

Behind him, Starbrow emerged from the portal, followed by the others in short order. The moon elf warrior halted in surprise, a look of consternation on his face.

"I know this place!" he said. "We're near the Burial Glen, only half a mile or so from Myth Drannor."

"Myth Drannor! Are you certain?" Ilsevele said. She quickly drew an arrow and laid it across her bow, scanning the vicinity for any enemies.

"Trust me," Starbrow said. "I know this place."

"Aren't the ruins supposed to be overrun by devils and dragons, monsters and ghosts of the worst kind?" Maresa asked, obviously uneasy.

"So it is said," Ilsevele replied.

"Myth Drannor . . . of course," Araevin said.

Where else would the daemonfey go? Saelethil Dlardrageth and the rest of his accursed House had arisen in the ancient realm of Arcorar, which had become Myth Drannor. He'd already seen that Sarya knew how to use mythals to anchor demons to Faerûn and compel their service—and there was a mythal here, one even more powerful than the mythal that had stood over Myth Glaurach. And mythals often served to absolutely block scrying, which would explain why no one had been able to divine the whereabouts of Sarya's defeated army.

"Be careful," he told the others. "I think there is a very good chance we have found Sarya's hiding place."

"So what now?" Ilsevele asked. "Make certain that they're here, or return and report what we've found so far?"

"Press on," Araevin said at once. "If nothing else, I need to get a look at the mythal spells and see if Sarya is manipulating this mythal as she did the other one."

"The mythal stone is in the heart of Castle Cormanthor," Starbrow said. "I can't imagine how we can reach it, if the whole fey'ri army is here."

Araevin looked at Starbrow. "You know Myth Drannor well. Mythal stones are usually hidden with care."

"I've spent some time here." Starbrow shrugged and looked away, searching the trees for danger, Keryvian's hilt in his hand.

"I don't need to see the stone itself, at least not right this moment. I just need to be within the bounds of the mythal's influence."

"That's easier, then," the moon elf said. "We need only walk a couple of hundred yards in that direction—" he pointed toward where the old spires could still be seen over the trees—"and we'll be within the mythal."

"We might be walking into the middle of Sarya's legion," Maresa said. "Anything could be in there. Hells, even if she isn't here, I've heard enough stories about Myth Drannor to think twice about setting foot in that place."

"I'll conceal us, at least for a short time," Araevin promised.

He drew out a tiny pinch of spirit gum from his bandolier of spell components, and plucked out one of his eyelashes, wincing. Pressing the lash into the gum, he carefully spoke the words of a spell. The forest around them seemed to grow dimmer, more distant.

"Araevin, what did you do?" Filsaelene asked.

"A spell of invisibility. It covers all of us, but you must remain close to me. If we run into enemies, do not strike unless you're sure it can't be helped, because you'll break the spell if you do." He looked over to Starbrow. "Lead the way, since you know where we're going."

Starbrow nodded grimly and took the lead. They followed an old, winding path that led from the portal glen toward the city, taking pains to move quietly and avoid talking. Many things could pierce a spell of invisibility, but if they were quiet and careful, they might be able to avoid trouble of that sort.

They reached the outskirts of the city, and took cover behind a low stone wall. Araevin sensed the moment they entered the mythal. His skin tingled with the power of the ancient magic.

"Let's stop here. I have a couple of spells to cast, now that we're inside the mythal. Keep watch for me."

Ilsevele crouched beside him, an arrow on the string of her bow. Starbrow stood behind a tall pile of stones, sword in hand, watching the ruins with his face set in an unreadable expression. Maresa and Filsaelene guarded the other side.

Satisfied that they were ready, Araevin first cast one of his divinations. Myth Drannor's magical aura made scrying impossible, but he hoped that a different sort of divination might work. He spoke the words of the spell that conjured up unseen drifting eyes, hovering above his head like a halo.

"Spread out and search for the daemonfey," he instructed them. "Return when you sight any."

The intangible sensors whirred away out of sight, each dodging and darting its way into the ruins and the forests around him.

He waited patiently for several minutes, as his spell-creations went about their searches. Then they began to return, one by one. Araevin caught each in his hand as it came back, closing his eyes to see played out in his mind's eye the things the magical eyes had seen. He glimpsed buildings with broken windows, fallen-in roofs, and piles of masonry inside; streets overgrown with vines and wild trees; proud old manors and schools still surprisingly intact, though their windows were dark and empty. And he also found the daemonfey—glimpses of fey'ri companies bivouacked in whichever buildings were best preserved. The demonspawn were hard at work in repairing their weapons and armor, forging new weapons, drilling with spell and blade, or simply patrolling the ruins, fluttering from building to building like oversized bats.

"Well?" Maresa asked.

"Yes, they're here," Araevin said. "This is the fey'ri army, I'm certain of it."

"We have to leave, then," Starbrow said. "I have to get word of this back to Gaerth and Seiveril."

Araevin nodded. "In a moment," he said. "There is one

more thing I want to see here." The others shifted nervously, watching the ruins for any sign of approaching enemies, but Araevin moved his hands in arcane passes and murmured the words of another spell, the spell of mythal-sight that Saelethil had taught him.

He closed his eyes, and when he opened them he perceived Myth Drannor's ancient and mighty mythal as a golden vault filling the sky, a huge dome of drifting magic threads that slowly orbited the whole city. The beauty and power of the thing astonished him. Araevin trained his vision closer in, studying carefully to see what the mythal's effects were. He glimpsed protections against scrying—well, he knew about those already, didn't he?—and wards to suppress spells of compulsion and domination. There seemed to be no modifications to the drifting strands of magic.

Sarya hasn't figured out how to manipulate this mythal yet, he decided. *Maybe it takes her a while to determine how to attune herself.*

He allowed himself a confident smile, and spoke the words of a spell that would allow him to gain access to the mythal so that he could raise defenses against Sarya. But even as he spoke the last syllable and reached out to grasp at the magical strands he saw around him, he realized that he had made a mistake.

From the drifting golden strand hovering in arm's reach, a shimmering red-gold thread suddenly emerged, appearing from nowhere. Araevin yelped and stumbled back, but not before the new strand hummed angrily. A scarlet veil descended over him, dancing across his body in a thousand motes of painful pinpricks, jabbing and sharp. With each pinprick, a spell vanished from his mind, draining away at a horrendous rate.

"Araevin!" Ilsevele cried.

She sprang to her feet and backed away as he jerked and flailed in his crimson cocoon of light motes.

The great golden dome of Myth Drannor's mythal wavered and faded from Araevin's view. He desperately tried to speak a counterspell, but before he had even said the third word of the enchantment, the spell was sucked out of his mind in mid-casting. He tried to quickly think of another, but then there was no more time—every spell he held prepared in his mind was gone, drained away.

I am powerless, he realized. Sarya set a trap for me!

"Araevin! What's wrong? What has happened?" Ilsevele asked. "Are you hurt?"

"Not physically," he managed. He steadied himself against the wall. "But I've been drained of magic. I have no spells. We have to flee, before the daemonfey come for me."

Starbrow drew back from his post, and glanced at Araevin.

"Can you walk?" he asked.

"I don't know," Araevin answered.

He hugged himself, feeling a strange ache in the center of his body, as if something had been torn out of him. He wasn't sure exactly how he'd been injured, but he prayed to Corellon that it wasn't permanent. He couldn't imagine being powerless for the rest of his days.

He forced himself to look up at Starbrow and say, "Yes, I can walk. But I think we ought to run."

CHAPTER SIX

21 Mirtul, the Year of Lightning Storms

"Lord Seiveril Miritar, Your Highness," the major domo announced, ringing her ceremonial staff once on the stone floor.

Seiveril inclined his head to acknowledge the courtesy, and strode into the Dome of Stars amid the golden glow of the fading daylight. The dark marble of the floor caught the pale rose sky and mirrored its serried colors, so that the council table drifted in the darkness between gold-glowing floor and brilliant sky, a white ship adrift in the shadows between the two. Seiveril almost hesitated to set foot on the floor before him, as if he might disturb the sky's reflection with a careless step, but he continued without a pause and approached the high table where he had sat in council for so many years.

Amlaruil greeted him with a cool smile. The

queen wore a silver gown, and her face shone like moonlight in the shadows.

"Welcome, Lord Miritar," she said. "We did not expect you this evening; what brings you before us?"

"I am afraid something has come up, my queen," Seiveril replied. He halted two paces before the outswept arms of the council and bowed to Amlaruil. "I must conclude my business here in Evermeet and return to Faerûn immediately."

Amlaruil met his eyes, and her brow creased. "What news from Faerûn, my friend?" she asked.

"I have received a sending from Lord Vesilde Gaerth, Your Highness. He tells me that a hidden portal network has been found under Myth Glaurach, portals through which Sarya Dlardrageth's army may have made their escape."

"Portals?" said Keryth Blackhelm. The stern-faced marshal frowned. "Why, the daemonfey might be anywhere by now!"

"The portals are being searched even as we speak. Rest assured I will not give up until we have destroyed the daemonfey root and branch," said Seiveril.

"The daemonfey have been defeated, have they not?" Ammisyll Veldann asked. "How much longer will you persist in this interminable folly, Miritar? While you chase after ghosts and garrison gloomy old ruins, Evermeet itself remains vulnerable to attack!"

"Clearly, Evermeet was vulnerable to attack before I called for my Crusade," Seiveril replied. "My efforts in Faerûn are your best defense, Lady Veldann."

Veldann scowled and began to frame a response, but Amlaruil interceded.

"The Dlardrageths are the enemies of all the elf race," she said. "I will pray to the Seldarine for your success." The queen did not glance at Ammisyll Veldann, but the highborn sun elf frowned and subsided, leaning back in her seat. Instead, Amlaruil studied Seiveril. "Have you given more thought to Lady Durothil's proposal, Lord Miritar?"

Seiveril glanced up at the pale sky overhead. An empty chair stood at the foot of the left-hand side of the table, opposite the seat occupied by the high admiral.

It would be easy to take my place there, he thought. I would certainly wield power at least equal to the power I held as Lord of Elion—perhaps even more, since I would hold a high office indeed, with no one within three thousand miles to countermand my commands. I could do a great deal of good, if I chose to take that seat.

But how long would that good last? he wondered. Evermeet might set a shining example for the young human lands of Faerûn to follow, but ultimately Evermeet is a refuge, a retreat. All the troubles that were foremost in his mind—the daemonfey, the phaerimm, the assaults on Evermeet, even the fall of the realms of Eaerlann and Cormanthor hundreds of years ago—seemed inextricably linked with the pattern of Retreat and flight that had been established for a dozen elf generations.

The empty seat at the table was inviting. It was familiar, comfortable. And it might undo everything he had accomplished so far.

"Lady Durothil's suggestion has great merit," he finally said. "I wholeheartedly endorse the notion of appointing a minister or a marshal to sit on this council and speak for those of the People who remain in Faerûn. But I respectfully decline to hold any such office, or to answer to anyone who does."

"I don't understand," Keryth Blackhelm growled. "You tell us to raise up a councilor for the east, and you say you will pay no heed to him? What is the point?"

"If I accepted the seat you offer, I would be honor-bound to answer to Evermeet's authority and conform my actions to the will of the throne and the council. I do not have confidence in this body's ability to take the actions I deem necessary in Faerûn. Therefore I must decline to be so bound."

"Isn't it arrogant of you to decide that you, in the solitude of your own heart, are better suited to make such decisions than anyone else?" High Admiral Elsydar asked.

"Perhaps, but I have work that is not yet done in Faerûn," Seiveril said. "I will remain until I know that I have done all that I can, and I will not let Evermeet's isolationists to tell me otherwise."

"Wander around in Faerûn's dying forests as long as you like, Miritar," Ammisyll Veldann hissed, "but send home the sons and daughters of Evermeet you have inveigled with your promises of glory!"

"Each elf who followed me into Faerûn is free to return to Evermeet whenever he or she chooses," Seiveril said, standing as straight as a fine blade. "I compelled no one to follow me to Faerûn, and I will not allow you to compel anyone to return, Veldann. If I have to, I will found a realm of my own to prevent it."

The council fell silent for a moment, astonished. Even Amlaruil's eyes widened.

The queen said, "Seiveril, think of the People who follow you. You are not the only one who must accept the consequences of your crusade."

"By what authority?" snapped Selsharra Durothil. "By what authority do you name yourself a king, Seiveril Miritar? Where is your realm?"

"By what authority?" Seiveril repeated. "By the authority of each elf who chooses to follow me, Lady Durothil. I claim no crown. All who remain with me shall have a voice in choosing who we name as our lord and how we do so."

He looked at each of the councilors and went on, "As far as our realm . . . how many of our lands lie empty now? Who would argue with me if I raised a city in the High Moor, where Miyeritar once was? Or the wild lands west of Tun, where the towers of Shantel Othreier stood? The Border Forest, where once the sylvan realm of Rystallwood lay? Or the Elven Court, or Cormanthor itself?" He paused, and said again, "Why not Cormanthor itself?"

Seiveril looked up at the sky overhead, where the first stars were beginning to glimmer in the darkening sky.

Corellon, guide me, he prayed silently. *Hold me to the course you have set for me.*

Then he turned his back on the council, and strode from the Dome of Stars, leaving Evermeet behind him.

☯ ☯ ☯ ☯ ☯

The portal near the Burial Glen failed to work, as Araevin knew it would. The spells that had powered the device for centuries were designed to allow intermittent functioning only—once used, the portal could not work again for hours. He knew a spell or two that might suspend that particular property and allow the instantaneous use of the gate, but with all his spells drained, he did not have a chance of opening it.

"I am sorry," he told his companions. "We can't escape through this portal. It will be hours before it opens again."

"Damn! Why build a magical door that's nothing more than a dead stone most of the time?" Maresa snarled.

"Among other things, it makes a portal much harder to sneak an army through," Araevin answered. "We'll have to wait for it to activate again."

"We certainly can't wait here," Starbrow growled. The moon elf looked around the clearing, his hand on Keryvian's hilt. "Let's keep moving. There's a lot of forest to hide in, and maybe we can circle back in a few hours to try it again."

"Agreed. The farther we are from this place, the better," Araevin said. If she were in Myth Drannor, Sarya would certainly have sensed his attempt to manipulate her mythal defenses and the pounce of his spell trap. He couldn't believe that she would not order her fey'ri to hunt him down, especially if she knew that her trap had drained away all his spells. "Starbrow, you know this place. Take the lead."

The moon elf nodded curtly and set off at once, leading the small party away from the portal clearing along a small footpath. Ilsevele followed behind him, her bow in her hand, and Araevin trotted behind her, his disruption wand clenched in one fist. He was fairly sure that the wand would still work for him—wands didn't draw on any spells held in the mind, they simply contained spells of their own that any competent mage could make use of. It was a good weapon, and he had two more wands at his belt with equally destructive spells. But he normally held dozens of spells in his mind, many of which were significantly more powerful than any he could build into a wand. Without the power and versatility of his normal repertoire, he was in no position to invite a battle against Sarya's fey'ri or any of their infernal allies.

How did she do it? Araevin wondered. If she knew a spell to secure the mythal-weave from another mage's examination or touch, why didn't she guard the mythal at Myth Glaurach in the same manner? He could only think of three possible answers: Sarya Dlardrageth was simply careless at Myth Glaurach, which seemed scarcely credible; there was something different about Myth Drannor's mythal; or Sarya Dlardrageth had learned something new about mythalcraft in the relatively short time since he had bested her at Myth Glaurach.

But she doesn't have the Nightstar. Where could she have learned the necessary spells? Is there another *selukiira* she might have access to? Or . . . did Sarya find a tutor? Araevin's frown deepened, and he rubbed at the gemstone in his chest.

"This way," Starbrow said. He turned from the path, striking off into the forests. He slid down a leaf-covered slope, muddy and wet with the spring, and splashed across a small stream at the bottom of the dell. But before they scrambled up the far side of the stream bank, Araevin sensed a terrible, icy cold in the air, and a crawling *wrongness* that turned his stomach.

He looked back up the short hillside they'd just descended. A pair of nightmarish monsters bounded down after them. They were a pale bluish-white in color, the hue of dead flesh, and they were big—each easily the size of an ogre, with insectile features, clacking mandibles, and long, lashing tails studded with terrible barbs. They carried great spears of black iron frosted with supernatural cold.

"Behind us!" he cried. "Ice devils!"

The devils hissed and clicked at each other, slowing and spreading apart as they realized their quarry had been brought to bay. Araevin and his companions turned to face them.

"We have to kill them," Starbrow said. "Don't let them teleport away, or they'll be back with more of their kind in a matter of moments."

"Right," said Ilsevele.

Her hands blurred and her bow sang its deadly song, thrumming deeply. A silver arrow struck the first devil just above its cold, faceted eye, splintering against its chitinous hide, and a second arrow stuck in the tender joint between its armored torso and its bony arm.

The two fiends halted, gathering their infernal power. Araevin started to shout a warning, but even as he drew breath the monsters let loose with a terrible, scathing blast of unearthly cold. The stream iced over at once, and tree and fern alike turned white and died under the deadly frost.

Araevin ducked down under his cloak, hoping its enchantments would help protect him. Cold so fierce that it felt like a white-hot poker seared his hands, his feet, and soaked through his cloak, wrenching away his breath and burning in his nose and mouth. He heard Ilsevele cry out in pain. Then the cold eased, and he threw off his cloak, shaking off a mantle of deadly white hoarfrost as he stood again.

The whole hillside was white and frozen from the ice devils' wintry blasts. The monsters stalked forward, iron spears smoking with cold. Before him, at the bottom of the dell, Filsaelene stood frozen. She had been in midstream when the devils attacked, and the ice on the creek held her immobilized at the knee.

"I'm stuck!" she cried.

Araevin leveled his disruption wand at the nearest of the two devils and barked out the command word. A bolt of azure energy, shimmering and crackling, lanced out from the wand to knock the devil off its feet. The second devil approached Filsaelene, who stooped down to smash the edge of her shield against the ice covering the creek, trying to free her feet from the ice. But then Maresa suddenly slipped out from behind a tree, leveled her crossbow, and shot the ice devil in the side of its thick neck. Blue-black gore spattered the frost-covered ground, and the monster whirled on her, moving with impossible speed for something so large and powerful. Maresa yelped and gave ground, ducking back into a young stand of alders and trying to keep as many of the slender white trees as possible between her and the devil.

"Is there a good way to kill these things?" Maresa called.

"Holy weapons!" Filsaelene replied. "You need a holy weapon to really hurt them!"

"Anything else?" the genasi demanded.

The ice devil stalked closer and rammed the point of its black spear through the trees, missing Maresa by a hand's breadth.

Araevin blasted that devil with his wand, staggering it for a moment, then he risked a quick glance back at Ilsevele. He found her fumbling to pick up her bow again with frozen hands. Starbrow knelt by her, trying to help.

"I can't shoot!" she said.

The first devil regained its feet and charged at Filsaelene, who finally managed to pull her feet free of the ice. She parried the first strike of its spear with her shield, twisted out of the way of the second, but then the monster's barbed tail came sweeping in fast and low, lashing her across her knees. Her feet flew out from under her, and Filsaelene fell on her back in the icy stream, her sword clattering out of her grasp. The monster straddled her, one clawed foot on either side of her torso, and raised its great black spear in both hands.

Then Starbrow came dashing down the slope, Keryvian alight in his hands. The sword gleamed in one perfect arc that took off the ice devil's leg at the knee. The creature let out a high-pitched, whistling shriek, and toppled into the creek, even as it slashed and gouged at Starbrow. The big moon elf followed the monster to the ground, blocking its claws and mandibles with lightning-swift parries. Then he set one foot on its chest and rammed Keryvian's point through the monster's mandibles, pinning its head to the streambed. Keryvian's pure white fire flashed from the ice devil's eyes. The thing shuddered once and lay still.

The second ice devil whirled at the cry of the first, and abandoned Maresa to rush toward the others. But when Starbrow killed its companion, the ice devil halted, its eyes glittering with cold malice. It abruptly vanished, teleporting away.

"Damn," Starbrow said. "It's gone for help!"

"Quickly, then. We must be away from here before it returns!" Araevin replied. He turned and helped Ilsevele to her feet, shivering at the icy touch of her flesh. "Can you walk?" he asked her.

She winced with pain, but nodded. "Yes. Let's go."

They scrambled up the other side of the dell, and ran at their best speed through the woods beyond, following Starbrow as he dashed ahead. He led them for several hundred yards, through tall groves of magnificent trees that resembled nothing so much as the pillars of a great cathedral above a floor of green ferns, into tangled thickets and past old ruined walls and roads, before they reached a small shrine or chapel half-hidden by the hillside it was built against.

"In here," Starbrow said. "I think we'll be safe."

"Are you sure this is a good idea?" Ilsevele asked. "Wouldn't it be better to stay out in the woods, where we can try to keep ahead of the pursuit? If they track us to this place, we'll be cornered."

"The fey'ri have wings," Starbrow answered. "If they find us in the open, we won't be able to outrun them. Hiding is probably our best option. And if I remember right . . ." The moon elf warrior moved into the ruined shrine, and studied the floor carefully.

"Whatever you're doing, do it quickly! The fey'ri are coming," Maresa hissed. She flattened herself beside the door, watching the path along which they'd just come.

"There are at least a dozen of them back there."

Starbrow swept aside a small bare patch, then knelt to flip up a flagstone and open a hidden catch. Behind the altar, a hidden door slid open.

"Into the passage," he said, and stood aside to motion Araevin, Ilsevele, and Filsaelene through. Maresa followed, hurrying across the chapel, and Starbrow stepped in and slid the door closed.

The chamber beyond was absolutely lightless, but then Filsaelene spoke the words of a minor prayer and summoned up a magical light. Araevin looked around and saw that they were in a natural cave hidden within the hillside. A small pool of clear, still water lay in the center of the cave, and soft moss that glowed faintly blue-green covered the floor. "What is this place?" he asked.

"A secret refuge, hidden beneath the shrine of Sehanine Moonbow. There are a few such places scattered around Myth Drannor and its outskirts," Starbrow said. "Once they were also guarded by spells designed to keep them concealed, even against magic, but I don't know if those work any longer. The moss has healing properties, if you are hurt."

He set Keryvian down on the ground, and lowered himself to the moss, stretching out as if on a bed.

"How did you ever find this place?" Ilsevele asked. She sank down onto the mossy floor nearby.

Starbrow shrugged and looked over to Araevin. "How long before we can use that portal to return to Myth Glaurach?"

"Several hours, I think," Araevin replied. "Of course, Sarya may be guarding it now. For that matter, we'll have to figure out a way to reach it without fighting our way through her entire legion."

"Can you prepare any spells that would help us reach the portal unseen?" Filsaelene asked.

"Not until I rest. Then, I could ready the invisibility spell again," Araevin said. He frowned, and added, "That is, assuming that I can commit spells to my mind at all. I think that Sarya's trap only depleted my mind of the spells

I knew at the moment, but if she somehow drew out my ability to cast spells at all. . . ."

"*Aillesel Seldarie*," Ilsevele breathed. "Araevin, I didn't realize how the mythal had affected you."

"Well, we will cross that bridge when we come to it, as my human friends say." Araevin looked over to Starbrow. "If we were thinking of hiding here for several hours to allow the portal to recharge, we might as well remain here long enough for me to prepare spells, if I can. It will make things much easier if we have trouble getting back to the portal glade."

They settled down to rest from their exertions, lying quietly in the moss-filled cave. Filsaelene used her spells to heal the worst of their injuries, though her healing spells could do nothing for Araevin's magic. Stilling his thoughts to silence, Araevin stretched out and let himself drift into Reverie, trying very hard not to dwell on what would happen if he found he could not wield magic. While he composed himself to rest, he listened to his companions conversing in low voices.

"When did you explore this place, Starbrow?" Ilsevele asked the moon elf.

"A long time ago."

"It can't be that long ago. You're not more than a hundred and fifty or so, are you?"

"That's about right," Starbrow said.

"That is certainly long by my standards," Maresa observed. "Because you elves live so damned long, you have no idea of the value of *time*."

Ilsevele smiled in the dim light. "That might be true, but I note that Starbrow here hasn't answered my question. You've said before that you were from Cormanthor, but where exactly?"

"I thought the elves abandoned this place," Maresa said, surprised.

"For the most part, we did," Filsaelene told her. "Certainly no elves live near Myth Drannor any longer. But there are still a few small elven settlements in different places in this forest. Cormanthor stretches from the

Thunder Peaks to the Dragon Reach, and from Cormyr to the Moonsea. It's a big forest."

"How did you come to meet my father?" Ilsevele asked. "Until he embarked on this crusade against the daemonfey, I never knew him to have visited Cormanthor."

Starbrow remained silent for a long time. "You will have to ask your father about that," he finally said. "It's not a question for me to answer."

"Now what does that mean?" Ilsevele asked, rather sharply.

"Ask your father," Starbrow said again. Then he fell silent, and said no more.

Araevin finally stirred fully from his Reverie some hours later, and felt surprisingly refreshed. He ran his fingers over the blue moss of the cavern floor, and wondered what kind of healing magic the folk of Myth Drannor had imbued in it long ago. He found Starbrow sitting with his back to the wall, watching the secret door that led back out to the chapel. Ilsevele and Filsaelene were deep in their own Reveries, and Maresa was simply asleep, snoring softly.

Lying still, he closed his eyes and touched the Nightstar embedded in his chest, seeking the spells the *selukiira* stored as ably as his own spellbooks. He chose a simple spell of minor telekinesis first, the sort of thing that almost any apprentice could master, and concentrated on it until its mystic symbology and invocations were pressed into his mind, like a melody he could not get out of his head.

Then he sat up, moved his hands in the appropriate gestures, and muttered the words of the simple spell. To his great relief, he felt the magic, soft and familiar, streaming through his mind and his fingertips, as he picked up a small stone and carefully moved it over to drop into Starbrow's lap.

The moon elf looked up. "You did that?"

Araevin nodded. "Yes. Sarya's defenses simply emptied my mind of readied spells. They didn't damage my ability to study and memorize more."

"That's a relief, then," the moon elf said.

"You don't know the half of it," Araevin replied. He

focused his attention on the *selukiira* again, and began furiously memorizing spell after spell, rebuilding his repertoire from nothing. He felt as if his mind were humming with arcane energy, a sensation that he had become so accustomed to in centuries of practicing magecraft that he could not begin to guess when he might have stopped noticing it.

"How long will you need to ready your spells?"

"An hour, perhaps two," said Araevin. "Then we will see about getting out of here."

☙ ☙ ☙ ☙ ☙

Sarya Dlardrageth stood by a ruined wall near the city's old Burial Glen, and studied her handiwork with the mythal-weave. The dark bronze strands of her crafting drifted past her outstretched fingers, winding in and among the invisible golden net that comprised the city's ancient magic field.

"Here," she said. "He was here when the mythal's defenses struck him."

Xhalph waited nearby, towering over her. The daemonfey prince stood well over eight feet tall, with four powerfully muscled arms and just the slightest canine cast to his features—both inherited from his demonic father.

"The sun elf mage?" he asked. "The one who marred your weaving at Myth Glaurach?"

"Yes," Sarya hissed.

In her long life she had learned to hate many adversaries, to nurse smoldering anger and cold fury for years upon years, but rarely had she been dealt such a reverse as Araevin Teshurr had dealt her in the heart of her own citadel. The very notion that he had somehow followed her to her new lair and had attempted to evict her from yet another mythal was enough to fill her with a wrath so hot and bitter than even Xhalph shied from meeting her eyes.

"Araevin was here," she went on, "and he attempted to take this mythal from me, too." She allowed herself a cold smile. "But my new defenses were more than he expected.

I was ready for him this time. If I read the mythal right, he received a nasty little surprise when he started plucking at my threads."

"Do you think he knows we are here?"

Sarya's smile faded at once. "It is almost a certainty," she admitted. "I want him caught before he carries word of our presence back to his friend Seiveril Miritar and the rest of Evermeet's knights and mages."

Xhalph glanced around the wooded glade. "Our fey'ri and baatezu have been scouring the area for hours, and the only sign they've turned up is a dead gelugon about half a mile from here. He has had ample opportunity to escape by now."

"My mythal trap drained him of most, if not all, of his magic," Sarya said. "Without his spells, he must flee on foot or hide somewhere until his magic returns. In either case, we can still catch him." She looked up at Xhalph, and lightly leaped into the air, snapping her leathery wings until she hovered ten feet above him. "Take charge of the pursuit, Xhalph! Spare no effort to prevent the mage's escape."

The daemonfey swordsman bowed his head, and sprang into the air, arrowing off into the woods, calling for the fey'ri who attended him. Sarya wheeled and flew in the opposite direction, back to Castle Cormanthor. While she certainly hoped that Araevin was lying powerless and vulnerable somewhere nearby, it was clearly foolish to simply hope that he would be caught before he carried word of her tampering in Myth Drannor to her enemies. She would have to presume that he had already escaped, and that Seiveril Miritar and all who stood with him would soon learn of her new retreat.

She needed to speak to Malkizid.

Alighting on a high balcony, Sarya passed a pair of fey'ri who stood guard there. The proud daemonfey warriors knelt and spread their wings as she passed, grounding their long-headed spears in salute. She swept by them into the hallway beyond, and quickly made her way to the chamber of the mythal stone.

With the ease of long practice, Sarya whispered the words

of a spell and woke the mythal's magic to her hand.

"Malkizid!" she called out. "Answer me! I would speak with you."

Her words reverberated in the dense magical fields dancing around the mythal stone. Then she felt Malkizid's presence in the conduit, as the devil-prince responded to her call.

"I am here, Sarya," he said in his melodious voice. "What is it you desire?"

"The mage Araevin Teshurr has visited us here," she said.

"Ah! Did the spell trap I showed you snare him?"

"He triggered it, but he apparently made his escape on foot before my warriors could catch him. But it did empty him of spells, and he was completely unable to tamper with my mythal-weaving here."

Even though she could not see him, she felt Malkizid nodding in satisfaction on the other side of the conduit.

"Good, good. You see what we can do when we combine my knowledge of these things with your special heritage and talent for sorcery?"

"Do not patronize me, Malkizid," Sarya snapped. She paced anxiously in front of the stone, her tail twitching from side to side. She had had little use for confined spaces since escaping from her prison beneath old Ascalhorn three years ago, and even though the mythal chamber beneath the castle's great hall was large and spacious, she still did not care for it. "If Araevin has discovered me here, he will certainly carry word to Evermeet's army and anyone else who cares to listen."

The devil-prince fell silent a moment.

"You fear Evermeet's army will pursue you even here," he said at last.

"Twice now I have been denied the realm that is mine to rule—once in ancient Siluvanede, and a second time at Myth Glaurach. This city is the seat of my third realm, Malkizid, and here I will raise a mighty kingdom indeed. All I need is time, time to master more of your mythal spells, time to build my armies again."

"You need not fear that possibility, Sarya," said the demon-prince. "With the right mythal spells, you could stand a siege of centuries within Myth Drannor's ruins."

Sarya stopped her pacing and turned to face the mythal stone through which Malkizid spoke, even though she knew that he was not physically present.

"I have spent ages uncounted buried in traps and prisons! I am not going to simply sit within these crumbling ruins and allow my enemies to contain me here forever."

"Then you must destroy Evermeet's army. Since you cannot reach them where they are now, perhaps matters will turn to your advantage if they place themselves within your reach here." Malkizid paused a moment, then asked, "Are you certain that Evermeet is your only foe? What of the Jaelre or Auzkovyn drow? Or the human lands near this city?"

Sarya barked in bitter laughter. "The drow have not seen fit to show themselves yet, and I doubt they will do so. Vesryn Aelorothi tells me that some demonic nemesis has all but harried them from the old Elven Court entirely. As for the humans . . . the humans have dreaded these woods for a thousand years or more. Why, the memories alone of old Cormanthyr have been sufficient to keep them from expanding into the forest."

"A kingdom stands on four pillars, Sarya: magic, steel, coin, and allies. You can do without one pillar, but your realm will not survive long if you lack two or more. Here you have magical power, and soon an army to be reckoned with, when we bring more of my infernal warriors to your banner—under the terms of our existing bargain, of course. What of the other two pillars?"

"Commerce is for humans," Sarya growled. "But allies . . . allies could be useful. Unfortunately, the nearest orcs or ogres of any number are in the lands of Thar, across the Moonsea."

"I was speaking of the human powers that surround this forest. Or even the drow, for that matter."

Sarya turned slowly to gaze into the aura of dancing golden light.

"I have no use for the drow," she said. She was inclined to discount the rest of Malkizid's suggestion, too, yet there was something in the archdevil's words, wasn't there? Even if she had no use for the humans, she certainly did not want to see Evermeet's army ally with any of those powers against her. "But the humans . . . Sembia or Zhentil Keep have no interest in seeing Evermeet's army in Cormanthor, do they? Perhaps these enemies could be turned against each other. But what would you gain from such a development, I wonder?"

"Your success is my success, Sarya Dlardrageth. You are the ally I have needed for five thousand years, the missing pillar in my kingdom. And I am the missing pillar in your new realm." Sarya felt the archdevil's keen hunger and ambition glinting through the mythal almost as if she were gazing into his eyes. "I have waited a long time for my freedom. You can help me gain it."

CHAPTER SEVEN

22 Mirtul, the Year of Lightning Storms

Anticipating trouble, Araevin and Filsaelene wove a number of spells, wards, and abjurations over their companions in the safety of the hidden cave. Araevin warded them from blades and talons with his spell of stoneskin, and finished by once again weaving the spell of invisibility over the small band.

"The spells will not last long," he said. "We should head straight for the portal glade, and avoid any delay."

He nodded to Starbrow, and the tall moon elf set his shoulder to the hidden door leading out into Sehanine's shrine, gently opening it a handspan to peer outside.

"No one in sight," Starbrow said. "Follow me, and stay close."

One by one they slipped out of the refuge. Daylight had long since faded, and the night was overcast with only a hint of moonshine glowing behind the clouds. Starbrow lingered a moment to slide the door shut behind them and quickly scuff up the signs of their passage.

"No sense letting the daemonfey find it," he said in a low voice.

They set off at a quick jog along the old forest roads, heading back toward the jagged spires of the city that rose above the trees.

They hurried on through the night-black forest, until Araevin sensed that they were quite close to the portal glade. He started to whisper a warning to Starbrow, but the moon elf slacked his pace and raised one hand in warning before Araevin could speak.

He looked back to Araevin and whispered, "Do I go on ahead, or do we all go together?"

"Together," Araevin whispered back. "My invisibility spell won't work if we spread out too far."

Starbrow nodded, and moved carefully out into the clearing, his hand on Keryvian's hilt. Araevin followed him, peering into the dark shadows that gathered around the edges of the clearing. Nothing stirred in the small clearing. He felt Ilsevele a step behind, and Filsaelene and Maresa bringing up the rear.

"The portal," Araevin said to his companions, and he hurried over to the blank stone face where the magical doorway opened. He checked it quickly, searching for signs of a sealing spell or trap, and found none.

"Just a moment," he told the others, and he fished out the tiny white blossoms needed to open the gate.

A sinister voice hissed somewhere in the air above him, and Araevin felt his invisibility spell suddenly shredded into useless scraps of fading magic.

"Ambush!" he cried to his companions.

"I knew you would return to this door, paleblood!" cried a harsh, booming voice from above the glade. "You have troubled us for the last time."

Araevin whirled and looked up. Descending from some unseen perch high above, a band of armored fey'ri appeared in the night sky and dropped down toward his small company. At their head flew a terrible scion of darkness, a huge, powerfully built demon-elf with four arms and a curving scimitar in each hand. His eyes burned like balls of green flame in the darkness.

"What in the black pits of the Abyss is *that?*" Maresa snarled.

Her crossbow snapped, and a stubby quarrel glanced from the huge swordsman's breastplate. Ilsevele's bow sang beside Araevin, and silver-white arrows killed in midair a fey'ri sorcerer about to cast a spell. The creature's wings crumpled and he plummeted headlong into the clearing.

A stabbing bolt of lighting darted down from another spellcaster, but Araevin expertly parried the spell with a quick spell-shield, batting its baleful energy aside to detonate in the forest nearby. Then from another fey'ri a small knot of absolute darkness streaked down into the center of the glade. In the space of two heartbeats the black ball blossomed out into a wide cloud of roiling blackness, shot through with purple-white bolts of energy. Frigid, cloying darkness closed in around Araevin, and jabbing lances of unclean fire seared him across his limbs and torso, as if icy filth had been shoved under his skin. He gasped and staggered.

"Araevin, get the gate open!" Starbrow called.

Keryvian leaped from its sheath like a brand of white fire, burning away the foul blackness that had descended over the glade. He dashed forward and met the daemonfey swordmaster.

With a roar of fury, the four-armed monster dropped down on top of Starbrow, his two lower blades flashing in a vicious cross-cut, followed an instant later by a double down-cut from his upper arms. Yet somehow Starbrow, with his one blade, parried both cross-cuts with a single great shock, and quickly spun aside from the overhand attacks, finishing his turn with a whirling backhand slash that beat through the massive daemonfey's right-hand guard and slashed a deep cut across the back of the monster's calf. Keryvian gave off a shrill, high ring as it tasted demonflesh.

The huge swordsman roared again, then turned and sprang straight at Starbrow, unleashing a dizzying fusillade of slashes with his four blades. Then Araevin wrenched his eyes away from the furious duel as more fey'ri attacked, scouring the clearing with gouts of green sorcerous fire and deadly curses and blights. Filsaelene stumbled and fell to her hands and knees, blinded by a fey'ri spell, then Maresa swore a vile oath and scrambled back away from a boiling nest of magical, ruby-colored scorpions that erupted from the ground all around her, each the size of a human hand.

"Damn it! I hate scorpions. I hate them!" she snarled.

Araevin spied a fey'ri warrior swooping down at the blinded Filsaelene. He snapped out the arcane words of a deadly spell and fired a bright emerald beam of magical power at the demon-elf. The spell caught the fey'ri on her right side, and with a terrible green flash of light, she disintegrated into sparkling motes that rained down over the clearing. He searched for another foe and found Ilsevele firing furiously at several fey'ri who swooped and dodged, trading magical blasts for her arrows. Already two black scorch marks smoked at her hip and left arm, but an arrow-feathered fey'ri lay crumpled in the clearing nearby.

Araevin calmly chanted the words of a spell that illuminated the whole clearing with lights of a dozen different colors. Yellow arcs of lightning incinerated one fey'ri, while another was turned instantly to stone and fell so close to Maresa that the genasi had to dive aside to keep from being crushed. She swore again and returned to her work of skewering scorpions on the point of her rapier.

Araevin turned to help Starbrow with his foe, but a battery of fiery bolts from an invisible spellcaster he had missed rained down all around him. Flames seared his chest, his thigh, and his outflung arms, just missing his eyes. He staggered back, flailing at the smoldering fires.

"Araevin! Is the door open yet?" snarled Starbrow.

His duel with the massive daemonfey swordsman continued unabated. He'd been wounded at least twice, with long lines of scarlet trickling down his fine elven mail, but he battled grimly on, somehow ducking and dodging and parrying blow after blow his opponent rained down on him. The hulking daemonfey bared his fangs in pure frustration, hacking his heavy scimitars one after another at the moon elf warrior.

Filsaelene scrambled to her feet, quickly chanting a holy verse that wiped away the blindness curse that had felled her before. She looked for a foe, and blanched.

"There are devils coming! A lot of them!"

"Closer!" Araevin called back. "Everybody, move closer!"

Then he waited for an awful moment, afraid to activate the portal if one or more of his companions could not reach the door in time, yet dreading any spell or attack that might make it impossible for them to escape. Filsaelene was close by. She backed toward the door, sword point weaving in front her. Ilsevele and Maresa fell back as well, Ilsevele still firing arrows at enemies who swooped and dodged in and among the trees. Starbrow tried to back away from his ferocious opponent, but the daemonfey lord roared in answer and followed him closely.

"Araevin, the portal!" Ilsevele cried.

"A moment," he said, watching Starbrow and his foe.

The moon elf danced back three steps to the side as the swordsman launched a furious assault, and Araevin saw his opportunity. He quickly chanted a spell, even as he felt enemy magic lashing against his spell-shield, and raised up from the ground a great arching dome of white frost. In the blink of an eye the frost thickened and spread, making an impenetrable barrier of pure white ice that shut their enemies outside.

"We have only a moment," he told his companions. "It won't take them long to dispel or destroy the ice. Follow me through the portal as quickly as you can!"

Then he turned and barked the words of the ancient Elvish pass phrase, waking the portal from blank gray stone to a glowing silver door in the side of the hill. Without another word he leaped through, trusting to his own example to encourage his comrades to hurry after him.

He stumbled into the barrel-vaulted mausoleum chamber, his ears ringing from the sounds of the battle he had just left behind. Automatically he moved away from the portal, making sure that he was not in the way for the next to follow. The portal flashed silver, and Ilsevele and Filsaelene tumbled through together, followed by Maresa, and finally Starbrow. The moon elf picked up Filsaelene by one arm, and waved Keryvian toward the far end of the room.

"Stand back!" he cried. "The ice wall gave out, and they are on our heels!"

"Not if I can do something about it," Araevin muttered.

The portal was intermittent and unreliable, but there was always the chance that the daemonfey might get lucky, and succeed in activating the portal again. Fortunately, he knew a spell to shut down a portal, at least for a time. He retrieved a pinch of spidersilk and mortar dust from his bandolier of spell reagents, and quickly spoke the words of a sealing spell.

It might have been because he hurried the spell, or simply because the magic of the portal was so old, but whatever the cause, Araevin shattered the ancient spell of the portal. The blank stone face of the doorway cracked like a thick pane of glass struck by a hammer, creating a jagged spiderweb of fractures. He staggered back, hands and arms burning with the shock of the broken spell, and bit his tongue hard enough to draw blood.

"Damn!" he gasped.

"That," said Starbrow, "seems to be a very well-sealed door. I don't think they'll follow us through that."

"I ruined it," Araevin groaned. "The portal's gone."

"Right now, I don't count that a loss," Filsaelene said. "They're on that side, and we're on this side. I don't know if we could have held them off for much longer."

"You don't understand," Araevin said. "I stopped them from following us, yes, but when we want to use this doorway again, we won't be able to." He sighed, furious with his own clumsiness. All questions of practicality aside, he hated to be the mage responsible for wrecking a work of magic that might have been a thousand years old. It made him feel like a vandal.

"I don't know if that is a loss worth regretting, Araevin," Ilsevele said. She stood up and gingerly looked down at the scorch marks on her armor. "After that fight, the daemonfey are certain to guard that portal exit heavily. We probably couldn't have used it again, even if we wanted to."

"So, what now?" Maresa asked.

"Back to the mountain fortress, and Myth Glaurach," Starbrow said at once. "We have to tell Seiveril and the others where the daemonfey are hiding."

"Agreed," Araevin said. "And Sarya has found herself another mythal to twist to her own purposes. We have to stop her before she gathers a new army here."

Ilsevele looked over at Starbrow, and offered him a small smile. "For what it's worth, Starbrow, that was some of the finest swordplay I've ever seen. I can't believe you're still in one piece after standing in front of that four-armed monster."

The moon elf winced, looking down at the slashes he hadn't turned aside. "It's not the first time I've fought such as him," he remarked. "Now, let's get going before they think to gather some teleporting demons and come here looking for us."

❂ ❂ ❂ ❂ ❂

The Citadel of the Raven stood on a high, windswept hilltop many miles to the north of Zhentil Keep itself. Legend had it that the forbidding walls and deep-delved halls beneath the ground had been made by giants, and Scyllua had never managed to think of a better explanation for stairs better than two feet tall and doorways sixteen feet in height. She climbed through the glowering black ramparts, taking the wooden risers that had been fitted between the fortress's cyclopean stairways. It was bitterly cold, despite the weak spring sunshine. The citadel was dozens of miles north of even the northern shores of the Moonsea, and the high elevation and lack of cover seemed to invite cold, shrieking winds from the vast wilderness beyond.

She paid little attention to her own discomfort. She rarely did, after all. Her mind was fixed on other things, and she had long ago discovered that clarity and determination could overcome any bodily weakness, such as fatigue or hunger or pain. *Purpose* was all one needed, and that was something that Scyllua Darkhope had in abundance.

She reached the gates to the Stone Court, the inmost bailey of the great keep, and swept past a dozen mailed guards who wore the black-and-yellow surcoats of Zhentil Keep, not even noticing their nervous salutes. Within the high court stood several large, strong towers, armories and barracks and banquet rooms fit for a royal seat, but Scyllua walked past these to a squat round bulwark at the far end of the keep. This sturdy tower housed the Temple of the Black Lord, the citadel's shrine to Bane, the fearsome patron of the Zhentarim and Scyllua's absolute lord and master.

Temple guards in black and green stared straight ahead as she climbed the steps, refusing to acknowledge her presence—as was only right and proper. As warriors of Bane entrusted with their sacred post, they bowed to no one. Scyllua passed into the fane beyond, where a towering idol of black stone carved in the shape of a mighty armored lord stood. Without hesitation, she threw herself down on the cold stone floor and abased herself.

"Great lord," she murmured, "Favor your worthy servant, and destroy any who displease you. At your word the heavens tremble and the earth groans. I am a sword in your hand. Let me be the instrument with which you smite your enemies."

"You stand high in the Black Lord's favor, Scyllua," came a voice from above her. "Some mouth the words of that prayer and secretly hope that our dread master never takes them up on the offer. You, however, possess true zeal. The Black Lord has plans to do just as you ask, I am sure of it. Now, what brings you to the Citadel of the Raven? The last I heard, you were busy fortifying the vale of the Tesh."

Her prayer finished, Scyllua easily climbed to her feet despite the heavy armor she wore, and turned to face the speaker. He was a tall, powerfully built man, with thick arms and a broad, square jaw. A mane of deep red hair framed a pale face dominated by a long, drooping mustache.

"I crave an audience with the Anointed Hand of the Black Lord, Lord Fzoul," she said, bowing deeply.

Fzoul Chembryl smiled coldly, an expression that failed to warm the measuring malice in his hooded eyes.

"Such formality is hardly necessary between us, Scyllua. You are no mere novice or underpriest, after all."

"We are all novices before the Great Lord Bane, Lord Fzoul."

"Yes, of course. But you must take care, Scyllua, to avoid the sin of humility. The Great Lord demands abasement in the face of one's betters, true, but he also requires us to govern absolutely those who stand below us in the grand hierarchy Bane has prescribed for mankind. To suggest that any novice or initiate is your equal in the eyes of the Mighty King of All is to deny Bane's will."

Fzoul inclined his head to the idol that towered over the shrine, and descended to the chapel floor.

"Yes, Lord Fzoul. I submit myself for correction."

"I deem no more necessary—this time. Now, I doubt that you came here to seek my instruction on minor matters of the Black Lord's tenets. I am going to take some air on the walls. Consider your audience granted, and join me on my walk."

Fzoul strolled out of the temple into the citadel's courtyard, pausing in the doorway to hold his arms outright while a pair of attendants quickly draped a heavy mantle over his garments to keep him warm. He paid them no mind, nor did Scyllua. "There is something very odd going on in Myth Drannor," she began.

Farthest Reach • 123

"There is *always* something odd going on in that dreadful elven wreck. It's the nature of the place."

Fzoul climbed slowly up a nearby stairway to the top of the wall, ignoring the fiercely cold wind. In the distance, long, knifelike peaks still held flanks full of snow. The High Priest of Bane paused to survey the view.

"I would not report a routine occurrence to you," Scyllua said. "A few days ago, the wizard Perestrom of the Black Network came to me in Yûlash. He told me that the ruins of the city are now occupied by an army of demonspawned sun elves. He guessed that better than a thousand of these creatures occupy the ruins, and he also said that a great number were competent sorcerers as well as swordsmen."

"Demonspawned sun elves?" Fzoul asked. He pulled his gaze from the distant peaks.

"I rode to Myth Drannor to see for myself, leading a small company of trusted soldiers." Scyllua possessed an unusual steed, a nightmare of ghostly white. The demon-horse could gallop through other planes at need, and gave her the ability to ride fast and far by strange roads indeed. "Perestrom's observations were accurate. There is an army of these fellows gathering in Myth Drannor. I took the liberty of instructing the clerics and mages in my command to scry and divine what they could of this, and they gave me a name: the daemonfey."

"Now that is interesting," Fzoul said. He pulled on one side of his mustache, thinking. "You may not have heard, yet, but I have just learned that the elves fought some kind of fierce campaign in the Delimbiyr Vale over the last couple of months. Soldiers of Silverymoon were sent into the High Forest to confront orcs led by demonic sorcerers, and an army of demons appeared near the ruins of Hellgate Keep and marched south into the trackless mountains where the elven city of Evereska is reputed to lie. A great battle was fought on the Lonely Moor only a few tendays ago."

Scyllua nodded. The Delimbiyr Vale was more than five hundred miles distant, but Zhentarim spies and merchants were firmly established in the towns of Llorkh and

Loudwater, which were not too far away. And Zhent agents had a way of gathering rumors from the savage races of the North, the orcs and goblins and such. If elf armies were marching around in the wilds of the Graypeaks, the orcs would have noticed.

"Were these daemonfey involved with that, my lord?"

"Our sources passed on stories of demon-elves and such, but I had frankly discounted them. But now . . . hearing of demonspawned elves twice in the course of only a few days, I am much less inclined to treat this as groundless rumor." Fzoul resumed his pacing, his hands clasped before his chest. "So you say they are in Myth Drannor. What is the significance of an army in Myth Drannor?"

"It menaces any of the northern or central Dales," Scyllua replied. "It serves as a check on any designs that Sembia or Hillsfar might have in the region. And it certainly might constitute a threat to our own holdings on the south shore of the Moonsea."

"They are enemies of the elves. That suggests they are no friends of the Dalesfolk."

"There is something more. Perestrom also claimed that these daemonfey had the allegiance of the devils of Myth Drannor."

Fzoul frowned deeply, and continued his walk along the ramparts, passing guards posted along the imposing walls. No enemy was likely to approach the citadel unseen, so the sentries were little more than ornamentation, but Scyllua approved. Discipline and regimentation were the foundations of an army's strength, and soldiers inured to onerous duties in times of peace would not balk at them in times of war.

"How many devils are there in Myth Drannor?" he wondered aloud. "One hundred? Two hundred?"

"There could be many more than that, if they have been keeping their true strength a secret. And baatezu are certainly clever and patient enough to conceal their numbers if it suits their purposes."

The lord of Zhentil Keep halted suddenly, looking sharply at his high captain. "I had not considered that possibility." He glanced off toward the south, as if he might catch a glimpse of the distant elven towers, forest-mantled. "Could this herald the beginning of a fiendish invasion of the Dales? Infernal hordes have brought down more than one kingdom in Faerûn."

"Myth Drannor itself was destroyed by such an invasion six hundred years ago," Scyllua observed. "At least, powerful fiends captained that army. If they appeared in Cormanthor once, it could happen again."

Fzoul grinned fiercely and struck one gauntleted fist into the other. "North of Myth Drannor lies Hillsfar. South, east, and west lie sparsely settled Dales. Any way a fiendish army in Myth Drannor turns, one of our enemies stands in the way. If we stood by and did nothing, we could hardly help but to profit from our enemies' discomfort. How much more could we gain if we actively sought to turn events to our advantage?"

"You have a plan, my lord?" Scyllua asked.

"I will soon," Fzoul promised. "I want you to march an army to Yûlash, and be prepared to strike east toward Hillsfar or south toward the Dales, as events demand. In the meantime, I must seek Bane's will in this matter. Opportunities such as this do not come along every day, and I want to be certain of the mark I'm shooting at before I loose my bolt."

❂ ❂ ❂ ❂ ❂

Araevin protected the portal in the mountain fortress with a powerful spell of sealing, just to make sure that the daemonfey would find it difficult to make use of the portal nexus even if they managed to somehow repair or restore the damaged gate at Myth Drannor. Then they gathered up for burial the body of the dead human mage whose ghost had attacked them, and returned to Myth Glaurach, four days after they had set out to chart Sarya's portal network.

Starbrow went at once to report their findings to Vesilde Gaerth and the other captains of the Crusade. Weary and wounded, Araevin and the others trudged back to the ruined shell that had been set aside for their campsite, shucked their packs and armor, and tended to their injuries with spells of healing and restoration. Then they went in search of hot baths, eventually finding the city's old bathhouse down in the main body of the elven camp. Though little more remained of the building than its pools and its crumbling walls, the forest that had grown up in and around the city roofed the bathhouse well enough, and elves had arranged several screens for privacy. The pools had been cleaned and filled with fresh water, well-heated by stones kept warm in a big brazier nearby. Araevin parted from his female companions and enjoyed a long, hot soak in the pool set aside for men.

When he returned to the company's campsite, he found a messenger awaiting him, a young moon elf who wore the colors of a squire in the Eagle Knights.

"Mage Araevin?" the fellow asked. "I have been sent to bring you to Lord Seiveril's quarters. He has returned from Evermeet, and wants to see you and your companions."

"Seiveril's back?" Araevin sat up, shaking off his fatigue. "I'll be there soon. You'll find Ilsevele and the others at the bathhouse."

In a little less than an hour, Araevin, Ilsevele, Maresa, and Filsaelene found themselves back in the old library that served as the headquarters of Seiveril's army in Myth Glaurach. Starbrow reappeared as well, still dripping wet from a hurried bath to clean the grime and blood from his body.

"Sorry to keep you from resting now," he said to Araevin and Ilsevele, "but Seiveril wants to hear this straight from you."

"I simply want to make sure that I understand the tale as best I can." Seiveril Miritar came into the room, dressed in simple traveling clothes. Vesilde Gaerth followed him. Seiveril embraced Ilsevele, and took Araevin's hand in a strong clasp. "Welcome back. I understand you have been busy while I was away on Evermeet."

"We have, Father," Ilsevele said. "We followed the daemonfey to Myth Drannor. They're encamped in the ruins of the city, gathering their strength again."

"Worse yet, Sarya Dlardrageth has another mythal to pervert," Araevin added. "This one she has guarded more carefully than the last. I attempted to wrest control of it from her, and discovered that I could not contest her authority."

Seiveril's eyes darkened. "Start from the beginning, and tell me everything. I want to hear this story in its fullness."

Together, Araevin and Ilsevele described how they navigated the chain of portals to Myth Drannor and what they found in the ancient capital of Cormanthyr. Maresa and Starbrow added details as they came up. Then they answered question after question put to them by Seiveril and Vesilde, until Seiveril finally nodded.

"All right," he said, "I have heard all I need to hear. If you are confident that Sarya has hidden her army in Myth Drannor, I am as well. We will pursue them without pause, and put an end to the daemonfey once and for all."

"Are you certain that is a wise idea?" Vesilde Gaerth asked. "You may have trouble persuading Evermeet's sons and daughters to go a thousand miles farther east and fight another campaign in a place where there are no living elven realms to defend."

"The daemonfey are our enemies. If we drive them into the middle of peaceful human kingdoms and leave them alone to turn their evil against non-elf neighbors, how will the humans and other folk of Faerûn thank us?" Seiveril asked. He paced away from the others to gaze out at the snow-capped mountains, gleaming in the morning light beyond the forests that surrounded the old city. "Besides, Vesilde, consider this: Sarya Dlardrageth has already demonstrated that she can and will attack Evermeet from Faerûn. I think the warriors of Evermeet who march under our banner will be willing to fight some more to make sure that doesn't happen again."

"Cormanthyr is a long march indeed. It would be many hundreds of miles on foot, and we would have to cross Anauroch as well," Vesilde said. "I doubt the phaerimm have forgotten their defeat in Evereska. For that matter, the Shadovar might not permit our passage."

"There are elfgates leading to Cormanthyr from Evermeet, aren't there?" Ilsevele asked. "Return to Evermeet by means of the gate in Evereska, and go from Evermeet to Cormanthyr."

"I do not think that will be possible," Seiveril said. He turned from the window with a small frown, his hands clasped behind his back. "The council will not permit me to launch another crusade from Evermeet's shores."

Seiveril fell silent, and no one else spoke for a time. Maresa fidgeted, but for once the genasi kept her opinions to herself. Finally Starbrow looked up and addressed Seiveril.

"Presuming that our warriors are still willing to follow you in sufficient numbers that we can field an army," Starbrow said, "there is still the question of how to get them from here to there. Is the march across Anauroch possible, or not?"

"I don't know," Seiveril replied. He looked to Araevin. "Can we bring an army through the portals you explored?"

"The portal leading to Myth Drannor's Burial Glen was destroyed when we fled," Araevin answered. "You cannot bring your warriors to Myth Drannor through that door."

"It would have been impossible to force our way into the daemonfey stronghold through that portal, anyway," Starbrow added. "It only worked once every few hours."

Ilsevele glanced over at Araevin. "What of the portal before the one leading to Myth Drannor? Starbrow said that the mausoleum stands in Semberholme or somewhere in western Cormanthor."

"Cormanthor is a very large forest," Starbrow said. "That portal might be a hundred or more miles from Myth Drannor."

"Still, it would save you the march across Anauroch," Ilsevele said.

"It won't go quickly," Araevin cautioned. "The portal in the mountain fortress requires the casting of a spell, and each casting would only permit a handful of soldiers to pass through. You'll need a mage to activate the portal for each four or five soldiers, and even a competent mage won't be able to activate the portal more than a dozen times in a single day. If you have twenty wizards in your army who can cast the proper spell, it would take you at least four or five days to pass your army through the portals."

"That assumes perfect organization and timing," Ilsevele added. "Better count on twice that time, to be safe."

"But there is no enemy waiting for us in the Semberholme portal?" Seiveril asked.

"No, Father. At least, we spent the night in the woods outside the mausoleum two nights ago, and no one troubled us."

"Then it doesn't matter if it takes us two days or a tenday. The Semberholme gate is clearly the best choice available to us." Seiveril fixed his eyes on the unseen dangers ahead, looking away to the east as if he could see the spot where he meant to move his army despite the intervening mountains, deserts, and forests. "Summon the captains, Starbrow. I must explain to them what I propose to do—*all* of what I propose to do—so that those who choose to come with me can begin to march as quickly as possible."

CHAPTER EIGHT

24 Mirtul, the Year of Lightning Storms

After resting a night in the company's improvised quarters, Araevin spent the next two days instructing the half-elf mage Jorildyn and several other high-ranking wizards of the Crusade in the pass phrases and spells necessary to use the old portal network. The mages retraced Araevin's steps through the mountain fortress and the forest crypt to the woods of Semberholme, and confirmed that the door leading to Myth Drannor was beyond repair.

"A shame," Jorildyn muttered as they stood in the vault beneath the mausoleum. "It would have been useful to be able to slip spies directly into the city through that door."

Araevin shook his head. "The daemonfey were waiting for us when we sought to return. If the portal was working, they would guard it heavily with spells and infernal monsters." He thought for a moment then added, "Also, I would not discount the possibility that Sarya might prepare deadly spell traps in the city's mythal. When my friends and I entered the city before, there were spells to prevent me from inspecting the mythal. If Sarya could do that, she might be able to weave other spells into the mythal—for example, curses to afflict anyone who isn't a daemonfey."

"Lord Miritar means to move on Myth Drannor and attack the daemonfey in their lair, if they don't come out to fight," Jorildyn said, frowning. "How will Sarya's control of the mythal effect a battle in Myth Drannor's streets?"

"Consider the effect that Evereska's mythal had against the phaerimm a couple of years ago, once the city's high mages repaired it. Certainly the daemonfey army didn't attempt to enter the mythal during their attack two months ago, but they probably just didn't have the opportunity."

The battle mage looked at Araevin, his face troubled, and asked, "Does Sarya have sufficient skill and ability to do that with the mythal?"

"I don't know," Araevin replied. "I don't believe she has the ability to sculpt the mythal as she pleases, at least not yet. But a month ago I was able to best her at Myth Glaurach, and three days ago I could not do so at Myth Drannor. Either she was simply careless the first time I attemped to contest her access to a mythal—something that doesn't really seem to be in her nature—or she has learned something new about mythalcraft in a very short time. That possibility terrifies me."

"I don't care for the idea of marching our army into Sarya's mythal and hoping for the best," Jorildyn said.

"Nor do I."

Araevin narrowed his eyes, thinking. The magical might and lore of the Crusade was formidable indeed, but would it be enough if things came to a battle for Myth Drannor?

He set aside the question for a time, as he and Jorildyn charted out the other portals from the mountain fortress. First they blocked the trapped portal and marked it as such, so that there would be no mistakes while moving soldiers through. Then they examined the other two functioning portals. One led to a sunlit glen in a warm, southerly forest, with thick moss hanging from the trees and the humming of countless insects in the air. The other opened into a ruined wood elven watchtower, a great tree that had once been a living fortress. Araevin guessed that that portal likely opened in the forests of the Great Dale, though none of the other wizards assisting in the task knew for certain.

Within hours of their return, Seiveril summoned all the captains of the Crusade to his headquarters: Jorildyn, master of the battle mages; Edraele Muirreste, the captain who had succeeded the fallen Elvath Muirreste as leader of the Silver Guard of Elion; Ferryl Nimersyl, commander of the Moon Knights of Sehanine Moonbow; Daeron Sunlance, ranking Eagle Knight of the small company of aerial warriors; and Rhaellen Darthammel, the Blade-Major of Evereska, who led a stout company of Evereskan Vale Guards in order to repay the warriors of Evermeet for their stand on Evereska's behalf. They were joined by Keldith Oericel, who had taken over as leader of the infantry of Leuthilspar after Celleilol Fireheart's death at the Battle of the Cwm. A dozen lesser captains from smaller companies, orders, clans, houses, and societies came as well, each the leader of anywhere from a couple of dozen to a few hundred elf warriors. Finally, Seiveril also invited a score of the most prominent heroes and champions. Even though they led no companies of soldiers, powerful wizards and noted bladesingers wielded great influence over the opinions of many warriors in the Crusade.

The commanders and heroes filled the great hall of Myth Glaurach's ruined library, gathered together beneath soft lanternlight. The night was clear, cold, and breezy, with stars glimmering above the roofless white ruins, and a constant cool murmur of wind in the branches of the surrounding forest. Araevin and his companions stood near an open arch leading out to the overgrown balcony beyond.

When the leaders of the Crusade stood assembled, Seiveril strode to the front of the room and climbed three steps up the remains of the grand staircase that had once swept down into the room from the missing upper floors.

"Welcome, friends," he began. "I have summoned you here because our next campaign is at hand. As you have no doubt heard by now, we have learned that the daemonfey legion has retreated to the ruins of Myth Drannor in ancient Cormanthor. I propose to bring our might against the Dlardrageths there, and finish the daemonfey once and for all.

"You may wonder how we will get to the forests of Cormanthor from the ruins of Myth Glaurach without months of difficult and dangerous marches. There is a simple answer: We will pursue the daemonfey through the same portal network they used to make their escape. We cannot follow them into Myth Drannor itself—that last portal has been destroyed—but, thanks to the efforts of Mage Araevin Teshurr and his companions, we can move our army swiftly and safely to Semberholme, which is only a hundred miles or so from our destination.

"My friends, I hold no one here sworn to join me in Cormanthor. You and your warriors came to Faerûn to defend Evereska and the High Forest from invasion, and we have succeeded in doing that. But I want you to consider the question of whether we should content ourselves with having defeated one daemonfey attack, or should seek to eradicate forever the threat they pose to realms of the People here in Faerûn, as well as Evermeet itself—for we should not forget that this war began when the daemonfey attacked Tower Reilloch."

"Leuthilspar is with you, Seiveril!" called the moon elf Keldith Oericel. "We will not allow the daemonfey to escape unpunished!"

Seiveril conceded a hard, thin smile, and nodded toward Keldith. "Do not be too quick to answer, my friends," he cautioned the others. "You must lay this choice before all who serve under your banner. I asked Evermeet's warriors to follow me to Evereska, but I will not take them farther without asking again."

"I, for one, do not like to leave a job half-done," said a

sun elf swordsman that Araevin didn't know by name. "You have my answer, Seiveril."

"For those who choose to follow me to Cormanthor, then, I have another question to ask you," Seiveril said, raising his hands to still any more outbursts. "So far you have regarded this campaign as a Crusade, a war against the daemonfey. I want you to consider this: Are we engaged in a Crusade, or a Return? For myself, this is my Return. I will remain in Faerûn, even after the daemonfey are defeated, and seek to rebuild a realm on this shore that will prove strong enough to prevent threats such as House Dlardrageth from rising unchallenged for generations to come."

The assembled captains and heroes looked to one another, as if to confirm that they had heard Seiveril's words right. Some shouted out their approval, raising fists and bared blades in the air. Some remained silent and thoughtful, weighing the meaning of Seiveril's words. Others were openly troubled, frowning or whispering to their neighbors.

"Has the queen given her blessing to this?" called a bladesinger who stood near Araevin.

"The Council of Evermeet frankly opposes it," Seiveril said, "but Amlaruil has not forbidden me from asking you—each of you—whether you would consider aiding me in rebuilding a lasting elven presence in Faerûn."

"Where will you raise this realm?" asked the Eagle Knight Daeron Sunlance. "Here, in Myth Glaurach?"

"If it proves the wisest course, then yes, I will come back to Myth Glaurach to found a realm here," Seiveril said. "But first we have unfinished business with the daemonfey in Cormanthor. Once we have driven them out of our fathers' lands, we might find that old Cormanthyr is the place to which we will Return."

"What of the humans? Their kingdoms surround Cormanthor. They may fight to keep us from our ancient homelands," Sunlance said.

"We would be better neighbors than the daemonfey, wouldn't we?" More than one elf laughed at Seiveril's words. The sun elf lord raised his arms again. "As I said before, I ask for no one to swear allegiance to a new realm tonight.

The Crusade has work to do before the Return can truly begin. But I hold this dream in my heart, my friends, and it is long past time for me to share this vision with you, in the hopes that it will kindle the same passion and determination in your hearts that it has kindled in mine.

"Now, go back to your warriors, and tell them what you have heard here tonight. Starbrow, Thilesil, and I will begin to order our march through the portal to Semberholme under the assumption that most or all will follow us against the daemonfey, if no farther. Sweet water and light laughter, friends."

Seiveril descended from his steps, and was promptly surrounded by several of the captains, besieging him with questions or demanding to march first.

Araevin, Ilsevele, and their companions moved onto the balcony nearby as the captains and commanders walked out into the starlight, many already engaged in arguments about whose company should march first, how and when to break camp, or whether it was even possible to contemplate a march on Myth Drannor. The sun elf mage looked over to where Seiveril, Starbrow, and Vesilde stood, besieged by others who were unwilling to leave without seeking more answers.

"Your father has a talent for making trouble, doesn't he?" Maresa asked Ilsevele, with a mischievous grin. "Didn't any of it rub off on you?"

"It's a skill he's learned late in life," Ilsevele retorted. She looked up to Araevin, who simply stared off into the dark skies to the east, his hands on the ruined balustrade. She moved up beside him, and laid her hand on top of his. "Something troubles you?"

"I think my path lies elsewhere, Ilsevele." Araevin glanced back at his companions, and touched his hand to his breastbone, feeling the hard form of the Nightstar beneath his robes. "I have to decipher the last of Saelethil's lore in this *selukiira*. If Sarya turns the mythal into a weapon, Saelethil's magic may be the only answer we have."

"What do you propose, then?" she asked, her voice small against the sounds of the night.

"To find out who the star elves were, and where they lived, and whether some record of what Morthil brought back from Arcorar still exists. There is a rite I must master before the Nightstar will open the rest of its knowledge to me."

"That might be the work of years, Araevin! You are speaking of secrets that were hidden five thousand years ago. That is a terribly long time, even by our standards."

"It might also be the work of months, or days," he replied. He looked back up at the starry sky, watching the dance and flicker of lanternlight bobbing in the breeze. "I can always seek to invoke a vision if I turn into a blind alley. My heart tells me that Saelethil's lore will be the key to any battle in Myth Drannor. There are many skilled wizards marching in your father's army, but I am the only one who can do this. Even if it proves to be fruitless, I have to make the attempt."

She sighed and looked down at her hand atop his. "Are you asking me to choose between going with you or going with my father?"

"I do not mean to." He allowed himself a small smile. "But there is more of Faerûn to see, if you haven't gotten your fill of it yet."

Ilsevele pulled her hand away from his, and drifted away across the cracked and weathered stone of the old balcony. She stared off into the green shadows beneath the trees, hugging her arms against her body. Araevin gazed at her back, waiting. Finally she seemed to give herself a small shiver, and turned back to him.

"All right. Now that I have seen Myth Drannor with my own eyes, I find that I cannot argue against doing everything in our power to sever Sarya Dlardrageth from the city's mythal. But I fear for you, Araevin. I think it is a perilous path you intend to walk. I will come, if only to guard you from yourself."

Araevin started to reply, but then he thought better of it, and kept his argument to himself.

Instead he looked over to Maresa and asked, "What of you?"

Maresa leaned against the old wall, her arms folded. Her hair drifted softly against the breeze, glimmering like silver in the starlight.

"I see no reason to walk toward a battle when I've got an excuse to head away from one," she said with a snort. "And I like the idea that your magic might be a stiletto we can stick in Sarya's back while she's watching Lord Seiveril march his army at her fortress. I'm with you, Araevin."

Araevin looked over to Filsaelene and asked, "And you?"

The sun elf girl shook her head. "I think I should march with the Crusade. If Evermeet's soldiers are heading into battle against the daemonfey, many will have need of healing. Lord Miritar needs every cleric he can find." She frowned and raised her eyes to meet Araevin's. "But . . . if you ask me to help you in this new quest, I will do so gladly. I can never repay you for saving me from captivity in Myth Glaurach."

"You helped us in the mausoleum of the ghost and in the fight at the portal glade," Araevin pointed out. "I'm inclined to think you have little left to repay."

Ilsevele looked at her and smiled sadly. "Follow your heart, Filsaelene. You should serve as you think best, and I am afraid you are right about where you will be needed." She stepped forward and embraced the young cleric. "Be careful. And do not be afraid to send for us if we are needed in Cormanthor. We will come if we can."

Maresa turned back to Araevin. "So, more portals leading into the godsforsaken wilderness? Maybe a dragon's lair this time?"

The sun elf mage shook his head. "No, no portals this time. If you're willing, I will teleport us to where we need to go."

👁 👁 👁 👁 👁

Sarya climbed the steps of the First Lord's Tower, and tried not to allow crawling disgust to mar her composed features. Hillsfar was a city of humans, a hundred miles north of Myth Drannor, on the shores of the Moonsea. It was filled with the reek and clamor of humankind, and everywhere she looked humans carried on with their senseless commerce, bickering, squabbling, and bullying each other.

She was shrouded in a magical disguise, a simple spell of appearance-changing that made her resemble a human woman—perhaps somewhat slighter of build than normal, but graceful and beautiful nonetheless, with hair of deep auburn and eyes of bewitching green. She wore a pleated emerald dress of human design, decorated with delicate gold embroidery. She had entered Hillsfar in a small coach driven by disguised fey'ri, and passed through its crowded streets unnoticed until her carriage clattered to a stop before the stern, tall citadel that stood at the heart of the city.

She glanced up at the banners and pennants snapping overhead, and frowned despite herself. In her day the humans had known their place. None dared challenge the power of the great elven realms. They had been a race of simple barbarians, suitable for use perhaps as mercenaries in the wars of greater races. Yet it was an inescapable fact of the age in which she found herself that humankind must be reckoned with.

That can be set right, she told herself. *Soon I will be able to hurl an army of devils, yugoloths, and demons at any foe who dares to challenge me. I will lay this city under tribute—or have it torn down stone by stone and its people driven away from the borders of my new realm.*

Six stern warriors in heavy armor with red-plumed helmets stood by the archway leading into the tower. It was more properly a small keep, really, with an interior courtyard and high, strong walls.

"Halt and state your business," the guard sergeant demanded.

"Why, I seek an audience with First Lord Maalthiir," Sarya said, her voice and smile cold and dripping with contempt. "I am Lady Senda Dereth. I believe he expects me."

The man-at-arms—actually a woman-at-arms, though one could hardly tell beneath the heavy armor—turned her back on Sarya and glanced at an orders book on a standing desk in a small alcove by the doorway.

After consulting the book for a moment she grunted and said, "You're to be shown to the Conservatory, and await the first lord there. Come with me."

Sarya inclined her head without allowing her cool smile to slip, though the ill manners of the guard sergeant deserved a sharp rebuke indeed. She followed the stocky woman as she clomped along in her armor, passing through barren, cheerless halls that were almost devoid of decoration. Another guard followed at her back, a good three paces behind her.

"Is this truly necessary?" she asked.

"No one goes into this tower without a Red Plume escort," the guard sergeant replied. "The first lord has made that absolutely clear. It is a standing order."

She came to a tall, paneled door, and opened it for Sarya. Inside was a large parlor or sitting room, with several empty bookshelves along the periphery, and a number of old portraits hanging from the walls—mostly of elves, it appeared, though with the crude human artistry it was hard to be sure.

"Wait here," the sergeant said, and withdrew to the hallway, closing the door behind Sarya.

Sarya composed herself for a long wait, and she was not disappointed. It was well over an hour before she heard measured footfalls in the hall outside, and the rough clatter of the guards coming to attention. She turned to face the door as Maalthiir, First Lord of Hillsfar, strode into the room.

He was a human of middle years, tall but thin, with a heavily lined face and a scalp shaved down to gray stubble. He wore a long goatee of iron gray, and dressed in a high-collared tunic of gleaming black, chased with dragon designs. In one hand he carried a short staff or long scepter of dark metal, with its head in the shape of a draconic claw. Four more guards followed him into the room, pale and silent warriors who seemed human at a glance, but positively reeked of planar magic to Sarya's keen sense for such things.

"Well, you must be Lady Senda," Maalthiir rasped, his voice completely humorless. "I've never heard of any Dereths around here. Who are you, and what do you want with me?"

"Who I am does not much matter," Sarya said. "And I want nothing more than to give you a warning, First Lord."

Maalthiir's scowl deepened. "I react poorly to mysteries and threats. Choose your next words carefully."

"You have a new enemy on your doorstep, Maalthiir."

The first lord snorted and crossed his arms, tucking his scepter under his arm. "Oh, do I? And I suppose you have come to tell me all about my new adversary. Very well, then—who is this dreadful new foe?"

"Evermeet, my lord," Sarya said.

Whatever the first lord might have been expecting her to say, that was not it. Maalthiir glared at her for a long moment, measuring her.

"What in the world does Evermeet want with me?" he demanded.

"An army from Evermeet is returning to Cormanthor. They mean to recapture Myth Drannor and restore the kingdom of Cormanthyr. I wonder what they will think of a neighbor who purged his city of elves years ago, having them slaughtered in bloody games?"

Sarya's eyes glittered like green ice as she delivered the barb. She had not yet managed to insinuate many fey'ri spies into the lands around Myth Drannor, but it had not taken her long to learn that Maalthiir had come to the throne of Hillsfar many years ago by deposing a council dominated by elves.

A momentary uncertainty glinted in the human lord's face before he bared his teeth in a fierce grin.

"Cormanthyr is dead," he stated. "The elves have Retreated. It took them five hundred years to reach that decision, Lady Senda. They will never overturn it in only fifty years."

"Do not take me at my word, Maalthiir. Investigate for yourself. You are reputed to be a mage of no small talent. Scry the woods of Semberholme and see what you find there. Or send for your spymasters and ask them what passes in the western Dales of late. You will find an army of elves better than five thousand strong—sun elves, moon elves, bladesingers and champions, mages and clerics, making ready to march north," said Sarya. "It is a formidable array."

"Assuming for the moment that you are telling me the truth—who are you, and why tell me?"

Sarya glided forward a step, and glanced at the expressionless guards with their black eyes.

"Do you wish me to speak freely here?"

The first lord did not even look at the black-clad swordsmen.

"Oh, yes," he said. "Do not mind my guards. They will not repeat anything they hear, and they are completely incorruptible. I see no one alone, Lady Senda. Ever."

"As you wish, then." Sarya glanced at the impassive guards again, wondering exactly what they were, then dismissed them as unimportant. "Who I am is not important. As far as why I am carrying tales to you of an elven army in Cormanthyr, it is simply a matter of self-interest. The elves are my enemies. Since it seems that I must deal with them, I naturally thought it wise to consider who else might regard an elven Return to Cormanthyr as less than desirable."

"Now it becomes clear," Maalthiir snorted. "You picked a fight with the elves, and now that they have come for you, you hope to hide behind Hillsfar's army."

"Do you really wish to see a Coronal in Myth Drannor, Maalthiir? A power in the forest to shield the weaker Dales against you, to bar you from the timber and resources of the woodland at your very doorstep, and perhaps to restore elves to the rule of this city?"

"You will have to do better than that, if you hope to frighten me," the first lord said.

"I do not expect to frighten you. I expect you to examine

the situation for yourself and act in your own interests as you perceive them." Sarya turned her back on him and paced away, pretending to admire the portraits on the walls. "You have designs on the northern Dales, do you not?"

"It is none of your business if I do," Maalthiir snapped.

"And your ally Sembia has interests in the southern Dales," Sarya glanced back at the mage-lord. "An elven army in Myth Drannor would make both of those goals immeasurably more difficult. I submit to you, First Lord, that you would be well advised to think of how you could encourage the elves to Retreat once again, and leave you to the business of ordering this region as you see fit."

"I tire of this verbal fencing, my lady," Maalthiir said. "You still have not explained who you are and why you are in my tower. I will have answers, real answers, now."

Sarya inclined her head. "Not until you verify that I have told you the truth so far, First Lord. See for yourself the army of Evermeet, marching to your doorstep. I will return in a few days to resume this conversation when you have had an opportunity to confirm the truthfulness of my words."

"I have not given you leave to go," Maalthiir said. He made no motion or sound, but the pale swordsmen beside him set hands to sword hilts in unison and fixed their dead gazes on Sarya. "You will answer my questions one way or another, Lady Senda."

"Another day," Sarya said, and she teleported away from Maalthiir's parlor, vanishing in the blink of an eye.

The last she saw of the first lord, his face was set in a scowl of displeasure—but not surprise.

❂ ❂ ❂ ❂ ❂

On the morning following Seiveril's Council of War, Araevin, Ilsevele, and Maresa gathered their belongings, armed themselves with swords and spells, shouldered their packs, and drew their traveling cloaks over their clothes.

Then, as Filsaelene stood by to see them off, Araevin incanted his teleport spell and grasped the hands of the two women. The ruins of Myth Glaurach faded away into a golden, sparkling haze, only to be replaced a moment later by the cool green shadows of the old hillside shrine overlooking Silverymoon—the same hillside where he had met Ilsevele before. Silverymoon's graceful Moonbridge glimmered in the sun below them.

Maresa glanced down and patted at her torso and arms, as if to make certain that all of her was present.

"I've always thought that was an extremely useful spell," she observed. "Why bother to walk anywhere once you know it?"

"In the first place, it's somewhat inappropriate to use magic of that sort on a whim," Araevin replied. "More than a few wizards have managed to forget that their feet must serve when their magic won't do. Secondly, the spell is not particularly easy. I have a difficult time holding more than one or two teleport spells in my mind at a time without giving up other spells that are equally useful. Finally, it's wise to never use the last teleport spell you have in your repertoire unless you are in dire peril. You never know when you might earnestly wish to be somewhere else."

"There is also the chance of a mistake," Ilsevele told Maresa.

The genasi shot a sharp look at her. "Mistake? What sort of mistake?"

"It would not ease your mind at all if you knew, Maresa." Ilsevele patted her arm and walked past her, following the path down to the city below.

The three travelers found their way back to the Golden Oak, and took rooms there again. Then, after shucking their packs and traveling gear, they went straight to the Vault of Sages.

"I left Calwern with a list of references and texts to search for me," Araevin explained as they walked through the tree-shaded streets of the city. "Before we do anything else, I want to see if he has learned anything important."

"What will you do if the knowledge you seek has simply been lost?" Ilsevele asked. "It has been a very long time. The spells you need may not exist any longer."

"Spells rarely vanish all together, at least in my experience. The gods of magic often intervene to ensure that knowledge does not disappear from the world." In truth, Araevin dreaded that very possibility, but he did not want to dwell on it until he had to. "If Morthil has been forgotten by history, it may be that his spells remain. Clerics of Mystra, Oghma, or Denier hold many old spellbooks in their libraries. And if all else fails, I can attempt to reinvent the spells myself, though that would take many months, perhaps even years, of research. I think I am in too much of a hurry for that."

They arrived at the Vault. The great library's gray stone turrets and narrow windows made it seem more like a castle sitting in the center of Silverymoon than a place of learning, but the library's doors stood open. They mounted the worn stone steps to the wood-paneled foyer inside. Bright dust motes drifted in the yellow sunlight that slanted through the windows.

"Why, Master Teshurr, you have returned! And Lady Miritar, too—how good to see you again!" Brother Calwern straightened up from his desk, a broad smile creasing his seamed face. "You concluded your out-of-town affairs to your satisfaction, I trust?"

"Not entirely. I dealt with the question I was called away to look into, but I fear it only led to more questions."

"In my experience, difficult questions are like hydras' heads," Calwern said. "Each one you vanquish leads to two more. If it's any help, I have set aside those tomes you asked me to look for. Do you want me to bring them out for you?"

Araevin nodded. "Yes, please, Brother Calwern."

"The second reading room is open. Make yourselves comfortable, and I will bring them out directly."

Araevin bowed to the human cleric, and led Ilsevele and Maresa to the reading room. In a few minutes Calwern appeared, wheeling a small cart stacked with musty old texts and scrolls.

"Here you are," the human said. He handed Araevin a parchment letter, a list of the tomes with cryptic notes and marks accompanying it. "The list you requested. You'll find some notes about what is here and what isn't, as well as a few sources I added as I thought of them."

Maresa eyed the stack of books with suspicion. "I like reading as much as the next person, but that is a formidable stack of paper. Are you going to read all of those, Araevin?"

"As many as I need to," he said. "Make yourself comfortable, Maresa. Or, if you'd like to help, I'll explain what I'm looking for, and you can try your hand at it too." He looked over to Brother Calwern. "Thank you, Brother Calwern. This should be an excellent start."

They spent the rest of the day plowing through the collection of ancient texts and histories compiled by dozens of different authors, some human, some elf, and even a couple written by dwarves or halflings. Then they returned to the Golden Oak, ate, rested, and returned the next morning to resume their efforts, and again on the following day.

By the morning of the third day, Araevin had learned some things he hadn't known before. Morthil, the star elf wizard, was said to live in a realm named Yuireshanyaar. Araevin had never heard of any such land, and so he broadened his search, looking for anything he could find about a realm so old or so far off that even the sun elves had forgotten about it. He asked Calwern to look into it as well, and resumed his reading.

Late in the afternoon, Brother Calwern brought Araevin a heavy ancient tome bound in dragon hide.

"Good afternoon, Master Teshurr," he said warmly. "I believe I may have found your missing kingdom."

Maresa looked up from an old tome she had been examining. "Thank Akadi," she muttered. "My eyes can't stand another hour of this."

The Deneirrath cleric set the heavy book on the reading table, and opened it with care. It was an ancient atlas with page after page of old maps, all marked in script Araevin could not read.

"Is this Untheric?" he asked.

"Yes, it is. The atlas dates back almost two thousand years. Fortunately its makers protected it with spells of preservation long ago." The white-haired Deneirrath carefully paged through the atlas, finally settling on a spread that showed, in fading ink, a long peninsula jutting into an island-studded sea. "The Yuir forest, where the realm of Aglarond now stands," the cleric said.

Ilsevele leaned over Araevin's shoulders. "Aglarond's forests hide many secrets, but a fallen kingdom no one has ever heard of? That stretches credulity."

Araevin studied the ancient map and said, "I see no realm or cities marked on the map."

"Ah, but look at the Untheric caption, here." Calwern pointed with one stubby finger. "It reads, 'Here of old stood Yuireshanyaar, which is now hidden from the world.'"

Araevin glanced up to the Deneirrath. "Do you have any older maps of the Aglarondan peninsula here?"

"No, I checked already. The ancient empire of Unther was the first human realm to settle the peninsula's shores, and this is the oldest Untheric text we have in the library." Calwern rubbed his chin. "But there is something here that puzzles me, Master Teshurr. Why does the map say that Yuireshanyaar used to be here, but has been hidden? If one hides something in a certain place, it is still there, isn't it?"

"That is odd," murmured Araevin. "I might expect it to say 'Here of old stood Yuireshanyaar,' which would imply that the realm was there and has now fallen. Or I might expect it to say, 'Here is Yuireshanyaar, which is now hidden.' Which interpretation is correct?"

Calwern shrugged awkwardly. "I fear my understanding of Untheric may be insufficient to the task."

"It could be an error on the part of the cartographer," Araevin offered. He stood up from the desk and paced around the room, thinking. Morthil, the star elf—whatever that was—inherited the spellbooks and magical devices of Grand Mage Ithraides, hundreds of years after the coronal of Arcorar moved against the Dlardrageths. The last anyone recorded, Morthil returned to his people, taking Ithraides's lore with him. The star elves lived in Yuireshanyaar, and here was a map claiming that Yuireshanyaar might once have stood in the forests of Aglarond.

"Does anything of Yuireshanyaar survive in Aglarond?" he wondered aloud.

"*Tel'Quessir* have lived in Aglarond for a long time," Ilsevele observed. "It is said that many half-elves still live in the Yuirwood."

"I have heard stories of old ruins and strange magic in Aglarond's forests," Calwern offered. "It is entirely possible that better records of Yuireshanyaar are preserved in the Simbul's realm."

"I am inclined to think so too," Araevin said. He looked to Calwern. "Can I have a copy made of that map, and translations of the captions and names? By tomorrow?"

The cleric nodded. "Of course, Master Teshurr. I will set our scribes to the task immediately."

Ilsevele looked over Araevin's shoulder at the map with some interest. "So, how far is Aglarond from here?" she asked.

"It is quite far—two thousand miles, perhaps more," said Calwern.

Ilsevele's eyes widened. "That is two months' journey, at the least!"

"It is not as bad as it sounds," Araevin said. "A long part of that would be over water. We can hire a ship in one of the Dragon Coast ports and cross the Sea of Fallen Stars in a tenday or so. So, the question is how to reach the Sea of Fallen Stars quickly and easily." Araevin leaned back in his chair, looking up at the ceiling in thought. "The portals we found under Myth Glaurach might serve. One led to the Chondalwood, another one to the forests of the east—"

"What of the portal to Semberholme?" Ilsevele interrupted him, tracing a path on Araevin's map. "That would bring us within a few days' ride of the ports in Sembia or Cormyr, wouldn't it?"

Araevin allowed himself a small grimace. He was supposed to be the veteran traveler and the expert on portals, but Ilsevele had found the answer before he'd even started to consider the question.

"I think you're right," he said. "The other portals might get us closer to our goal at the first step, but then we would have to find our way to a port on strange shores. Riding from Semberholme to Suzail or Marsember seems much easier than finding our way out of the Chondalwood."

Ilsevele patted his shoulder. He could feel her smirking behind his back.

"What are Cormyr and Sembia like?" she asked. "And how likely is it that we will find a ship bound for Aglarond in their ports?"

Araevin shrugged. "I haven't been to that part of Faerûn before, but I know they're both regarded as civilized lands. Sembia is a land where gold is king, a league of cities governed by merchant princes. They're suspicious of elves, I hear, but as long as we have coin to spend, we should have no trouble there. Cormyr is a smaller realm, but well spoken of by many travelers I've encountered. As far as passage to Aglarond, well, I suppose we will learn more when we reach the Sea of Fallen Stars. If nothing else, it seems likely that we could take passage to Westgate or Procampur, and go from there to Aglarond."

"The quicker, the better," Ilsevele said. "I have a feeling my father will need us in Cormanthor before too long. I do not want to tarry an hour longer than we need to."

Maresa shut the ponderous tome in front of her and smiled crookedly. "I've never been to Aglarond," she said. "I wonder if their wine's any good."

◈ ◈ ◈ ◈ ◈

They returned to their rooms at the inn, making ready to depart on the following day. Araevin left the details in Ilsevele's hands. He had something to do, and the time had come to do it whether he wanted to or not. At sunset he left the city's gates and retraced his steps to the shrine of Labelas Enoreth, seeking quiet and solitude. The night was cool and breezy. Spring in the North faded fast once the sun set, and the woods around the old temple sighed and rustled in the wind.

Araevin seated himself cross-legged, looking out over the lights of the city below. Then, drawing a deep breath, he began to chant the words of a powerful vision spell. Before he set off for a kingdom as distant and exotic as Aglarond, he wanted to *know* that he could find what he sought there.

He focused on the tale of Ithraides and his allies, conjuring the images he'd seen preserved in the ancient *telkiira* stones: Ithraides, the ancient moon elf, with his younger apprentices around him. Morthil, he thought. Star elves. Yuireshanyaar. The *telmiirkara neshyrr*, the Rite of Transformation.

"I wish to know!" he called to the wind.

The vision seized him at once, powerful and immediate. Araevin felt himself flung out of his body, his perception hurtling eastward across land, sea, and mountains. He glimpsed a palace of green stone, a great woodland, a circle of old menhirs in a sun-dappled clearing in the forest. Then his vision lurched and leaped. He reeled, dizzy, setting a hand on the cold flagstones to steady himself.

When he looked up again, he saw that he stood in a great, lightless hall. Wrecked balustrades of stone lined the walls, the remnants of high, proud galleries that once encircled the place. In the center of the hall a drifting spiral of white magic hovered in the air, turning slowly. Araevin gazed at the odd apparition, trying to make out what exactly it was—and his vision leaped again, diving into the white spiral.

He stood in a strange room of gray mist and shining light, gazing at a great old tome of golden letters, lying open on a stand.

"Ithraides's spellbook," he gasped.

All at once the vision whirled away from him, and Araevin was left cold and hollow on the windswept terrace above Silverymoon.

He climbed shaking to his feet, only to give up and sink back down to the ground. The spell was neither easy nor forgiving, and he would not be himself for quite some time. But the vision was usually truthful.

A silver door of mist in a black hall, he wondered. *Ithraides's lore has not been lost.*

With a sigh, he climbed again to his feet, and started back toward the city and his companions below.

CHAPTER NINE

28 Mirtul, the Year of Lightning Storms

They spent their last night at the Golden Oak much as they had the last time they left Silverymoon, enjoying a good meal, drink, and dancing beneath the lanternlit boughs of the great old tree. Then, in the morning, the three travelers returned to the Vault of Sages to pick up the copies Araevin had commissioned from Brother Calwern before leaving the city again. It was another warm spring morning, and flower beds all over the city were in bloom around them.

They climbed the steps to the Vault's entrance, and found Brother Calwern waiting for them with a new leather scroll case, secured for travel.

"The Untheric map you requested is ready," the aged Deneirrath told Araevin. "I wish you luck in your travels, Master Teshurr. Come back when you can and tell us about them."

"Thank you," Araevin replied, accepting the map in its leather case. "Until we meet again, Brother Calwern."

He bowed and turned to go, but then someone called his name from nearby. The voice was human, though raspy and somewhat deep. Araevin turned and found himself looking on a man who sat by one of the desks. The fellow stood slowly, pushing himself to his feet with a jangle of mail beneath his surcoat.

"I am Dawnmaster Donnor Kerth, of the Order of the Aster," he said. "I have been waiting for you."

The same order that Grayth served in, Araevin recalled. He inclined his head to the fellow.

"Well met, Dawnmaster," he replied, studying the Lathanderian. He was young—a grown man, certainly, but no more than his mid-twenties, if Araevin was any judge of it—and he had a hard manner to him. His eyes were bright blue and intense, and his hair was hacked so short that it was little more than dark stubble covering his dusky scalp. He wore the rising sun symbol of Lathander on his breast, and a big-hilted broadsword hung at his hip. "What can I do for you?"

"You were the companion of Mornmaster Grayth Holmfast?" the human asked.

"Yes, I was," Araevin said. He frowned, taking the young man's measure. "We traveled together in the Company of the White Star some years ago, and again this very spring."

"Grayth Holmfast was my mentor in the Order. I understand you were with him when he was killed." His fierce manner grew even harder as his eyes narrowed, and a scowl crept across his features. "He was like a father to me, Master Teshurr. Tell me what happened to him."

Araevin searched Donnor Kerth's eyes. "Grayth was a true friend to me as well, Dawnmaster. I will do as you ask." He reached out and set a hand on the big human's shoulder. "But, I have to warn you—it will be hard to hear. He fought valiantly at my side through many perils, but in the end he was murdered in cold blood by the daemonfey."

"I mean to hear your tale, Araevin Teshurr, whether it is good or ill."

Araevin glanced at Ilsevele and Maresa, then nodded. "Give me a moment to finish my business here, and we will go somewhere to talk. Dawnmaster, this is my betrothed, Ilsevele Miritar, and our companion Maresa Rost, who has also shared many dangers with us. We all rode with Grayth."

Ilsevele offered her hand in the human way, and Kerth surprisingly did not seek to crush it in his mailed grasp. He drew off his gauntlet to touch her fingers, and bent down to kiss her hand.

"My lady Miritar," he murmured. Then he turned to Maresa, who made a show of daintily extending her hand for the same treatment. "Lady Rost."

"Dawnmaster Kerth," Maresa intoned gravely. The genasi regarded the serious Lathanderian with a solemn face, but Araevin caught a glimmer of humor in her eyes. Maresa was not used to such displays of courtesy, it seemed.

"Let us go outside," he suggested.

The human assented with a nod, and Araevin led him outside to the green boulevard that ran past the Vault. Many of Silverymoon's streets would have passed for parks in other cities. They found a row of cherry trees in full bloom, and sat on a pair of stone benches beneath the soft pink blossoms. Araevin related to Donnor Kerth the story of his return to Faerûn and quest for the missing *telkiira*. From time to time, Ilsevele or Maresa interrupted with details of Grayth's valor and their adventures together.

Araevin went on to tell of their continued quest in search of the last *telkiira*, the battle against Grimlight the behir, and the daemonfey treachery that snared them all in Sarya Dlardrageth's clutches. Then he came to the end of Grayth's tale in the demon-haunted halls beneath Myth Glaurach.

"The daemonfey demanded that I lead them to the last of the treasures they sought, and so they threatened Grayth's life if I did not comply." He paused, struggling with the words, as the grief of the moment welled up again in his chest. "I hesitated, because I did not want to put such a weapon in Sarya's hands. She ordered Grayth killed, and one of her fey'ri cut his throat. My resistance failed, and she caught me in a spell of dominion, commanding me to do as she asked."

Kerth's fierce eyes softened for a moment. "You did what you could, Araevin Teshurr. Your lives were forfeit from the moment such monsters captured you. As far as you knew, they would kill you anyway."

"I know. But if I had yielded sooner, they might have saved Grayth for later use against me, as they did Ilsevele and Maresa. In which case, I might have been able to rescue him as well."

"How did you escape the domination spell and free your comrades?"

Araevin frowned, and rubbed unconsciously at the Nightstar embedded beneath his shirt. Some things should not be lightly shared.

"Sarya's captain commanded me to attempt something that risked grave harm. That gave me the strength to break the spell. After that, I returned to Myth Glaurach, which had been mostly emptied, as the daemonfey were busy with their war against Evereska and the High Forest. I found Ilsevele and Maresa, and teleported away."

"He also managed to sabotage Sarya's control of the city's mythal, and banish a few hundred demons while he was at it," Maresa added. "Don't let Araevin convince you that he isn't at least a little bit heroic."

The human glanced at Araevin again, and leaned back to digest the tale, hands locked in front of his chest. After a long moment he sighed and looked up.

"Does Grayth's murderer still live?" he asked.

"No. I killed the one who wielded the knife," Araevin said.

"But as far as we know, Sarya Dlardrageth still lives," Ilsevele added. "She is the one who ordered Grayth's death. We think she is hiding in the ruins of Myth Drannor."

"Then, if you will permit me, I offer you my service in Grayth Holmfast's stead." The Dawnmaster bowed deeply, his arms spread wide. "These daemonfey, whoever they are, have made an enemy of the Order of the Aster, and I intend to see Lord Holmfast's work through to its end."

Araevin frowned, not sure what to make of the offer. He exchanged looks with Ilsevele and Maresa. The genasi shrugged, but Ilsevele studied the human closely, her green eyes narrowed in thought.

"Evermeet's army is marching against the Dlardrageths in Myth Drannor," Araevin finally said. "However, our path does not lead there yet. We are about to set out in search of some ancient lore that we need to defeat the mythal defenses Sarya is erecting around Myth Drannor. It is my intent to travel swiftly and return to the fight against the daemonfey as quickly as I can, but I can't say where my quest will lead me, or how long it will take."

"A long and difficult march may prove more important than a single glorious charge in deciding a war," the human knight said. "Honor is served equally by both. Until such a time as you know that you will have no need of my sword, I would like to aid you in whatever way I can. If Grayth would have followed you, I will follow you."

Araevin considered his reply. As far as he knew, he might be wandering in and out of libraries for months in search of the spells he needed. But Ilsevele answered for him. As a captain in the Queen's Guard, she understood a warrior's honor better than he did.

"For the sake of Grayth Holmfast's memory, we will accept your service," she told the human. "The only conditions I place on you, Dawnmaster, are these—if Araevin or I tell you that something you see or do is not to be spoken of to those who aren't elves, you will not do so, and you will not abandon us in danger. Other than that you are free to judge for yourself when honor has been served."

The human crossed his right arm over his heart. "I so swear," he said.

"Good," said Araevin. He stood and faced the Lathanderian. "If you have a bedroll and a pack, go get them and meet us by the river gate. We need to get a mile or so beyond the city walls, and I will teleport us all to Myth Glaurach."

◉ ◉ ◉ ◉ ◉

Curnil Thordrim stood his ground, and prepared to meet his death shoulder-to-shoulder with five more Riders of Mistledale. He and his fellows crouched in the common room of a farmhouse, staring out through the open door and the half-shuttered windows. Skulking closer through the forest verge came shapes out of a nightmare—snarling, hissing devils with snakelike tails, wide mouths full of foul, jagged teeth, and huge saw-toothed glaives of rust-red metal. Fearsome yellow light glimmered in the fiends' eyes, and they cackled and snarled horribly in their terrible voices.

"Why don't they just get on with it?" muttered Rethold.

The tall archer stood beside Curnil, a silver-tipped arrow held on his bowstring. He had only three arrows left, and he was waiting until he was sure of a shot. For the better part of a tenday, the Riders of Mistledale had been embroiled in a deadly fight that worsened every day, defending their vale against what was first a marauding devil or two, then murderous gangs of the creatures. In the past few days a dozen of Curnil's fellows had died, torn apart by fiendish talons, skewered on hell-forged hooks or spears, or blasted to smoking corpses by devil-wrought hellfire.

"Be patient, and wait for your shot," Curnil told him. "If we are going to fall here, we have to take as many of these foul hellspawn with us as we can."

"What I'd like to know," remarked Ingra, who was keeping watch by the window, "is how these monsters got out of Myth Drannor."

She stood with a powerful crossbow in her hands, a highly enchanted quarrel laid in its rest. Curnil knew that she'd account for one of the devils, when the moment came. But that wouldn't be enough, would it?

"They're coming!" cried Ingra.

Curnil raised his paired short swords and crouched by the doorway, ready to kill the first devil to enter the room. Rethold's bow thrummed to his left, as the archer fired through one of the shuttered windows on that side of the house, and Ingra's crossbow snapped sharply on his right.

There was a sudden rush of footfalls, the clicking of taloned nails on the floorboards of the porch outside—and a furious devil leaped in the door, eyes ablaze with battle-lust. It was so quick and reckless in its rush that it nearly skewered Curnil with its barbed glaive before the swordsman could move. He cursed and threw himself aside, then parried two more jabbing thrusts as the monster pressed in, two more of its fellows crowding in close behind it.

"For Mistledale!" Curnil cried, and he heard his fellow Riders take up the call.

He slipped inside the glaive's point and launched a furious assault of his own, slashing and stabbing with his swords as the devil snapped at him with its fangs. The other Riders crashed into the doorway with him, and for a few moments the whole fight came down to a savage press right in the farmhouse's door, blades flashing, fangs sinking into flesh, hisses of anger, and sudden grunts or cries of pain.

Curnil roared in anger as the devil he battled sank its teeth into his forearm, snarling and worrying at him like a great fierce hound, but he managed to slip his right hand free and stabbed his enchanted blade into the monster's torso over and over again, until the devil finally slipped and went down in the doorway. He stumbled to the floor, saw Rethold killed by a glaive-thrust that burst the weapon's point half a foot out of the archer's back, and from all fours awkwardly parried the attack of yet another devil leaping through the press.

His new opponent hissed in savage glee and drew back its weapon for a killing thrust, even as Curnil tried to gain his feet—and a silver-white arrow sprouted from the devil's neck. Curnil took advantage of the devil's distraction to gain his feet again and gut the creature with a wicked low slash under its guard. More silver arrows struck all around him, a deadly sleet of archery that took the devils in their backs until the creatures finally scattered and dashed away, seeking escape.

Curnil found himself standing with Ingra and two of the other four Riders, staring in disbelief at the evidence of the archery around them.

"Someone has an excellent sense of timing," he said.

He ventured out onto the porch, looking to see who or what had just saved his life.

Arrayed around the farmhouse stood dozens of elf archers, some kneeling behind the undergrowth, others standing in the shadow of tree trunks. With easy grace they glided forward, loosing arrows at the fleeing devils as they came, until the skirmish line swept past the farmhouse and into the fields beyond.

"Who are they?" Ingra asked. "I thought I knew most of the wood elves of Cormanthor, but I've never seen these fellows before."

"Nor have I," Curnil said. He limped out into the open—somehow, during the fighting in the farmhouse door, he seemed to have been slashed across the leg without even noticing it—and raised a hand in greeting to the archers' captain, who trotted up to the house. *"Well met, friend!"* Curnil said in Elvish. *"My companions and I owe you our lives!"*

The captain—a wood elf whose silver-green garb seemed to shimmer and shift as it constantly adjusted for the green and dappled shadows the elf passed through—looked at Curnil in surprise.

"You speak Elvish!" he said. "And not very badly, either. You must know some of the *Tel-Quessir!*"

"I do. My name is Curnil Thordrim. I spent several years in the service of Lord Dessaer of Elventree."

"Are these his lands?" the elf asked.

Definitely not from around here, Curnil noted. "No, Elventree lies a hundred miles or more to the north and east. You are near the human settlement of Mistledale."

"Ah, I think I have heard of it," the elf answered. His eye fell on the dead or dying devils sprawled on the farmhouse's stoop and doorway, and he nodded. "I am glad we were able to help. You fought with great valor against more numerous foes."

"Not to seem ungrateful, sir, but—who are you? And what are you doing in Mistledale?"

The elf looked back to Curnil, and inclined his head. "I have forgotten my manners. I am Felael Springleap. My warriors and I belong to Lord Seiveril Miritar's host. We have come from Evermeet to destroy the daemonfey in Myth Drannor."

"Lord Seiveril? Daemonfey?" Curnil shrugged. "Do you mean to tell me that an army from Evermeet is in Cormanthor?"

"I mean that very thing." The elf—Felael, Curnil reminded himself—turned away for a moment to quickly confer with some of the others, who trotted off after the rest of the company. Then he turned back to the weary Riders. "Have you seen many of these hellspawn here, Curnil Thordrim?"

"For a tenday or more they've been raiding our settlements and slaughtering our people. We always knew there were creatures like this lurking in Myth Drannor, but they have never escaped to the larger forest to trouble us before."

"Then it may be that we can help each other," Felael said. "We are here to defeat these creatures and their masters, and it seems to me that you must know much about the lands and happenings nearby. Do you think your leader would be willing to meet with us?"

Curnil took in the skilled and graceful company with a glance. How many more companies of elf archers were roaming around Cormanthor, looking for devils to slay? he wondered. Whatever the answer, it was certainly the best news Mistledale had heard in quite some time.

"Yes," he said. "I think he would."

◈ ◈ ◈ ◈ ◈

Donnor Kerth seemed a grim and serious traveling companion, putting Araevin in mind of some dwarves he'd known in his day. But his gruff and fierce manner had a way of melting away whenever he addressed Ilsevele or Maresa. Donnor hailed from southern Tethyr, the son of a mid-ranking noble, and he had been brought up with an exacting sense of chivalrous behavior, particularly in regards to the opposite sex. Some of the more conservative sun elf houses embraced similar romantic ideals, but humans had a way of fixing their minds on something and carrying it to extremes that elves would never practice.

At Myth Glaurach, they joined in with the stream of elves passing from the Delimbiyr Vale to Semberholme. Since Araevin was perfectly capable of navigating the portal network by himself, they didn't have to wait for an elf mage to lead them through, as the rest of the warriors did. They rested for the night in the growing camp by the shores of Lake Sember, surrounded by the lanternlight and cookfires of Lord Seiveril's army.

Araevin and Ilsevele went to see Seiveril when they had settled on a place to camp. They found him sharing the evening meal with Jerreda Starcloak's wood elves, who sang and danced with abandon as if to show the elflord that their high spirits were sufficient for the whole army. The wood elves greeted both Araevin and Ilsevele warmly, and it was some time before the three sun elves managed to disentangle themselves from the songs, games, and bawdy wit of the wood elf encampment.

As they walked back to Seiveril's pavilion, Ilsevele took her father's arm. "Did you feel in need of some song and dance tonight?" she asked.

"A little music never hurt anyone," Seiveril replied. "I try to make it a point to take at least half my meals with the troops, choosing a different company each time. I want to know what's on their minds, and take some time to remind them why they're here. But I have to say, the wood elves don't give one much of a chance to talk, do they?"

Araevin smiled. Wood elves were notoriously garrulous,

but then again sun elves were supposed to be distant and reserved. He suspected that his wood elf friends went out of their way to act the part when he came to visit, simply because he was a sun elf.

"Their spirits seem high, anyway," he observed.

"It cheers me to pass an hour with them, I'll admit," Seiveril said. "So, you have returned much sooner than I expected. Did you forget something?"

"We're only passing through," Araevin told him. "We need to head south from here, toward the ports in Sembia or Cormyr. We'll be taking a ship to Aglarond."

"Aglarond?" Seiveril paused, his eyes thoughtful. "That makes sense. The People have lived there for a very long time, perhaps even as long ago as the dawn of Arcorar. But it is so far away! Do you really think you will find what you are looking for there?"

"I don't know," Araevin admitted. "But it is the best guess I have at the moment."

"What of you, Father? Have you found any sign of the daemonfey yet?" asked Ilsevele.

"We have companies already marching north and east toward the Standing Stone. I have heard from some of our scouts that they have met demons and devils of various sorts in the forest. Apparently the human folk who live in the forest verge have been greatly troubled in the last few tendays by the fiends that Sarya has released from Myth Drannor, or summoned on her own."

Ilsevele frowned. "I do not like the idea of bringing our own war into the middle of their homeland," she said.

"Sarya made that decision, not I," Seiveril said. "Even if we had chosen not to follow her here, the Dalesfolk would still have to reckon with the daemonfey army and Sarya's summoned hellspawn—and they would not have our swords and spells to help them." They reached Seiveril's pavilion, and the elflord stopped and kissed Ilsevele on the cheek. "I am afraid I have to set our marching orders for tomorrow, and make ready to meet with some human emissaries from the nearby lands who want to know why an army of elves has suddenly returned to this ancient forest. If you like, I will have Thilesil provide you with mounts to speed your journey."

They thanked Seiveril, and Ilsevele kissed her father again. Then they returned to their camp.

The next morning, they found Seiveril's aide Thilesil and obtained riding horses for the four of them—not the elven coursers from Evermeet itself, of course, since they did not know if they would be able to embark the horses when they reached Cormyr's ports. Then they set off for the human lands south of Cormanthor.

From the wilderness of Semberholme, they made their way south for a day to the land of Deepingdale and its chief town Highmoon. The next morning, they rode to the town of White Ford at the northern end of Archendale, and passed along the length of the dale to the town of Archenbridge in a long, hard day of riding made a little easier by fine weather and good roads. Two more days of riding brought them across Sembia's broad farmlands and well-ordered hamlets to the great old city of Saerloon, on the shores of the Sea of Fallen Stars.

Saerloon had long ago over-spilled its city walls, and for miles outside the old city, inns, taverns, stockyards, and stables lined the road. The aroma of the place was overpowering, a mix of cookfires, animal dung, and industry such as tanning, papermaking, and smelting. Busy humans everywhere were noisily engaged in their trades with little regard for their neighbors. Few passersby took any notice of the four riders approaching the city, but those who did looked hard at Araevin and Ilsevele, saying little.

"Why do they stare at us so?" Ilsevele asked Araevin in Elvish.

"Not many human cities are as welcoming to our people as Silverymoon," he replied. "The humans who settled these shores learned little from elves, unlike the human lands you passed through in the North. The Sembians have long regarded elves as rivals, perhaps even enemies."

"Enemies? Why?"

"Long ago the Sembians were checked in their northward expansion by the might of elven Cormanthyr. Even after the fall of Myth Drannor, elves remained in the forest for centuries, enough that the Sembians still did not dare to defy them. The last Houses of Cormanthyr abandoned the Elven Court only within the last forty years or so."

"Will the Sembians claim the forest, now that it has been abandoned?"

"I do not know. The Dalesfolk still stand in their way, even if they are no match for Sembia's strength." Araevin glanced at Ilsevele with a thin smile. "Besides, your father may have other ideas on the question now."

They finally reached the old gates, so deeply buried within the city that there seemed to be no difference between the districts outside the walls and the ones inside the walls, and rode through. Now that they were in old Saerloon, the city's native architecture became apparent. Great stone buildings centuries old rose high overhead, distinguished by needle-like spires, bladelike flying buttresses, high pointed arches, and an incredible wealth of statuary—crouching, leering gargoyles seemed to adorn every rooftop. It was magnificent in its way, but more than little sinister as well.

Araevin gazed up at the threatening, monstrous figures captured in stone, and wondered what had led the long-dead sculptors to adorn their city so.

"Let's find a good inn," he suggested, "and we'll see what ships are in port and where they are bound."

❖ ❖ ❖ ❖ ❖

The waters of Lake Sember glowed with the golden sunset, and a dark line of storm clouds gathered around the distant Desertsmouth Mountains to the west, promising rain before long. Seiveril stood near the lakeshore, absently noting that the camp was smaller than it had been. Many of his companies were already well on their march to the north and east, and soon he too would be gone from there.

"Lord Miritar? The Dalesfolk emissaries are here," Thilesil told him.

The efficient sun elf was a priestess of Corellon Larethian, and one of the clerics subordinate to Seiveril in the hierarchy of Corellon's Grove. But more importantly she had proved to be an exceptionally competent administrator and secretary, helping him to attend to the myriad details of moving, feeding, and planning for an army numbering in the thousands.

"Excellent," Seiveril replied. "I will be there in just a moment."

He would have liked Starbrow or Vesilde Gaerth to be present for the council, but the moon elf warrior was leading the vanguard of the march, and Gaerth was behind him, in charge of the main body.

Seiveril turned his back on the sunset and found his way back to an old, stone colonnade beneath the trees. The slender white pillars had once ringed a great table where the old lords of Semberholme had feasted on summer nights. Like many of Semberholme's ruins, they were not really ruined at all, just abandoned for a time. Since Seiveril's folk had had a few days to set things in order, golden lanterns hung once again from the branches overhead, and the table was set much as it might have been five hundred years ago. Three humans and a half-elf awaited him.

Thilesil stepped forward and announced, "Honored guests, the Lord Seiveril Miritar of Elion. Lord Seiveril, this is High Councilor Haresk Malorn of Mistledale, Lord Theremen Ularth of Deepingdale, Lord Ilmeth of Battledale, and Lady Storm Silverhand of Shadowdale."

"Welcome, friends," said Seiveril. "I thank you for consenting to meet me here."

He bowed, and took a moment to study his guests. He'd sent couriers to all the nearby lands after discovering the troubles besetting Mistledale, even dispatching mages with teleport spells to speed their journeys if necessary.

Haresk Malorn, High Councilor of Mistledale, was a tall, balding human with a heavy body, dressed in garb Seiveril might expect of a small town merchant, which was exactly what Malorn was. For all his evident lack of martial bearing, he had a surprisingly direct and strong look to his face, even if he seemed a little overwhelmed in the present circumstances.

Lord Ilmeth of Battledale, another tall human, was the second of Seiveril's guests. He had a thick, dark beard and a grim, almost sullen manner to him. He also shifted his feet nervously, his powerful arms folded across his broad chest.

His third guest was the half-elf Lord Theremen Ulath of Deepingdale. Theremen evidently had some moon elf blood in him. He was quite fair of skin, with dark hair and a build that was almost elf-slender. He seemed somewhat more at ease than the Malorn, but Seiveril would have expected that from a lord whose demesnes included both human towns and elf settlements in the southern margin of Cormanthor. It helped that Seiveril and Theremen had spoken several times already in the days since the Crusade had emerged in the forests not far north of Deepingdale.

"It has been a long time since an elflord has invited Dalelords to his table in Cormanthor," Theremen said. "I, for one, am honored to be here."

Seiveril inclined his head to acknowledge the compliment, and turned his eyes to the fourth of his guests—none other than Storm Silverhand, one of the Seven Sisters, Bard of Shadowdale, Harper, Chosen of Mystra, and a dozen other things more. She stood watching him, her eyes dark and thoughtful in a face of tremendous beauty. She wore a mail shirt and a leather jacket, and a long sword rode at her hip. Her silver hair, long and straight, gleamed in the lanternlight. Seiveril had not expected her, believing Shadowdale would send its lord Mourngrym Amcathra or another representative, but he was not about to tell a Chosen of Mystra that she was not welcome.

"Well, Seiveril Miritar, you've certainly stirred up a hornet's nest in Myth Drannor," Storm said. "I suppose I would like to know what in the world is going on there, and why a whole army from Evermeet has suddenly gated into this forest."

"I will explain," Seiveril said, glancing to Thilesil, "but first, I was expecting a representative from Archendale too."

166 • Richard Baker

"The Swords declined to come," Thilesil said. "They sent word that they are not concerned with 'elven matters,' but will not obstruct your movements in any way, as long as you do not approach their land."

Malorn shook his head. "Trust Archendale to look out for itself first. You won't get much from them, Lord Miritar."

"In all fairness, High Councilor, the Swords are mightily concerned by Sembia, which sits at their southern doorstep," Lord Theremen replied. "They do not want to give Sembia a reason to pick a quarrel with them."

Seiveril shook his head. The human ability to ignore their own common good always astonished him, but he supposed that if the rulers of Archendale wanted to be left alone, he could certainly leave them alone. He looked back to Storm Silverhand, sensing that she was the one he would have to convince. The legendary Bard of Shadowdale might not hold any titles or govern any lands, but her words went a long way in the Dalelands.

"I promised to explain our presence," he began. "We have spent the last three months marching and fighting in the Delimbiyr Vale, where we fought a bitter campaign against a legion of daemonfey—winged demons who wear the shapes of elves. They are an ancient evil long ago defeated and imprisoned in the High Forest. But earlier this year they mounted a raid on Evermeet itself, and freed a great legion of their kind to launch an attack against the elves of the High Forest and nearby realms."

"Evereska," Storm said.

Seiveril nodded. He hadn't wanted to name the city, not knowing the Dalelords with whom he spoke well enough to speak of such a secret.

"Yes, Evereska," he allowed. "In response, I gathered a host of warriors from Evermeet to go to the Delimbiyr Vale and destroy the daemonfey threat. We stopped them at the gates of Evereska and in the deep refuges of the High Forest, and broke their army on the Lonely Moor. But the daemonfey fled through hidden gates to Myth Drannor, where they are now rebuilding their strength." He faced Councilor Malorn and spread his hands in apology. "In truth, we did not mean to drive an army of our foes into your lands. But now that they have fled here, we have come to finish what we started at the Lonely Moor."

"That explains your army's presence," Storm Silverhand said, "but perhaps you can also tell me why the forest is suddenly thick with creatures of the infernal planes. Have these daemonfey of yours broken the wards trapping those monsters inside Myth Drannor?"

"We think so, yes." Seiveril paused, to make sure that the Chosen understood him. "One of my mages, an expert on mythalcraft and the daemonfey spells, surveyed Sarya's handiwork at Myth Drannor. He found that she has assumed control over the mythal, and is now working to twist it to her own purposes. In the High Forest she used the wards over Myth Glaurach to summon up a whole army of fiends. I fear she will do so again in Myth Drannor if we do not stop her."

"Damn." Storm turned away to stare out over the lake. "We've allowed Myth Drannor to fester for decades, and now it seems we'll have to pay the price for it."

Haresk Malorn looked to Storm and asked, "Can the Sage of Shadowdale do something about a demon queen tinkering with Myth Drannor's old magic? Or the Knights of Myth Drannor? They would not stand aside and let this happen, would they?"

The Bard of Shadowdale frowned, and her face grew dark. "Elminster took the Knights off through a magical gate months ago on some perilous errand. I haven't seen them since. My sister—the Simbul—grew so sick with worry that she appointed a regent in Aglarond and went seeking them. She said something to me about the Srinshee before she left, but now I haven't heard from *her* since. I would like to know where they are, too."

"I know that Elminster and the Knights have proven their friendship to the Dales many times over," Malorn said. "But still . . . what in the world is more important than what's going on right here?"

"The world is full of troubles, my friend, and we who are Chosen can only deal with a very few of them." Storm looked up at the twilight skies overhead. "For my own part, I have always hated choosing which things to do and which to leave undone."

The high councilor frowned and looked down at his feet, perhaps regretting his words. The gathering fell silent for a long moment, as the other Dalesfolk chewed over Storm Silverhand's tidings.

Then Ilmeth of Battledale stirred and looked over to Seiveril. "So you're just going to march your army up to Myth Drannor, kick out the daemonfey, and ride off back to Evermeet?"

"As directly as we can, though the mythal wards may prevent us from an outright assault. We may have to invest the city and batter down its defenses, or work powerful magic of our own to contain the daemonfey." Seiveril hesitated, then added, "After that, many of us will likely return to Evermeet. But I intend to remain here and keep some strength in this forest. We have been surprised by threats originating in Faerûn too many times. I cannot speak for all who march under my banner, but I at least have Returned."

The Dalelords did not attempt to conceal their surprise. Councilor Malorn exchanged looks with Ilmeth of Battledale, and both surreptitiously glanced to Storm Silverhand to see how the Bard of Shadowdale responded. Storm, for her part, was still staring out over the lake. After a long moment, she spoke over her shoulder.

"Turning back the march of years is rarely a good idea, Seiveril Miritar," she said. "It took the lords of the Elven Court nearly five centuries to decide on Retreat. Are you telling me that in a few short months they've suddenly decided otherwise?"

"The decision was not without debate."

Storm snorted softly in the twilight. "Sun elves make an art of understatement. Do you have any idea of the trouble that will come from this?"

"Whatever trouble comes, it must surely be less than that which will come to this land if we leave Sarya Dlardrageth in Myth Drannor," Seiveril answered.

"Lord Miritar, not all of the Dales hold to the old Dales Compact anymore," High Councilor Malorn said. "The four Dales represented here still abide by the promises made fourteen centuries ago by our forefathers to yours, but the Compact is not remembered with much fondness in Archendale, Tasseldale, or Scardale. Even Harrowdale is questionable."

"And there are powers encroaching on the borders of Cormanthor that never agreed to any Compact with the elves," Lord Theremen pointed out. "Realms such as Zhentil Keep and Hillsfar—or Sembia, for that matter—are not at all unhappy with the elves' Retreat. They might resist your Return to Cormanthor."

"I have no designs on their lands," Seiveril protested.

"No, Seiveril Miritar, but they certainly have designs on yours—and ours," Storm Silverhand said. The silver-haired bard turned back from Lake Sember and fixed her eyes on Seiveril. "Cormanthyr long shielded the Dales and the forest lands from the ambitions of kingdoms nearby. But since the final Retreat of the Elven Court thirty years ago, the realms surrounding the Dalelands and Cormanthor have been growing ever bolder. In the absence of the elves' strength and determination, the forest has become a great borderland, a frontier that all are eager to claim.

"Fortunately—" Storm smiled humorlessly as she spoke—"we live in interesting times. The Zhents would have overrun the northern Dales long ago, but they have murdered each other in at least two great bloody purges. They have now recovered from those feuds, stronger than ever. The Sembians might have bought Tasseldale and Featherdale and who knows what else lock, stock, and barrel—but Cormyr under King Azoun would have none of that. Well, Azoun is dead now. Hillsfar was a city friendly to the Fair Folk, respectful of the old Compact. Now it is ruled by the tyrant Maalthiir, a man known to hate elves.

"For a decade now, the only thing keeping the aspirations of these ambitious powers in check is the fear that should one of them move too quickly, the others would certainly join forces to drag down the leader from behind." Storm frowned at Seiveril, her eyes narrow and thoughtful. "Now you tell me that there's an army of demonspawn in Myth Drannor, who no doubt plan to seize a realm to rule for themselves."

"That, at least, I mean to prevent," Seiveril replied. "As for the other realms, I recognize that the years have passed since the Standing Stone was raised, and that a new Compact may be necessary. But I see no human cities standing here on the shores of Lake Sember, or rising in the silver groves of the Elven Court. I will not be told that elves cannot raise a realm under Cormanthor's branches."

Storm sighed and looked over at the glimmering lanterns and campfires of the elven army, which were beginning to flicker into life as the twilight deepened.

"Before the Retreat, no one would have dreamed of challenging an elven army in Cormanthor," she said. "I do not think you can trade on that old fear and respect any longer. Whether you meant to or not, Lord Miritar, you have brought war to Cormanthor, and I cannot yet see who will take up arms against whom."

CHAPTER TEN

4 Kythorn, the Year of Lightning Storms

Saerloon was one of the busiest ports on the Sea of Fallen Stars. Two days after Araevin and his companions arrived in the city, they boarded *Windsinger,* bound for the city of Velprintalar on Aglarond's northern coast. *Windsinger* was a graceful three-masted caravel under the command of a captain named Ilthor, a wiry, sun-darkened Aglarondan. She had carried great tuns of wine, cords of fine hardwood, and small coffers full of rich amber from the Yuirwood to Saerloon, and was taking on Sembian pewter, ironwork, copperwork, and tooled leather to carry back home again.

The day was warm and the skies streaked with rain as two longboats pulled *Windsinger* from Saerloon's wharves. Once in open water the caravel let down her sails, and set her course south-southwest for the whole day in order to clear the great southern cape of Sembia. Then, with a northwest wind at their back, they turned due east and made for the Isle of Prespur, sighting its town-dotted shores early on the third day of sailing. After that Ilthor turned *Windbringer* sharply to the northeast, striking across the mouth of the Dragon Reach for the city of Procampur, on the northern shore of the Inner Sea. It would have been far swifter to simply continue due east for Aglarond, crossing the center of the Sea of Fallen Stars, but the Pirate Isles and the dangerous shoals south of Altumbel lay astride that course, and Ilthor had no intention of trying his luck with either.

Araevin found the sea voyage an easy way to travel. There was little room to spare for passengers, and the deck was cluttered with cargo and stores, but the voyage offered ample opportunity to find a cargo hatch or coil of line to sit on, watch the sea or the distant shorelines, make entries in his journals, talk with his friends, or simply sit and reflect. *Windsinger* was too small to boast cabins exclusively for the use of passengers, so Ilsevele and Maresa shared the pilot's cabin in the sterncastle, while the pilot bunked in the forecastle with the other crewmen. Araevin and Donnor were given the best sleeping places on the open deck. Covered from the weather by the quarterdeck overhead, the after deck was actually quite pleasant in warm weather, if not particularly private.

By night Ilthor found various small anchorages along the coastlines, dropping anchor each night in a different cove or bay. Only once did he run at night, when he crossed from Prespur to Procampur.

"The sea is too cluttered with islands and shoals to sail in the dark," he explained. "Out on the Sword Coast or the Shining Sea, they'll keep their course by day and night. But here I drop anchor when it gets dark, unless I'm certain I've got an open pitch of water all around me or the moon is bright enough to sail by."

For the next few days they sailed eastward along the shores of Impiltur, passing cities such as Tsurlagol, Lyrabar, and Hlammach. Then Ilthor turned southeast, striking across the mouth of the Eastern Reach for Cape Dragonfang.

On the seventh day of their voyage, Araevin found himself sitting with Ilsevele at the stern. He studied his spellbooks in the bright sun, puzzling over the notations and concepts of a spell he had recorded months before but had not yet mastered, while she gazed back at the green shores of Impiltur, slowly sinking into the sea behind them. Her ivory skin had acquired a golden bronze hue in the past few days, as sun elves often did in warm climes. Even the fairest tanned quickly and easily, unlike moon elves, who could never gain more than the faintest hint of color to their skin. After a time Araevin realized that Ilsevele had been staring out over the sea for a long while, her brow faintly furrowed, her eyes distant.

He set down his spellbook and reached to place a hand over hers.

"What is it, Ilsevele? You've been staring at the sea all morning. Where are your thoughts?"

She didn't reply for a long time, long enough that someone who didn't know her as well as Araevin might have wondered whether she had heard him. But finally she took her eyes from the bright horizon, and looked down at the slender white wake streaming from behind *Windsinger*'s rudderpost.

"Where will we marry?" she asked.

"Where?" Araevin blinked, considering the question. In truth, he hadn't given a single thought to any sort of wedding preparations—and especially not since the night the daemonfey had raided Tower Reilloch. "Your father's palace at Seamist, I suppose. Everyone in Elion will want to come." He managed an awkward shrug. "I hadn't really thought about it."

"Do you think we will return to Evermeet in time for our wedding day? It is less than two years from now—Greengrass in the Year of the Bent Blade. That is the promise we made in the Year of the Prince."

"I remember," Araevin said. "Why wouldn't we return for our wedding day?"

"What if my father's army is laying siege to Myth Drannor? Or the daemonfey escape again, and we pursue them to some even more distant land? What if your search for high magic takes you to some realm on the other side of the sunrise, a road whose end you won't reach for years and years?"

"Even if all those things happen as you say, Ilsevele, I don't see why we could not stand in the arbor at Seamist and speak our promises before the Seldarine," Araevin said.

"So we would abandon our battles and our journeys for a day, in order to honor our betrothal?"

"If that is the way we must do it, then yes."

Ilsevele sighed. "And back to your studies, my father's battles, whatever desperate journeys and adventures we must face. That is not much of a marriage, Araevin, and not much of a life together."

Frustration hardened his words more than he intended, but Araevin spoke anyway. "If it is all we are to be permitted now, it will have to do. In time there will be years for us, Ilsevele. We won't always be called away."

"It isn't enough." Ilsevele glanced up at the cloudless sky overhead, her eyes as bright as emeralds in the sunshine. "When we met, Araevin, there was such passion in our hearts! There is nothing we would not abandon for an hour in each other's company, stealing away for a walk in the glades of the forest, an evening's dance in the wine rooms of Elion, a morning together in the woods by the sea . . . but when was the last time we did something like that?"

"You came to find me at the House of Cedars only a few months ago," he protested. "For a few days, at least, I certainly did not think of anything other than you."

"So you say. Yet even then you were aching to set out for Faerûn again. I would catch you staring off to the east at sunset, looking out over the darkening sea toward Faerûn, wishing with all your heart to tread those roads and wander those lands again, even though your mind did not want to hear your heart's whispering."

"If you had asked me, Ilsevele, I would have stayed. You know that."

"If you had stayed, you would have wished I had not asked you."

Araevin looked away, gazing at the empty sea as the breeze played with his hair, listening to the soft sound of water slipping past the hull, the ruffling of the sails in the breeze, the rhythmic creaking of lines and tackle as *Windsinger* rode the waves.

"But you came with me," he said. "You have seen only a thimbleful of these lands, Ilsevele. We could roam the world for a hundred years, and still you would not have seen it all."

She smiled and said, "I am not a roamer, Araevin. I have enjoyed our travels—the parts that weren't difficult or deadly, anyway—and I am not done with them. But my heart turns to home, to familiar places, to the people I love. You, on the other hand . . . when you are at home, wherever that is, your heart turns to the things you have not seen. Tell me the truth: Can you close your eyes and imagine our life together? Can you picture fifty years in the House of Cedars, an end to your journeys, a life of *being* instead of a life of *doing?*"

He started to tell her yes, but Ilsevele held up her hand. "Try it before you answer."

"All right, then."

He closed his eyes, and did as she asked, imagining days of springtime sunshine in the House of Cedars, the sea storms of fall and the dark clouds of winter, the sound of the surf in his ears, nothing to do but pass his days a perfect and complete hour at a time. He might spend a hundred years there, two hundred perhaps, with Ilsevele and the children that might come. Yet he could not seem to envision Ilsevele in that house, or himself for that matter. He frowned and tried again. He was a high mage, and he wandered the halls of Tower Reilloch or the courts of Leuthilspar, while Ilsevele stood at her father's right hand or perhaps even sat at the council table in the fullness of years. But that left the House of Cedars empty again, and he could not fill it with all his imagination.

"You can't do it, can you?" Ilsevele said. "I can read it on your face."

Araevin opened his eyes and looked at his betrothed. There was strength and unflinching wisdom behind her eyes, so bright and perfect. She had changed in the years of their betrothal. Wisdom and confidence, poise and determination, had gathered around her since he had first met her. She was not the timid young woman who had once been content to lose herself in his love, swept away by his stories of far-off places and the restlessness he had learned from a century among humankind.

There, on the sun-bleached deck of *Windsinger,* it occurred to Araevin for the first time that Ilsevele perhaps held a destiny and a passion that might eclipse his own, even if she had not yet found it.

"Give me a year," he pleaded. "Let me walk a few more miles down the road I have to walk. When I know that the daemonfey have been dealt with, when I know that your father has done what he has set out to do, things will be different."

"How do you know?" Ilsevele said. She looked away from him, her red-gold hair gleaming in the sunshine.

"Because you are waiting for me, and I would have to be a fool to let you slip through my fingers." He pulled his hand away from hers, standing up slowly. "I have only a little farther to roam, Ilsevele. Then I will be coming back with you."

Ilsevele pulled herself to her feet, and searched his face for a long moment.

"I know," she said. "I know."

She leaned on the rail, gazing at the sea astern of them. Araevin followed her eyes. Nothing but empty ocean and sweeping sky surrounded them, and they remained there, looking at nothing for a long time.

"I can't see the land anymore," Ilsevele finally said.

Araevin nodded. He had long since lost sight of Impiltur's capes.

"We're well in the Easting Reach now," he said. "We should sight the shores of Aglarond tomorrow."

❂ ❂ ❂ ❂ ❂

The street lanterns of Hillsfar glowed orange in a light evening smog of smoke from thousands of homes, the banked furnaces and forges that had burned all day long, and the cold sea mist from the dark Moonsea, less than two miles from the city walls. Sarya Dlardrageth contemplated the cluttered streets and ramshackle buildings as her hired coach clattered over the gleaming, wet cobblestones.

"What a stinking sty of a city," her son observed. The hulking swordsman wore the aspect of a tall, broad-shouldered human, but the daemonfey lord had little liking for hiding his true nature in a lesser guise. "Do all human cities reek so?"

"Mind your manners in the First Lord's Tower, Xhalph," Sarya said. "Maalthiir is a cold and arrogant man, quick to take offense. I want him as an ally, not an enemy."

Xhalph scowled, but nodded. Sarya glanced out the coach's window. The driver pulled up before the First Lord's Tower, set the brake, and hopped down to open the door for Sarya and Xhalph—two foreign nobles, as far as he knew. Sarya descended, Xhalph at her side, and they climbed the steps to the tower.

"I am Lady Senda Dereth," she told the guard captain. "Lord Maalthiir does not expect me, but I believe he will wish to see me."

The guard captain consulted his order book, then looked up sharply. "The first lord will be notified of your arrival," he said. "You will await him in the banquet room."

He gestured to four of the red-plumed guards, who led Sarya and Xhalph through the keep's winding passages and broad halls to a large room with a great table of oak and dozens of chairs arrayed neatly behind it. The windows were mere slits only a hand's-breadth wide, and the two sets of doors leading into the chamber were made of four-inch thick oak bound with iron bands.

"Do they think this will hold us, if we should choose to leave?" Xhalph muttered to her, as the door closed behind the guards.

"I doubt it," Sarya said. "Maalthiir at least knows that I am a mage. I suspect that the first lord simply wants to remind us of where we are."

To Sarya's surprise, Maalthiir did not keep her waiting. After only ten minutes, the first lord threw open the doors and strode into the banquet room, flanked as before by the four pale swordsmen with the dead black eyes, as well as two more Red Plumes. There was another lord with him, a heavyset man with an exquisitely trimmed mustache and goatee to go along with his long, curled locks of black hair and dark, narrow-set eyes. Sarya decided that he had the look of a warrior who'd let himself go. Despite his evident paunch, the man's shoulders were broad, and his hands were large and strong beneath the delicate lace cuffs of his tunic.

Maalthiir paused on entering, studying Sarya intensely, and motioned to more guards stationed in the hall. The thick oak doors swung shut, and the first lord smiled coldly.

"Good evening, Lady Senda," he said. "You left without answering my questions last time you visited my tower. I hope you will not do so again tonight."

Sarya inclined her head to the human lord. "I hope I will not need to, Lord Maalthiir," she said, ignoring the threat. "May I present my captain-at-arms Alphon? He advises me on military matters."

Maalthiir studied Xhalph for a moment, and his lips twisted into a small, humorless smile.

"Captain Alphon," he answered, then indicated the dark-bearded lord who had accompanied him into the room. "This is High Master Borstag Duncastle of Ordulin. He represents Sembian interests concerned with trade, settlement, and industry in the Dales and the Moonsea."

Sarya nodded to the Sembian lord—more likely nothing more than a jumped-up merchant, she reminded herself—and looked back to the First Lord of Hillsfar.

"I hope you have had an opportunity to confirm for yourself the incursion of Evermeet's army to these lands?"

"I have indeed. The elven army was exactly where you'd

said I would find them." Maalthiir crossed the room to the head of the large, empty table, kicked out the chair there, and sat down in an unconcerned slouch. The oddly pale swordsmen who accompanied the first lord moved to stand behind him. "My spies added some important details you neglected to mention, Lady Senda. They spoke with Dalesfolk who in turn spoke with emissaries of the elven army, and they learned that the leader of the elves—a Lord Miritar, I believe—has discovered that an ancient enemy of elf-kind has occupied Myth Drannor. Apparently these foes of the elves recently waged a furious war in the vales of the Delimbiyr, attacking elven kingdoms in the High Forest, but fled to Myth Drannor when they were defeated a month or two ago."

High Master Borstag folded his thick arms in front of his chest. "My own spies confirmed the first lord's report," he said in a deep, rumbling voice. "In fact, I learned a name for these adversaries of the elves: The daemonfey."

"You are well-informed, Lord Maalthiir."

"Perhaps more well informed than you think, Lady Senda." Maalthiir raised a hand and pointed at his own eyes. "I took the liberty of casting a spell of true seeing before I entered the room. You, dear lady, are not what you appear to be. Nor is your Captain Alphon, for that matter. In fact, were I to hazard a guess, I believe that I am speaking to a pair of Lord Miritar's daemonfey at this very moment."

Xhalph shifted beside Sarya, and his hand stole down to the sword at his side. The four mysterious swordsmen behind Maalthiir mirrored his move in unison, swiveling to direct their dark, dead gazes at Xhalph.

Sarya glanced up at him in irritation and said quietly, "Not yet."

Xhalph growled softly deep in his throat, but he took his hand from his sword hilt and subsided. Sarya looked back at Maalthiir, who still lounged in his chair at the head of the table.

"You are more astute than I had thought you would be, First Lord," she said. "I am Countess Sarya Dlardrageth, of House Dlardrageth. This is my son Xhalph. I hope you will forgive me for taking steps to keep my identity a secret in order to avoid any undue alarm on your part."

"I am by nature a suspicious man," Maalthiir replied. "There is no such thing as undue alarm. Now, with all that behind us . . . what precisely do you want with Hillsfar, Lady Sarya?"

"I want to drive Seiveril Miritar out of Cormanthor entirely. As I said in our previous meeting, it seems to me that you might share that desire. Hillsfar would not profit from an elf coronal in Myth Drannor."

"It is not at all clear to me that Hillsfar would profit from a demon-queen in Myth Drannor, either."

"Well, among other things, I certainly have no interest in guaranteeing the Dales against the natural and logical growth of Hillsfar's power . . . or Sembia's. On the other hand, Miritar will stand in your path. If you ever hope to raise Hillsfar's banner over Harrowdale or Battledale—or if the high master here ever hopes to see Featherdale or Tasseldale under Sembia's dominion—you would be well-advised to make sure that Lord Miritar does not establish himself in Cormanthor."

"Whereas you would gladly stand aside while we seized the Dalelands that lie all around your forest city?"

Sarya walked over to the banquet table and seated herself a few chairs down from Maalthiir, ignoring the flash of irritation in the human lord's eyes.

"I mean to rule over most, if not all, of the old realm of Cormanthyr. That means the woods of the Elven Court, Semberholme . . . much of the forest Cormanthor, in fact. But the Dales were never a part of Cormanthyr, and I could care less what becomes of them. In fact, to help secure your assistance against my foe, I am willing to help you arrange matters in the Dalelands as you see fit."

"An elflord in Cormanthyr—whether you or Miritar—is not something that Sembia wishes to see," said High Master Borstag. "The southern Dales are Sembia's in all but name anyway. What I need are furs, timber, game, lands to clear and to settle . . ."

"Trees are trees," Sarya said. "I won't let you cut the whole forest, but I see no reason why I could not sell you a concession for logging and clearing a good portion of it." She smiled coldly. "Trust me, High Master, no such offer will be forthcoming from Seiveril Miritar."

Borstag narrowed his eyes, and Sarya nodded to herself. She could almost see the human merchant prince counting coins in his head. Someone would have the right to exercise those concessions. Whether she permitted the Sembians to take as much as they wanted or at the price they offered was something she could determine for herself later, but she had little use for a few miles of forest on her southern border.

Maalthiir stirred in his seat. "So you want my Red Plumes to help you defeat Miritar's army," he said. "In exchange, you are offering me the northern Dales, and High Master Borstag the southern. I am afraid it is not so simple, though. You have omitted three important factors from your calculations: Cormyr, Zhentil Keep, and the Sage of Shadowdale."

"Cormyr is in no condition to contest aggressive moves in the Dalelands," Borstag pointed out. "Between the death of Azoun, the goblin incursions, and the Shades in Anauroch, Cormyr is as weak as it has been in a hundred years. Lady Sarya has chosen an auspicious time to reclaim Myth Drannor."

"And I can aid you against Zhentil Keep and the Chosen of Mystra," Sarya said. "I may lack in sheer numbers, but through my control over Myth Drannor I wield great magical power. I can dispatch hundreds of sorcerous warriors against my foes, striking anywhere within hundreds of miles, with dozens of powerful demons or devils to lead the attack."

"If that is the case, I find myself wondering why you need me at all," Maalthiir observed.

Sarya leaned back in her chair and studied the first lord. "I am not entirely certain that I do," she said with a deceptively pleasant tone. "I believe that I could hoard my strength inside Myth Drannor and defy Seiveril Miritar forever. But I am not willing to take the chance that the powerful human lands surrounding Cormanthor might join forces with Miritar. That is why I have chosen to come to you, Lord Maalthiir, and through you your friends in Sembia. It is worth my while to make sure that you, at least, understand what you stand to lose from an elven Return to Cormanthyr. If you were to help Miritar overthrow me, I would simply melt away again, and you would be left with that army of elves to deal with. How many more centuries do you wish to spend under the shadow of elven power?"

Borstag glanced at Maalthiir, who simply studied Sarya in silence, a deep scowl etched on his face.

Then the Sembian looked back to Sarya and asked, "So how do you propose to go about removing Miritar's army from Cormanthor?"

"As you might expect, I have given that some thought." Sarya straightened in her seat, and focused her emerald gaze on Maalthiir of Hillsfar. The first lord brooded, leaning against the arm of his chair, one hand under his jaw. "The key, I think," Sarya began, "is the land of Mistledale."

❖ ❖ ❖ ❖ ❖

From the shores of Lake Sember, the Crusade marched north for three days on long-disused elfroads that few other armies could have found, let alone followed, through the heart of southern Cormanthor. The weather, which had been fine for the days of the portal transit, turned cold and wet, with sullen gray skies and a strong, gusty wind out of the north that seemed to carry the chill of the Moonsea down into Cormanthor's green, mossy heart.

Seiveril's army had come to include a small company of rangers and archers from Deepingdale, many of them moon elves or half-elves descended from those who had chosen not to Retreat from Cormanthor when the last leaders of the Elven Court had finally decided to abandon the great woodland thirty years ago. The Deepingdale elves knew Cormanthor intimately, the secret paths and lore of rock, water, and leaf, and they helped Jerreda's wood elf scouts guide the army northward toward the Standing Stone and Myth Drannor beyond that. Lord Ilmeth of Battledale had no strength to spare for such work, and little inclination to do so in any event. The lord of Essembra had fewer than a hundred men under arms in his whole demesne. Lord Mourngrym Amcathra of Shadowdale had more strength than that, but his land was much closer to Myth Drannor, and Storm Silverhand informed Seiveril that Mourngrym would not bring any soldiers to join the army of Evermeet until Evermeet's soldiers were in sight of Myth Drannor.

Seiveril sent a company of bladesingers and battle-mages ahead of his marching host to help the folk of Mistledale fend off the marauding demons and devils that harried their small land, and another company ahead to Shadowdale for the same purpose. He did not like to part with any of the Crusade's magical strength, especially when there was always the chance that hundreds of Sarya's fey'ri warriors might appear in the skies overhead at any moment, but the daemonfey lurked out of sight and out of reach, letting their conjured hellspawn do their work for them.

"I don't understand the point of harassing the Dalesfolk," Seiveril remarked to Starbrow on the morning of the third day. The sun elf lord and the moon elf champion stood on the banks of the Ashaba, which was running deep and swift after several days of rain, and watched the lead companies of Seiveril's host crossing the river on three bridges of glimmering magic, conjured by Jorildyn and the elf wizards under his command. "Shadowdale and Mistledale could lend us a couple of hundred trained fighters at best. Sending devils to harry them takes almost nothing away from our strength, and makes my quarrel with Sarya Dlardrageth their quarrel too."

"The demons and devils who have been prowling about in the forests around Mistledale and Shadowdale might not be a part of Sarya's army," Starbrow replied. "Lord Theremen of Deepingdale says that monsters of the infernal realms have haunted the ruins of Myth Drannor for centuries now.

Sarya's seizure of the city's mythal might have damaged the wards that held them trapped in the city, which would mean that this might be an unintended consequence of Sarya's actions, not a deliberate act on her part."

"Or . . . she might be doing nothing more than testing the strength of the humans who might ally with us," Seiveril said, thinking out loud. "If Sarya doesn't know these lands well, she might be worried about whether the folk of the Dales can give us as much help as Silverymoon's knights did in the High Forest."

Starbrow glanced up at the clouded sky above the river, then sighed and looked back to the elflord. "If you're right, it's a bad sign," he said. "It suggests to me that Sarya doesn't think she needs to hoard her demons for battle against our army. Either she's got an inexhaustible supply of the monsters, or she doesn't think we're going to be able to do anything about her stronghold in Myth Drannor. I don't know about you, but I certainly wonder why she'd think that."

The vanguard made camp for the night in the shadow of Galath's Roost, an old abandoned keep that stood little more than a mile from the Moonsea Ride. The rocky heights on which the old keep had been built offered a commanding view of the northern end of Mistledale and the great green sea of trees that rolled north, east, and south from the end of the open dale. Starbrow had the Crusade's companies set out a double guard, fearing a sudden attack of marauding fey'ri or yugoloths, but no enemies showed themselves.

Seiveril greeted star rise with the customary devotions to Corellon Larethian and the Seldarine, celebrating the rites he had observed for so many years as a high priest of the elven faith. He spent an hour praying for guidance, trying to catch a glimpse of what waited if he continued on his way north. Myth Drannor was only three days' march away, and he would soon test the strength of his host against Sarya's demonic power. But Sarya's mythal wards obscured his efforts to scry her fortress, and he had to content himself with minor auguries that promised little besides danger and uncertainty.

As he descended from the hilltop, still grappling with the incomplete visions he had seen, Seiveril found Thilesil waiting near his pavilion.

"Lord Seiveril," the cleric said with a small bow. "An emissary from the human city of Hillsfar is waiting for you."

"Hillsfar?" Seiveril said. He knew of the city, having walked in Cormanthor many years before, but from what he had heard, the city of Hillsfar wanted nothing to do with elves since the final Retreat from Cormanthor. "Very well, show him into my pavilion."

Seiveril stepped into his personal quarters, doffed his ceremonial mantle, and washed his hands in a basin of water. Then he emerged into the pavilion's sitting area, which doubled as his reception room. He did not have long to wait. Two of the guards standing watch by his door—both seasoned veterans of Vesilde Gaerth's Knights of the Golden Star—showed the human ambassador into his room, and unobtrusively took up their posts just inside the door.

The human was a surprisingly short man, so stocky and thick-shouldered that Seiveril found himself wondering whether the fellow had any dwarf blood in him. His head was shaven, but he wore a long, pointed goatee under his wide mouth, and his eyes were sunk deep beneath beetling brows. The Hillsfarian wore the elegant dress one might expect of a courtier in a lordly palace, a well-tailored garment of scarlet that did not conceal the supple links of golden mail he wore beneath his shirt.

"Welcome, sir," Seiveril said. "I am Seiveril Miritar, lately lord of Elion and high priest of Corellon's Grove. I speak for the host of Evermeet."

The human offered an obsequious grin that struck Seiveril as more than a little false. "And I am Hardil Gearas, High Warden of Hillsfar. I speak for my master, the First Lord Maalthiir."

Seiveril deliberately set aside his dislike of the high warden's facetious manner, and gravely offered his hand in the human fashion.

"Would you care for any refreshment, High Warden? Wine, or something to eat?"

"Not necessary, Lord Seiveril. I am anxious to get to business."

The elflord nodded. "As you wish, then, High Warden. What can I do for the First Lord of Hillsfar?"

The human crossed his powerful arms and looked up at Seiveril. "The first lord would dearly love to know what you intend to do with this army, Lord Seiveril. It does not escape Lord Maalthiir's notice that you are drawing closer to Hillsfar with every march."

Human diplomacy may take different forms than I am used to, Seiveril reminded himself. I must be patient, even in the face of discourtesy. "Lord Maalthiir need not worry, High Warden. I am bringing my army to Myth Drannor in order to finally root out the evil that has taken hold there. I do not expect to come within thirty miles of Hillsfar."

"Some things are better left alone," Hardil Gearas answered. "Your people haven't seen fit to do anything about Myth Drannor for six full centuries, but now you seem to have stirred up much evil in a land you abandoned thirty years ago. Evermeet might be far enough from Myth Drannor to ignore the depredations of the city's fiends, Lord Seiveril, but Hillsfar is not."

"You have the course of events confused, High Warden. We are here to deal with the evil that has stirred in Myth Drannor. We did not cause it to stir with our approach."

The human snorted. "So you say now, anyway."

Seiveril studied the human emissary. If this is the way humans conduct their diplomacy, the elflord thought, it is no wonder that they get into so many wars. "Did Maalthiir of Hillsfar have anything else to say to me?" he asked.

"In fact, he did," Hardil Gearas replied. "The first lord instructed me to advise you of three important facts. First, in conjunction with our allies in Sembia, we are moving strong forces into place to safeguard the upper stretch of the Moonsea Ride and Rauthauvyr's Road. We are concerned that your reckless marching about and warmongering may jeopardize our crucial, legitimate commercial interests in this vital route, and the various minor settlements and communities that lie along the way.

"Second, Hillsfar and Sembia recognize no other power as sovereign over the forest of Cormanthor. Your people gave up any claim to ownership over the woodlands when you left some three decades ago. Hillsfar now claims all lands within fifty miles of the city's walls. We will clear, settle, log, or otherwise use these lands as we see fit. We will regard the presence of any foreign soldiers within this area as nothing less than an invasion of Hillsfar itself.

"Finally, the first lord offers this for your consideration: In Myth Drannor's day, the elven realm of Cormanthyr was surrounded by human states too small and weak to do anything other than what the coronal told them to do. That is no longer true. Humans have grown strong in the centuries since Myth Drannor's fall, Lord Seiveril. We were not party to the Dales Compact, and we see no reason to abide by an agreement made centuries ago by people who had no right or authority to speak for us." Hardil Gearas bared his teeth in a cold, reptilian smile. "It is in the nature of humankind to grow, to expand, to become more numerous and more powerful with the passing of a few short years. You might as well shout at the incoming tide as try to check our natural increase. We need room to grow, Lord Seiveril, and we will have it."

Seiveril folded his arms in front of his chest, and consciously made himself wait a full minute before he responded, in order to keep his anger in check.

"I wish no quarrel with Hillsfar or Sembia, High Warden, and I should hope they wish no quarrel with me. But your First Lord Maalthiir must understand that I will not countenance the occupation of Dales who have no interest in being ruled from Ordulin or Hillsfar, and I will not surrender a claim to the Elven Court. If Hillsfar needs room to grow, I hope that we could reach some agreement over the responsible use of the woodlands in question. As for your master's third point . . . well, it may be human nature to expand, but you should not assume that it is in an elf's nature to Retreat. With the host of Evermeet in this forest, there is a greater strength of elf warriors in Cormanthor today than there has been at any time since the Weeping War."

"Elven armies stronger than your own failed to stop the Army of Darkness in the Year of Doom, Lord Seiveril," the High Warden said, not even bothering to conceal a smirk.

The elflord watched the sneering Hillsfarian. What was his purpose in coming here? he wondered. Is he trying to provoke me with these threats and demands? Or is this simply a façade, a ploy of bravado to mask true fear?

"I mean to save my arrows for the daemonfey," Seiveril told the first lord's emissary. "Whether you know it or not, they are your enemies as well as mine. For all our sakes, do not interfere with my work in Myth Drannor."

"For your own sake, think long and carefully before you attempt any work at all in Myth Drannor," Gearas growled. "You will not be warned again."

The stocky human inclined his head a bare inch and glowered at Seiveril before turning on his heel and stomping out of Seiveril's presence, waving aside the door guards with a curt gesture.

Seiveril stared after the Hillsfarian lord.

"Corellon, grant me patience," he whispered into the night.

CHAPTER ELEVEN

12 Kythorn, the Year of Lightning Storms

Windsinger dropped anchor in the round bay of Velprintalar, surrounded by the steep green hillsides and graceful, airy buildings of the city. Araevin could see the elven influences in the city's flower-covered verandas, tree-shaded boulevards, and elegant palaces high above the bay. High up on the slopes above the city's center stood the palace of the Simbul, the ruler of Aglarond, a rambling structure of beautiful green stone that gleamed like emerald in the sunshine.

"Is this truly a human city?" Ilsevele wondered aloud. She stood beside him at the ship's rail. Smiling, her eyes were warm when she looked at him, but there was a distance hiding in her thoughts, a searching quality to her gaze that he could not miss. "I didn't know humans could be so . . . elven . . . in their work."

"Aglarond is the union of two lands under one crown," Araevin answered, glad of an opportunity to speak without addressing the anxiety he knew was growing in his own heart. "Centuries ago the young human kingdom of Velprin settled the northern coasts of the Aglarondan peninsula, while a race of forest-dwelling humans, half-elves, and wood elves held the woodlands of the interior. Velprin tried to bring the whole of the peninsula under its rule, but the forest folk defeated Velprin's ambitious rulers. The lords of the forest folk governed both the forests and the coastlands from that day forward."

"My homeland has a similar history, but a more tragic outcome," Donnor Kerth said. Araevin glanced at him in surprise. Their new companion had proved more than a little taciturn, a fellow who rarely used two words when one would do. "In Tethyr elves and humans fought for centuries. Elves still roam the deeps of the Wealdath, or so I am told, but they have nothing to do with the human lands beyond their forests, and humans do not venture very far into their woods." He dropped his gaze from Araevin and Ilsevele. "I am sorry to say that I have known very few elves. And I believed things that were said about your kind that I have since learned are not true."

Ilsevele reached out and set her slender hand atop the Lathanderian's. "I have spent most of my years on Evermeet, Donnor, and I have known very few humans. I, too, am learning that not all that I have heard is true."

Maresa laced up her crimson-dyed leather armor, and adjusted her sword belt. "I thought you said you hadn't been here before, Araevin," she said. "You seem to know a lot about this place for a stranger."

"I haven't. But I've had a long time to pick up odds and ends about a lot of places I haven't been." Araevin picked up his pack, and quickly checked to make sure he had everything he needed. "Come, let's go ashore."

The four travelers thanked Master Ilthor for their passage and paid him handsomely. Then they were rowed ashore in *Windsinger*'s longboat. They landed along the city's stone quay, and climbed up the seawall's steps to the harborside streets. For all Velprintalar's elven grace, the dock district seemed human enough, filled with carts and longshoremen, and dozens of workshops, warehouses, and merchant's offices, all crowded together in buildings faced with white stone.

"Well, where now?" asked Maresa.

"We'll find a place to stay then we'll ask after sages, colleges, wizards' guilds, and such things," Araevin said. "Someone will have an idea of who I can ask about star elves and ancient Yuireshanyaar."

They found a comfortable but expensive inn within an hour of landing, a fine establishment called the Greenhaven, high up on one of the hillsides overlooking the harbor. Araevin asked the proprietor about sages or libraries he could visit, and the inn's proprietor directed him to several locales where he might confer with learned folk.

With his companions in tow, Araevin spent much of the next two days visiting Velprintalar's houses of learning. He visited the temple of Oghma and spoke with the high loremasters there. He conferred with a local wizard held in high regard by the Oghmanytes. And he also found a small chapel dedicated to the Seldarine, where he and Ilsevele were able to speak at length with the presiding priest. Several times Araevin confirmed that the ancient realm of Yuireshanyaar had indeed stood within the Yuirwood, and that some at least of its ruins might still be found there, but no one knew anything about star elves or a mage named Morthil who had lived long ago in that realm.

At the end of their second day, Araevin returned to the Greenhaven, resigning himself to a long and arduous effort to unearth the knowledge he sought. He suspected that some at least of his inquiries had simply been evaded, and he was wondering how he could proceed if that turned out to be the case. But as he and his companions ate a light supper on the Greenhaven's veranda, drinking watered wine and watching the shadows lengthen over the city, a dark-haired, deeply tanned half-elf dressed in an elegantly embroidered doublet appeared at their table, flanked by a pair of human guardsmen who wore the green-and-white tabards of the Simbul's Guard over coats of mail.

"Araevin Teshurr and company?" he asked pleasantly.

Araevin sensed his companions exchanging puzzled looks behind him, but he stood slowly and nodded to the fellow.

"I am Araevin Teshurr," he said. "To whom am I speaking?"

"I am Jorin Kell Harthan. I serve the Simbul." Harthan's manner remained easy, but Araevin did not miss the keen alertness in his eyes, nor the businesslike demeanor of the two guards who accompanied him. A long sword was sheathed at the half-elf's hip, and a long dagger was tucked into his left boot. "You have been inquiring after things that few people ask about, Master Teshurr. We would like to know more about the nature of your interests. Would you kindly accompany me to the Simbul's palace?"

"Careful, Araevin," Maresa whispered under her breath. "I don't like the looks of this."

"I assure you, I mean no harm to Aglarond or anyone in it," Araevin told the half-elf.

"If we did not believe that to be true, Master Teshurr, our invitation would leave you little opportunity to decline," Jorin Kell Harthan said. He bowed and gestured toward the door. "You may find answers in the palace that you will not be given outside it. If you please?"

Araevin could see the alarm in Maresa's face. From what he knew of her, she had reason to be suspicious of city guards and officials of the court. Ilsevele, on the other hand, was herself an officer of the Queen's Guard in Leuthilspar.

She glanced up at the half-elf and asked, "May we accompany Araevin?"

The Simbul's servant considered for a moment then said, "Very well."

They rose and followed Harthan to an open carriage waiting outside the inn. Araevin had half-feared a sealed coach that would double as a cell in a pinch. They climbed in—the half-elf sat opposite Araevin, with Donnor beside him, while the guards stepped up onto the running boards—and clattered off through the winding, dusk-dim streets. In a few minutes they rolled into a small courtyard below one of the palace's green stone towers, and followed the half-elf past more guardsmen into the tower.

The palace of Aglarond's queen was not so large or ethereally beautiful as Amlaruil's in Leuthilspar, but it was easily the grandest and most elegant building Araevin had ever set foot in outside of Evermeet itself. Despite his two and a half centuries and familiarity with the uses and exercises of power, he could not entirely quell the uneasy awe that settled over him. Maresa was positively petrified, marching stiffly as if she expected to be arrested on the spot, while Donnor Kerth lapsed into a silence so deep and sullen that Araevin feared he might try to fight his way out of the place given the least provocation to do so. Ilsevele, though. . . . She strode along confidently, her chin high, her eyes straight ahead, refusing to be intimidated by the setting. She was the daughter of a lord of Evermeet, after all, and she had been born to palaces.

Jorin Kell Harthan led them to a comfortable hall with a great fireplace and a large banquet table. He spoke a quiet word to the guards walking with them, and the two warriors withdrew to flank the door.

"There's wine on the table," the half-elf said. "Help yourselves, if you like."

"Well, if we are being arrested, it's starting well enough," Maresa muttered. She went over and poured herself a goblet.

"Are we under arrest?" Donnor Kerth asked the half-elf.

"Most likely you are not, Dawnmaster. We will see soon." Harthan leaned against a credenza, and spoke no more.

They all waited anxiously for a short time, but just as Araevin was about to question the Aglarondan again, the door at the far end of the hall opened, and a regal woman swept into the room. She was tall and dark-haired, with striking green eyes as bright and keen as a serpent's. She wore a gown of deep green, and Araevin noticed at once that she was quite skilled in the Art, girded with subtle spells and enchantments he would be hard-pressed to match.

"Greetings," she said in a cool voice. "I am Phaeldara, apprentice to the Simbul. I am currently serving as regent in her stead. Now, do not be alarmed, but I am going to cast a spell. Be still."

With no more warning, the enchantress skillfully cast a powerful divination that Araevin recognized, a spell that would give her the ability to reveal false things and unearth magical deceptions. Phaeldara studied Araevin and each of his companions for a long moment, taking their measure, and she allowed the spell to fade away.

"Forgive me for that. We have learned that we must be careful of strangers. The zulkirs of Thay have tried to slip assassins in magical guise into the palace before."

"What is this all about, Lady Phaeldara?" Araevin asked. "If we have given offense to you or your people in the last two days, we sincerely apologize."

"It has come to my attention that you have been making inquiries throughout the city about Yuireshanyaar and star elves. I would like to know why you are interested in such things."

Araevin studied the Simbul's apprentice for a moment, considering his answer. He could see no reason not to be reasonably forthright with the Aglarondans. They did not need to know about the *selukiira* embedded over his heart, but it certainly would not hurt for more people to know of the threat posed by Sarya Dlardrageth and her fey'ri legion.

"An old enemy of the People returned to Faerûn this year, Lady Phaeldara," he began. "They are known as House Dlardrageth—or the daemonfey, a family of sun elves tainted by demonic blood. Long ago they were driven out of Cormanthyr, in the early days of that realm. Later they and their followers caused the Seven Citadels' War between Siluvanede, Sharrven, and Eaerlann. They were imprisoned for thousands of years by high magic, but they have escaped. The daemonfey raided Evermeet itself, and launched a war against the High Forest and Evereska."

"We heard of war in the High Forest," Lady Phaeldara said. "But what does this have to do with Aglarond, Master Teshurr?"

"Ilsevele's father—Lord Seiveril Miritar of Elion—gathered a host in Evermeet to battle the daemonfey. His army drove the daemonfey out of Myth Glaurach, but they fled to Myth Drannor and began to fortify the ruins of that city as their new stronghold. More importantly, Sarya Dlardrageth, the queen of the daemonfey, has learned how to manipulate the wards and powers of mythals, so she has surrounded Myth Drannor in magical defenses of great power. Lord Miritar's army followed the daemonfey to Cormanthyr, but I fear that they will be unable to defeat Sarya unless we find a way to contest her control of Myth Drannor's mythal."

"And you think that this can be found in Aglarond?"

"I *hope* that what I seek exists in Aglarond," said Araevin. "We have come to believe that the key to unlocking the high magic secrets Sarya Dlardrageth now wields might lie somewhere in your realm. Specifically, we know that a great mage of early Cormanthyr carried away many Dlardrageth spellbooks when the coronal and the court mages first drove the Dlardrageths out of that realm. That mage was a star elf named Morthil. We are attempting to trace his footsteps."

Phaeldara said nothing, but her eyes flicked to Jorin Kell Harthan.

The half-elf straightened and said, "So you came to Aglarond in search of star elves?"

"We were unfamiliar with that kindred of the People, but in researching the question, we learned that their realm was known as Yuireshanyaar, and that it stood in the Yuirwood long ago."

"How long ago did this Morthil leave Cormanthyr?" Phaeldara asked.

"Five thousand years, give or take," Araevin said.

"Five thousand years?" Jorin Kell Harthan said, his voice incredulous. "You can't seriously expect that any spellbooks have survived that long!"

"It is an immense span of time, I know. But time means less to elves than it does to humans. I do not hope to find the original spellbooks, but I hope to find more durable records such as *telkiira* stones, or mages who have studied a tradition that is founded on this missing lore without even knowing where it once came from, or possibly even books that were copied from copies made from the original tomes." Araevin spread his hands helplessly. "I admit that I have little prospect for success, but there is no telling what horrors Sarya Dlardrageth will inflict on the lands around Myth Drannor if we do not find a way to stop her."

Ilsevele addressed the Simbul's apprentice. "Do the star elves still exist? Can they be found in Aglarond?"

Phaeldara turned away without answering. She paced over to a row of elegantly arched windows, gazing out over the glimmering lamps and lanterns that were coming to life all over the city below, sparkling like a sea of fireflies.

"I wish the Simbul were here," she remarked. "She would be a better judge of this than I. But she has left the realm in my hands for better than a month now, and I do not know when she will return. I suppose I must decide as best I can."

She looked back to Araevin and his companions. "It seems that your need is pressing, so I will share a secret that few know, and trust that two of the *ar Tel-Quessir* and anyone they trust enough to call friend know the value of keeping secrets. Yes, the star elves exist, but they are not exactly in Aglarond."

"Great," Maresa sighed. "I suppose we'll have to sail off to Kara-Tur or Selûne itself to find them, right?"

"You won't find them in any other land, either," Jorin Kell Harthan said.

Donnor Kerth frowned. "Are they ghosts, then?"

"Nothing like that, Dawnmaster," Phaeldara said. "Their kingdom lies entirely within the Yuirwood, but it is not of this world. You could crisscross the peninsula a hundred times, but you would never set foot in it. Only a few of us outside its borders have been entrusted with Sildëyuir's secret." The Simbul's apprentice looked over to Jorin Kell Harthan, who still lounged by the door. "But Master Harthan knows the way. He can take you there."

The half-elf frowned. "The paths to Sildëyuir have grown wild and strange in recent years, Lady Phaeldara. And the star elves might not welcome the Dawnmaster and the genasi."

"We will answer for them, if need be," Ilsevele said. "Maresa has walked in Evermeet and Evereska, and Donnor Kerth has sworn by Lathander to accompany us wherever our quest takes us. They will not betray your trust."

Phaeldara nodded. "I believe you, Ilsevele Miritar."

Jorin shrugged and stepped forward to clasp Araevin's hand. "I'll meet you at the Greenhaven an hour after sunrise. Be ready for a couple of days of walking."

☙ ☙ ☙ ☙ ☙

The city of Yûlash had been a ruin for decades. It sprawled atop a great, shield-shaped plateau overlooking the fertile lower vale of the Tesh, with the Moonsea a dark shadow in the eastern distance. From its battered walls a sentry could see the black towers of Zhentil Keep a little more than twenty miles to the north and the white-tipped peaks of the Dragonspires a hundred miles past that on a clear day.

The mountaintops floated like a distant phalanx of blunt spears in the sky, but Scyllua Darkhope ignored the view. She stood, sword in hand, beside her lord and master Fzoul, vigilantly watching the ruins around them. The two Zhents stood amid the foundations of a ruined tower that had once been the home of Yûlash's greatest wizard. That mage was long dead, assassinated in the early years of the fierce civil war that had eventually consumed the city, and his tower had the distinction of being the largest and most prominent structure located between the Zhent-fortified districts remaining around Yûlash's old citadel and the Hillsfarian-held districts located in the vicinity of the city's great eastern gate, and the fortifications there.

Fzoul Chembryl, on the other hand, stood near a gap in the wall, gazing northward at the city he ruled, small and distant at the mouth of the Tesh. Half a dozen of the Castellan's Guard, the most dedicated and skilled warriors of Zhentil Keep, stood watch around the clearing, and Scyllua knew that other unseen guardians hovered nearby, cloaked by magic.

"You may put up your sword, Scyllua," the Chosen of Bane said amiably. "This is a parley, after all, and we are supposed to show some small sign to indicate that we won't fall on our guest the minute he sets foot in the door."

"This place is dangerous," Scyllua replied. "I do not like to take chances with your life, my lord."

"It's neutral ground, Scyllua. It's the best we could do." Fzoul glanced at his zealous captain, and Scyllua submitted, sheathing her blade.

The air in the center of the broken tower rippled, and half a dozen figures materialized out of thin air: Maalthiir, First Lord of Hillsfar, his four black-clad swordsmen, and the stocky High Warden Hardil Gearas. Scyllua kept her hand on her sword hilt, but took care to remain still, unwilling to provoke a fight without her lord's express permission.

Maalthiir gazed around the ruined tower, and snorted. "Trying to impress me, Fzoul?" he asked.

"Not at all," the Lord of the Zhentarim answered. He turned away from broken walls and the view to the north, arms folded confidently across his black breastplate. He studied the first lord, his expression mild enough, even though his eyes glittered with the avid hunger that Scyllua knew burned within him. "Since I judged that you would be unwilling to come to Zhentil Keep, and I found myself unwilling to call on you in Hillsfar, I deemed Avandalythir's Tower a good middle ground."

"Indeed," the first lord said. "It does not escape my attention that your army still occupies half of Yûlash to deny Hillsfar control of this place."

"I might say the same thing about your Red Plumes, Maalthiir. And I'll add that Yûlash lies much closer to my city than it does to yours." Fzoul held up his hand to forestall Maalthiir's retort, and continued, "Let us agree to disagree about Yûlash for the moment. I did not ask you here to discuss this dilapidated ruin, First Lord. I wished to speak to you about Cormanthor and the Dalelands."

"I am a busy man, Fzoul, so make your point quickly."

Fzoul smiled humorlessly. "You *are* busy these days, Maalthiir. I have learned that a strong force of your Red Plumes is even now marching down the Moonsea Ride toward Mistledale and Battledale. And your Sembian friends are moving whole armies of mercenaries up Rauthauvyr's Road through Tasseldale and Featherdale. I take it you have decided to seize those lands before the elven army in Cormanthor contests your actions?"

Maalthiir scowled. "I am simply taking steps to defend our commercial interests in these lands, Fzoul. I can't have the elves throw humans out of the forest for another thirteen hundred years."

"I certainly wonder what possible interests you might have in Mistledale or Battledale," said Fzoul, "but I suppose your exact motives are not as important to me as the facts of your military movements."

"The last time I looked, there weren't any Zhentish outposts in those lands," the first lord said. "I do not have to justify myself to you, Fzoul!"

"If you intend to build yourself an empire in the Dalelands, you certainly do," Fzoul said. "Why should I stand aside and let you seize for yourself a prize that I have long desired?"

"Do you think you can take those lands from me?" Maalthiir demanded.

"Whether I can or I can't, I am fairly certain that I can make sure you don't get them, Maalthiir. If I can't have them, you and your friends in Sembia can't either."

The lord of Hillsfar gave Fzoul a look so black that Scyllua took half a step forward, prepared to draw her blade in Fzoul's defense. But Maalthiir controlled his anger with a visible effort.

200 • Richard Baker

"The Dales are incidental to my first purpose, Fzoul. I intend to drive the elven army out of Cormanthor. Neither you nor I will benefit from the return of elven power to the forest."

The lord of Zhentil Keep nodded. "On that point I do not disagree. Do you really believe you have the strength to beat an elven army in Cormanthor?"

"I have acquired some useful allies lately." Maalthiir shrugged. "They have a long and bitter quarrel with the elves."

Fzoul measured the first lord, and he grinned fiercely. "Why, you have struck a deal with those fiendish sorcerers who have appeared in Myth Drannor! That is why you think you can risk a battle against the elves."

"And you, if need be," Maalthiir said.

"Do not threaten the Chosen of Bane!" Scyllua snapped, stepping close to Maalthiir.

The pale, silent swordsmen who stood beside the first lord fixed their cold gazes on her, hands dropping to sword hilts as one.

"Enough, Scyllua," Fzoul said. "I must consider this."

"As I said, Fzoul, I do not need your approval to act in Hillsfar's best interests." Maalthiir sketched a small bow, and without any other cue or command, his swordsmen gathered close around him. "I agreed to a parley because you have never troubled me with such a request before. Do not expect me to come at your beck and call in the future."

"A moment, Maalthiir," the high priest of Bane said. Fzoul raised a hand, palm outward. "If Hillsfar and Sembia insist on fighting Evermeet's army to seize Cormanthor and the Dales, then I will have no choice but to make sure you fail. If I must choose Hillsfar or an elf coronal to be master of the Dales, I will choose the elves."

The first lord glared at Fzoul. "Then I suppose it is a good thing that I have not put the choice in your hands," he grated. "If that is all . . . ?"

Fzoul swept an arm at the ruins around them and said, "Consider these ruins, Maalthiir. Is the lesson of this place lost on you? Two factions vying for rule over this city accomplished nothing but their own destruction, and neither side won."

"Make your point swiftly, if you have one!"

"I will not let you have Cormanthor and the Dales to yourself. But I am willing to collaborate with you and your newfound friends in return for a share of the prize." Fzoul stepped forward, and allowed ambition to creep into his voice. "For thirty years we've been waiting to carve up the Dales, but no one has made a move because of the threat posed by the other powers. Now Cormyr's attention has been drawn westward by the Shadovar of Anauroch, and you have reached an understanding with Sembia. The two of us are now in the position to apportion these lands as we see fit, are we not?"

"Perhaps," the first lord admitted. "Your proposal?"

"You take the eastern Dales, I'll take the western, and Sembia can have the southern Dales. The great human powers of this land acting in concert present a threat that the elf army cannot hope to overcome. None of us gets all of what we want, because the others would not stand for it. But we could all wind up with significant gains, and more importantly we'd send the elves back to Evermeet empty-handed."

Maalthiir hesitated, studying Fzoul. "Even if events fall out as you suggest, I think we will have a difficult time in sharing the Dales."

"That is a problem for some other day." The Chosen of Bane grinned again, his red mustache framing a predatory smile. "But that is a problem for the two of us to decide between us. We do not need any elven armies to complicate the question."

The first lord nodded slowly and said, "Very well. I must confer with my allies, Fzoul, but in principle I agree to what you suggest. If you wish to help in our campaign, you should plan on marching against Shadowdale and Daggerdale as soon as possible. Your armies on the western flank of the Dales will draw crucial strength away from the center, where the decisive blow must fall."

"Excellent. High Captain Darkhope and her army can march with a day's warning. I am eager to know more about your plan for the campaign, and what Zhentil Keep can do to help." Fzoul motioned to the guards who stood nearby, and two of the soldiers brought up a folding camp table and a couple of large chairs. "Now, why don't we see if we can agree on which Dales clearly fall in whose sphere of influence, and how we can bring them under civilized rule?"

֍ ֍ ֍ ֍ ֍

As promised, Jorin Kell Harthan met Araevin and his friends at the Greenhaven an hour after sunup. The half-elf had replaced his well-tailored tunic with leather armor studded with copper rivets and a long gray-green cloak he wore thrown over his shoulder. He had his long, dark hair tied back in a simple ponytail, and he carried a curved bow and a quiver-full of green-feathered arrows on his back. Jorin took one glance at Araevin and his friends, arrayed by the inn's courtyard, and nodded.

"I see you're no stranger to travel," he observed. "Good. The Yuirwood can be difficult."

The half-elf looked over to Donnor Kerth, and frowned. The Lathanderian wore his mail shirt over his thick arming-coat, keeping his heavier plate armor on a pack horse.

"Are you sure you want to wear all that iron?" Jorin asked. "You'll be swimming in sweat within an hour. Once we enter the forest, you won't have the sea breeze to cool you off."

The Lathanderian shrugged. "I grew up in Tethyr," he said. "I'm accustomed to wearing armor in warm weather."

"Suit yourself," Jorin said. "We may have to set free your pack horse before we cross to Sildëyuir, though. Do you want to leave the rest of your armor here?"

"If I have to, I'll wear it," Donnor said.

Araevin opened his own tunic another handspan, thankful that the mail shirt he wore was made of elf-wrought mithral, so light and fine that he hardly noticed its weight or its warmth. In bright sunlight it sometimes grew hot, but he did not expect much of that within the Yuirwood's bounds. Ilsevele's armor was somewhat heavier than his, since she wore a more complete suit, but it was also made of elven mail, and she was more accustomed to the weight of her armor than he was to his.

They followed the coastal road south and west out of Velprintalar, marching for an hour before they reached the River Vel. There they turned aside onto a dusty cart-track that followed the river south, toward its headwaters in the forest beyond. In a long, hard day of marching, they reached the small town of Halendos, hard under the eaves of the Yuirwood, and stayed the night in a comfortable roadside inn.

In the morning, they resumed their march, but Jorin soon led them away from the Vel, turning eastward on a narrow footpath that soon vanished into the warm green gloom of the Yuirwood. It was hot and still in the great forest, and Araevin was surprised to find that the undergrowth was exceedingly dense and difficult. It embarrassed him to admit it, but he would quickly have become lost without a track to follow or Jorin Kell Harthan as a guide.

For all its difficulty, the forest possessed a green and wild beauty. Colorful birds soared and chattered in the higher branches, and from time to time the trail wandered into sun-dappled clearings free of the thickets and underbrush, or stone-bounded forest pools of cool, inviting water. The old forests of the North that Araevin knew were distant, in some ways reserved, majestic but deeply asleep. The Yuirwood's slumber was not deep at all, and Araevin could feel its watchfulness, its wild wariness, lurking as close as the brambles that scratched their faces and the vines that seemed eager to trap their footsteps.

"This forest is restless," Ilsevele said as they rested beside a forest pool, eating their midday meal. "I do not think I have ever walked in a forest so wakeful."

"There are parts that are even more wild," Jorin said. "Many of my people live within the forest, but even those of us with elf blood avoid the truly wakeful places. And I think things have been growing worse over the last few years."

"Worse? How so?" asked Araevin.

"There have always been fierce beasts in the wood, things like barghests and gray renders, ettercaps and sword spiders, even a few bands of gnolls in the eastern parts, but the unnatural creatures have been growing more prevalent . . . and bloodthirsty." Jorin gazed off into the woods, frowning. "I would give much to know what dark power is stirring in these woods."

"Maybe the star elves know something," Maresa remarked.

Jorin shrugged. "I suppose it's possible," he said. "But they do not walk in the same forest that we do. It might be different for them."

"They don't walk in the same forest? What does that mean?" the genasi asked. "Are they here, or not?"

"They're here, all right. I can't easily explain it, but you'll see for yourself soon enough," Jorin said. He stood up, brushing off his hands, and looked up at the forest canopy overhead. "We should keep moving—I want to get a few more miles behind us before it gets dark. We're going to find ourselves in some of the more perilous parts of the forest before we reach Sildëyuir."

CHAPTER TWELVE

16 Kythorn, the Year of Lightning Storms

Company after company of Sembian soldiers marched over the Blackfeather Bridge, a disorderly river of steel-clad warriors, horses, and creaking wagons that stretched for miles over Rauthauvyr's Road. The day was warm and heavy, drowsy under the morning sun. The summer was still young, and though the days were long and bright, the air held only a dim promise of the stifling heat and great thunderstorms that would come to the southern Dales in a few tendays.

Sarya Dlardrageth stood by the shaded porch of a large stone inn on the bridge's northern end, with a small band of her fey'ri beside her: Teryani Ealoeth, one of her closer relations among the fey'ri Houses, and four more fey'ri who served Teryani as guards, spies, or messengers. Sarya wore her guise as the human Lady Senda, while the fey'ri had all likewise assumed human appearance. Borstag Duncastle certainly had half an idea of Sarya's true nature, but none of the other Sembians did. The daemonfey queen deemed it best to let them continue in ignorance.

Teryani Ealoeth watched the marching soldiers with studied disinterest. She was short and slender, with a dark-eyed, heart-shaped face of exceptional beauty. One of the first spies Sarya had sent out into the human lands surrounding Cormanthor, Teryani's task had been to insinuate herself into the councils of those Sembian lords who were most concerned with Cormanthor and the Dalelands. Unlike other fey'ri, who saw no reason to hide their heritage behind shapechanging tricks unless they had to, Teryani delighted in deceit as an end in and of itself. More than a few of the human soldiers passing by the inn yard leered at her or offered various lewd suggestions, which she simply ignored with a cold, scornful smile.

"Are these really worth the trouble, my lady?" Teryani asked Sarya. Her voice was girlish and sweet.

"They are," Sarya said. "Remember, Teryani, I could hardly care less whether the army of Evermeet scatters them in an hour of fighting. The important thing is to set Sembia against Evermeet. If Miritar's host butchers this army like bleating sheep, we will have our Sembian friends gather more swords and throw them at Miritar. Evermeet's soldiers are precious, but I have no shortage of Sembians, do I?" She paused, and added, "In fact, it might not be bad if these companies blundered into an utter disaster in Cormanthor. Sembia is too strong for my liking, and I'd like to see it bled dry in these little flyspeck lands they call the Dales."

"I will see what I can do," Teryani promised, and she returned her attention to the human soldiers marching past.

The Sembian army wasn't Sembian at all, really. Companies of Chondathan crossbowmen, Chessentan swordsmen, and Tethyrian cavalrymen in half-plate armor made up most of the army's fighting power. All had been hired by a league of Sembian noble Houses with interests in the Dales and the Moonsea trade routes, headed up by House Duncastle. In fact, some of the mercenaries had been in the employ of Duncastle for years, engaged in such tasks as the occupation of Scardale and the protection of House Duncastle's Moonsea caravans. Others had been quickly hired under the authorization of Sembia's Great Council of merchant lords, ostensibly for the purposes of restoring good order and protecting Sembian investments in the Dalelands.

Native-born Sembians themselves were not very common among Duncastle's soldiers, but then again, Sembia didn't really have an army. Instead, the largest and most powerful of the land's various noble merchant Houses each fielded their own private army, some numbering many hundreds in strength. Any Sembian city or town had a small civic guard and town watch, of course, and the Overmaster of Sembia—the elected leader of Sembia's Great Council—commanded the loyalty of the Ordulin Guard, a small but well-equipped army that defended the capital and served to check any unreasonable ambitions on the part of the more powerful noble Houses. But by and large, any Sembian lord was free to raise and provision an army, if he saw the need for one. The troops of House Duncastle were the largest Sembian contingent in the whole army, and they made up no more than five hundred of an army whose strength was more than ten times that number.

"Mercenaries," Sarya Dlardrageth murmured, not bothering to conceal her disdain.

She glanced over at the shade of a nearby oak, where Lord Duncastle stood beneath the broad branches, consulting with the chief captains of his army.

The merchant prince Borstag Duncastle finished with his captains, and sauntered over to watch the army pass by with her and Teryani. Sarya wrinkled her nose, unable to ignore the stink of his human blood so close to her, but with an iron effort of will she smoothed her face. Like it or not, humans were allies she needed to entice and persuade. In her war against the High Forest and Evereska she had been able to simply intimidate and browbeat the wild orcs and ogres of the Nether Mountains into marching at her command, but humans required more subtlety. Until she managed to bring them to blows with Miritar's army, she needed to consider her words and actions carefully. Long ago in ancient Siluvanede she had learned how to whisper a word in one ear, begin a rumor somewhere else, plot a skillful murder in another place, bringing one elven House after another into her growing web of influence. Her work among the human powers of Cormanthor was not very different, really . . . except in this case she regarded her tools as eminently disposable.

Duncastle glanced at her, let his gaze linger on Teryani's slender form for a moment, and looked back to Sarya.

"Good afternoon, Lady Senda," he said in his deep voice. "You will be pleased to know that I have come to value Lady Terian's counsel quite highly in the last few tendays, especially in martial matters. For such a delicate creature, she has a mind of steel."

Sarya forced a smile to her face. "She enjoys my full confidence, Lord Duncastle. And in turn I am pleased by Terian's reports of your army's progress. I did not expect you to assemble such a large force in so little time."

"As they say, my lady, he who hesitates is lost." He looked at Teryani again, and his eyes glittered. "While I am personally delighted by Lady Terian's company, I must say, I am concerned that an army marching into battle is no place for a young lady of such high breeding. Are you certain that you wish her to accompany our army on this campaign?"

"I am confident that you can look after me, Lord Duncastle," Terian said, inclining her head to the Sembian lord. "And I have my guards, as well. I will be safe, I think."

Sarya couldn't help but smile at Teryani's winsome manner. In truth the Ealoeth noblewoman was a deadly swordmaster, skilled in the arts of stealth, subterfuge, and poisoning. Even if Duncastle was half the swordsman he might once have been, she wouldn't have been surprised if Teryani Ealoeth could have carved him like a trussed

Farthest Reach • 209

pig in any kind of swordplay—or more likely, killed him in any of a dozen other ways that the human lord never would see coming.

She decided to change the subject before Teryani carried on her coquettish little act any further.

"You need to increase your pace, Lord Duncastle. Events are moving quickly in Battledale and Mistledale. I would not want you to miss out."

"Do not fear, Lady Senda," the Sembian lord said with a broad smile. "We've already got five full squadrons of cavalry in Essembra. We won't miss our date in Mistledale."

"The sooner your whole army reaches Essembra, the better," Sarya answered. "We have to halt Miritar's host and draw them into a fight in open ground. You are in a race, Lord Duncastle."

In Essembra, the Sembian force would threaten Miritar's right flank. If the elven army continued north from Mistledale's borders toward Myth Drannor, Duncastle's Sembians could move west on the Essembra-Ashabenford trail and cut Miritar off from his base in Semberholme, as well as any aid from his human allies in Mistledale and Deepingdale. In fact, Sembia's army would be ideally positioned to crush those allies if Miritar chose not to meet Duncastle's threat. Meanwhile, the Red Plume army from Hillsfar descending the Moonsea Ride could come in to block him from a move to the north. And Fzoul Chembryl's Zhentish army was sweeping far to the west, marching from Voonlar toward Shadowdale to seal the western side of the trap as Duncastle's Sembians sealed the eastern side.

Sarya had been absolutely enraged to find that the first lord of Hillsfar had presumed to allow yet another petty human tyrant to ally with him, but she had made herself wait one full day before attacking the First Lord's Tower with a hundred devils and fiends and a thousand fey'ri. After considering exactly how to raze Maalthiir's tower and execute the first lord of Hillsfar in an appropriately gruesome manner, a few hours for thought had helped her to see that Fzoul Chembryl's grandiose ambitions and Maalthiir's underhanded dealings played perfectly into her hands.

Maalthiir is too clever for his own good, she reflected. *Either he is foolish enough to think that dealing with another power proves that he is not beholden to me, or he thinks himself prudent in providing himself with an ally whom he might turn against me if we should have a falling out. The question, of course, is who will betray whom first?*

Sarya was an old and practiced hand at that particular game.

"Bane's brazen throne," Borstag Duncastle muttered, disturbing her from her ruminations. "What is *he* doing here?"

Sarya followed the direction of the Sembian lord's glance, and spotted a small party of well-appointed horsemen riding over the bridge alongside the columns of Duncastle soldiers. The man at the head of the company was a handsome lord with hair of close-cut black ringlets, attired in a fine doublet of dove-gray under which mail glinted. A score of armored riders followed him, all wearing surcoats or doublets that featured at least a splash of the same dove-gray.

"Who is this?" she asked, intrigued by Lord Duncastle's reaction.

"Miklos Selkirk and his accursed Silver Ravens," Duncastle growled. "He is the overmaster's son, and his chief agent and defender in any enterprise that catches his eye." He looked at Sarya, and scowled. "He'll be here to spy on our every move and carry tales back to his father, mark my words."

"Does this overmaster have the power to recall your soldiers, Duncastle?" Sarya asked with icy calm.

"He can certainly call my actions into question, and perhaps persuade the Great Council to issue such an order."

"Then I suggest you avoid giving this Selkirk offense." Sarya folded her arms and watched the riders in gray approach.

Miklos Selkirk and his company passed abreast of the inn. The overmaster's son caught sight of Borstag Duncastle and turned his horse aside. He dismounted with easy grace and handed his reins to one of his Silver Ravens.

"Ah, there you are, Duncastle!" he called. "I've been riding all up and down this column looking for you."

"Selkirk," Duncastle said. He made a shallow bow, never taking his eyes from the younger lord's face. "I was not expecting you, or else I would have left word that you were to be brought up to me."

"No matter. The ride gave me a good opportunity to size up your army." Miklos Selkirk turned to Sarya and Teryani, and he offered a deep flourish and bow. "I am afraid I have not had the pleasure, dear ladies. I am Miklos Selkirk, of the House Selkirk."

"Lady Senda Dereth," Sarya answered. "This is my lady-in-waiting, Terian."

Sarya offered her hand, and despite her deep-rooted loathing of humans and all their works, she had to admit that Miklos Selkirk was a handsome fellow, gifted with almost elven grace and self-possession. She looked into his eyes, and saw nothing but keen steel there.

Here is a worthy adversary, Sarya thought. She would have to amend Teryani's instructions, if Selkirk was going to be near the head of the Sembian army for any time at all.

"A pleasure to meet you, Lady Senda," the human said. A flicker of interest crossed his face—a moment's glance as Selkirk fixed her face in his mind, perhaps, and reminded himself to find out more about her later—then he looked back to Lord Duncastle.

"My father asked me to accompany you for a while, Lord Duncastle," he said. "As you know, the council has expended no small sum in adding to the forces at your command, and they want to make sure that their investment is in good hands." Selkirk glanced toward the south and shrugged, as if to imply that he thought it was all nonsense, but Sarya did not mistake the sharp calculation in his eyes. "The expedition is entirely in your hands, I assure you.

My only function is to ensure that accurate and timely reports reach Ordulin."

Duncastle's scowl deepened, but he held his temper in check. "Very well," he rumbled. "You are, of course, welcome to observe as long as you feel necessary, Selkirk."

"Good," said the younger noble. "I knew you would be reasonable about this, Duncastle. Now, if I may be so bold . . . might I ask you to explain your plan of march? I see thousands of Sembian soldiers invading the Dalelands, and I find that I am not at all sure I understand *why*."

Duncastle fumed, thunder gathering on his brow, but Sarya intervened. "The plan, Lord Selkirk, is to bring three armies against one, and demonstrate to Seiveril Miritar and the rest of Evermeet's army that the days of elves dictating terms to human kingdoms are over. Now, do you have the steel for the game, or not?"

Miklos Selkirk's easy manner froze on his face. He looked back to Sarya, and studied her more closely.

"You are playing with dangerous powers, Lady Senda," he said in a more serious voice. "I don't pretend to know what sort of old elven spells might still be sleeping in Cormanthor, or what the heroes who defend the Dalelands might do about a concerted threat such as that we're offering them now, and so I fear the remedying of my ignorance. But yes, I agree that the stakes are . . . enticing."

"I do not know what to tell you about any heroes defending these lands," Sarya said, "but I can tell you this, Miklos Selkirk: *I* wield Cormanthor's magic, and as long as Sembia's army is moving against my enemies, you need have no fear of old elven spells."

❖ ❖ ❖ ❖ ❖

Jorin Kell Harthan's prediction proved uncannily accurate. Araevin and his comrades passed a cold and rainy night in the ruins of an old elven tower buried deep in the forest, and when they pressed forward from the place in the morning, the drizzle followed them, soaking the party in a dripping fog that quickly became a bright, steaming bath when the sun burned through the clouds overhead. The normal sounds of the forest died away over the course of the first three miles of walking, replaced with the insistent dripping of water from countless branches and leaves. Soon it seemed they were passing through a world of emerald and silver-gray, a silent world that resented their presence.

They hiked on in single-file, following the Aglarondan along the narrow trail. Araevin fell into the rhythm of the walk, his thoughts drifting. How long will it take Sarya Dlardrageth to detect the approach of Evermeet's army? he wondered. And what will she do when she does? Sarya might attempt to sabotage the army's march by striking at the portal nexus in the frozen fortress. He frowned, wondering if he should have advised Seiveril and Starbrow to keep the windswept mountaintop guarded against a sudden demonic assault. Or was there some other way for Sarya to strike at the host of Evermeet? He paused in mid-stride, examining the thought.

"Araevin! Look out!" Ilsevele reached forward and jerked at his arm, dragging him back from his reflections. Something crashed through the dense underbrush not more than a dozen yards from where he stood, a hulking gray mass of hairless flesh that grunted and thrashed furiously through the thorn-studded vines, snapping arm-thick saplings in half as it charged toward the small company.

"*Aillesel Seldarie!* Where did that come from?" Araevin gasped.

He quickly backstepped, trying to keep out of the thing's reach while he considered the spells he held ready.

It went on two thick legs, with a hunched-over posture and a blunt snout that held row after row of sharp black teeth. A double row of small, yellow eyes dotted the front of its head, and its forelimbs were long, powerful arms that ended in strong crushing claws. The thing snuffled loudly, and roared in bestial rage.

No one offered an answer to his question, but beside him Ilsevele's hands blurred as she sent a pair of arrows winging at the monster. The arrows sank into the side of its thick neck, but there was nothing but muscle there—the creature swatted at the arrows like they were insect bites, and bellowed with such anger that the leaves shook overhead.

"It's a gray render!" Jorin called from up ahead. The monster had broken onto the trail between the Aglarondan and the rest of the small company. "Be careful, it can crush an ogre with those arms!"

The creature hesitated an instant, then turned its back on Jorin and thundered up the trail at Ilsevele and Araevin. The spellarcher fired several more times, trying for its eyes, but the front of the beast's head held a mass of bone so dense that her arrows simply glanced away. The creature reared up, drawing back one huge taloned hand to crush Ilsevele—and Araevin barked out the words of a simple teleport spell and caught hold of the back of her tunic, whisking them both twenty yards aside.

The render's claws stripped a foot-wide row of furrows four inches deep through the trunk of a cedar next to the spot Ilsevele had been standing, and the beast screeched in frustration. Ilsevele stumbled, unprepared for the spell, but she looked back at him, eyes wide.

"Good timing," she managed.

Jorin Kell Harthan sprinted down the trail behind the render, and skidded to a halt behind the monster, slashing at its hamstring with his long sword. The render howled again as its leg buckled beneath it, but it whirled with astonishing speed and batted the Aglarondan ranger into the underbrush with a single off-balance swing of one claw. Then Donnor Kerth, who had been behind Araevin and Ilsevele on the trail, charged the monster from the other side, mail jingling and armor rattling, his face hidden behind his heavy helm. He landed a heavy cut on the back of the monster's shoulder, grunting with the force of his swing. The gray render wheeled drunkenly back toward the Lathanderian, and clubbed him with its other arm. Kerth caught the blow on his sturdy shield, but the monster was so strong that it drove him to his knees, and began to rain down mighty blows like the pounding of some berserk smith's hammer.

"Donnor's in trouble!" Ilsevele snapped. She scrambled to her feet and drew her own long sword, gliding toward the fight with a rapid but balanced advance, ready to dart forward or give ground as she needed.

"I see it!"

Araevin snatched for the zalanthar-wood wand at his belt, and leveled the device at the monster, pausing only long enough to make sure none of his companions were in the way. The wand erupted in a hazy blue bolt of sonic disruption, blasting the render's flank with a terrible *crack!* that echoed in the dripping wood. Behind Kerth, Maresa pointed her own wand at the beast over the shoulder of the kneeling human warrior, and scorched the monster with a jet of flame that caught it full in the face.

The gray render hissed and reared back, raising its head and turning its face away from the searing flame—and Donnor uncoiled from beneath his shield and brought his heavy broadsword up under the render's jaw, sinking the point of the weapon deep into the base of its throat. The Lathanderian warrior surged to his feet and wrenched his blade free, ripping open a terrible wound across the render's throat.

The render's hissing rage drowned in a horrible gurgle of dark gore. It wheeled around and bolted back down the trail, away from Kerth and Maresa. Blood splattered the leaves and left a crimson trail in the creature's wake. Ilsevele quickly backed away, giving the render plenty of room to flee, while Jorin Kell Harthan, who had been circling back in to attack again from behind the monster, literally threw himself into a dense briar bush to avoid being trampled.

The creature went thrashing its way down the trail, burbling its misery, and vanished into the gloom of the forest.

Donnor Kerth climbed to his feet and watched the monster flee. He shucked his helmet, and looked down at his sword, clotted with the render's gore for a full two feet from its point. He stared in amazement, as the crashing and pained howls of the monster receded into the distance.

"It's still running," he muttered. "By the Morninglord, what does it take to kill one of those things?"

Jorin slowly picked himself up and began extricating himself from the briars. "Maybe a big dragon could manage it, but other than that, there isn't much in the forest that a gray render fears. It's best to avoid them."

Maresa blew out her breath, and sheathed her wand at her belt. "I'll keep that in mind. Are there a lot of them around here?"

"It seems there have been more of them about in the last year or two," Jorin replied. "I used to go two or three years at a time without hearing of anyone running into a render, but I've heard of seven attacks already this year—not counting this one."

"Is that what you meant when you said that parts of the forest were growing more wild?" Ilsevele asked.

"In part, yes." Jorin spotted his sword lying under the briars, and with a grimace he knelt and reached his arm through the thorns, groping for the blade. "Gray renders aren't natural beasts, really. They're dimly intelligent, and foul-tempered beyond belief. They'll tear down cabins and rip up trails on a whim, but then they can be devilishly patient when stalking prey."

The Aglarondan reached his blade and pulled it out of the briars, but not without a good armful of scrapes.

"Are there more gray renders in the forest than before, or are the ones that were always here just growing more aggressive?" asked Ilsevele.

"There are more of them, I'm sure of it. But I certainly wonder where they're coming from. Some infernal plot of Thay, I suppose." Jorin wiped his sword on the mossy trailside, and sheathed it. "I am sorry that I failed to spot that one before we wandered into its path. I won't let it happen again."

"Make sure you don't!" Maresa said. "I don't ever need to see a gray render any closer than that."

Donnor Kerth tended their injuries—mostly Jorin's and his own—with a few healing prayers, and they continued on their way. They pressed on through the afternoon, encountering no more gray renders, though on one occasion Jorin pointed out troll-sign on the trail, and led them on a long, circuitous detour by a streambed to skirt the trouble if they could. The detour evidently worked, for they saw no trolls and ran across nothing else dangerous.

They camped for the night in the high branches of a great shadowtop overlooking a swift, cool stream. Some of Jorin's folk had built a small, railless platform in the tree's middle branches, a good sixty feet above the forest floor, and a tug on a well-hidden lanyard brought down a rope ladder to reach the lower branches, from where other concealed ladders led up to the hiding place. Kerth's packhorse they had to leave on the ground, but Araevin wove a skillful illusion to hide the animal's makeshift corral and keep any forest predators from finding it.

The next morning dawned hot, still, and clear, the forest sweltering in the humidity left by the previous days' rain and mist. They descended from their aerial camp, found the packhorse unmolested, and set off again. But only a couple of hours into the march, the trail broke out into a large, grassy glade in the heart of the forest, a clearing the better part of a hundred yards wide. Bright sunlight flooded the open spot, and the air hummed with darting insects. In the center of the clearing stood an old ring of standing stones, each almost ten feet tall, arranged in a lopsided circle. Thick moss mantled the ancient stones, and Araevin sensed at once the presence of old and potent magic in the clearing.

"What is this place, Jorin?" he asked.

"The doorway to Sildëyuir," the half-elf answered. He led them between the leaning menhirs, into the center of the old ring, where a large square block stood like a great altar. "This is your last chance to turn aside, all of you. Once I take you through the door, there is no guarantee that you will be permitted to return. The folk of Sildëyuir are not cruel, but they do not tolerate intrusion, and they will not permit a stranger to carry their secrets back to the realms of humankind. Araevin and Ilsevele will likely have little trouble, since they are both *ar Tel'Quessir*. But this is a perilous journey for Donnor and Maresa."

Maresa gazed at the old stones leaning in the sun. Despite the warmth of the day, it was cool and quiet within the circle.

"I've walked in Evermeet," she said, her manner serious. "I think I want to see what's on the other side of this stone ring."

Donnor Kerth stood holding the reins of his packhorse. He glanced up at the bright sky, shading his dark face with a hand, and nodded once to the half-elf.

"Donnor, you don't have to follow us here," Araevin said in a low voice.

"If you go, I'll go," the human rasped. He glanced back at the dense wall of green behind them, then looked back to Araevin and flashed a startlingly bright smile. "Besides, it's a long, hot walk back from here."

Jorin indicated the square stone altar in the center of the circle and said, "All right, then. Everybody set a hand on the stone and keep it there. Donnor, hold your mount's reins in your other hand, there. Now be still a moment."

The half-elf hummed a strange tune under his breath, and Araevin felt the magic of the place waking, stirring, shaking off its sun-drowsed slumber as cool shadows began to grow within the ring.

He looked across the altar stone at Maresa, who stood with her eyes squeezed shut and her teeth bared.

She still doesn't trust magic of this sort, he thought with a smile. *You would think that she'd become accustomed to it sooner or later.*

Then strange silver shadows seemed to burst out of the great old stones, whirling and darting all around the company, and the sunny clearing in the Yuirwood whirled away into nothingness.

❦ ❦ ❦ ❦ ❦

Seiveril Miritar stood in the heart of a grove of mighty shadowtops at dusk, and prayed earnestly to the Seldarine for guidance, as he had every night at star rise since he had embarked on his great crusade against the foes of the People. He was distantly aware of the ring of vigilant guards who stood nearby, watching in case his enemies tried to strike at him while he walked alone in the forest. But the knights of the Golden Star respected his communion with Corellon Larethian and the Seldarine. They waited a short distance out of sight, giving Seiveril the silence and privacy to speak to his gods with his whole heart.

Here, in the heart of old Cormanthor, Seiveril felt the presence of Corellon Larethian almost as clearly as he did when he stood in Evermeet's sacred groves, but at the same time, doubt darkened his heart. His divinations whispered of disaster and warned him that a narrow way indeed threaded the perils that lay before him.

Three days now, and the same shadows of danger hover in my auguries, Seiveril thought. Our army stands motionless while our enemies move against us, and still Corellon warns me that to march on Myth Drannor now courts terrible danger. "I cannot remain in Galath's Roost while my enemies encircle me, Corellon, and yet you warn me against marching from this place," Seiveril said aloud, speaking up at the silver starlight that glimmered in the treetops far above. "I am afraid that I do not see what it is you want me to do."

A soft breeze sighed in the high branches, but no answer came to Seiveril. The gods of his people had bestowed many blessings upon the elf race, but they wished for the elves to find their own path through life. While Corellon and the rest of the Seldarine were unsparing in the divine magic they placed in the hands of priests such as Seiveril, they had the habit of keeping their silence even when great matters were at hand, so that elves' hearts and minds might reach their full flowering and growth by striving to set right the griefs of the world and overcome the challenges life offered. To do otherwise would be to diminish the People, to make them something less than they otherwise could be, and that the Seldarine—wise even among gods, or so it was said—would not do.

"I am reaching the point at which I wouldn't mind a little help," Seiveril said.

At his order, the Crusade had held its position near Galath's Roost and the Standing Stone for several days. Myth Drannor lay only forty miles to the north, not far beyond the Vale of Lost Voices, but as long as the auguries against marching onward were so dark and dire, Seiveril hesitated to advance, or to even share with his captains the reason he chose not to march.

One more day, he decided. *If nothing changes, then I will have to confide in Vesilde and Starbrow, at the very least.*

With a weary sigh, he bowed before the glimmer of early stars, then shrugged his chasuble from his shoulders and rolled it carefully, slipping it into his tunic.

"Corellon, if there is something I am supposed to be doing, I hope you will find a way to tell me," he said to the dusk. Then he straightened his shoulders and strode back toward the place where his guards waited.

To his surprise, Seiveril found several of his guards hurrying up the path to meet him, led by Starbrow.

"Seiveril?" called the moon elf. "I apologize for disturbing your prayers, but Storm Silverhand has returned with news from Shadowdale. She wants to speak with you at once."

"It is fine, my friend," Seiveril answered. "I have just concluded my devotions for the evening anyway. Please, take me to her." He fell in alongside Starbrow as they hurried back to the camp. "Did she say anything more?"

Starbrow nodded. "She told me that we've got a new enemy to deal with."

Is that why you wanted me to wait here, Corellon? Seiveril wondered. *To hear what Storm Silverhand has to tell me tonight?*

There was no answer within his own heart, but Seiveril still felt comforted by the thought, even as he dreaded whatever dire new development had brought Storm back to his encampment with such urgency. *Perhaps there is a design at work here after all,* he thought. *I was meant to* be here at this hour, whatever trials await me, and all who followed me from Evermeet as well.

Starbrow led him back to the large pavilion that served Seiveril as both headquarters and personal quarters, and held the tent flaps aside as the elflord strode in. Two guests waited inside: Storm Silverhand of Shadowdale, dressed in gleaming mail and dark leather with her long, silver hair bound from her brow by a slender circlet, and a tall, stern-looking human lord of middle years with dark silver-streaked hair.

"Ah, there you are," Storm said. She indicated her companion with a curt nod. "This is Mourngrym Amcathra, the Lord of Shadowdale."

"I am honored to meet you, Lord Miritar," said the Lord of Shadowdale. Mourngrym offered his hand to Seiveril, who remembered to take it in a firm clasp.

"And I, you, Lord Amcathra," Seiveril answered. He glanced at Storm. For all her years, she hasn't lost the human habit of haste, he noted. Still, if Storm Silverhand was in a hurry, that was good enough for him. "What it is, Lady Silverhand? What has happened?"

"We've got trouble," Storm said. "Zhentilar are marching on Shadowdale. A strong army out of Zhentil Keep started moving south yesterday, making for Voonlar. The companies garrisoning Yûlash have joined them, as well as mercenary bands of ogres and orcs from Thar." Storm's anger glittered in her eyes. "Better than five thousand soldiers are no more than five days from the Twisted Tower."

"Aillesel Seldarie," Seiveril breathed. His stomach ached with cold dread.

Behind him the Sembian army from the south was pressing up Rauthauvyr's Road and had closed to within twenty miles of his camp, occupying Battledale in the process. Ahead of him, Red Plume soldiers from Hillsfar descended the Moonsea Ride, building their strength on the far side of the Vale of Lost Voices. And the Zhentarim were moving to close him on the west. Two armies he might hope to avoid through maneuver in the green fastness of Cormanthor,

222 • Richard Baker

but three? Even his elves' skill and swiftness in woodland marches would not suffice to avoid battle for long.

"Sarya Dlardrageth had a hand in this, I know it," he murmured. "Why do they aid her? Don't they understand that if they help the daemonfey to repel Evermeet's army, she will destroy them in turn?"

"Maalthiir and Fzoul will turn on each other sooner or later, never you fear," Storm promised. "It's in their nature. But that doesn't mean they won't lay waste to half the Dales before they're done."

Starbrow looked to Mourngrym Amcathra and asked, "How much strength do you have in Shadowdale, Lord Amcathra? Can you halt the Zhents?"

"Three hundred men under arms, plus a thousand stout archers when I call out the militia. And I have no small amount of help from friends of the Dale such as Storm, here, or Those Who Harp." Mourngrym sighed and shook his head. "But this is the strongest Zhentarim army we've seen since the Time of Troubles, and I don't know if I can stop them."

"It certainly doesn't help that Sembia and Hillsfar have decided to move at the same time," Storm added. "If only one threatened the Dales, the Dalesfolk would set aside many of their quarrels and band together against the threat. But Harrowdale won't do anything with Maalthiir's army on the march. The folk of Tasseldale, Battledale, and Featherdale might have mustered against the Sembians given a little help, but Mistledale is sorely pressed by the fiends out of Myth Drannor, and Archendale is content to let the rest of the southern Dales hang." She shook her head. "I'd never realized the extent to which the great powers bordering the Dalelands kept each other in check, but with Cormyr so weak now, the old balance of power is gone. The Dales Compact is dead as the stone it's carved on."

Starbrow studied Seiveril, his strong arms folded across his chest. "Like it or not, Seiveril, we are going to have to bring these human armies to battle, or they will certainly bring us to battle at a time and place of their choosing. They simply aren't giving us any choice. You can't let them bring all three armies, along with whatever fiends and fey'ri Sarya Dlardrageth can muster, against us at the same time. That is a fight I do not think we can win."

"I do not want to spend our strength fighting humans instead of Sarya Dlardrageth's daemonfey," the elflord answered. "And I do not want to fight humans at all unless we absolutely must. Bloodshed between elf and human will stain these lands for centuries."

"Abandoning the smaller Dales to foreign occupation won't win you many friends, either," Storm pointed out.

"I know."

Seiveril turned away, staring out into the lanternlit dusk that lay over the elven camp as he considered his path. He wanted nothing more than to take to the forest and simply march directly on Myth Drannor, leaving the Sembians behind him and circling the roadblock Hillsfar had thrown up ahead of him—but he could see at a glance that the Sembian army could turn west and fall on Mistledale behind him as soon as he marched, and he could not abandon Shadowdale to the Zhents. At least the Sembian army had simply marched through Tasseldale, Featherdale, and Battledale without devastating those lands. The Sembians were not so foolish as to provoke the southern Dalesfolk into full resistance against their army and its vulnerable lines of supply. But he had no such hopes for how the Zhentilar would treat Shadowdale, if Lord Amcathra's warriors failed to stop them.

Storm is right, he realized. *Refusing to help Dalesfolk defend their homes against tyrannical powers such as Hillsfar or Zhentil Keep is just as bad as refusing to help Dalesfolk standing against Sarya Dlardrageth and her hell-born marauders. This is the task I shouldered when I called for a Return to Cormanthor.*

He sighed and turned back to the others.

"We cannot remain here and allow our enemies to gather against us while they subjugate the free Dales. If we have to fight, then it is clear that we must attempt to defeat our foes in detail. So which enemy do we confront first? Hillsfar, Sembia, Zhentil Keep, or Sarya Dlardrageth?"

"If we attack Hillsfar in the Vale of Lost Voices, we'll have to deal with Sembia too," Starbrow said. "They'll turn west behind us and cut across our lines of communication, which will bring Mistledale under their fist as well."

Seiveril replied, "The same is true if we try to avoid Hillsfar's army and march straight against Myth Drannor, except we might be dealing with Sarya Dlardrageth, too. So we have to turn against Sembia's army in Battledale or Zhentil Keep's army in Shadowdale."

"The people of Battledale will fare better with the Sembians than the folk of Shadowdale will with the Zhents," Storm said.

"There is likely a better chance to negotiate a settlement with the Sembians, too," Mourngrym added. "Their adventurism might reverse itself if they see that no one else is still in the game."

"That leaves the Zhents, then," Seiveril said. He glanced at Starbrow, and smiled crookedly. "For what it's worth, I think that a fast march to the west is the last thing our enemies expect. We'll leave Hillsfar and Sembia miles behind us."

"They'll certainly join forces by the time you can march back," Starbrow warned. "And Mistledale will be exposed to attack."

"We'll leave at least some strength here, to help the folk of Mistledale repel any attack. As for the combination of our foes, well . . . maybe turning west will give us an opportunity to bring more of the Dalesfolk to our banner."

Storm nodded slowly. "We might be able to talk sense into the Swords of Archendale, once they open their eyes and see the danger that Sembians in Battledale poses for their own independence. And we might raise Tasseldale, as well."

"Then it is settled," Seiveril said. He looked back to Mourngrym. "We will march before sunrise, Lord Amcathra. You can expect Evermeet's soldiers at your side in three days' time."

CHAPTER THIRTEEN

18 Kythorn, the Year of Lightning Storms

The stars of Sildëyuir were brilliant and strange, so bright that the shadows beneath the great old trees were silver and luminous. The land beyond the stone circle's mystic gate existed in a perpetual twilight, a magical hour of pale dusk that was cool and perfect. The sky above the tree crowns was a soft pearl-gray, as if the sun had set a short time ago and still brightened the world somewhere beyond the horizon, but in Sildëyuir there seemed to be no west or east. In any direction Araevin looked, the skies glimmered along the hillcrests and forest-tops with that same sourceless illumination. But as the eye roamed upward into the sky and approached the zenith, the skies darkened into true night, and countless brilliant stars danced in the firmament.

He stood motionless for what seemed to be

hours, drinking in the eldritch beauty of the place, his companions likewise silent beside him. Jorin Kell Harthan simply waited with a small smile on his handsome face, allowing them to sate their wonder.

Araevin didn't need his magesight to tell that they stood on another plane, a world that lay beyond the world he knew, and yet somehow remained bound to it. The starry realm's forests and hills matched the landscape he remembered from the Yuirwood's sunny glade almost perfectly. The forest was not as dense, taller and more majestic, but they stood in a starlit clearing instead of a sun-warmed one, and the ancient ring of standing stones seemed exactly the same. He looked again at the forest; the trees were tall and silver-trunked with very little undergrowth, a great living colonnade that stretched as far as the eye could see. Strange phosphorescent lichens clung like shelves to the trunks, and a sweet, rich odor hung in the air. The trees reminded Araevin of the mighty redwoods of the Forest of Wyrms, but how could they grow so tall and perfect with no sunlight?

He finally found his voice, and glanced at Jorin. "I never suspected . . ." he managed. "It's extraordinary. Not even Evermeet itself compares. How far does this realm extend?"

"Sildëyuir is about the size of the Yuirwood, though direction and distance are a little hard to judge here." Jorin tilted his head to one side, thinking. "Perhaps two or three hundred miles from end to end?"

"End to end?" Maresa glanced up at the pearl aura of dusk above the treetops. In the twilight, her pale white skin seemed to shine like the moon. "It just stops somewhere?"

"Not really. At the borders the forest grows thicker and thicker, and any track you care to follow—or make for yourself, for that matter—simply bends back on itself. There isn't an edge you can fall off." Jorin paused, and added, "I know that it is eldritch and wondrous and beautiful, but I must warn you all: Sildëyuir is not as safe as it looks. Strange monsters wander these forests, creatures that you do not find in the sunlit world. Do not relax your vigilance here."

"Have you been here often?" Ilsevele asked Jorin.

The Aglarondan shook his head. "Only a couple of times, and the last was ten years ago or more. Finding a stone circle that will let you reach this place is hard, because not all circles work all the time." He gazed into the woods, but beneath his bemusement there was wariness in his eyes.

"Now I understand what was meant by the note on my map," Araevin told Ilsevele. " 'Here of old was Yuireshanyaar, which now is hidden.' The star elves removed their kingdom from the Yuirwood to this twilit plane alongside the forest. " He turned to Jorin. "Are they still here? Can you take us to them?"

"Yes, they are still here. But it is a wide land, and not many star elves remain, and I do not know where we are." Jorin shrugged, a look of embarrassment on his face. "I am afraid I have no better plan than to pick a likely direction and start walking."

"I may be able to help," Donnor Kerth said. He handed the reins of his warhorse to Ilsevele, and drew a golden medallion out of his tunic. He raised Lathander's holy symbol in his powerful hand; the gold gleamed softly in the shadows. "Pick a direction, Jorin."

The Aglarondan studied the forest for a moment then indicated a trail that led away from the stone circle into the shadows of the trees.

"I suppose I'm inclined to head that way first," the guide said.

Kerth peered down the path, and closed his eyes as he carefully spoke the words of a prayer to Lathander. Araevin felt the warm glow of divine magic suffusing the air, and the human opened his eyes and held up his holy symbol.

"Lord of the Dawn, aid me! Will this path lead us to those whom Araevin must find, or should we go another way?"

The members of the company watched as the holy symbol in Kerth's hand grew brighter, warmer, until it seemed almost as if a small sun was caught in the cleric's grasp, throwing out dazzling rays of radiance that lit up the dim forest around them. Then the magic faded, the golden sunburst symbol becoming nothing more than a piece of metal again. Donnor shook himself slowly, closed his eyes, and murmured a prayer of thanks.

"Well?" asked Maresa. "Will it?"

The Lathanderian nodded and replied, "Yes. My divination indicates that this path will serve. But as Jorin warns, we must be careful. We will meet with danger on this road."

The small company set off down the broad path into the forest, passing into the eerie gloom beneath the gleaming silver trunks. The cool air was a welcome change after the warmth and humidity of the Yuirwood, and the absence of dense undergrowth made for good visibility and long, open views from the trail. At times it was so still and solemn that Araevin felt almost as if he was simply lost in some enormous temple, wandering among the works of dreaming gods. At other times they caught sight of the forest's creatures: white owls high in the branches above, silver-gray deer that vanished quickly into the gloom, black squirrels that darted along the pale trunks, and once a great gray-furred bear that snuffled and snorted at something that had caught its interest on the forest floor, a good eighty yards off the path.

Araevin soon came to realize that travel within the realm of Sildëyuir would be more than a little deceptive. The opalescent twilight that pervaded the woodland offered no hint as to how long they had traveled—it might have been an hour, or it might have been four. Gradually he noticed that the day, such as it was, had darkened somewhat, so that the purple velvet of the sky overhead had deepened into pure inky darkness, and in time a soft rain began to fall, so fine and thin that he did not even bother to draw up his hood.

After a long spell of marching, they came to a moss-grown bridge of stone that spanned a gloom-filled ravine through which swift white water rushed forty feet below.

"That's a good sign," Ilsevele remarked. "Someone built this bridge. I was beginning to wonder if this whole place was empty."

"We've been walking for quite a while," Araevin said, "and we began our day with a march in the Yuirwood. Maybe we should find a place to rest, and make camp for the night."

"The night?" Maresa asked.

"Such as it is," Araevin said. "We'll halt a few hours, long enough for you and the others to get a good sleep. Ilsevele and I can keep watch. We need less rest than you."

"I won't say no," the genasi said.

They walked a short distance past the bridge before they found a good clearing away from the path. Jorin built a small fire in order to prepare a hot meal from their stores, and Donnor unloaded his packhorse and brushed it down while Araevin took a few minutes to weave some magical wards around their campsite—spells of concealment and protection. So far they had seen nothing dangerous in Sildëyuir's forests, but he remembered Jorin's warning and decided to take no chances.

While Donnor, Maresa, and Jorin slept the deep and helpless sleep that Araevin had always both envied and pitied in his non-elf friends, the two sun elves sat and talked softly in Elvish or simply waited together in the comfort of each other's company, leaning back-to-back against a young tree so that they could watch all around the small camp. After a long silence in which Araevin had actually started to slip into Reverie, Ilsevele reached back to set her hand on his.

"I am glad I came here, Araevin," she said. "Regardless of what comes next, I do not regret the circumstances that brought me to Sildëyuir, even for a day."

"Nor do I," he agreed. He started to say more, but then Ilsevele squeezed his hand twice, hard and quick. Araevin froze, peering into the shadows under the trees.

"On your left, sixty yards," Ilsevele whispered. "It will be almost behind you. Move slowly."

"What is it?" he whispered back, slowly turning his head and letting his eyes slide farther and farther over his left shoulder.

"I don't know."

Carefully, Araevin allowed himself to lean just a little, getting a better look behind him—then he saw what Ilsevele had spotted. It was wormlike in shape, with a dark, glistening hide of blue-black skin, but smaller tendrils or limbs branched from its body. It slithered through the forest, passing along the path they had been following, moving with a rolling corkscrew gait that brought different limbs to the ground at different times. Three golden orbs projected from its blunt, bulbous head, if it was a head. Behind the monster came a pair of hulking, snakelike monstrosities, pale worms whose beaked maws were surrounded by four strong, barbed tentacles. Araevin couldn't say what gave him the impression, given the startling alieness of all three creatures, but something in the motions of the corkscrew monster suggested purpose and intelligence.

"What do we do?" Ilsevele asked.

"Let's see if it will pass by. I'll watch, and you be ready to rouse the others."

The creatures' progress had brought them from Ilsevele's side over to Araevin's, and he had a good view of all three. Carefully he eased his lightning wand into his hand, and reviewed the spells held in his mind just in case.

The sinister creatures continued on their way, the forest silent around them, but then the dark corkscrew creature halted, right at the spot where Araevin and his comrades had left the path to set up their camp off the trail. It seemed to feel around, groping like a caterpillar seeking the next place to set its feet, and it gave voice to a strange, shrill whistling sound. It began to sway and weave its limbs in a strange, coiling motion.

Araevin peered closer, trying to discern what it was up to—and he saw the magic at work.

Corellon preserve us, he thought in horror, *it's casting a spell! The thing is a sorcerer of some kind.*

"What is it, Araevin? What's going on?" Ilsevele hissed.

"Ready your bow," he said. "When I give the word, you must shoot the dark one."

He couldn't see it, but he felt her nod of assent. She

moved softly behind him, drawing an arrow and laying it across her bowstring.

Has it found my spell wards? he wondered.

He watched for ten terrible heartbeats as the monster sniffed at and studied the concealing spells he'd woven around the camp, and for one moment he felt certain that the thing had detected his illusions—but then it whistled again, and curled itself away, resuming its serpentine progress along the forest path. The large pale tentacled things snuffled and followed, undulating after the first one. In a few moments, they disappeared from view, and Araevin breathed a sigh of relief.

"You can relax," he said to Ilsevele. "They're gone now."

"What were those things?" Ilsevele sighed and leaned around the tree to meet his eyes.

"I have no idea," Araevin said. "Whatever they were, they were intelligent, and one at least could wield magic." He stared off into the gloom after the monsters, still trying to make sense of the whole scene. "Let's give the others another hour of sleep if we can then get moving. I don't like the idea of waiting here for those creatures to return."

❧ ❧ ❧ ❧ ❧

Three days of swift marching put Mistledale and Galath's Roost nearly eighty miles behind the Army of Evermeet, as Seiveril and Starbrow led their host westward toward Shadowdale. Seiveril rode at the head of his troops, his spirits lifting as they left the Sembians and Hillsfarians behind. Regardless of what might come, the days of indecision had passed, and the shadow of disaster in his divinations had retreated for a time. His course was not without risk—he weighed that much every day with his auguries and prayers—but events were once again in motion, and Seiveril was content with that for the time.

Despite the fact that he knew better than to divide his forces in the face of more numerous enemies, Seiveril had decided to leave a strong force behind him in Mistledale. Six full companies of infantry remained near Ashabenford, under the command of Vesilde Gaerth and a small contingent of the Knights of the Golden Star—two companies from Seiveril's own Silver Guard, one from Evereska, and three companies of the volunteers who had mustered at Elion and had been forged into real fighting units by the furious battles at Evereska and the Lonely Moor. Seiveril did not expect Vesilde to repel the Sembians or Hillsfarians if they moved on Mistledale in strength, but he hoped that the elven infantry would deter the Sembians from attempting to follow his main body to the west, and perhaps convince them that Mistledale would not be yielded without a fight. If matters came down to it, Vesilde was to retreat southwest down the Dale, covering the Dalesfolk as best he could and giving up land rather than meeting a stronger enemy in battle—but Seiveril hoped that the Sembians and Hillsfarians would be slow to attack a resisting Dale outright.

The army's track followed a human-cut footpath along the river's north bank that linked Ashabenford and Shadowdale-town. In other times it might have been a picturesque journey, with the broad, shallow ribbon of the river close to Seiveril's left hand, its waters often swift and boulder-studded, so that the river's voice filled the forest nearby. But Seiveril urged his captains to march long and quickly each day, exhorting his host for more speed. The warriors who followed him responded with swiftness that no human army could hope to match, often trotting for hours at a time to make better speed. Seiveril was not sure if he could reach the northern borders of the dale before the Zhentilar, but forty miles lay between Shadowdale's northern border and the Twisted Tower. He was certain that he'd have his army waiting in the village of Shadowdale for the invaders if he failed to meet the Zhents before they entered the dale.

Seiveril rode at the head of the army among the Silver Guard, the cavalry who had served House Miritar in Evermeet. The Silver Guard was the largest body of mounted soldiers in Seiveril's host, three full squadrons of lightly-armored knights who rode under the banner of Edraele

Muirreste. Edraele was a young and slightly built moon elf, so small that it seemed ludicrous that she should have taken up the sword. Edraele might have been young for her command, but she was also the single finest equestrian that Seiveril had seen in his four hundred years, and she possessed a fiery charisma that her warriors adored. He'd placed her in command of the vanguard on leaving Galath's Roost, and she and her Silver Guard had vigorously patrolled ahead of the army, searching for any sign of the enemy.

In the evening of the march's third day, they fought their first skirmish against the Zhentarim's soldiers.

The track broke out of the forest Cormanthor proper, crossing a narrow neck of open land along the southern border of the Dale, less than twenty miles from the town of Shadowdale. As the glittering elven cavalry rode between fields of chest-high grain straight and still in the calm hour before sunset, a pair of scouts appeared from behind a stone farmhouse, riding hard for the banner.

"What is this?" muttered Captain Edraele from beside Seiveril.

She stood up in her stirrups and cantered forward to meet the scouts. Seiveril restrained his impulse to go and see what news the scouts brought, and made himself wait. He didn't want Edraele to think he lacked confidence in her.

As it turned out, he did not have long to wonder. Edraele wheeled away at once and spurred back to the company of Golden Star knights and Silver Guard officers who rode by Seiveril.

"Zhentarim cavalry!" she snarled as she pulled up abreast of Seiveril and Starbrow. "A large company, about a mile off on our right front. They're chasing after a scouting party of our own warriors."

"The Zhents are here already?" Seiveril said.

He glanced back at the twilight woods behind him, thinking of the miles-long column of marching elves who followed behind the cavalry. The forest wouldn't stop him from deploying from the march into a line of battle, but still

. . . he'd thought he would have two days more, at least.

Starbrow read the concern in his face, and shook his head. "It won't be the main body, Seiveril. The Zhentarim likely have bands of marauders and scouts ranging all over the open dale, looking for us and causing trouble where they can. It's what I would do in their place."

Edraele pranced her horse around, and looked to Seiveril. "They likely don't have any idea that we've got the vanguard of the army at our backs, Lord Seiveril," she said. "Unless you object, I'll take the Silver Guard and drive them off."

"I agree," Starbrow said. "I don't see any reason why we shouldn't teach them a hard lesson about getting too close to us."

Seiveril hesitated. Somehow, he found that he had been hoping that it would not prove necessary to meet Zhentil Keep in battle. He felt Starbrow and Edraele waiting on his words, and frowned. Regardless of his wishes, the Zhentarim had picked a fight, and the fact that they were willing to employ orc, gnoll, and ogre mercenaries spoke volumes about the sort of realm they would raise over northern Cormanthor if he avoided battle.

"Very well," Seiveril answered. "Drive them off, but be wary of ambushes, Edraele."

Edraele did not wait an instant longer. She plucked the standard from her bearer's stirrup-rest and waved the banner in a fluttering circle.

"Silver Guards, follow me!" she cried, and she dashed off into the dusk. All around, the Silver Guards spurred their own mounts after her, thundering away across the fields.

Seiveril looked at Adresin, the sun elf knight who commanded his personal guard, and said, "Let's follow after them. I want to see what we're up against."

Adresin winced. "Lord Seiveril, I can't risk losing you to a chance arrow in a simple skirmish—" he began, but Seiveril decided to make it easy on the poor fellow. He simply spurred his own horse after the Silver Guard, making sure to leave a good space so that no one could accuse him of riding right into the fray on their heels.

He felt Starbrow close up beside him, and looked over to see the moon elf champion grinning broadly. "That was not fair, Seiveril," he called over the drumming of the hooves. "He is only doing his duty!"

"I'll be careful," Seiveril promised.

He slowed his pace a little, and allowed Adresin and his bodyguards to close up around him. To the young knight's credit, he did not bother to argue the point any longer. He simply slammed the half-visor of his bright helmet closed, and stayed close to Seiveril.

They passed through a broken line of wind-stunted poplars and scrub, then emerged into a broad field. The Silver Guard galloped away, lances lowered, charging at a ragged line of human riders dressed in surcoats of black and yellow. The numbers seemed equal, or close to it, and the Zhentilar did not waver. They couched their own spears and turned to meet the elf riders who flashed over the field toward them. For one terrible moment they thundered toward each other in the bright field, stained crimson by the setting sun, and the skirmish lines met with shrill ring of steel and the terrified whinnying of wounded horses. Riders in black and yellow fell, but so too did elves in silver and white, and the charge disintegrated into a furious, swirling, spurred melee as any kind of battle order failed.

"They've got courage," Starbrow said. "I'll say that for them. And that's at least two full companies over there."

"I see them." Seiveril watched the battle for only a moment before glancing back to Adresin. "Captain, let's see if we can lend a hand. This looks to be a closer thing than I'd thought."

Adresin nodded behind his visor. "We'll do what we can, sir," he said.

He motioned for two of his soldiers to remain close to Seiveril then he gathered the rest of the guards and raced off to join the skirmish. Seiveril approached more cautiously, anxious to lend his guards' help to the battle, but not sure of where he could make himself most useful.

The fight raged on. The Zhentarim cavalrymen fought

furiously, keeping their heads and working to cover their allies as best they could. Their armor was substantially heavier than the elf knights', but the elves were faster and more nimble, and they fought with a skill and élan that the humans were hard-pressed to match. Time and again, elf riders danced close to their foes to slash with silver sabers or lash out with long-pennoned lances, only to parry the cuts of heavy broadswords or spur away from hard-driven lance-thrusts. Elf warriors with some skill at magic peppered the skirmish with darting blasts of golden magic or confused the human horsemen with shifting illusions and quick enchantments, confounding the Zhentilar's efforts.

That's a season of fighting the daemonfey, Seiveril thought with a fierce burst of pride. *Our warriors have become a well-tempered blade indeed!* He angled toward the right flank, drew his silver mace, and spurred forward to join the fight, shouting a wordless battle cry.

He crossed the last hundred yards in the blink of an eye, his mount's hooves flashing like silver fire in the dusk, and Seiveril found himself in the fray. He batted aside a Zhentish lance and hammered the warrior out of the saddle with a great overhand swing, then wheeled his horse to meet another Zhentilar behind him in a furious rain of ringing blows as their weapons met with shock after shock, their horses stamped and whinnied, and cries of anger, pain, and triumph filled his ears. Seiveril dueled his swordsman to a standstill and was about to hammer down his guard, but an elf lancer took the man from behind and knocked him out of the saddle. The elflord spun around, searching for the fight. Starbrow battled close by, cutting an awful swath through the Zhentilar ranks with Keryvian's pure white blade.

A shrill, terrible sound tore through the twilight, and the black earth around Seiveril erupted in a great blast. His horse was thrown sideways and fell, but Seiveril managed to hurl himself clear of the saddle before the animal rolled over him. Ears ringing, he found his feet and looked up.

Overhead a sinister, bat-winged shadow swooped down low over the battlefield. The monster's long, blunt snout held a blind, gaping smile, and a long lashing tail twisted behind it. Between its humpbacked wings a black-clad human wizard sat in an ornate saddle, hurling down blasts of scorching fire as the huge monster winged over the fight. It opened its mouth again, and another shrill shriek flayed a pair of elf riders with an awful blast.

"What kind of abomination is that?" snapped Starbrow. He ducked away from a fiery bolt, and turned against another horseman nearby.

Seiveril didn't have an answer for Starbrow, but he quickly intoned the words of a holy prayer to Corellon, invoking the divine power with which he was entrusted. Holy power seethed around his hand, and he hurled a blast of supernal light up at the monster. The brilliant white ray chewed into the flying monster's flank, charring it, and the creature croaked in pain and awkwardly reeled away. But then a second flying monster appeared, also with a battle-mage riding between its wings. The wizard hurled a great blast of fire down at Seiveril.

Seiveril threw himself flat as the fireball burst over him and searing heat washed across his body. His cloak and surcoat smoking, he slowly picked himself up. All around him Zhentilar and elves alike had been scorched and scoured by the attack of the wizards on their flying beasts. With heavy, slow beats of their vast wings, the creatures circled for another pass, spurred on by their riders.

"Archers!" called Edraele Muirreste. "Get some arrows on those accursed wizards!"

The Silver Guards were outfitted for lance-work and sword play, but they were elves; every one of them carried a shortbow in a saddle holster, and knew how to use it. Many of the guards were still busy with the melee, but dozens quickly spurred clear of the fighting and drew their bows. As the flying monsters turned back toward the fray, elven bows began to thrum, and white arrows soared up into the crimson sky—at first a few, then a heavier and more accurate storm.

With another great croaking cry, the flying beasts turned away and flapped off, but not before their riders raised a long line of green fire across the trampled fields. Behind the leaping wall of magical fire, the Zhentilar horsemen quickly mustered, and retreated from the field, leaving dozens of dead and wounded behind.

Edraele rode up beside Seiveril, and took in his scorched clothing with a quick glance. "Lord Seiveril, shall we pursue?" she asked.

Seiveril watched the flapping beasts drawing away. "No, I think we've done enough for tonight. We'll need to keep some Eagle Knights nearby from now on, just in case the Zhents have more of those flying wizards. And more archers among our troops would be a good idea."

Starbrow also rode up, his eyes fixed on the departing wizards. "I am thoroughly tired of fighting flying creatures armed with magic," he declared. "I had enough of that with Sarya's daemonfey legion and their demons."

"I agree," Seiveril said. He sighed and ran a hand through his hair. "At least this is a threat we know how to face—one more thing that Sarya Dlardrageth has taught us this year." He looked around at the field of the skirmish, and frowned. Many of the Zhentilar had fallen, but so too had more than a few of the Silver Guards. "See to the army's camp tonight, Starbrow. I will join you after I have done what I can for the wounded."

☉ ☉ ☉ ☉ ☉

Curnil leaned against the gray wheel of an old oxcart, exhausted beyond all endurance. The farmyard was littered with dead gnolls, but two of his Riders lay still on the ground. One band of bloodthirsty raiders would slay no more, but his squad was down to himself and Ingra. He looked over to Ingra, who sat holding a blood-soaked bandage to an arrow wound in her left arm.

"I hope to all the gods that things are better somewhere else," he said. "We're getting butchered out here."

"Tell me something I don't know," Ingra replied. "So what do we do now?"

"Damned if I know." For half a tenday, Curnil and his

Riders had battled across the forest north of Mistledale, fighting their way right up to the very eastern edge of Shadowdale. He'd meant to turn back for home an hour ago, but the smoke of burning homesteads had caught his eye. The fighting had been fierce, but they'd saved the folk of one freehold from a death too terrible to contemplate. "Ride for Ashabenford, I suppose. We've done all we can here."

Ingra started to nod in agreement, but then she looked up sharply. "Riders coming," she hissed.

Curnil straightened and looked over the side of the cart. At first he couldn't see anything through the green cornstalks, but then he glimpsed sunlight glinting on spear points. A double column of mailed horsemen came trotting into sight, led by a tall, slender woman whose long white hair was gathered in a single braid that trailed down to her waist.

"Grimmar," he told Ingra. He raised one arm to catch their attention, and stepped out into the open.

The cavalrymen turned toward Curnil and rode into the farmyard, taking stock of the dead gnolls and fallen Riders. Their captain studied the scene for a moment, and doffed her helm, shaking the sweat and dust from her face.

Curnil looked up, and blinked. "You're Storm Silverhand!"

"So I'm told," the woman replied. She dismounted with an easy motion, hung her helm on the saddle horn, and turned to size up Curnil. "Riders of Mistledale?"

"Yes—though there were more of us a few moments ago."

"So I see," Storm said with a sigh. "You're a long way from home, aren't you?"

"We've been watching for Red Plumes or fiends from Myth Drannor passing north of Mistledale," Curnil answered. He waved a hand at the dead gnolls. "We found their sign this morning, and followed them here. I . . . I didn't know if any Grimmar were nearby to deal with these marauders, so I decided to take care of them."

"I wish we'd been here a few minutes sooner," Storm said. "I guess you couldn't have known we were near. My thanks for what you and your companions did here, friend."

"What else could we do?" Curnil sighed. He ran a hand through his grimy hair. "If you don't mind my asking, Lady Silverhand—what are you doing out here? Aren't the Zhentarim marching on Shadowdale?"

Storm gave him a sharp nod, and glanced off toward the west. "Yes. They're not far off now. In fact, I should have turned back already, but I wanted to see for myself how things stood in the eastern part of the dale. I don't like to leave such as these—" she toed a dead gnoll "—free to pillage and plunder in the east just because our eyes are fixed on the Zhentilar coming down from the north."

"Will you be able to stop the Zhents, Lady Silverhand?" Ingra asked.

"We're facing a hard fight tomorrow or the day after, but we've beat them before," Storm said. Cold steel danced in her eyes as she gazed off toward the smoke-stained skies to the north. Then a weary smile crept back across Storm's face. She held out her hand, and took Curnil's arm in a warrior's clasp. "Well, Riders of Mistledale, you might as well come back to Shadowdale with us. We'll have work for you soon enough."

CHAPTER FOURTEEN

21 Kythorn, the Year of Lightning Storms

Jorin Kell Harthan led Araevin and his friends along the forest road for a day and a half more, leaving the circle of standing stones thirty miles behind them. It was hard to gauge the passage of time in Sildëyuir; the subtle darkening and lightening of the sky was no substitute for a true sunrise or sunset, and the hours simply had a way of slipping away. Araevin would find his mind turning to some thought or another as they traveled, only to come to himself with a start only to realize that miles had passed by under his feet while his mind was occupied. He began to wonder whether the great magic that had created this world beyond the world had also altered the flow of time in the place—but of course, he could not really test that without returning to the Yuirwood and Aglarond to find out how long he had been away.

On two more occasions they encountered strange creatures abroad in the woodland. The first time they met a wheeling, darting flight of great dragonflies whose gemlike bodies glowed in soft emerald and sapphire hues beneath the trees. Each insect was better than a foot long, which caused no small consternation on the part of Donnor's horse, but the glittering swarm seemed merely curious about them, following the company for a time as they filled the air with whirring wing beats and soft light. On the second occasion, they sighted another one of the blue-black worm creatures crossing their path a couple of hundred yards ahead. It flew through the air on slick, gleaming wings, its spiraling motion twisting its flight into a strange aerial weave as it went. But the monster did not sight them, and simply continued on its way.

As the dimming hour approached and the skies began to darken again, they finally emerged from the great band of forest through which they had walked, finding themselves on the edge of a long stretch of low, rolling hills, crowned with waving silver grasses beneath the stars. There another large stone circle stood, which Jorin examined with great interest.

"I think I know where this place is," he told Araevin. "Distance here correlates to distance in the Yuirwood. We've come more than forty miles to the south, as much as directions mean anything here."

"Do you know where to find the star elves?"

Jorin nodded. "If I remember right, there is a citadel about ten miles in that direction." He pointed over the bare, starlit hills. "It lies on the far side of this clear space."

They made camp for the darkest hours within the circle of standing stones. Araevin could not detect any wakeful spells or magic within the circle, but he sensed old and powerful wards around the ring, and he judged them as good a defense as his own spells. He composed himself for Reverie, sitting cross-legged at the foot of a great stone with his back to the cold, smooth granite, and drifted off into strange dreams.

"Araevin."

Farthest Reach • 243

He roused to full wakefulness with a start, and found Ilsevele touching his shoulder.

"What is it?" he asked.

"A rider approaches. Two more of those dark creatures pursue him."

Araevin climbed to his feet. Donnor Kerth stood beside one of the outer stones, murmuring calming words to the hitched packhorse and looking back along the forest path they'd recently passed. Ilsevele stooped to wake Jorin and Maresa next, while Araevin joined the big human by the stone. He followed Donnor's gaze and spied the rider, galloping along the path. The trail ran alongside the stone circle for a time before doubling back, so they had an excellent opportunity to watch the fellow as he raced past them perhaps three hundred yards downhill, appearing and vanishing as he passed behind trees and steeper embankments along the trail. At that distance, he was little more than a glimmering white figure, tiny and distant, but Araevin quickly spied the flying monsters that followed him, twisting their way through the air above the trees . . . and gaining on their quarry.

"He'll pass close by in just a minute or two," Donnor said. "What do we do?"

"Hail him and make ready to stand against the flying creatures," Araevin replied.

He didn't know who or what the rider was, but he didn't like the looks of the sorcerous worm-monsters at all, and he was not about to abandon anyone to them. Besides, the longer he watched, the more certain he was that the rider was an elf.

Donnor nodded. He drew his broadsword and pressed himself against the stone next to him, trying to stay out of sight. Ilsevele took up a position against another stone, her bow of red yew in her hands, and Maresa joined her. Jorin drew his own swords and slid down the slope a little to a boulder closer to the trail, crouching low to keep out of sight. Araevin took a moment to whisper the words of a spell of shielding, and waited.

The rider rounded the bend close by the ring of standing

stones and spurred his mount—a fine dappled-gray destrier, stretching out its long legs with an easy grace that belied the speed of its run—up the hillside, following the trail as it wound past the old menhirs. The flying monsters shifted their own course and climbed over the trees, cutting the corner against their quarry. Araevin decided that he'd waited long enough. He stepped out from behind the stones and waved at the rider.

"Here!" he cried. "Into the standing stones!"

A momentary astonishment crossed the rider's face, but he wasted no time at all. He wrenched the reins to the left and took his horse scrambling up the steep, grassy hillside. He was indeed an elf, though not of any kindred Araevin knew. He had skin as pale and fair as a moon elf's, but his hair was a pale gold that didn't often appear among the *teu Tel'Quessir*. He wore a gray cloak over a shirt of gleaming mithral mail and a quilted white doublet lavishly embroidered with gold thread.

"Beware the nilshai!" he called in Elvish. "They are fearsome sorcerers!"

The winged worm-monsters did not miss the rider's change of course. They veered toward the hilltop ring and arrowed through the air. One of them whistled and piped loudly, twisting its limbs in a strange fashion, and a sizzling green orb of acid appeared before it. With a flick of its long torso, the monster hurled the acid ball at the company sheltering among the stones.

Great glowing gouts of emerald fire exploded around Araevin and his friends, searing flesh and burning foul, smoking holes in cloaks and clothing, but the stones served as good cover—Araevin ducked under the spattering acid, and he saw Ilsevele throw herself forward out of the ring, escaping the worst of the blast. She rolled upright and fired three quick arrows at the nearest of the monsters. One shivered to pieces in midair, broken on some invisible shield of magic the worm had raised, but two others pierced its long, serpentine torso. It fluttered and twisted, its weird whistling taking on a shriller note.

Araevin incanted the words of a potent lightning spell,

Farthest Reach • 245

and blasted up at the two creatures with an eye-searing bolt of blue-white. One darted aside, but the wounded one could not escape. The bolt burned it badly, bringing it spinning to the ground, smoke streaming from charred patches on its hide. Donnor and Jorin charged it at once, blades bared, but the monster had fight in it yet—it pulled the Lathanderian's feet out from under him with one swift jerk of its curling tail, and at the same time it enmeshed Jorin in a gleaming black spell-web of freezing shadows. Jorin's charge came to a stumbling halt ten feet short of the creature.

"Damn it!" he snarled, gasping with the bitter chill that snared him. "I can't get to it!"

Araevin turned his attention back to the nilshai that remained airborne, and managed to quickly parry the monster's next spell, batting the alien magic aside with a quick countering spell. He exchanged two more spells and counter spells with the monster in the next few heartbeats, again astonished by the speed with which the nilshai worked its magic while continuously weaving and dodging against Ilsevele's rain of deadly arrows.

On the hillside below him, Donnor gained his feet again and approached the wounded nilshai more cautiously. The monster lunged at him, battering at his shield with powerful blows of its whipping tentacles, but Donnor slashed it twice with his broadsword, weaving a glittering cage of steel with his blade. The nilshai recoiled from the human knight—and Maresa lunged in from behind it, fixing her rapier in the center of its torso between two of its three wings. The monster leaped and bucked, carrying Maresa's rapier from her hand and knocking her to the ground. It shrieked a single high, harsh note, then drew into a tight coil on the ground and lay still.

Maresa rolled to her feet, and grinned fiercely. "This one's done!" she called.

Araevin parried another spell from the one that remained, but then the creature managed to slip a spell through by virtue of its uncanny quickness, trapping him in a bitter, freezing fog of silver mist. He fumbled with his disruption wand with fingers that were suddenly stiff and numb, and fought to utter the words of a dismissing spell, but then he heard a high, clear voice ringing behind him. A brilliant white arc of magic swept out of the old stone ring and lanced upward to blast the remaining nilshai, scouring the monster's dark flesh with silver power.

Araevin struggled to look over his shoulder to see what had happened, and he saw the elf they had rescued standing within the stones and *singing,* hands clenched at his sides, eyes fixed on the winged horror overhead.

The winged worm hissed and tried to climb out of the reach of the arcing magic, but then a pair of arrows from Ilsevele brought it down. Its wings folded in midair and it dropped to the ground like a stone. The rider held his song for one more moment then allowed the eldritch music to fade. He leaned against a menhir in fatigue.

Araevin finally managed to shake off the clinging silver fog that had numbed him. He turned to Jorin and dispelled the shadow-web with a quick word and motion of his hand, then looked at his companions.

"Is anybody hurt?" he asked.

"Singed a little from that acid, but I'm fine," Ilsevele answered. She looked down at her side, where a handful of holes in her tunic still smoked.

"I can tend to that," Donnor said. He picked his way back up the hillside and began to chant a healing prayer to Lathander, holding his hand over Ilsevele's side.

The rider straightened and turned to face Araevin. "I don't know how you came to be here, sir, but I am indebted to you," he said. His Elvish was a little strange to Araevin's ear, due in no small part to the remarkable voice the fellow possessed, a rich tenor in which every word held music. "I am Nesterin of House Deirr, and I believe that I owe you my life."

"I am Araevin Teshurr of Evermeet. This is my betrothed, Lady Ilsevele Miritar. Our companions Maresa Rost of Waterdeep, Dawnmaster Donnor Kerth of the Temple of Lathander, and our guide Jorin Kell Harthan of Aglarond."

"I am pleased to meet all of you, especially considering the circumstances." Nesterin bowed to each of them.

"Might I ask what brings your company to Sildëyuir? We rarely see folk of other races here."

"I guided them here," Jorin said, stepping forward.

"You are of the Yuir?"

Jorin nodded. "I am. They have an errand of some importance. The Simbul's apprentice decided that they needed to speak with the star elves."

Nesterin studied Araevin and his companions more closely.

"Very well," he said at length. "The masters of the Yuirwood do not lightly give strangers their trust, and I am indebted to you all in any event. My home is only a few miles away. I would be greatly pleased if you would allow me to offer you the hospitality of House Deirr."

☙ ☙ ☙ ☙ ☙

The First Lord's Tower gleamed in the sunset, tall and slender as a sword blade over the center of Hillsfar. The evening was warm and still, and the lamplighters hurried through the streets to perform their duties as the city's bustle and commerce guttered out for the day. A whisper of magic danced in the air, and Sarya Dlardrageth and Xhalph appeared on a balcony amid a dull thump of displaced air.

As before, Sarya and Xhalph wore their human guises. She glanced at the balcony around them, and nodded in approval. As promised, Maalthiir had left it bare of any awkward spells or arcane defenses so that she or her messengers could simply teleport directly to his home. There was even an iced ewer of wine by the door leading into the tower. Sarya approved; the less she had to see of the human squalor surrounding Maalthiir's tower, the better.

Two Red Plume guards stood nearby, straightening to attention and smoothing the surprise from their faces.

"I see we're expected," Xhalph noted.

Sarya looked at the nearer of the guards. "You, there—tell your master that Lady Senda and Lord Alphon are here, and desire a few words with him."

She went over to the table and poured herself a goblet of wine, first taking a moment to work a minor spell to reveal any poisons that might be waiting for her.

The Red Plume muttered a word of assent, and ducked through the door leading into the tower proper. He returned a few minutes later with a short, burly human warrior in fine court clothes. The fellow dressed like a dandy, but his eyes glittered coldly within deep, dark sockets.

"Lady Senda," he said, bowing obsequiously. "I am Hardil Gearas, High Warden of the First Lord's Tower. If you'll follow me, I will lead you to Lord Maalthiir."

"Of course," Sarya purred.

The high warden bowed, and led her into the tower. They proceeded through sparsely furnished hallways of polished stone, eventually reaching a conservatory of modest size that seemed like it had seen little use. Though the harps and recorders in their fine glass cases showed not a hint of dust on them, the whole chamber seemed too carefully arranged for actual recitals. Besides, Sarya doubted that Maalthiir was much given to music, let alone practicing or performing himself.

She composed herself for a lengthy wait, but Maalthiir swept into the room almost on her heels, his four pallid swordsmen a pace behind him, and another pair of Red Plumes following. The first lord was dressed in a scarlet coat emblazoned with a Draconic emblem, and he carried his dark iron dragon claw scepter in his hand. He paused in the doorway to study Sarya, and something less than humor creased his stern features.

"Lady Sarya," he said. "To what do I owe this unexpected call?"

"Lord Maalthiir." Sarya kept her voice neutral, and did not lower her gaze an inch from Maalthiir's dark eyes. "I am concerned by the progress of our campaign in Cormanthor, and I hoped you might be able to reassure me."

"I am widely regarded as the very font of optimism," Maalthiir rasped. "What specifically concerns you, Lady Sarya?"

"Evermeet's army has marched west a hundred miles

in the last three days, in order to meet Fzoul's Zhentarim army descending on Shadowdale," Xhalph answered. "We have dispatched several messengers instructing you to bring the Red Plume army north of Mistledale westward, so that you and Fzoul might combine and effect the destruction of the elven army. Yet Hillsfar's army has not yet moved."

Maalthiir's eyes flashed, but he kept his temper in check. "Of course. I have not ordered them to march."

Xhalph squared his shoulders, a low growl rumbling deep in his throat, but Sarya set a hand on his arm and silenced him. She folded her arms and paced across the room, finding the space confining and small.

"This is an excellent opportunity to destroy the elven army, Maalthiir," she said. "Your Sembian friends have led Seiveril Miritar to leave a good quarter of his strength sitting in Mistledale. Between your Red Plumes, the Zhentilar, and my own warriors, we can crush Miritar. However, if you do not move, you will expose Fzoul to defeat in detail."

"Lady Sarya," Maalthiir said, "that is exactly what I intend. It would suit my purposes very well indeed if Evermeet and Zhentil Keep were to maul each other in Shadowdale. Therefore I see no reason to send help to Fzoul Chembryl."

"I do not care about your petty little spats with Fzoul!" Sarya hissed. "I will not allow your machinations to upset my opportunity to destroy Miritar. Betray Fzoul later if you like, but today I need your army in Shadowdale, and you will not delay an hour longer."

Maalthiir measured Sarya for a long moment, making no reply. His coterie of dead-eyed swordsmen stood unmoving at his side.

"I am not your servant, Sarya," he said. "In fact, I see no reason to continue our association. Should Evermeet and Zhentil Keep fight to exhaustion in Shadowdale, my Red Plumes and Duncastle's Sembians will be the only powers left in the Dales. I see no reason to share that prize with a hellspawned harpy such as yourself."

"You treacherous dog," Sarya snarled. "You have no idea of the might I have gathered at Myth Drannor. I will destroy you for your perfidy!"

"You would be better advised to save your strength for Evermeet's army," Hardil Gearas sneered.

"If you will not take the field against Evermeet, then I will," Sarya promised. "I will crush Miritar with my own power, Maalthiir, and I will use Fzoul Chembryl to destroy you!"

She snapped out the words of a teleportation spell, reaching out to take Xhalph's arm. But to her astonishment, nothing happened; the spell simply failed, leaving her standing in the middle of Maalthiir's conservatory.

"The chamber is warded against teleportation," Maalthiir observed. He smiled, a hard and cheerless expression that did not touch his eyes. "I have no idea whether you can even begin to make good on your threats, Sarya, but as I have said before, I take few chances. Prudence would dictate that I not allow you to leave this room alive."

With a curt gesture of his dragon-clawed scepter, Maalthiir vanished from sight, and the swordsmen swept out their blades as one. Sarya bared her fangs and crooked her hands to cast a spell—but an instant later she was battered by a whole array of deadly magic, as Maalthiir suddenly reappeared, surrounded in a shimmering spellshield. A scintillating blast of vibrant colors embraced her in magical destruction, sending sheets of crimson fire racing over her body, while at the same time a sinister black ray struck her over the heart like a spear of ice, draining life and power from her, and a dancing sword of emerald green energy appeared above her head and slashed at her with dizzying speed. Xhalph was struck by a yellow ray that sent crackling yellow lightning racing over his body, charring and stabbing him.

He froze time to cast all those spells! Sarya realized. The sudden assault filled her with anger beyond measure. The fires burning on her skin troubled her not at all. She was the daughter of a balor lord, and no flame could harm her, magical or otherwise. But the other spells were dangerous.

With a savage snarl, Sarya conjured an orb of hell-tainted fire and detonated it in her hands, scouring the whole room with the sinister flames. The cabinets exploded in shards of hot glass, and the Red Plumes were virtually incinerated before they even took a step. But Hardil Gearas threw himself into a corner and survived, and Maalthiir's swordsmen, while scorched badly, did not even break stride or show the slightest reaction to the clinging hellfire that burned on them. Maalthiir himself stood unharmed, protected by his spell-shields.

"You will have to do better than that, Sarya," he called.

Xhalph abandoned his magical guise with a roar of rage, instantly gaining two full feet in height as his scarlet-scaled form appeared. He leaped straight for Maalthiir, sweeping his swords out in one quick motion, but two of the pale swordsmen interposed themselves with uncanny swiftness. The daemonfey lord tried to simply bull his way through the unearthly guards, but their sword points darted and stabbed, drawing blood at thigh, hip, and shoulder before Xhalph even began his first parry. The daemonfey swordsman whipped around to confront one of the pair and drove four swords into the fellow at once, ripping the blades free with a shout of bloodlust—but nothing except strange black mist came from the wounds, and despite being almost ripped apart, the pale swordsman made no sound. He only staggered a bit with the force of the blows, and came on again, moving a little slower and more awkwardly as slashed tendons and rent muscle failed him.

Sarya found the other two swordsmen closing on her, while the blazing blade of green energy slashed and darted at her face. She quickly backstepped and managed to dispel the emerald sword before it did more than give her a couple of shallow cuts, but while she did that, Maalthiir intoned another spell, hurling a deadly blast of scathing cold at her. The thin white beam grazed her left arm and turned a solid foot of her forearm white and dead. Sarya screeched in pain, and nearly died on the sword point of the first of Maalthiir's strange guardsmen to reach her.

Maalthiir cannot be beaten here and now, she realized. The First Lord's Tower was the heart of his domain, and he had prepared for a fight, while she had not. As much as she longed to rip the human dog to pieces with her own talons, she risked destruction with every moment she remained.

"Xhalph!" she shouted. "The window!"

Xhalph wheeled away from his antagonists at once, and hurled his heavy form at the row of narrow windows along the wall. They were not large enough to permit him to pass, but Xhalph's strength was immense, and he was caught up in the fullness of his wrath; nothing could stand in his way. Lowering his shoulder, he battered the lintel with such force that he sent a shower of masonry out of the tower's side and burst through into clear air.

Sarya darted after her son, abandoning her human appearance in midstep. Swords slashed and hissed through the air only a step behind her, and Maalthiir's last spell—a great, golden hand of magical energy that tried to snatch her out of the air—faltered and broke against the power of her demonic heritage, fizzling into nothingness. She spread her dark wings wide and soared away from the tower.

"I will tear him to pieces with my naked claws!" Xhalph bellowed, hovering in the air. "I will feed his entrails to rutterkin while he watches!"

"Yes, but not today," Sarya snapped.

She caught hold of Xhalph's hand and barked out another teleport spell. In the space of an icy instant, they hovered in the air above the green vastness of Cormanthor, with Hillsfar's spires and towers dimly visible in the warm haze far to the north and east. Sarya glared at the distant city, her eyes glowing red with pure hate.

"I should have known better than to try to find a use for stinking humans," she muttered. "Maalthiir thinks he is strong enough to defy me? He will learn otherwise. I will teach the humans to fear the wrath of House Dlardrageth!"

❧ ❧ ❧ ❧ ❧

As he had promised, Nesterin Deirr led Araevin and his companions toward his home. They walked over silver-grassed hilltops beneath the open, starry sky, leading the star elf's mount and Donnor's packhorse. As they walked, Nesterin questioned them about their presence in Sildëyuir and their travels in the realm—though he was fairly courteous and indirect about it, so much so that Araevin doubted whether any of his companions other than Ilsevele noticed that they were being skillfully interrogated as they walked.

Araevin decided to turn the tables on their host after Nesterin succeeded in drawing out of Maresa a good account of their meeting with the Simbul's apprentice and their journey through the Yuirwood. As the company fell silent for a moment, he asked, "What were those monsters you were fleeing from, Nesterin? We saw several others like them in the forest."

"They are the nilshai, and as you have seen, they are formidable sorcerers. They haunt the lonelier stretches of our forests." The handsome star elf glanced toward the dim line of trees, a dark tide washing against the hills by starlight, miles behind them. "It does not surprise me that you met them on your way here. They have been trying to poison our realm for many years now, loosing monsters in our forests and pulling the outlying reaches of Sildëyuir into their own sinister realm."

"Where do they come from? What do they want with you?" Ilsevele asked.

Nesterin shook his head. "We do not know. Some of our sages say that the nilshai are creatures of the Ethereal Plane, the spectral reality that infuses all the rest of existence. But Sildëyuir was disjoined from the Ethereal when our mages created this domain long ago. I cannot fathom why they would go to such lengths to bore gates into this realm, when the daylight world that you all come from is far more accessible to them."

"These things are even closer to our world than they

are to yours?" Maresa asked. She shook her head. "I don't like the sound of that."

"What business did you have in the forest we passed through?" Ilsevele asked Nesterin. "It seemed to be wild and desolate. You are the first person we've seen since crossing over from Aglarond."

The star elf was slow to answer. Araevin glanced over his shoulder at Nesterin, who was leading his horse as he walked alongside the rest of the company. The mage wondered for a moment whether Nesterin intended to keep his errand a secret, but it seemed that the star elf was simply organizing his thoughts.

"I had ridden out to the seat of House Aerilpé, where my cousin Leissera has lived for many years," Nesterin began. "It is a strong tower far to the south, overlooking the Shimmersea that marks the bounds of our kingdom in that direction. The nilshai have always been strong in that region, and their taint has filled vast tracts of the forest there with strange and dangerous creatures—things like plants or great funguses, but alive and hungry, and monsters to suit.

"I followed a road I thought to be safe to Aerilpé, but a few miles from the tower I found that the nilshai had been busy since last I passed that way. The forests were choked with creeping, groping tendrils and pallid, eyeless beasts that hunted in the shadows. And the very realm itself seemed to be, well . . . fraying. Sluggish streams or rivers of bright gray dust sliced through the landscape, and as I struggled to find my way through to Tower Aerilpé, the damnable stuff would close in behind me, trying to surround and trap me.

"In any event, I managed to find my way through to Aerilpé, but I found the tower utterly abandoned. Everything seemed as it should be—furnishings stood where last they had been used, clothes still filled the chests and drawers, food still lay almost fresh in the kitchens—but there was not a sign of another living soul. I lingered no more than an hour in that place, because it was simply so unnerving to be alone amid such silence, then I set out at once for home.

"I decided to try a different road on my return—the path that led past the old gate ring two days' walk behind you. The nilshai caught my trail, though, and they pursued me closely for the better part of a day." Nesterin glanced over at Ilsevele, and shrugged. "So there is my tale, Lady Ilsevele. A great House of our people has vanished, the distant reaches of my world seem to be coming undone, and I cannot explain why or how."

They walked on in silence for a while longer, and they crested another low hilltop. Before them on a high knoll overlooking a shining river stood an elegant tower of pale white stone. It was ringed by a tall, sturdy wall, and its lower galleries and bastions were carved from the dark gray granite of its natural footing. Dozens of softly glowing lamps gleamed in its windows and treetops.

"My home," Nesterin said. He glanced to Araevin and the others. "No one who has battled the nilshai will come to harm here, my friends, but I must warn you: Few who aren't star elves have ever walked in Sildëyuir. You will be asked to give an account of yourself, and you may be required to accept a geas or enchantment to ensure that you will guard our secrets well. I will speak on your behalf, but I cannot say how our lord will rule in your case."

Maresa scowled. "I'll be damned if I let you put a geas on me. Why shouldn't we just walk away now?"

Nesterin shrugged. "You saved my life today; you should know what awaits you. Araevin and Ilsevele, as *Ar Tel'Quessir,* have little to worry about. Nor does Jorin, though his judgment in bringing you here may be questioned. But you and the Dawnmaster have no elf blood, and are not known to us. If you choose to depart now, I must tell my lord that you are abroad in Sildëyuir, and he may very well decide that you are not to be allowed to wander about the realm."

Donnor Kerth's brow furrowed deeply, but the Lathanderian did not speak. Maresa, on the other hand, stopped dead in her tracks.

"I don't like jails," she said.

Ilsevele turned to her and set her hand on Maresa's

arm. "I promise you, Maresa, whatever they would do to you, they must do to me as well."

Maresa looked up to Ilsevele, and after a moment she snorted and shook her head. "You've got too much trust for any ten people, Ilsevele, do you know that?" She shrugged off Ilsevele's hand and started down the path again. "All right, then, let's see what Nesterin's folk make of us."

They followed the path down the silvered slopes of the grassy hillside, crossed the river on a bridge of luminous stone, and came up to the mithral gates of the tower. There half a dozen elf warriors in knee-length hauberks of white-scaled armor stood guard, armed with long halberds and slender bows.

"Welcome back, Nesterin," the captain of the gate guard said, but her eyes were fixed on Araevin and his companions. She searched for words, evidently more than a little surprised. Finally she frowned and said, "I see you have been far afield in the last few days. Who are these people?"

"I did not find them; they found me," Nesterin answered. "They slew two nilshai and saved my life in the process."

"Two nilshai?" The captain glanced at Araevin again before looking back at Nesterin. "I will tell Lord Tessaernil of your return, and inform him that you have brought guests back to the tower."

"Good," said Nesterin. "They have a strange tale to share, and I have much to tell him of what I found at Tower Aerilpé. We will be in the high hall."

The captain sent a messenger off into the tower, and detailed two guards to attend to Nesterin's graceful destrier and Donnor's warhorse. Ilsevele flicked her eyes to Araevin, and the mage immediately grasped her unspoken thought—the gate guards treated Nesterin with an air of deference. Their host was an elf of some importance, one of the masters of the House.

"This way, my friends."

Nesterin gathered up Araevin's company and led them into the tower proper. It was a comfortable elven palace, though quite strongly built—more a citadel than a home, really, with high, well-made walls of stone. It was large enough to be home to a hundred or more people, but Araevin quickly formed the impression that substantially fewer folk than that lived in Tower Deirr. They passed other elves only at odd intervals, and the echoing halls and corridors seemed too perfect and bare to have been lived in much.

Nesterin showed them into a small banquet room at the top of a winding flight of steps that ascended the rocky pedestal of the tower's hilltop.

"Please, lay down your packs, doff your cloaks, and make yourselves comfortable," he said. "I will send for refreshments for you."

"Thank you," Araevin murmured.

He shrugged his backpack from his shoulders and rested his staff by the door. The others followed suit. In the space of a few minutes they were dining on platters of fruit and warm bread. Nesterin joined in as well, with an apologetic smile.

"I fear that I haven't eaten in a couple of days," he said between bites. "I left Aerilpé in a hurry, as you might imagine."

As they ate, a tall, lordly star elf dressed in elegant robes appeared at the hall's door. Araevin sensed a deep and studious mastery of the Art in the elflord, a strength of spirit that reminded him of the might of Evermeet's own high mages. He had eyes of pure jet, with not a hint of iris, and his elegant features seemed to be graven with the weight of long care. His long white hair was bound by a platinum circlet at the brow, and hung loose to his collarbone and the nape of his neck.

"Jaressyr told me you'd returned, Nesterin," he said, his voice inflectionless. "I see that you have company."

Nesterin stood and bowed. "Lord Tessaernil," he said. "May I present Araevin Teshurr and Ilsevele Miritar of Evermeet, Maresa Rost of Waterdeep, Donnor Kerth of the church of Lathander, and Jorin Kell Harthan of the Yuir? My friends, this is Lord Tessaernil Deirr, my mother's elder brother and the master of this House."

The star elf lord nodded gravely to them. "I have heard that you aided Nesterin in a desperate hour. You have my thanks for that. I want to hear what brings you to our land, but first—I did not expect you back so soon, Nesterin. Is everything well at Aerilpé?"

The younger elf frowned, and shook his head. "No, my lord, I fear that it is not." He quickly recounted the tale he had told Araevin and his friends, and went on to tell how he had encountered the company in the old stone ring at the edge of the hills as he fled from the nilshai. "These travelers may very well have saved my life," he finished. "The nilshai pursuing me were more than I would have cared to face alone, and they were close to overtaking me when Araevin and his friends intervened."

"We would have done the same for anyone in your circumstances," Donnor Kerth said gruffly. "How could we have stood by and done nothing?"

Jorin looked to the two star elves and spoke. "My lords, I hope you will forgive my curiosity," he said. "I visited Sildëyuir once, many years ago. I do not recall meeting such dangerous and fell creatures abroad in your realm. Have these monsters always been here?"

"They have been getting much worse of late," Tessaernil admitted. His habitual frown deepened until his face seemed almost empty of hope. "There are portions of the realm that have been drawn almost completely into their influence. We are not a warlike people, but it is clear that we face a threat that we cannot hide from any longer. If the nilshai have learned how to assault our Towers, we face a dark and desperate battle indeed." He sighed, and turned to face Araevin. "Now, sir, you have already seen and heard more of this realm than I would like. I must ask: What brings you to Sildëyuir? Who are you, and what do you want here?"

"I am in search of knowledge that has been lost in the world outside your realm," Araevin said. "I hope that it still exists here, though."

"Knowledge?" Tessaernil folded his arms. "What sort of knowledge?"

"Thousands of years ago, a star elf mage named Morthil lived among the elves of Arcorar," Araevin answered. "He helped the grand mage of that realm to defeat an ancient evil. I have reason to believe that Morthil returned to his homeland with magical lore that he removed from the enemies of Arcorar. I need to find out if anything of what Morthil removed from Arcorar still survives."

"There must be some reason you have come all the way to Sildëyuir in search of this old lore," Tessaernil observed. "What do you need with it?"

"I need it to defeat the enemies that Morthil once fought," Araevin said. "They are called the daemonfey, and they are an abominable House of sun elves who consorted with demons long ago."

He decided that Tessaernil was not an elf to be trifled with, and chose to tell him the story of events since Dlardrageth's return as completely and openly as he could.

When the tale was told, Nesterin and Tessaernil stood in silence for a long moment. The older lord finally moved to a seat at the head of the table and sat down heavily, his gaze troubled and distant.

"First Nesterin's tale, and now this," he murmured. "It has been a long time since I heard two such stories in the same day. We keep abreast of doings in Aglarond and the Yuirwood, but news of the wars and perils of the distant corners of Faerûn rarely find its way to our realm."

Araevin paused, steeling his nerve to ask the question. "I perceive that you are skilled with the Art, Lord Tessaernil. Do you know of magical lore brought out of Arcorar to Sildëyuir? Have you heard the name of Morthil before?"

Tessaernil looked up at Araevin, his dark eyes unreadable. "I know that name," he said. "And I think I know where you might recover at least a remnant of Morthil's ancient lore. But you will find that it is a dark and difficult journey, son of Evermeet. Morthil's old tower lies in the farthest reach of our realm, in the borderlands where things have been slipping away into strangeness for many years now. Even if the place has not vanished entirely, I do not see how you can get there without passing into the domain of the nilshai. Few indeed return from that journey."

CHAPTER FIFTEEN

23 Kythorn, the Year of Lightning Storms

For two full days, Seiveril waited for the Zhentarim army to attack Shadowdale-town and the Twisted Tower. Forty-five hundred elf warriors of the Crusade held the woodlands and fields a couple of miles north of the town, standing alongside more than a thousand humans gathered from all corners of Shadowdale, a strong company from Deepingdale, and even a few dozen veterans from nearby Daggerdale. But having lost the foot race to crush the Dalesfolk before the elves of Evermeet arrived in Shadowdale, the Zhentilar settled for a very deliberate and cautious approach. Instead of pressing forward to the attack, they advanced at a snail's pace. By night the Black Network had fortified their camp with great earthworks and palisades.

On the evening of the third day, Starbrow found Seiveril standing among the pickets at the northern end of the elven camp, gazing out across the fields toward the distant campfires of the Zhentarim camp. The moon elf joined him in studying the enemy entrenchments for a time.

"You understand what the Zhents are trying to do?" Starbrow asked.

"I didn't until this morning, when I saw that they were not marching today," Seiveril replied. "But I see it clearly enough now. They are going to make us come to them if we want to force a battle. And I have to do it, because the longer I sit here waiting on the Zhents, the more likely it is that the Sembians and Hillsfarians will overwhelm Mistledale or march against our rear." Seiveril ran a hand through his fine silver-red hair, and sighed. "I should have anticipated this response. Clearly our best strategy is to defeat our enemies in detail, and that means I must fall on the Zhents while their allies are still far behind us. The burden of action is on me."

Starbrow nodded. "You're learning. So when do we fight?"

"It has to be soon," Seiveril admitted. "Tomorrow is as good a day as any. What do you think?"

"Tonight, an hour after moonset," Starbrow said. "We'd have three hours until sunup. We see in the dark better than the humans, and we need less rest. It's the best time for elves to fight humans, and our Crusade makes up better than three-quarters of the fighting strength we have gathered in Shadowdale."

"A good part of their army consists of orcs, gnolls, and ogres. The darkness won't bother them."

"True. But if the Zhentilar break, the humanoid mercenaries in their camp might follow. It's the best we can do. We could wait another day and plan a more deliberate attack for the day after tomorrow, but why give Sarya and her human pawns another day to close the noose around our necks?"

"All right, then. Tomorrow morning." Seiveril clapped Starbrow on the shoulder. "Pass the word to our captains. I have to speak with Lord Mourngrym and Lady Silverhand, and tell them what we intend."

He glanced once more at the open fields before him, wondering briefly how many elves and humans would meet their ends in those common farm fields by dawn the next morning. Then he turned away to go in search of the lord of Shadowdale and Storm Silverhand.

He found Mourngrym Amcathra inspecting the old ditch-and-rampart earthworks that lay a few hundred yards north of the town, barring passage against any invader approaching along the northern road. The ramparts had been raised fifteen years past to defend the town against another Zhentarim invasion. The elven army was bivouacked a mile to the north, astride the road, but the Grimmar—as folk from Shadowdale preferred to be called, after the old Castle Grimstead that had once stood in the Dale—were readying the ramparts as a second line of defense. Mourngrym was pounding sharpened stakes into the ground with his own hands, hard at work with a whole crew of townsfolk, as Seiveril rode up.

"Lord Miritar," he said with a nod, wiping the sweat from his brow. "The Zhents are staying put?"

"Yes, for now," Seiveril said. He dismounted and left his reins with the knights who served as his guard. "They are not going to move, not as long as they hope to catch our army between the Red Plumes and their own force. Yet we have to scatter or destroy the Zhentilar as quickly as possible, so that we can turn back to deal with the Red Plumes and Sembians in Mistledale and Battledale. We will have to take the fight to them, I am afraid."

Mourngrym gave a stake two more taps with the wooden sledge he held then set down the hammer and said, "I'd rather stand on the defensive, but I understand your predicament. Shadowdale isn't the only realm you're fighting for. What do you have in mind?"

"We will march against their camp and attack an hour after moonset."

The lord of Shadowdale glanced sharply at him. "You'll have to start marching in a matter of hours. Can your captains organize an attack on a fortified camp that quickly?"

"Yes," said Seiveril, and he felt a pang of pride in his heart as he realized that he was not boasting. "It will be hard, but we have faced worse in the last few months." He paused then added, "There is an advantage to a hasty attack. If there are any spies around—daemonfey or Zhent—they will not have much of an opportunity to discover our intentions and report."

"I wish that were not a consideration, but you are right." The human lord looked off toward the north, where the ruddy glare of watch fires drew a broad red smear across the northern sky. "Elven archery in the night is a fearsome thing, but my folk will be hindered by darkness until the skies start to lighten. Could you detail a company of your scouts to march with the muster of Shadowdale? A few of your elves will go a long way toward guiding my folk to the fight in the dark, and helping them until it grows light enough for humans to see well, too."

"A wise idea, Lord Amcathra. I will make sure that a good number of Jerreda Starcloak's wood elves march in your ranks in the morning." Seiveril looked around, and asked, "Is Lady Silverhand nearby? She should be told, too."

"She's out in the eastern dale with a party of riders—Harpers and such folk," Mourngrym said. "She saw an opportunity to waylay a Zhentilar cavalry squadron and a couple of sky mages that have been causing trouble out there, and I asked her to make a sweep of the forest border to make sure that the Zhents weren't looking to march east and outflank our lines. I'll send a couple of her Harpers after her tonight." He offered Seiveril a grim smile. "You know, Storm told me before she left that she thought you'd move against the enemy camp within a day or two. I think she knew your mind before you did."

"It would not surprise me," Seiveril answered. He stepped forward and gripped Mourngrym's forearms. "I must return to our camp. We will send the wood elves soon, and the moment I know where and when we will strike, I will send word."

Mourngrym nodded. "If we can drive them out of their camp, there's no place for the Zhents to stop running before they reach Voonlar. I like the thought of that."

◈ ◈ ◈ ◈ ◈

Six hours later, Seiveril sat on his courser, armed and armored for battle. He had managed only half an hour of Reverie while the rest of the camp was rising and arming, since he spent his whole night hammering out the best plan of attack he and Starbrow could come up with. Yet he did not feel tired. The hour having come for him to test his strength against Zhentil Keep, he was anxious to be about it.

"Edraele Muirreste reports that the Silver Guard is in position, Lord Miritar," said Adresin. The young captain was Seiveril's herald and adjutant on the field of battle. As much as Seiveril relied on Thilesil as his aide-de-camp, she was not a skilled fighter. Instead, she remained with the other healers and clerics to tend to the inevitable tide of the wounded and dying, and Adresin served as his voice and messenger on the battlefield.

"Very good, Adresin."

Seiveril looked up and down along the line. Concealed with illusory mists that mimicked a low ground fog hovering over the damp, cold fields in the chill night air, the Crusade was arrayed for battle. In the center marched Seiveril's best infantry, the Vale Guards from Evereska he had not left behind in Mistledale. Seiveril had also massed most of his magical might in the center. His bladesingers, spellarchers, and battle-mages marched among his heavy infantry, some openly, others disguised as common footsoldiers. To his left, on the west side of the dale, Jerreda Starcloak's wood elves were already slipping through the dark forests. On his right, where the land was somewhat more open, the Grimmar had gathered under their lord Mourngrym. Seiveril was surprised to find the townsfolk arrayed in quiet, purposeful ranks, with none of the sloppiness or empty bravado he might have expected of a hastily gathered militia. More than a few of those farmers and merchants knew their way around the battlefield, and the elflord realized that he had misjudged their strength. Then again, the Zhents had done exactly that more than once, hadn't they?

Seiveril twisted in his saddle—an awkward motion in his plate armor—and verified once again the companies of knights and cavalrymen who waited behind the infantry. Ferryl Nimersyl and the Moon Knights of Sehanine, along with the remaining Knights of the Golden Star and Lord Theremin's men-at-arms from Deepingdale, made up most of that force. If Seiveril's hammer blow on the center carried the Zhentish earthworks, it was their job to stream through the hole and devastate the camp.

"All right, Adresin," he said. "Pass the word: Forward, march!"

Adresin softly called out the order, and the banners of Seiveril's command company dipped once. All along the line, keen-eyed elves watched for the visual signal. Seiveril had no intention of announcing the attack with horn blasts or battle cries. With an uneven surge, the elves flowed smoothly out into the misty fields before the enemy's own earthworks. The Zhentilar had raised their last camp only five miles from the town itself. The elves and the Grimmar had closed to within a mile in a cold, dark march they started three hours after midnight.

Corellon, grant us a swift and easy victory, Seiveril prayed fervently. *Lull the Zhents to slumber for just a little longer. I do not want to send any more of your sons and daughters to Arvandor than I must today.*

Their mail muffled with strips of cloth, silent in the dim fog, the army pressed forward. The elves were taking care not to march in step, and did not have heavy footfalls in any event, so all that met Seiveril's ears was an ominous rustle and creaking, punctuated by the occasional soft whicker of a horse or a low cough. Steadily the ramparts drew closer, and in the morning mist Seiveril found himself entertaining the curious conceit that his army was standing still, while the waiting battle at the ramparts was slowly advancing on him instead of the other way around.

A brilliant stroke of lightning flashed overhead, followed by a peal of thunder. Seiveril looked up at once, and saw in the fading brilliance the shape of a great, winged monster wheeling overhead. He glimpsed a dark figure astride the flying monster, a staff clutched in his hands. The Zhentilar sky mage hurled another blast of lightning down at the Grimmar off to his right, but then a pair of Eagle Knights streaked down out of the dark skies, lances couched. The monster croaked and turned away as a furious melee erupted in the skies over the elves' march.

"Well, I didn't really think we would reach the camp undetected," Seiveril muttered. "Adresin, wind your horn! Now is the time for speed!"

In the crude earthworks ahead a flat iron gong began to sound, beating an alarm. But a moment later it was drowned out by the high, clear ringing of dozens of elven horns. From the Crusade came a great roar in answer, and the elves and Dalesfolk broke into a run, hurrying to cross the last few hundred yards of ground before the Zhents could fully man their palisade.

A barrage of battle-magic blasted out from the Zhentilar camp, streaking fireballs and scathing ice storms, but Jorildyn and the other battle-mages were ready for that. They quickly countered most of the Zhentish magic, dispelling deadly invocations or raising magical shields to ward off battle spells. Many of the Zhentish spells faltered, broken on the elven defenses, but a few streaked through and detonated amid the onrushing elf and human soldiers. Horses screamed in the cold air, and battle cries became shrieks of pain, but the elves' rush swept on unbroken. From a dozen places in the elven lines mages halted their advance for a step to reply with spells of their own, scouring the enemy earthworks.

"Archers!" cried Seiveril. "Cover the ramparts!"

Trained to fire on the move, elf archers began to shower the palisade with a silver storm of arrows. Even though the Zhentilar rushing up to take up station behind their staked

Farthest Reach • 267

ditch-and-berm were well hidden by their earthworks, all an elf archer needed was a glimpse of a foe to send an arrow winging his way with uncanny accuracy. Seiveril was close enough to see bands of gnoll archers gathering behind the ramparts to fire back, as companies of ogres, bugbears, orcs, and black-clad human pikemen streamed up to defend their ramparts. But they were slow to form ranks, and several large gaps beckoned, places where Zhentil Keep's soldiers had not yet reached their posts or elven battle-magic had seared the ramparts clear.

We have them! Seiveril thought, and he started to give Adresin the order to charge.

But at that moment the air all around Seiveril and his guard rippled and boomed with dozens upon dozens of sulfurous belches. Demons and devils by the score appeared all around Seiveril's banner, grinning with needle fangs, eyes ablaze with hellish glee as they teleported to attack Seiveril's standard. Elves surrounding Seiveril cried out in panic, and horses screamed in sudden terror.

"'Ware the demons!" cried Adresin. "To the banner! To the banner!"

The center of the charging elven line was thrown into chaos. Seiveril found himself beset by a pair of insectlike mezzoloths, fearsome hellspawn who carried great tridents of iron. He danced his mount aside from the stabbing points, and barked out the words of a prayer that unsummoned one of the monsters, hurling it back into the foul netherworld from which it had come.

The other monster lunged and nearly impaled the elflord with a low belly thrust that Seiveril barely blocked with his shield. He reared his warhorse and battered at the monster with his courser's deadly silver-shod hooves, then wheeled around and caught the dazed yugoloth off-guard, smashing at it with his holy mace. The weapon burned with a pure white light as it struck demonflesh, and the mezzoloth's beak clicked and hissed in pain.

The mezzoloth reeled back out of reach and vanished in the confusion of the fray. Seiveril looked around desperately, trying to see what had become of the attack.

The Zhentish ramparts were only sixty yards away, and he could see that on both the right and the left that the wood elves and the Dalesfolk were already sweeping up and over, laying down a storm of arrows. Whole companies of elven infantry from the center continued their attack as well, already ahead of the demons who had suddenly teleported into their midst. And behind him the Moon Knights and Knights of the Golden Star were falling upon Sarya's demonic minions. Seiveril had wanted to use them to wreck the camp, but they had to drive off the demons and devils, and Ferryl Nimersyl knew it.

A gout of fearsome hellfire washed over Seiveril, and he staggered in his saddle as his mount reared and screamed. The elflord wrestled with the animal, speaking a quick healing prayer to salve his mount's injuries, and looked up just in time to catch the heavy blow of a nycaloth's brazen sword on his shield. The hulking monster snapped at him with its awful maw, and caught Seiveril's right arm in its teeth. Elven plate crumpled in the force of its bite, and Seiveril cried out as the foul fangs pierced his flesh. His mace dropped from his fingers, and the nycaloth wrenched him out of his saddle, shaking him like a dog worrying at a rabbit.

"Get away from me, hellspawn!" Seiveril snarled.

He ignored the agonizing pain in his arm and the bruising and battering, finding the clear still center in his soul where Corellon Larethian's divine power waited, and he shouted out a holy word of great power. In a burst of supernal white light Seiveril blasted a circle twenty yards wide clear of demons, devils, yugoloths, and all other sorts of foul creatures from the lower planes. The nycaloth shaking him vanished with an ear-splitting howl, so suddenly that Seiveril dropped to the ground and went to all fours, shaking his head.

Wincing inside his helm, he looked at the blood streaming from the punctures in his arm, and took a moment to whisper another healing prayer, staunching the wound. Then he groped for his silver mace and clambered to his feet, looking for his mount.

"Lord Seiveril! Are you hurt?" Adresin rode up, his golden armor badly scorched on one side, but seemingly unhurt otherwise.

Ferryl Nimersyl of the Moon Knights followed him, his gleaming white armor spattered with black gore.

"I've lost my mount, but I am all right," Seiveril managed.

He spied another horse nearby, its owner nowhere in sight, and hurried over to swing himself up into the saddle. The Golden Star knights and the Moon Knights were all around him, battling furiously against those hellspawn that still remained. He groaned in frustration, seeing the chaos that had come from the daemonfey intervention . . . but then a ragged shout of triumph from the right caught his ear. He looked toward the ramparts, and saw that only a few dark islands of Zhentilar soldiers remained on the ramparts. Left and right, wood elf and Dalesfolk archers held the earthworks and rained arrows down into the camp from point-blank range, and even in the center, the Evereskans had managed to seize their line as well.

"What kind of unholy alliance has Sarya forged with the lower planes?" Ferryl Nimersyl snarled. "Demons, devils, yugoloths all fighting together—they are supposed to be the most implacable of enemies!"

"I have no answer," Seiveril replied, though it was a question that troubled him too. There was no time to answer it just then, however. "Ferryl, rally your knights to my banner. I mean to take that camp."

The commander of the Moon Knights nodded and called for his riders to gather at Seiveril's banner. In the space of a hundred heartbeats, better than fourscore knights of both the orders assembled in a dense knot around Seiveril. Then they rode forward, veering to make for the gap where the Evereskans had breached the rampart. Seiveril kept his eyes away from the elf warriors who lay still among the stakes of the ditch and the steep berm, spurring his new mount to scramble up the rampart.

At the crest of the earthwork, he paused to take in the scene. There was little fighting along the rampart.

The elves had seized the camp's fortifications. But a furious melee still raged among the tents and wagons of the Zhentish camp. The first gray gleam of the coming dawn lightened the sky to the east, and by its faint light Seiveril could see to the far side of the camp—where hundreds of Zhents were streaming north, abandoning their encampment. But waiting for them along the road to Voonlar was the Silver Guard of Elion, with Starbrow and Edraele Muirreste at its head, five hundred elven cavalry to ride down and harry the Zhents as they fled.

"Well done, Seiveril," said Ferryl Nimersyl. "Even with the demon attack, your plan worked. We've got half their army trapped between us and the Silver Guard."

Seiveril nodded. "Corellon has favored us again. Come, my friends, we have hard and ugly work to finish here."

With a high battle cry he spurred his way down from the earthworks into the camp, followed by the knights of Evermeet.

❂ ❂ ❂ ❂ ❂

Araevin and his comrades remained at Tower Deirr for several days, guests of Lord Tessaernil, Nesterin, and their folk. They were not prisoners—at least, they were not disarmed or confined—but Tessaernil was very clear that they were not to leave without his permission. Maresa prowled the tower continuously, more than half-convinced that they were prisoners who simply didn't know it yet, but Araevin availed himself of the opportunity to study the elflord's library of old tomes, and Ilsevele studied the star elves themselves.

They were an ancient people, the descendants of the old kingdom of Yuireshanyaar that had once stood in Aglarond's forests thousands of years ago. In appearance they were very much like moon elves, though they tended toward fair hair instead of the dark brown or blue-black of most moon elves. But Araevin found their reserve and serious demeanor more reminiscent of many sun elves he knew. They had a love of song and music that was remarkable, even among elves, and when a truly skilled singer such as Nesterin raised his voice, the effect was so unearthly and beautiful that time itself seemed to fall still and listen.

As Nesterin had told them, the star elves had created Sildëyuir as a refuge, a place to which they could Retreat from the cruel and ambitious human empires that had arisen in the ancient east. More than a thousand years before the raising of the Standing Stone in the Dales, the human kingdoms of Narfell and Raumauthar, as well as Unther and Mulhorand, had fought furiously for dominion in the region. In western Faerûn many elves had retreated to Evermeet to avoid such ambitious human empires, but the star elves had decided to simply remove their entire realm rather than abandon it to flee elsewhere. All of Sildëyuir was a great work of high magic, an echo of the Yuirwood itself spun into starshine and dusk through mighty spells of old.

Since the creation of Sildëyuir, the star elves had slowly slipped farther and farther from Faerûn, leaving the daylight world to its own devices. Many still traveled through the old elfgates and roamed Aglarond or the Inner Sea, but they passed themselves off as moon elves, and did not speak of their homeland to strangers. Few elves remained in the forests of the east outside of Aglarond itself, and those who lived within the Yuirwood kept their silence regarding the star elves' secret.

Araevin spoke with Tessaernil at length, and discovered that after leaving Arcorar almost five thousand years ago, the wizard Morthil had returned to Yuireshanyaar and subsequently become that realm's grand mage. He had played a leading role in the affairs of the kingdom for several centuries. The former apprentice of Ithraides had gone on to become an even greater mage than his master in time, founding a society of wizards known as the *Seneirril Tathyrr,* or the Mooncrescent Order. The order survived all the long centuries from the time of Arcorar down to Sildëyuir's creation, three thousand years after the time of Ithraides and two thousand years before the present day.

"Even among elves, that is a very great span of time," Araevin said to Tessaernil and Nesterin as they sat together in the library. "How is it that Morthil has been remembered for so long?"

"His tomb lies in the rotunda of Mooncrescent Tower," Tessaernil said. "He was revered as the founder of the order. I saw it when I studied there in my youth."

Araevin's heart leaped in his chest. He set his hand to his breastbone, and felt the Nightstar murmur under his touch. Morthil's works had survived to within a single elf lifetime of the present day. Was it too much to hope that a *telkiira* stone or a spell passed down from master to apprentice over the years might still endure, too?

"Does any of Morthil's handiwork still survive? Loregems, spells he created, spellbooks he scribed?"

"When I was young, there were stories told in the *Seneirril Tathyrr* that the secret libraries and vaults of the tower might hold such things. But that was a long time ago—about three hundred years after the making of Sildëyuir and the translation of our kingdom into this plane."

Araevin stared at Tessaernil. "You told me before that Yuireshanyaar had been removed to Sildëyuir two thousand years ago. You have lived that long?"

"Time flows differently in Sildëyuir, Araevin. One year passes here for every two in the world outside." Tessaernil offered a small smile. "I was born over eighteen hundred years ago, but I am in truth not more than nine hundred years old."

"You may not find that remarkable, but few of my folk reach nine centuries, even in Evermeet," Araevin said. "Queen Amlaruil might be that old, but she enjoys the blessing of the Seldarine themselves."

"It is noteworthy among my people as well," Nesterin observed. He offered a crooked smile. "I introduced Lord Tessaernil to you as my uncle. It would have been more accurate to add a few 'greats' before that."

"You said before that you thought Morthil's tower lies in the farthest reach of your realm—you were referring to Mooncrescent Tower?"

"Yes," Tessaernil replied.

"So I need only speak to the masters of the tower, then," Araevin said. "They will be able to help me with Morthil's ancient lore."

"That is the problem," Nesterin said. "The order failed some time ago, and Mooncrescent Tower has been abandoned for centuries. It lies at the very border of our realm. Given what I recently discovered when I visited House Aerilpé, I fear that the place may no longer be accessible."

"As soon as you give me leave to, I certainly intend to try it, regardless of the tower's present circumstances," Araevin answered. "I have no small experience in dealing with ancient ruins and warding magic."

The older elflord nodded. "I cannot understate the peril you may face, Araevin, but I did not expect that you would depart without trying." He glanced to Nesterin and continued, "I have spoken with some of the other House lords of our land, taking counsel about you and your companions. I have decided to allow you to attempt Mooncrescent Tower. Nesterin here has agreed to guide you, at least as far as any road will serve."

"I thank you, Lord Tessaernil," Araevin said. He stood and offered a deep bow to the ancient elflord.

"You might not later, if things prove as dangerous as I fear they may," Tessaernil said. He stood as well, and gravely returned Araevin's bow. "You may set out when you like, Araevin. I wish you good fortune and a safe journey."

☙ ☙ ☙ ☙ ☙

For two days, Scyllua Darkhope fought with every inch of her zeal and determination to extricate something from the disaster on the borders of Shadowdale. By all rights, the Zhentarim army should have disintegrated completely in the retreat back to Voonlar, harried as it was by the slashing attacks of pursuing elf riders. But Scyllua personally commanded the rearguard action, turning at bay and standing her ground whenever the elves pressed too close, then wheeling away to gallop another mile or two down the road as soon as the elves had been repulsed again.

As she harangued the last weary companies of the rearguard, keeping them on their feet and moving north through nothing more than her own unswerving will, she found Fzoul Chembryl at a nameless ford ten miles south of Voonlar. The lord of Zhentil Keep and his company of guards came riding south, against the march of soldiers retreating north, breasting a path through the exhausted ranks with callous indifference.

When Fzoul caught sight of Scyllua, he said, "Ah, there you are. Come, Scyllua, I would like to have a word with you."

Scyllua dismounted and followed Fzoul into an old stone cottage that overlooked the ford. She did not fear punishment for her failure at Shadowdale. There was no point in dreading it. She had failed, and she would be disciplined. That was the way of the Black Lord. If she wanted to earn Bane's favor again, she must endure her punishment stoically, with no attempt at evasion or excuses.

Fzoul muttered the words of a spell and sealed the cottage from scrying or outside observation. Then, when he was satisfied, he turned to Scyllua and delivered a great backhanded slap to her face that spun her half around and left her reeling drunkenly, her ears ringing.

"How did you allow this to happen?" he demanded.

Scyllua spat blood from her split lip, and slowly straightened. She kept her hands at her sides, expecting that her lord and master would strike her again.

"I failed to take sufficient precautions against an attack on my camp, my lord," she said. "I expected to attack, not to be attacked."

"Did you not entrench your camp every night, and post a strong watch?"

"I did, my lord. But events proved those measures insufficient."

"Clearly," Fzoul muttered. "Recount all that happened as you marched south from Voonlar. Do not seek to conceal anything from me."

Scyllua did as she was told. When she had finished, she awaited Fzoul's punishment with open eyes. But the Chosen of Bane did not immediately lash out. Instead, he turned away, frowning, his thick arms crossed before his chest.

After a long time, he spoke. "Circumstances beyond your control contributed to your failure," he grudgingly admitted. "We had an excellent chance to crush the elven army, but the Red Plumes and Sembians did not take the steps that needed to be taken."

Scyllua looked up at Fzoul. "The Red Plumes did not move on Mistledale?" she asked in surprise. She'd simply *assumed* that Hillsfar would have moved against the elven army's rear. "Maalthiir is not stupid," she muttered, talking more to herself than to Fzoul. "He would not have missed that chance unless he *chose* to miss it. He has betrayed us, Lord Fzoul!"

"My spies in Hillsfar report that Maalthiir had some sort of falling out with his mysterious new allies. There were reports of a fearsome magical duel fought in the First Lord's Tower several days ago."

"Does Maalthiir still live?"

"Regrettably, yes. But this story of a falling out with Sarya intrigues me." Fzoul looked back to Scyllua. "The daemonfey agents who accompanied you and summoned the demons against Evermeet's army—what became of them?"

"They abandoned us after we were driven from the camp," Scyllua said bitterly. "As soon as they saw that we were beaten, Lord Reithel and his guards declined to offer any more assistance and left."

"It seems that we are no longer useful to them," said Fzoul. He scowled. "Now what? Do I hold back strength to counter Hillsfar . . . or Myth Drannor, for that matter? Do I strike a deal with the daemonfey and turn against Maalthiir? Or do Maalthiir and I hold to our agreement, and simply remove the daemonfey from consideration?"

Scyllua stood motionless, blood trickling from her damaged face. She would not be so forward as to offer an opinion. Fzoul was lost in his own dark thoughts, anyway.

He stroked his mustache, and nodded.

"We deal with Maalthiir," he decided. "That's the thing to do. As long as we have an understanding with Hillsfar and Sembia, we must profit by it. Let the elves worry about the daemonfey, and vice versa. In the meantime, Scyllua, you will repair this broken army as quickly as you can. I will have need of it soon."

CHAPTER SIXTEEN

26 Kythorn, the Year of Lightning Storms

Araevin and his comrades set out from the citadel of House Deirr on the day following Araevin's conversation with Lord Tessaernil. The elflord provided them with mounts for their journey; the horses of Sildëyuir were lightly built and graceful, with spirited manners. Donnor Kerth looked on their destriers with some suspicion, not entirely sure that the horses could keep up a good speed on a long ride, but the star elf mounts proved quick and enduring. They soon showed that they could outpace the heavily armored Dawnmaster, even if they were several hands shorter than the big roan Kerth had brought with him.

Nesterin rode at their head, leading the way along dim, shadowy roads of moss-grown gray stone that wound through countless miles of dusky forest. Araevin and Ilsevele rode behind the star elf, followed by Maresa and Kerth. Jorin Kell Harthan brought up the rear of the party, keeping a careful eye on the shadows behind them as they rode on. Tessaernil had warned them that no part of Sildëyuir outside the walls of an elven citadel was truly safe, and the Yuir ranger had taken the warning to heart.

They went on for several days, as near as Araevin could tell, halting to rest in the hours when the gloaming was at its deepest and the stars shone brightly in the velvet sky, then rising as the pearly gray of the lighter hours began to seep back up into the sky. From time to time they crossed over rushing streams on bridges of pale stone or came to silent crossroads in the forests, places where dim roads led off into the shadows beneath the silver trees. They even passed by several lonely citadels or towers, isolated keeps whose gleaming battlements looked out over the forest from rugged hilltops or slumbered in broad, grassy vales. Some of the towers glimmered with lanternlight and song, but others were dark and still, long abandoned.

As they rode past another of the empty towers, Maresa gazed up at the shadowed tower and shuddered. "Is this whole realm desolate?" she asked aloud. "We've gone sixty miles or more from Tower Deirr, and we haven't met a single person on the road. We've passed more empty keeps than occupied ones!"

Nesterin glanced back at Maresa and shrugged. "Most of the realm is like this," he said. "My people built true cities long ago, but our numbers have been dwindling for centuries. With the whole plane to ourselves, we never saw a need to crowd together into narrow lands and teeming towns. But I fear that the distances between our keeps and towers and towns are growing longer with each year."

"Do any towns or keeps lie ahead of us?" Ilsevele asked.

The star elf shook his head. "Our road doesn't take us near any towns," he said. "We are heading out toward the edge of the realm. In fact, I know of only one more keep on this road before we reach the place where Mooncrescent Tower once stood."

As it turned out, the keep that Nesterin remembered was also abandoned, with no sign of its People. Its walls were pitted and charred, as if by acid.

"The nilshai," the star elf said bitterly as they studied the ruins. "They must have come here, too."

"You are under attack, Nesterin," said Donnor. "Your foes are destroying you one by one. You must gather your strength, and soon, or you will be lost."

"We are not as warlike as you humans," Nesterin protested. "Sildëyuir has never had need of an army. We are the only realm on this plane!"

"War has come to Sildëyuir, whether you are ready for it or not," Ilsevele said.

Nesterin bowed his head, and did not answer.

They managed another day and a half of riding before they came to the first of the gray mist rivers. The road dropped into a dark, shallow dell, and in the bottom of the small hollow a silvery mist or dust flowed sluggishly across the road like a low fog. At first glance the stuff seemed innocuous, but as they drew closer, the horses stamped nervously and refused to set foot in it.

"Is this the mist you encountered when you rode to Aerilpé?" Ilsevele asked Nesterin.

The star elf frowned. "Yes, it is. But I did not expect to meet it so soon. We're many miles from Mooncrescent yet." He glanced around the shining forest, his eyes dark and troubled. *"Aillesel Seldarie!* What is becoming of my homeland?"

"It's just a little mist," Maresa snorted. "Just ride on through, and have done with it!"

"The horses don't like it at all," Ilsevele said. "And now that I'm here, I find that I don't like it either. Ride on through if you like, but I think we should look for a way around it if we can."

The genasi tapped her heels to her mount's flanks, and urged the animal forward until the mist lapped over the horse's hooves, and strange tendrils or streamers of the silvery stuff seemed to wind around its legs. The horse began to shy in fright, its ears flat along its head, its eyes wide and rolling. Maresa struggled with the animal, but then she gasped and drew away, backing the horse quickly away.

"The mist tried to grab me!" she exclaimed.

"I didn't see anything," rumbled Donnor. "Are you sure?"

"I *felt* it," Maresa insisted. "It's thick as molasses in there. And it was trying to pull me in deeper." She shuddered, her white hair streaming from her face as if she stood in a strong wind. "Have you ever stood in a high place and felt as if you might fall? As if you were about to slip over, but you didn't really want to stop yourself? It's something like that."

Nesterin nodded in agreement. "That's how I recall it. I discovered that I didn't dare cross more than a few feet of the mist, not even when the nilshai were on my heels."

Ilsevele looked over to Araevin. "What *is* this, Araevin? Do you have any idea?"

The wizard studied the weird, silver-gray mist, streaming slowly through the hollow's floor.

"I am not sure," he said. "One moment...."

He murmured the words of a seeing spell and studied his surroundings, searching for signs of magic. His companions all glowed brightly, armed as they were with various enchanted weapons or protective spells. Araevin ignored them and bent his attention to the sluggish silver-gray river of dust—or mist or smoke—that flowed across their path. Slowly he realized that the whole forest around him, and the sky overhead, was a vault of deep and powerful magic, a great silver artifice of staggering size.

High magic, he thought. Of course! Tessaernil said as much. The plane of Sildëyuir was called into being by high magic.

He couldn't even begin to imagine the difficulty and precision of the high magic ritual that had called a whole world into being, but the evidence was before his eyes. He tore his gaze from the faint silver vault of flowing magic that filled the sky and shaped the ground, and looked again at the gray stream of dust.

It was a crawling black gate, a ghostly portal that flickered and shifted beneath the mist. And it was growing. Whatever it touched was consumed, taken out of Sildëyuir to some other place. When the mist dissipated, its contents might return—or they might not. Like a great boring worm, the mist was chewing its way through the homeland of the star elves, devouring the magic and the very existence of the plane itself.

"Corellon's sword," Araevin whispered.

"Well, what do you see?" Maresa asked.

"You did well to turn away from the mist," Araevin answered. "It's a portal to another dimension, and if I am any judge of such things, not a dimension you would want to visit. We will have to avoid any such rivers we come across."

"That will become more and more difficult the farther we venture from Sildëyuir's heart," Nesterin warned. "In the farthest reaches of the realm, there is nothing *but* this cursed mist."

They turned their horses from the road and climbed up the side of the dell, simply circumventing the silver-gray pool roiling across the road. But as they continued on their way, they began to meet with more and more of the glimmering streams. Sometimes long tongues or arms of the mist seemed to shadow their path, twisting through the trees and glades of the forest beside the road. Other times pools or streams blocked their path, forcing them to detour away from the road and feel their way forward through the forest. The woodland fell ominously silent, with not a hint of birdsong or animal movement. Araevin realized that most of the forest creatures had long since abandoned the mist-haunted districts of the forest, seeking more wholesome environs.

At the end of Sildëyuir's dim day, they made their camp atop a small knoll in the forest. Araevin had observed that the silver mist tended to cling to low-lying areas, and it seemed prudent to seek a camp in some high place so that they would not be overcome while they rested. When they rose in the morning and studied their surroundings, they found that the knoll afforded a good view of the country around them.

A great gulf of silver-gray mist lay only a few miles away, carving its way through the forested hillsides like a fog-shrouded arm of the sea. Other inlets and channels glinted in the bright distance ahead and on all sides, as if they were approaching a sea coast of sorts.

"It's closing in behind us," Jorin murmured, looking back the way they had come. "I don't know if we could retrace our steps."

Araevin followed the Yuir ranger's gaze, and saw that large parts of the road they had passed along in their travel of the day before seemed to have been swallowed by the pearly streaks. He steeled himself and turned back toward the land ahead.

"We will find a way through," he told Jorin. "I know some spells that may help."

They broke camp quickly, unwilling to risk being stranded on the hilltop, and continued toward the edge of the realm. During the last hour of their ride great arms of silver-gray nothingness came to surround them on either side, so that it seemed that they were riding along a low, treacherous peninsula jutting out into a misty sea. Small patches and pools of mist began to appear in the road and in the woods to either side, slowly growing larger and more frequent as they pressed on, until they met and merged together. Finally they came to a place where they simply could go no farther. Ahead of them lay nothing but endless silver-gray mist, cold and perfect.

They halted and stood still for a time, looking out over nothingness. Finally Araevin shook himself and looked over to Nesterin.

"How much farther to Mooncrescent?" he asked.

The star elf looked around, studying those landmarks that hadn't been swallowed yet. "Five miles, I think. But there's no other way through. It's gone."

Araevin stared at the mist, and remembered the pure shining fountain he had seen in his vision many days and long miles before. The Nightstar was cold and hard in his chest, a dull aching weight that seemed to transfix his heart. He could almost hear Saelethil's mocking laughter, as this strangest of all obstacles checked his path toward high magic and the knowledge he needed to contest Sarya Dlardrageth's power in Myth Drannor.

I am not about to let Saelethil Dlardrageth laugh at me, he told himself.

Without glancing at his companions, he dismounted from his horse and began to undo the animal's saddle belt.

"Araevin? What are you doing?" Ilsevele asked.

"The horses are terrified of the mist," he said. "We can't take them in there."

"To the Nine Hells with the horses!" Maresa snapped. "We can't take *us* in there!"

"Nevertheless," Araevin said, "I am going forward. I ask no one else to come with me."

The rest of the company stared at him for a long moment, and Ilsevele slid wordlessly from her saddle and began to remove the harness from her own horse. A moment later Donnor Kerth and Jorin followed suit, and Nesterin as well. Finally Maresa swore and swung herself down from the horse.

"You're all mad," she snapped. "This is the worst idea I've heard in a long time!"

"I know," Araevin said. He tossed the saddle into the grass at the side of the road, and patted his horse's neck. "But it's the only one I have right now."

◉ ◉ ◉ ◉ ◉

The First Lord's Tower gleamed above the thin blanket of mist, smoke, and lanternlight that pooled in Hillsfar's streets. Despite the late hour, the city was not entirely asleep. The distant sounds of raucous shouts and bawdy singing drifted from those taphouses that were still open, apprentices worked to keep ovens and kilns stoked in workshops that needed their fires throughout the night, and folk were already rising to go to bakeries and smokehouses and begin their work for the morning. Squads of Red Plume guards patrolled the streets and kept watch from the battlements of Maalthiir's keep.

Sarya Dlardrageth looked over the rooftops of the human city and bared her fangs in a malice-filled smile. She'd spent days preparing her counterstroke to Maalthiir's treachery. Through her mastery of Myth Drannor's mythal she had summoned hundreds of yugoloths and demons to her banner. She commanded the allegiance of scores upon scores of Malkizid's devils, outcasts from the Nine Hells who followed the Branded King. Gathered around her was a small horde of infernal monsters: demons and devils stronger than ogres, and invulnerable to anything other than magic spells or enchanted weapons. Some were armed with fearsome claws, fangs, and stingers, others with brazen swords and cruel axes forged in the fires of the pit, and each of them was capable of summoning scathing blasts of hellfire, blinding, choking, or stunning their foes with words of evil power, or calling on even more terrible supernatural powers. And close beside her were three hundred of her most dangerous fey'ri warriors, skilled sorcerers and swordsmen who could fight with blade or spell with equal adeptness.

Maalthiir, the First Lord of Hillsfar, was about to wake to a city far less peaceful and secure than he'd imagined.

"Slay every soul you find in the First Lord's Tower," Sarya called to her fiendish horde. "Then tear it down and set the city afire. Now fly, my warriors! *Fly!*"

With a thunderous beat, Sarya's fey'ri warband leaped into the air as one. Those demons and yugoloths that could fly followed her fey'ri warriors, while the others simply teleported themselves directly to the battlements of Maalthiir's citadel. With the swiftness of a stooping dragon Sarya's winged warriors arrowed over the stout city walls, streaking toward the high tower gleaming in the moonlight.

Fireballs and gouts of hellish flame began to burst down in the city itself, and screams rose in the night as people awoke to a nightmare of fire and claws. Despite her orders, more than a few of her summoned demons had chosen to simply attack the sleeping city. Sarya scowled, but she didn't try to recall the fiends. Random slaughter and chaos in the streets would serve to confuse Hillsfar's defenders as to the true nature of the attack.

She and her winged warband reached the First Lord's Tower, and Sarya alighted on the high terrace that Maalthiir had formerly set aside for use in teleporting to his keep. An ironclad door sealed the tower interior from the open battlements. Sarya gestured to a nycaloth hovering nearby.

"Through there!" she commanded.

"Yes, my queen!" the monster hissed.

It dropped down in front of the iron door and clenched its great talons in the iron plate. With a mighty effort, the hulking creature wrenched the door from its pintle and hurled it across the battlements, sending it crashing to the street. Sarya watched the heavy door shatter the stone steps at the tower's gate.

Down below the battlements a large band of fey'ri stormed Maalthiir's front gate, leaving a dozen Red Plumes dead on the steps, hacked down by daemonfey swords or charred by daemonfey spells. More bands of fey'ri and demons assaulted other entrances to the tower, or simply teleported inside.

The nycaloth ducked down and pushed its way into the tower, but a terrible flash of blue light suddenly flared in front of the creature, and a potent symbol shone brightly before it. The nycaloth screeched once and staggered back, its talons raised in front of its eyes—and it froze, motionless, its green scaly hide suddenly growing clear and translucent. In the space of an instant the monster was turned into glass.

Sarya motioned to her fey'ri. "Get rid of that," she snarled.

A pair of vrocks wrestled the glass nycaloth out of the way, and hurled the petrified creature from the battlements in the same spot where the iron door had been dropped. The nycaloth exploded into countless shards of flying glass below, but Sarya paid the creature no mind. She turned her attention to the symbol guarding Maalthiir's tower, and she chanted the words of a powerful cancellation spell. The symbol glowed once under the force of her magic before it vanished.

"A potent defense, Maalthiir, but not sufficient to repel my attack," Sarya gloated.

She stepped aside, and her demons and hellspawned warriors poured into the fortress. Great gouts of hellfire exploded in the doorway, and she heard the ring of steel on steel and screams of terror. Maalthiir doubtless had many arcane defenses within his tower, but he likely had never planned on fighting off the attack of hundreds of demons and hellspawned warriors at one stroke. Towering constructs of stone and iron animated in defense of the first lord's sanctum. Yugoloths and demons shattered the living statues with their fearsome hellfire. Red Plume guards fought desperately to drive off the attack, only to fall by the score under fey'ri swords and demon claws.

"Find Maalthiir! Slay him!" Sarya cried. "Leave no one alive!"

Powerful spells and wards appeared to slay or block Sarya's minions, but she and her most skillful sorcerers struck down Maalthiir's defenses or simply overwhelmed them by hurling yugoloths and demons into the shrieking arcs of destruction until the spells were exhausted. Daemonfey magic shattered walls, broke open vaults, and set the tower burning with hellish red flames that leaped and spread, dancing through the First Lord's Tower.

For half an hour Sarya and her warriors tore Maalthiir's burning tower apart, searching for any sign of the first lord or his elite guards. But finally Sarya grudgingly gave up on destroying Maalthiir in person. Even if he had been present at the beginning of the attack, she had no doubt that he would have fled rather than stay to defend his citadel against her attack. She watched over the destruction, delighting in the screams of terror. Maalthiir would not soon forget her visit. And better yet, Xhalph was at that very moment leading an even larger attack against the Red Plumes encamped near the Standing Stone, fifty miles to the south. She had no intention of giving her foes any more set-piece battles, not when she commanded thousands of hellspawned warriors and demons who could appear out of thin air or strike like dragons out of the night sky. Xhalph was under orders to slaughter, not fight—to rake the standards and pavilions in the heart of the Red Plume camp with hellfire and deadly spells, then withdraw with chaos in his wake.

Next, she'd visit the same terror on the Sembians. Then she'd turn her infernal hordes against those wretched humans in Mistledale or Shadowdale, and Evermeet's accursed army. There would be no disaster at the Lonely Moor to save Evermeet's traitors from destruction at her hands. With each sunset her armies grew stronger. More and more demons and yugoloths answered her summons and poured through the gates she'd opened in Myth Drannor. The next time Sarya met Evermeet in battle, she did not intend to be defeated.

Maalthiir will not elude me forever, she decided.

She had other things to do that night, and she had harried Hillsfar enough for the time being. Sarya called for her captains and demons, and strode out of Maalthiir's burning tower into a night that had turned red with fire.

"Well done, my children! Well done!" Sarya cried. She looked back on the inferno that had been Maalthiir's tower, and the firelight danced in her malevolent green eyes. "Now come away. We have more slaying to do tonight."

☙ ☙ ☙ ☙ ☙

The first three steps into the swirling gray mist seemed harmless enough, though Araevin's ankles crawled at the sensation of the thick vapor tugging at him as he moved deeper. It felt as if he were wading into a sea, warm and thick as blood. He could see the white tree trunks and silver-green boughs behind him, the fair green hills of silver-tasseled grass rising not far behind him, the pale mossy stones of the road leading back into the luminous depths of the twilit forest. Then Araevin took another step, and he plummeted into darkness.

He cried out and flailed, his senses reeling, transfixed in a moment of endless falling—but then his foot fell on the next step of the road. He stumbled to his knees and found himself on all fours on a path made of dull paving stones covered over with thick, oily black moss. The stink of wet rot assailed his nostrils, and he looked up into a pallid, festering jungle. Sildëyuir's silver starlight was gone, leaving only a humid, cloying blackness, broken only by the sickly green phosphorescence of huge, rotting toadstools.

The trees are dead, he realized. The great silver-white boles of Sildëyuir's forest still surrounded him, but they were leprous and gray, choked by more of the black moss and sagging under the weight of parasitic fungi. He had not left Sildëyuir, not really. The gray vapors marked the border of a creeping blight, a monstrous disease consuming an entire world.

His gorge rising at the smell of the place, Araevin pushed himself to his feet and wiped his hands on his cloak. The foul moss left long black smears on the elven graycloth. He turned to look for his companions, and for a horrible moment he saw that he was alone—until Ilsevele suddenly appeared in midair, only an arm's-reach from where he stood. She gasped aloud and reeled, but Araevin caught her arm and steadied her.

"I have you," he said. "The disorientation will pass."

"It's horrible," Ilsevele gasped.

Araevin didn't know if she referred to the smell or appearance of the place, or her own nausea, but he held her while she found her feet. In the space of a few moments the rest of the company joined them, each appearing one by one. Donnor Kerth set his face in a fierce scowl and said nothing. Maresa winced and found a handkerchief, binding it over her nose and mouth.

Nesterin stared around the poisoned forest in horror. "This is what the nilshai have brought to us?" His voice broke, and he hid his face. "Better that it had been unmade entirely, than to be corrupted like this!"

"Nesterin, is this the road to Mooncrescent? Do we continue?" Araevin asked.

The star elf studied the landscape. "It could be. The lay of the land is right. But this is not Sildëyuir. It is a foul lie."

Araevin was not sure if the place was as unreal as Nesterin believed. Some great and terrible magic was at work, that much was plain to see. Maybe Sildëyuir's corrupted lands had acquired the traits of the nilshai world through some unforeseen planar conjunction. The creeping blight could have been a terrible spell or curse created by the nilshai to change the star elves' homeland into a place where they might exist comfortably. Perhaps some other force was at work—the presence of a malign god, the corruption of an evil artifact, *something*.

Whatever it was, Araevin knew for certain that he did not want to remain in the rotting forest a moment longer than he had to.

"Let's go on," he said to his companions. "The sooner we find the tower, the sooner we can leave."

They set out at once, picking their way along the overgrown roadway. The paving stones were slick and wet and made for difficult footing. Bulging, fluid-filled fungi dangled obscenely from the branches of the dying trees along the roadway, some overhanging the road itself. The whole place dripped, stank, and seemed to almost murmur and hiss with the rustlings and clicking of unwholesome things that wriggled and crawled in the slime and putrefaction of the forest floor. From time to time they encountered huge mounded balls of green-glowing fungus blocking the road, and when they set their swords to the stuff to clear a path, it broke with soft popping sounds and disgorged emerald streams of foulness across the path.

"We must put an end to this," Nesterin said. "When we return, I will have Lord Tessaernil send for the other great mages of the realm. Together they may be able to stem this foul tide. Or, if they cannot, perhaps they can rescribe the borders of Sildëyuir, excluding the corrupted parts."

"If I can help you, I will," Araevin promised. "This is an abomination."

"*Shhh!*" hissed Maresa. She stood still at the rear of

the party, looking back the way they had come. "There is something following us."

"What do you see?" Kerth asked, peering into the darkness behind them. His human eyes did not fare well in the thick shadows and witch-light of the place.

"It's not what I see, it's what I hear," Maresa said. "It's big, and it's coming closer. Can't you hear the toadstools popping back there?"

They all fell silent for a moment, straining to listen. Araevin caught the sound almost at once, a distant slopping or squelching as if someone had filled a bellows half full of water and was working it slowly. And as Maresa had said, there was an awful wet popping sound that preceded the other thing. He couldn't even begin to imagine what might make a sound like that, but there was no doubt that it was coming closer.

"Gods," murmured Jorin Kell Harthan. "What *is* that?"

"I prefer not to find out," Ilsevele answered. She tapped the ranger on the shoulder and pointed down the road. "Come on, let's pick up the pace. Maybe it's moving across our path instead of following us."

"Optimist," muttered Maresa, but the genasi did not disagree when Jorin and Ilsevele set off at an easy trot, pressing on down the road. They made another mile or more, by Araevin's reckoning. Abruptly they emerged from the closeness of the forest, and Araevin felt a great open space before him. He strained to see in the darkness, and gradually realized that sickly green luminescence marked out the great ramparts of a dark citadel before them.

Even though he could only catch a glimmer of its shape, Araevin recognized the place at once. It was the empty citadel he'd seen in his vision, the tower that Morthil raised long ago. Morthil's shining door was near, and with it the secret of the *Telmiirkara Neshyrr*. A lambent gleam stirred in the heart of the Nightstar, and sibilant whispers of ancient secrets gathered in the corners of his mind. Saelethil knew he was close, and the evil shade was watching him from the depths of the *selukiira*; Araevin could feel it.

"Is this the place, Nesterin?" Jorin asked.

The star elf gazed on the citadel's moss-grown battlements and said, "Yes. That is Mooncrescent Tower."

"Why in the world did your mages build it so close to the edge of your realm?" Maresa asked.

Nesterin grimaced. "It was not always like this. I think things have been slipping toward the mist for some time now. The tower disappeared from our realm decades ago. I suppose it has been here all that time."

"Inside, and quickly," Ilsevele said. "We are not alone out here."

They followed the road to a steep, climbing causeway that wound up the face of the low hill on which the tower sat. The air was warm, humid, and still, so thick that small sounds vanished in the darkness. At the top of the causeway, a great dark gate yawned open, leading into the lightless depths of the ancient stronghold.

"Be careful," Nesterin said to the others. "There were powerful spells in this place long ago, and the nilshai are drawn to magic."

Araevin drew his disruption wand from his belt, and paused to review the spells he held ready in his mind. Donnor Kerth slid his broadsword from its sheath, and shrugged his battered shield off his shoulder, while Maresa cocked her crossbow and set a bolt in the weapon. Then Araevin spoke the words of a minor spell, and illuminated the tower's open gateway. The surrounding darkness quickly smothered the light of the spell, but it carried a short distance at least.

Mooncrescent Tower was better described as a large castle than a simple tower or keep. High curtain walls and strong ramparts enclosed a broad courtyard in which a number of once-elegant buildings stood. At the far side of the bailey stood the keep proper, a sheer edifice of graying stone that disappeared into the oppressive darkness above Araevin's feeble light. The courtyard beyond the tower gates was choked by an orchard of once proud old fruit trees, all dead and rotting. Hanging curtains of green-black moss fouled the elegant arcade of arches that ran along the foot of the walls, and the trees were black with dank, sagging bark.

"This place is huge," said Jorin. "Where do we start?"

"The front hall of the keep," Araevin answered. "That's the place I saw in my vision. Morthil's Door is there."

They crossed the courtyard carefully, brushing through the wet hanging branches of the dead trees. Weed-choked fountains and mold-grown statues were hidden in the dark foliage, a reminder of the elf artisans who had once raised the place. At the far side of the orchard, they climbed up a broad flight of steps to the keep's doorway. Like the castle gate, it stood open, lightless as a pit. Araevin could hardly make out anything more than the silhouettes of his companions in the heavy darkness, despite his light spell. He couldn't imagine how Jorin or Donnor could see a thing.

He led the way up the steps and into the keep's hall, the Nightstar whispering in his mind. Once the place had been a great chamber indeed, with a soaring arched ceiling and high galleries overhead. The walls were painted with rich frescoes, but the foulness of the corrupt plane had had its way with the paintings and the majestic old tapestries. Thick gray lumps of gelatinous mold left the paintings mottled and leprous, and the tapestries drooped to the ground.

The shining silver door was nowhere in sight.

"Araevin, what are we looking for?" Ilsevele asked. "This is the right place, isn't it?"

"One moment," he said. He was certain the Door was there; visions did not lie, though it was possible that he had not understood what he'd seen. He fought down his sudden panic at that thought, and carefully pronounced his seeing spell, weaving his hands in the precise mystic passes of the casting.

The murk of the room lightened before his eyes, and the original shape of the ruined paintings and tapestries became clear to him. He had no attention to spare on the room's ruined splendor, though—before him, revolving slowly in the air, a spiral of dancing silver light shimmered with ancient magic.

"Morthil's Door," he breathed.

It was there, as his vision had predicted, simply hidden from hostile eyes by the star elf's old wards.

Araevin stepped forward, admiring the artistry of the ancient spell, but then he heard something strange. From the shadows overhead came a soft, fluttering, piping sound like the quick trill of a flute, followed by an odd crumpling or dull snapping beat. Araevin froze and stared up at the dark galleries in the top of the chamber, searching for the source.

"Beware!" cried Nesterin. "The nilshai come!"

The black hallways leading into the chamber erupted with the twisting blue-black forms of the alien nilshai, darting and swooping as they poured into the room. In the space of five heartbeats a dozen of the monsters appeared in the darkness, burbling and calling to one another in their weird piping voices.

Maresa's crossbow snapped, and one nilshai balled up in a dark tangle in midair, shrieking in anguish around the quarrel embedded in its wormlike body. Ilsevele and Jorin began to fire as well, sending arrow after arrow up at the creatures. But the nilshai were not so easily driven off. Two of the creatures flared their wings and hovered, stabbing down at Araevin and his companions with brilliant bolts of lightning. Araevin leaped aside and rolled on the flagstones, his cloak smoking from a shower of hot sparks, and the rest of his companions scattered.

He found his knees and hurled a blazing fireball up into the middle of the chamber. A great burst of crimson flame blossomed overhead with a frightful roar, blackening the old tapestries and sloughing the gray mold from the walls. Nilshai reeled wildly and shrilled in anger, but before Araevin had even climbed to his feet the monsters resumed their attack. One struck at Donnor with some kind of illusionary threat that only the Lathanderian could see. The human knight cried out in dismay and began to fend off an imaginary attacker with desperate parries of his heavy blade, backing across the hall and leaving his companions to fend for themselves. Another of the monstrous sorcerers created a whole writhing nest of blind, sucking lampreylike maws right at Nesterin's feet, and the star elf battled furiously to pluck the slavering mouths from his limbs as the things fastened themselves on him.

"Get them off me!" he shouted.

Arrows hissed in the darkness, and more nilshai trilled in pain or lunged out with their awful magic. Araevin spied one of the monsters hovering back out of the fight, engaged in a great summoning spell that it was completing with fearsome quickness.

I don't want to see what it's trying to conjure up there, he decided.

He threw out his hand and barked the words of a powerful spell, and before the nilshai finished its terrible conjuration a great golden hand materialized around it. The giant-sized fist closed around the monster, cutting off its spell and crushing the flying worm against the far wall, slowly grinding the life from the thing.

Araevin whirled to look for a new foe, but another of the nilshai seized his body in a telekinetic grip and hurled him into the air. He heard Ilsevele shout in terror, and the room spun end-over-end. As quick as he could, Araevin began a flying spell to save himself from the fall, but he was too slow—he hit the cracked flagstones with a bone-jarring impact before he finished. His skull bounced on the stone floor, and everything went black for a long, cold moment.

Damn, he thought. *They're quick.*

He started to fight his way back up through the darkness to his battling comrades, distant and strangely high above him. With a groan Araevin managed to roll over onto his elbows and knees, and pushed himself upright. His head swam and his left arm dangled at his side with a searing hot pain burning in his forearm.

He staggered to his feet and pointed his wand at the first nilshai he could see, barking out the command word for the device. A terrible shriek of tortured air split the darkness as the frightful blue bolt of disruption ripped the ancient hall, bursting one of the nilshai asunder and tearing the wing from another one behind the first. Araevin whipped around to blast at another one of the aerial sorcerers, but he missed the creature—in the blink of an eye it simply vanished from sight, teleporting away.

All around him, the sounds of battle slowly faded. He looked around, and realized that the nilshai had broken off the fight, fleeing back into the black depths of the old tower. Half a dozen of the monsters lay crumpled on the dark flagstones around the party, some burned, some riddled with arrows and bolts, one hacked into pieces.

"They ran off!" Maresa cried. "Come on back whenever you're ready, you foul flying slugs!"

"Is everybody all right?" Ilsevele asked. She straightened up, still searching the dark galleries overhead for any sign of the flying monsters.

Araevin glanced around. Nesterin bled freely from the ugly sucker bites on his legs and arms, and Jorin was hunched over, his clothes smoking from the lightning bolts the nilshai had thrown. But they all seemed alive, and no one terribly hurt. He looked down at his left arm. His hand trembled and ached when he tried to close his fist.

"I think I broke my arm," he said.

Donnor Kerth sheathed his sword and came over to examine his hand. "So it seems," the Lathanderian agreed. He chanted a healing prayer, setting one big hand firmly over Araevin's injured arm, and the hot ache faded somewhat. "It will trouble you some for a day or two, but you should be able to use it now," Kerth said.

"Thank you," said Araevin. He flexed his arm and made a fist. It hurt, but not as badly as before.

"Now what, Araevin?" asked Ilsevele. "Where do we go from here?"

"Morthil's Door," Araevin replied. He spoke a few arcane words, and revealed the floating aura for his companions to see. Nesterin's eyes widened in wonder. "What I'm looking for is in there."

"Do what you came here to do, and do it quickly," Jorin advised. "The damned nilshai might return at any time."

"Go ahead, Araevin," Ilsevele said. Her bow was still in her hand, and she shook the hair out of her eyes. "We will stand watch."

"I will be as quick as I can," Araevin promised. He turned to face the revolving cloud of silver lights in the room's center. It, too, was a portal of sorts. He whispered the words of an opening spell. The nimbus of magic slowed its turning, and grew brighter, so bright that his companions could make it out even without Araevin's help.

Without waiting, Araevin stepped into the gleaming spiral of magic. At once he felt himself carried away, lifted up into a marvelous chamber of streaming mist and translucent walls, a ghostly room that hovered in the air above the black courtyard. His companions stared at him in amazement, but they were dim and indistinct. He suspected that he'd become nothing more than a spectral blur of himself when he entered Morthil's Door, at least to the eyes of any who waited outside. But within the ghostly chamber, he felt completely solid. He glanced down at his hands, and found that his body had indeed grown somewhat translucent. He could see the lightless hall outside through his own garments and flesh.

Some sort of extradimensional space, he decided. Araevin was familiar with spells of the sort, though he had never studied any of them at length, and hadn't heard of any that endured as long or as perfectly as Morthil's evidently had. He turned his attention to the chamber's contents, and as he did so he felt himself drift farther into the ghostly walls. The world outside faded to a dull dark smear obscured by misty walls beneath his feet, and the ghostly chamber grew more substantial. Spectral shelves and tomes began to appear all around him, the secret library Morthil had preserved in the ethereal matrix so long ago.

Morthil did not want that knowledge to be lost, Araevin realized. He created a place where his books and tomes would be preserved forever, safe from harm or theft, yet accessible to anyone who entered without deceit. Even though Mooncrescent Tower had been swallowed entirely by the nilshai plane, Morthil's library survived unspoiled.

I have to find a way to bring this out of darkness. I cannot leave it here like this.

He glanced up, at the higher and better-defined floors overhead, and his eye fell on a great dome above him. Centered beneath the streaming mists stood a reading stand carved in the shape of two entwined silver dragons. In their outstretched claws they held a large, heavy tome of burnished copper plate, its pale vellum pages shining brightly in the muted light.

It was the tome he had seen in his vision, the tome in which Morthil had inscribed the words of the *telmiirkara neshyrr,* the Rite of Binding.

He approached the massive tome on its ornate stand. He could feel the magical power contained in the book. Golden glyphs crawled across its burnished pages, glowing softly in the sourceless light of Morthil's vault. He could no longer see or hear his companions in the black hall outside, but he paid that no mind. The tome absorbed his attention completely.

He touched the pages, and sigils of molten gold lifted from the tome and began to swirl around him. An eldritch melody of ancient notes thrummed in the air, as if the book itself spoke to him.

Eyes shining in wonder, Araevin began to read.

CHAPTER SEVENTEEN

1 Flamerule, the Year of Lightning Storms

Curnil looked ahead into the thick green woods, dark and damp with the second straight day of rain, and shook the raindrops from his hair. All around him rode the cavalry of the elven-host, a column of gray-clad riders moving quietly alongside the Ashaba like so many ghosts. The battle at the Zhentish camp was six days behind Evermeet's army. The elves and all the Dalesfolk who could be spared marched hard, retracing their steps back toward Ashabenford. Curnil was no strategist, but it was plain enough to him that Lord Miritar had no choice but to march the army back to Mistledale as fast as he could.

Since the skirmish at the farmhouse, Ingra and Curnil had stayed with Storm Silverhand, riding in a small company made up of all sorts of odds and ends. Some were plain-looking Grimmar who turned out to be former adventurers, murderously deliberate in the thickest of fights. Others were freebooters and travelers from all corners of Faerûn who had simply showed up to ride at Storm Silverhand's side. None of the twenty-odd riders who followed the Bard of Shadowdale wore a uniform or held a commission, but Curnil guessed that half of them at least wore the silver pin of the Harpers under their dirty jerkins and worn hauberks. They'd all fought like lions on the earthworks of the Zhentish camp.

Curnil glanced toward the head of their small company, where Storm Silverhand rode, her long white hair plastered to her back. She was laughing and speaking with one of the other riders in their odd little company, when she whipped her head up and to the left, searching the treetops overshadowing the narrow track alongside the river. He glanced that way, wondering what had caught her eye, when realization dawned.

"Ambush," he hissed.

From the treetops a dozen brilliant bolts of fire streaked down, exploding among the elven cavalry all around Storm's small company. Horses whinnied and screamed, fair voices cried out in pain or fear, and the dull gray drizzle of the day flashed into heat, steam, and mayhem. A fire-bolt blasted into a rider near Curnil, incinerating man and mount in one terrible, glaring blast that hurled gobbets of liquid fire throughout the small company. One thick gout splattered across his horse's face and clung to the animal's flesh, blazing fiendishly. The animal bolted off at once, fleeing in blind panic.

"Whoa! Whoa, damn you!" Curnil cried, but he realized that he would never get the animal under control with the fire clinging to its face.

Curnil kicked his feet out of the stirrups, and let the horse run out from under him. He stumbled into the mud on the trail, but a moment later he had his feet under him again, and he scrambled ten feet toward the river to crouch by a boulder and figure out what was going on.

The air was filled with winged swordsmen and sorcerers, armed for battle. Curnil stared in amazement. They were elves, of a sort, though their skin had a crimson hue and their eyes blazed with malice.

"The daemonfey," he breathed.

The first flight swooped past the panicked column, and Curnil saw that it was not a true ambush. The daemonfey had simply streaked in through the rain and drizzle, soaring low and fast over the treetops and falling on the elven column like a fiery thunderbolt. More spells and blasts came from above as the creatures wheeled in midair, scouring the track with emerald globes of acid and crackling yellow lightning. Curnil's ears rang with the fury of the explosions.

White arrows hissed up through the air at the flying sorcerers, and a few of the daemonfey warriors reeled or crumpled in flight. Storm Silverhand burned half a dozen of the sinister warriors out of the air with a great blast of blinding silver fire, carving an argent swath out of the rain-streaked sky.

Curnil swept his swords out of their scabbards and shouted defiance up at the sky. "Come on down and fight, you bastards!"

He had cause to regret his challenge only a moment later. A wave of strange, low booming sounds washed over him, leaving a foul acrid stink in the air. All around the column terrible demons appeared, teleporting into the elven ranks. Behind Storm Silverhand a pair of hulking monsters materialized, gripping huge cleavers in their horned claws. But the silver-haired swordswoman was already engaged in a furious melee with two more monsters in front of her, her sword flashing as she battled against them.

"Storm! Behind you!" Curnil shouted.

He hurled himself forward, charging at the demons attacking her. For one timeless instant the battle drifted motionless around him, his blood thundering in his ears, and Storm turned slowly to meet the new threat. Then he crashed into the closest of the ogre-sized monsters, ramming the point of his silvered sword into the small of its back. Curnil was not a small man, and even though the green-scaled monster towered over him, he sent the thing stumbling off-balance directly into Storm Silverhand.

With a single clean slash of her gleaming sword, she took the demon's head. She flashed Curnil one quick smile, the fierce smile of a warrior born, and her eyes flew open in horror.

A terrible blade of bronze flashed past Curnil's eyes and slammed into his shoulder, driving him to his knees. He grunted in cold shock, as the hulking demon wrenched its gore-spattered cleaver out of his chest. Hot metal grated on bone, and a horrible spurt of blood burst out of Curnil's collar.

"Curnil!" screamed Storm.

The demon's blade stuck for a moment, and with a growl of irritation the hellspawned monster shook Curnil viciously until he was flung off the axe. He landed badly, crumpled in the mud of the trail.

Get up, he told himself. You'll die if you just lie here.

But dark spots gathered at the corners of his vision, and he felt empty. His swords slipped from his grasp.

He tried to push himself upright, to stand, to clap a hand over the awful wound, even to call for help, but he had no strength in his limbs and no breath in his throat.

Damn, he thought. I don't think I can get up.

Then the darkness swallowed him.

☙ ☙ ☙ ☙ ☙

Araevin sat cross-legged on the floor of Morthil's vault. The great tome of the star elf archmage lay open on his lap, but he no longer looked at it. The *telmiirkara neshyrr* was upon him, and having begun it, he was powerless to draw back. Of their own accord the endless passages and phrases of the rite tumbled from his mouth, and the air of Morthil's library trembled with the magic he had unleashed.

Some small part of him wondered how long he had been engaged in the reading, how much time had passed since he had spoken the words Morthil had learned from Ithraides and left for others after him to find. With each word he felt his power, his strength, his vitality draining away, dissipating like frost misting away on a winter morning, leaving him empty, hollow and aching. He could not bear to continue another moment, and yet he realized that if he halted there he would not survive.

He pressed on, repeating the ancient prayers and supplications of the spell, even as his strength began to fail him and his chin drooped toward his chest.

I cannot stop, he told himself. I must not stop.

Yet even though his will was firm, his words began to slur, and his voice dropped to a mumble. He felt like a cold cinder, a graying coal reduced to nothing but an empty shell of ash.

Softly, slowly, he slumped to the mist-wreathed floor.

It feels as though I'm falling asleep, he thought. Falling asleep with my mind awake.

Am I dying?

He knew that he should care about dying, that he had great things to do and friends who needed him, but Araevin had no determination left to fend it off. He had lived long and well, he had traveled the world and left it a better place than he had found it. What was there to fear?

He surrendered to the soft gray blanket that was stealing over him. Darkness hovered within, strangely close and warm, but then he sensed a growing light. He felt a presence approaching, coming to him through the dark. It was a woman, radiant and beautiful, an elf in shape and features, yet incandescent with the power contained in her form.

He looked up to her, and saw her with his own eyes. She was a creature of starshine and wonder, a fey queen whose eyes shone like the sun. There was light and affection of a sort in her face, but there was something more besides—a terrible strength and willfulness that awed him. She was magic made flesh, the sudden power of the storm, the capriciousness of the wind, the delight of the ancient stars.

"An eladrin," he whispered. I have called a queen of the Court of Stars, a high lady of the fey lords!

She stooped over him, her eyes stern, and laid a hand

on his forehead. Her touch was frigidly cold.

Few have spoken the words you have spoken this day, she said with her eyes alone. *Is this truly what you wish, Araevin Teshurr?*

"It is what I have to do," he answered, his breath as faint as candlelight.

There is nothing that you have *to do,* she said. *That is the gift of the gods to mortals. To complete the* telmiirkara neshyrr *is to surrender something precious beyond words.*

He looked into her eyes, as brilliant as suns, and did not flinch.

The fey queen seemed to sigh. *You will learn the price of your power, Araevin,* she told him. *But this, too, you are free to choose.*

She leaned down and kissed him, her lips soft yet bitterly cold, and she breathed into his mouth a single whisper of breath.

Radiance, warmth, and life poured into his heart. He drew a great breath, and felt his soul kindle in unbearable fire. Yet it did not harm him, and it did not diminish. In the space of a dozen heartbeats the fire within had spread to the tips of his fingers and the bottoms of his feet, until it felt as though his entire body was a single sheet of steel-hard flame, dancing and flowing and burning and yet frozen into the shape of an elf.

He looked at the white lady in wonder. "What have you given me?" he asked.

It is not what I have given you, Araevin Teshurr. It is what I have taken away. She smiled sadly, and her eyes glimmered. *You will count this a great gift for now, yet you will also know regret.*

Then she vanished, fading away into golden light and leaving him alone in Morthil's ethereal sanctum.

Morthil's great tome was lying beside him, closed.

Araevin lay there for a long moment, trying to understand what it was he felt. Then, slowly, he pushed himself upright. He glanced up at the ethereal walls of Morthil's vault, and realized that he could *see* the threads of magic, the warp and woof of the Weave, woven with skill and care thousands of years ago. He reached out to touch a wall, and watched as his fingertips caused a ripple in the flowing magic just as a child might start a ripple in a still pool by brushing his fingers over the water.

Despite himself, he laughed out loud in delight.

He noticed that his fingertips seemed to glow in his mystic sight. Frowning, he drew his hand close to his face and studied it. Veins of magic pulsed beneath his skin, intertwined with his own blood. His flesh was possessed of an unmistakable radiance. It was still his own hand, warm, alive, and feeling, yet it was changed. Like a fine golden foil it served to indicate his shape and form, but it was delicate, paper-thin, nothing but a hollow shell of magic in which his sense of self existed.

Is this in my mind? he wondered. Only a perception of the rite's completion? Or have I really . . . changed?

He decided that he simply could not encompass what had happened during the *telmiirkara neshyrr,* not at that moment. In time he might make sense of it, weigh the words of the eladrin queen, sort out the strange sense of self and detachment he felt mingled in his own body, but he could not do it now. He could only continue on this desperate course, and finish what he had started. There would be time to comprehend and reflect later.

Araevin drew the Nightstar from his breast and held the gemstone in his hand. In his new vision he could hardly stand to gaze on the device, so great and dire was its power; it blazed like an amethyst fire in his hand.

Is this what Kileontheal and the others saw when they looked on the Nightstar? he wondered. Or have I gained powers of perception that even other high mages do not share?

He frowned, and effortlessly he hurled his consciousness into the gemstone, descending down through its lambent depths like a falling meteor. He sensed the vastness and the purpose of the thing, just as he had before, but this time he retained his bearings. He arrowed straight for the heart of the gem. The Nightstar no longer held the power to overwhelm him.

"I am coming, Saelethil," Araevin said, and he bared his teeth in challenge.

❦ ❦ ❦ ❦ ❦

Ilsevele studied the oppressive gloom that smothered the ancient hall, and shuddered. The air was hot and rank, and she felt a cold sick sense of danger beneath her ribs. The place was perilous; she could feel it, and she knew that the others sensed it as well. They'd beaten off two more nilshai incursions in the time since they'd entered the place, but above and beyond the danger posed by the alien sorcerers infesting the place, the nilshai world itself was dangerous. The longer they remained, the deeper they seemed to sink into the darkness, even though they hadn't moved from that spot for hours.

I fear that retracing our steps back to Sildëyuir will prove harder than finding our way to this tower, she thought.

"How much longer will Araevin need?" grumbled Maresa. She glanced over at the revolving spiral of faint white light hovering in the room's center. They'd tried several times to follow Araevin through the door, but apparently they lacked something the portal required. "He's been in there too long! I want to get out of this place."

"Unless the nilshai return in overwhelming force, we will remain here and guard Araevin's back," Ilsevele said. "He is counting on us, Maresa."

The genasi snorted and returned her attention to Ilsevele. "What if he's stuck in there, and can't get out? What if it's a one-way gate? How long do we give him before we leave?"

"We remain until we are forced to leave," Ilsevele repeated. She turned her back on Maresa and walked a short distance away, making a show of peering down a black corridor as if to check on it, but in truth she was avoiding the argument, and she knew it.

What happens if the nilshai come back? she asked herself. Is it worth our lives to protect what Araevin is doing?

Or do we abandon this expedition if the danger grows too great? It would be easier to answer that question if she were absolutely certain that Araevin's quest was something that *had* to be done.

If I knew there had been no choice but to come here, it would be easy to steel myself to stand and die in this black chamber if necessary, she thought. *But I wonder what Father is doing. Has the Crusade joined battle against the daemonfey in Myth Drannor? And just how might I have been able to help if I were there instead of here?*

"Something is coming," Jorin called in a low voice. The Yuir ranger crouched on the moss-covered remains of one of the higher balconies, his bow in hand. "The same thing we avoided in the forest, I think."

Ilsevele cocked her head to one side, and she heard it as well—a distant wet wheezing or sucking sound, slowly squishing its way closer.

Did the nilshai corral the creature to send it at us? she wondered. *Or did it follow us of its own accord?*

"Everyone, move to a new place," she called softly. "They're expecting to find us where they saw us last."

She followed her own advice, and darted across the hall to stand hidden in a narrow alcove. Maresa simply leaped up and levitated to the highest gallery; as a daughter of the elemental wind, she could take to the air when she liked. Donnor moved beside a pillar where he could watch the doorway leading back out to the courtyard of the keep. Nesterin flashed a quick smile at Ilsevele, and found an alcove opposite hers.

They waited in silence, listening to the approach of the unseen monster. Ilsevele laid a pair of arrows across her bow, and whispered the words of a spell to set them both smoldering with arcane power. The horrible squelching drew closer, and she heard the abominable piping voices of the nilshai, several of them warbling to each other in the black tunnels around the banquet hall. Peering into the dank gloom, she finally caught a glimpse of the massive creature drawing near.

Its skin glistened a translucent pink in the dim light of

the glowing doorway in the room's center. Its flesh oozed and rippled as it heaved itself closer, and Ilsevele glimpsed the indistinct outlines of a wormlike body and a ring-shaped mouth surrounded by small, rasping teeth. The thing was the size of a small inn, and she exhaled in relief. It was so large that it couldn't fit through the archway leading to the courtyard outside.

"Thank Corellon," she murmured, and straightened up.

The thing quivered for a moment, blindly groping for a way inside. Then it found the archway and began to press forward. Its flesh was so malleable that it squeezed through with ease, pouring itself into the room like a viscid stream of slime.

She looked over to Nesterin in horror, and found the star elf looking back at her with a similar expression on his face.

"I thought it couldn't get in!" he protested.

Ilsevele raised her bow and shot. Two arrows flew as one, each flaring into brilliant fire in mid-flight under the power of her spells. They struck the blank wall of glistening flesh and vanished, sinking deep into the monster before coming to rest with the fletching completely submerged. The shafts hung in the thing's body for all to see, burning with bright white light in the worm's snout. The creature quivered and recoiled, but still it groped onward.

"What in the world is that thing?" Ilsevele muttered as she drew two more arrows and readied another spell.

Across the hall from her, Nesterin stepped out of his own alcove and peppered the creature with arrows. More rained down from overhead, where Jorin shot over the edge of the gallery. And Maresa barked the trigger words of her wands, pummeling the worm's snout with bolts of magic.

The creature hesitated for a moment then it lashed out with astonishing speed, firing a pair of long, silky strands from pores in its head right at Nesterin. The star elf ducked under one, but the other struck him in the left thigh and clung to him. Nesterin cried out in revulsion and tried to pull away, but the giant worm gave a small toss of its head and jerked him off his feet. It started to reel in the star elf, retracting its strand and dragging him in with irresistible power.

Nesterin dropped his bow and struggled to draw a knife at his belt, grimly ignoring the terrible rasping maw of the worm as he sought to free himself.

"Let go of him!" Donnor Kerth called.

He stepped out from behind his pillar and dashed over to the strand by which the worm was dragging Nesterin. He gripped his sword and struck a mighty cut at the strand. It parted with a snap, sending Nesterin reeling backward. The worm moved farther into the room and fired two strands at Donnor. Both struck the Lathanderian's shield, and with a savage oath the human knight shook the shield off his arm before he was dragged off his feet. The shield skittered across the floor to the huge monstrosity in the doorway.

"Ilsevele!" Maresa cried. "It's too dumb to know that we're hurting it! What do we do?"

Ilsevele shook her lank hair out of her eyes and looked up at the genasi in amazement.

How in the world should I know? she thought. But she didn't speak her thoughts aloud. Instead, she paused for a moment then called back, "Try fire!"

She changed the spell she was about to lay on the arrows on her bow, and instead chanted the words to a fire spell. Her arrows glowed cherry-red and began to smolder. Quickly she raised her bow and let them fly. They struck together as flaming bolts, and the worm bucked and twisted, crushing masonry and shaking the whole building. Overhead Maresa changed to her fire wand and seared a great black swath across the monster's quaking flesh.

Donnor Kerth dashed at the huge monster, chasing after his shield. He sang out the words of a holy invocation to Lathander as he ran, and the broadsword in his hand burst into a brilliant yellow corona of flame.

"Burn!" he shouted. "Burn in Lathander's holy fires, foul monster!"

He hacked into the worm's snout, carving great black slashes through its body as his broadsword flared with the heat of the sun.

The worm shuddered and began to retreat, pouring itself back out of the room. It carried away Kerth's shield, shredding the metal war board to pieces with its teeth as it moved away. The Lathanderian howled in outrage and redoubled his efforts, but the worm flowed away and retreated into the darkness outside.

"It took my shield!" he snarled.

"Better your shield than our friend Nesterin," called Jorin from above.

Ilsevele lowered her bow and watched the creature flee. "Is everyone all right?" she asked.

"I will be, as soon as I get this damned stuff off my breeches," replied Nesterin.

The star elf continued to saw at the remnant of the strand that clung to his garb. The stuff was like a cable made of glue, tough and sticky at the same time, and his knife blade kept catching in the stuff. Ilsevele moved over to lend him a hand.

"Thank you," Nesterin murmured. "I hate to say it, Ilsevele, but the longer we remain here, the more likely it is that we will meet with disaster. Is there any chance you could hurry your friend Araevin?"

Ilsevele looked up to the shining mist in the center of the hall. "I would if I could," she answered. "But for now, he seems to be out of our reach."

❂ ❂ ❂ ❂ ❂

Araevin streaked over a hellscape of seething lava and billowing clouds of foul vapor. For the first time he perceived what lay outside the white walls of Saelethil's palace in the heart of the *selukiira*.

This is Saelethil's soul, he realized. This is the part of himself that he preserved for five thousand years in the Nightstar, hoping that his evil might endure long after his physical defeat.

I am the failure of a dark hope nourished for five millennia.

Araevin grinned to himself. He liked the thought of disappointing Saelethil Dlardrageth.

He caught sight of white walls and golden domes glinting amid the ruddy firelight below him, and he altered his course to descend into the heart of the place. With his cloak streaming behind him he alighted in the golden courtyard of Saelethil's palace. The monstrous mockeries of vines and flowers that filled the place shrank from his presence.

"Saelethil!" he called. "I have performed the rite of transcendence. Come forth!"

Behind him he felt a cold and sharp sensation, a gathering of malice that grew stronger in the space of a few heartbeats. He turned and watched as a column of black mist poured up out of the ground to the height of a man. It roiled violently before materializing in the shape of Saelethil Dlardrageth.

"I am here," he said.

Araevin gazed on him without lowering his eyes, and perceived the demonic corruption of the Dlardrageth high mage. Saelethil's very form fumed with intangible streams of spite and hatred, a black thundercloud of ancient anger hidden behind the veil of a noble-born sun elf.

I see more than I did before, he told himself. This is what the *telmiirkara neshyrr* has given to me.

Saelethil looked on him, and in that moment Araevin saw many things in his eyes: recognition, a grudging measure of respect, a bonfire of hatred and envy, and finally, a shadow of fear.

"I see you have followed the path I set you on," Saelethil said. "You have purged yourself of the flaws with which the gods have afflicted all lesser creatures. Only the most powerful of mages learn how to set right what the gods made wrong in the first place. I suppose I should congratulate you, Araevin."

"Save your congratulations," Araevin answered. "I am still myself."

The daemonfey archmage snorted. "You are no more an elf than I am. We are exactly alike, you and I. You have tempered yourself like steel in a smith's fire. I did no more or less than that when I chose my path."

"I am your antithesis, Saelethil." Araevin allowed himself a cold, hard smile. "Morthil's rite invoked the powers of Arvandor instead of the Abyss. I fear you no longer."

Saelethil's eyes flashed in anger. "Then you are a fool, Araevin Teshurr. You believe that you have not damned yourself with your pursuit of power, as if there were a difference between a demon's embrace and an eladrin's kiss! You have surrendered your soul. What does it matter to whom you surrendered it?"

"I did not come to bandy words, Saelethil. I came to study the spells of Aryvandaar, not debate your twisted views on good and evil. Now, show me what you have been hiding all this time."

The Dlardrageth glowered at Araevin for a moment, but then his face twisted into a cruel smile.

"Ah," he said to himself. "Now that I did not anticipate. The irony of it!"

He laughed richly, expansively, and the poisonous flowers of the garden quaked and trembled in reply.

Araevin frowned. Saelethil's persona in the Nightstar was bound by laws the archmage had laid down long ago. That was why the *selukiira* had been bound to him instead of destroying him when first he set his hand to the stone. Yet clearly Saelethil had discerned something new, something that pleased him greatly, and Araevin suspected that he would not like it at all.

"What is it?" he demanded. "I did not come here to be laughed at, Saelethil!"

"Oh, but you did, foolish boy!" Saelethil said. His eyes were cold with contempt as he laughed again. "You have no idea what you have done, do you?"

Araevin folded his arms and simply waited. He did not care to serve as the object of Saelethil's humor.

"When you chose Ithraides's path instead of mine," Saelethil hissed, "you severed yourself from your salvation.

I have not been able to destroy you because I was not permitted to harm one whose soul was marked by descent from my House, no matter how remote." He advanced a step on Araevin, and seemed to grow taller. "By infusing yourself with the celestial essence of the eladrin, you have removed the last thin vestiges of Dlardrageth blood. I am no longer required to serve you, which means that I am free to do with you as I wish."

Araevin stared in amazement. Then he stepped back and snapped out a potent abjuration, building a spell-shield to defend himself for a time while he figured out what to do.

The spell failed. The passes of his hand were nothing more than empty gestures, the words devoid of power.

Saelethil laughed aloud. "This is not a spell duel, Araevin! Your consciousness is enclosed entirely within my substance. Neither of us can work magic here. This is a contest of will."

Saelethil grew larger than a giant, shooting up into the air like a crimson tower, so tall that Araevin stumbled back in astonishment and fell.

"You have placed yourself in my power!" Saelethil boomed. "Now, dear boy, I will repay the indignities I have accumulated in your service!"

He strode forward and set one immense foot on Araevin, crushing him to the hot flagstones below, leaning on him with the terrible weight of a malicious and living mountain.

Araevin cried out in dismay as Saelethil's power gathered over him and crushed him down. Shadow rose up around him, and he felt his very substance, his life, his consciousness, compressed all around, being squeezed out of existence. Saelethil's cruel laughter lashed him like the winds of a dark hurricane, and the malice and power of the Dlardrageth's will filled the universe with black hate.

"Do not fear for your friends, Araevin!" Saelethil cried. "You will rejoin them in a moment—or at least your body will. I have yearned for flesh to wear for longer than you can imagine. You are not so handsome as I was in life, but Ilsevele will not know the difference, will she?"

"You will not lay a hand on her, monster!" Araevin screamed in empty protest.

Saelethil's scorn battered him. "I will do whatever I like with you, fool! You will bring me to my niece Sarya, and I will take up my rightful place as a lord of House Dlardrageth. I may even allow you to retain a glimmer of awareness so that you can perceive the extent of your defeat. I owe you that much after the servitude you have visited upon me."

Araevin despaired in the shrieking blackness beneath Saelethil's will. He had stumbled into the very fate he had first feared when he found the Nightstar; the *selukiira* would crush his sentience and seize his own empty body for its own use. The evils that might follow sickened him. What might a Dlardrageth high mage do, with the freedom of Araevin's own body? Destroy more of Evermeet's high mages? Lead the daemonfey legions against Seiveril Miritar's army? Or simply murder anyone Araevin ever loved?

He struggled to fight back, to find some purchase with which to gather his will and make a stand. For a moment he battled his way back to the palace of Saelethil's heart, struggling on the ground with the foot of a giant pinning him to the stone. But the Dlardrageth grinned at his struggles and caught him by his throat in one fine-taloned hand.

"This is *my* mind, *my* soul," Saelethil gloated. "Within these boundaries, my strength is limitless! Do you not understand that yet?"

Araevin said nothing, but grimly fought against Saelethil's grip, his feet kicking, his chest crying out for air. But Saelethil drew back his arm and hurled him straight down into the ground. The palace of white walls and venomous flowers shattered like a broken mirror, and Araevin plunged into the bottomless darkness underneath, tumbling and falling away from the light.

He shouted in outrage, trying to fight his way up out of the gemstone, escape, return to his own mind and body so that he could simply drop the damned stone and get away from Saelethil Dlardrageth. But he could not stop himself from sinking, falling, drowning in darkness as thick and heavy as a sea of black stone.

CHAPTER EIGHTEEN

3 Flamerule, the Year of Lightning Storms

The horrors of the last two days and nights had hardened Seiveril to death in a dozen gruesome forms, but at last he looked upon something that he could not bear. Not caring who saw him or what they might think, he staggered to his knees and covered his face.

"Ah, Corellon! How have you allowed me to fail your people so?" he cried.

Demons had fallen on a small company of wood elves—*his* wood elves, the merry band from Evermeet's forest who had followed him to Faerûn with such pluck and bravado—and flayed alive all they could catch. Seiveril stood in the center of the carnage, sickened by the sound of flies buzzing thickly around the dead and the mewling cries of those the demons had chosen not to kill. Starbrow let him grieve for a time, standing close by with Keryvian naked in his hand in case the demons returned. Over the past few days Sarya's infernal hordes had struck again and again, hammering at the Crusade as the army of Evermeet fought its way back toward Mistledale to rejoin Vesilde Gaerth. They were still ten miles from Ashabenford, but the smoke of the town's burning streaked the eastern sky.

Starbrow looked at the place where a handful of Seiveril's soldiers had fought and died alone, with no help at hand, and shook his head.

"Gods, what a scene," he murmured. Then he trudged over and set a hand on Seiveril's shoulder. "Come, my friend," he said wearily. "We cannot stay here any longer. The demons may return to attack our healers, and we cannot afford to lose any more clerics. Or you, for that matter."

"I have led us into disaster, Starbrow," Seiveril said. "My pride brought these wood elves to this place, and my stupidity killed them. How can I bear to live?"

"The measure of a general does not lie in victory, Seiveril. It lies in defeat. To continue after the worst has happened is hard, but if you do not lead us from this place, no one will."

Seiveril remained motionless, giving no answer. But then he slowly came to life again, and he nodded once. "If only we had been closer. . . ."

"Frankly, Seiveril, it is a miracle you have kept the army together as well as you have," Starbrow said. "Many have fallen, yes. But many have lived, too. We are not defeated yet." He looked around at the bloodstained clearing, and the gray-cloaked healers who worked silently among those who could still be helped. "Come. You can do nothing more here."

Seiveril followed Starbrow to the far side of the clearing, where Adresin and the rest of Seiveril's guard waited with their mounts. They climbed up into their saddles and rode away, passing through a narrow belt of trees before emerging into the open fields and groves of the Dale proper. The weather had warmed quickly since the fight at the river, and the day was hot and humid. Seiveril could smell a thunderstorm gathering in the air. Doubtless Sarya's demons would strike again in the storm, falling on some other part of his harried army to maim and kill and burn, melting away before he could bring them to battle. That had been the way of it for days.

"We should join up with Gaerth and the companies we left here soon," Starbrow offered. "That's almost two thousand bows, plus many of our best champions. Even Sarya's demons will be deterred by that."

Seiveril suspected that the moon elf was speaking simply to set Seiveril's mind on something other than the horror back in the clearing, but he allowed his friend to pull his thoughts to a new course.

"Vesilde has had an easier time of things than we have," he admitted.

The knight-commander had done as Seiveril had asked, giving ground instead of fighting. His footsoldiers had retired south and west down the Dale, covering the flight of the Dalesfolk and surrendering Ashabenford to the oncoming Sembians. Had the Sembians wanted to, they might have overrun the whole Dale with the help of the Red Plumes, and forced Gaerth to fight, but they had not moved farther into the Dale in days, and Seiveril could not fathom why.

Seiveril rode closer to Starbrow and lowered his voice. "There is something I need to know," he asked. "In the last days of Myth Drannor, when the Army of Darkness roamed Cormanthor . . . Was it like this?"

Starbrow did not look at him. He kept his eyes fixed ahead, gazing on the smoke from the burnings in the distance. "Yes," he said with a sigh. "Yes, it was like this. The orcs, ogres, and gnolls outnumbered us badly, yet we could have defeated them regardless of numbers. But not while legions of demons fought against us too."

"I was afraid you would say that."

Starbrow shrugged. He had always been reluctant to speak of his long-ago life in the days of Myth Drannor. "It's harder than you might think to pick your wars. The ones you least wish are the ones you often have to fight."

"I picked this one, didn't I?"

Starbrow halted and set a hand on Seiveril's reins, pulling the elflord around to face him. Seiveril's horse nickered in protest but turned.

"Sarya Dlardrageth picked this war, Seiveril. If you hadn't decided to stand up to her, she would have sacked Evereska and burned half of the North in her wrath. You answered the call to arms, yes. But that does not mean that you chose this fight." The moon elf looked into Seiveril's face, and after a moment he released the elflord's reins. "If it's any comfort to you, Sarya is not happy with her choice of enemies. She thought she was making war on a scattering of isolated wood elf settlements and a city weakened by a war against the phaerimm. She did not plan on you, my friend, and that is a cause for hope."

Seiveril considered that as they rejoined the column of weary elf soldiers who marched across Mistledale's open fields like a river of dusty steel.

"So what do I do now?" he asked Starbrow.

"Withdraw," the moon elf said. "We don't have the strength to move on Myth Drannor, and there's no point in staying here. The folk from Mistledale have fled to the southern parts of the Dale. We'd be defending empty farmland."

"I can't bear to turn my back on Myth Drannor, not when we're this close."

"What do your auguries tell you?"

Seiveril looked sharply at Starbrow. He hadn't realized that his friend knew the extent to which he had relied on his prayers and spells of guidance during the campaign.

He sighed and said, "This is not the hour to march against Myth Drannor, and disaster awaits us if we stay here. But I can't see what follows from this, Starbrow. If we retreat, what must change for the better before we can take the fight to Sarya again?"

"If we don't retreat, will any of our army be left to draw sword against her in the first place?" Starbrow asked. "There will be another day, Seiveril. The Seldarine did not bring you to this place—or *me* to this place, for that matter—without a purpose."

Seiveril nodded. He, of all people, was not likely to forget that. "Call the captains, Starbrow. We must plan a fighting retreat."

Starbrow clapped him once on the shoulder, and rode off, calling for the captains of the Crusade. The elflord watched him ride off, and looked again to the east. The thunderheads gathered there, moving lazily against the wind. Ominous rumbles rolled across the dry fields.

The storm is upon us, he thought. In more ways than one.

❖ ❖ ❖ ❖ ❖

Araevin plummeted through darkness, an infinite abyss in which the vast power of Saelethil's will threatened to swallow him completely. Grimly, he resolved to endure as long as he could. Even if he was to be extinguished in Saelethil's black hate, he would not go gently.

"You are not real!" he shouted into the endless night. "You are a ghost, a reflection, an echo of a mage who died five thousand years ago! You are not Saelethil Dlardrageth!"

He felt his fall begin to slow, and he turned his will toward arresting his plunge.

"You are nothing, Saelethil! A ghost!"

Saelethil's face appeared before him in the darkness, a titanic apparition that dwarfed Araevin.

"I am substantial enough to destroy you!" the Dlardrageth thundered. "And in your body I will be as real and alive as I ever was. You do not know my strength!"

"You do not know mine," Araevin replied.

He curled into a ball and closed his eyes, blocking out the maddening plunge and terrible vistas of purple towers and bottomless violet wells surrounding him. He envisioned himself as a shining white light smothered in darkness, a diamond glittering under the blow of a terrible black hammer, and he threw his full will into resisting Saelethil as long as he could.

"That will not avail you," Saelethil laughed.

He gathered up the force of his will, and hurled himself down on Araevin's last resistance with the force of a thunderbolt. Araevin screamed with the power of the attack, and darkness welled up to fill his being . . . but somehow he survived the blow.

Saelethil roared in frustration and attacked again, clutching at him, stabbing into his mind with dark blades that seared and cut Araevin's very soul, but Araevin battled on, repelling the blows. Saelethil's voice became the hissing of a demon, great and terrible, and black fires roared up out of the night to incinerate Araevin where he huddled, alone in the dark.

"Yield, curse you! You cannot endure me," Saelethil demanded. *"Yield!"*

"No!" Araevin cried. Saelethil redoubled his assault, but still Araevin refused to let himself be extinguished . . . and with that came the realization that Saelethil might not be *able* to crush him, not unless he allowed it to happen.

I am stronger than I was when I first encountered the Nightstar. I have completed the *telmiirkara neshyrr* and I have shaped high magic. Saelethil's *selukiira* could have destroyed me a few months ago, but no longer.

Saelethil's terrible will lashed Araevin again and again, but Araevin pushed the assaults to one part of his mind, and concentrated on gathering his own counterstroke. In his heart he conceived a white sword, a blade of purpose and perfection. He poured his determination, his hope, his love into the sword. He shaped its point with his pride and ambition, and he envisioned himself gripping the hilt with his hands and drawing back for the blow.

"I will not be extinguished!" he cried back at Saelethil, and with all the force of his will and mind he burst against the darkness, lunging out with his white sword.

In a single great cut he slashed a white gap across the encompassing darkness, and Saelethil screamed a high and horrible scream. The Nightstar trembled and thundered. Araevin lashed out again, and the white-hot fury of his wrath against Saelethil and Sarya, and all the evil the Dlardrageths had wreaked against him, drove him onward. He struck and struck again, until the great violet abyss within the Nightstar blazed with jagged lines of white lightning, and the purple ramparts crumpled in white fire.

The Nightstar's interior filled with an awful flash of white light, and Araevin found himself standing in the courtyard of Saelethil's garden, his sword in his hand. He wheeled about, searching for an adversary, but the horrid crawling vines were withered and dead. He looked at the ruddy fields of lava beyond the walls, yet nothing but cool black rock met his eye.

Saelethil Dlardrageth lay at his feet, a bloodless wound piercing his heart. Even as Araevin watched, Saelethil's form froze into a perfect statue of purple crystal then the crystal grew dark, gray, and brittle. Slowly it crumbled to powder and hissed away into nothingness. Araevin looked at the smear of lambent dust in the dead courtyard, and he turned away, gazing up at the white-shot sky overhead. The Nightstar was evidently damaged, possibly dying.

"The Aryvandaaran spells," Araevin whispered in a sudden panic, and whirled to look around him. But at the instant he conceived a desire to see the secrets within the loregem, he felt an artifice of magic awaken in his presence. Golden scrolls appeared around him, drifting in the air, each seeming to shimmer and tremble with the power of the spell it held.

He stared in wonder, surrounded by the secret hoard of lore. If Saelethil had not lied to Araevin, those spells were ten thousand years old, the legacy of the proudest and most powerful empire of elves that had ever existed in Faerûn. The things that the Aryvandaaran mages might have set down. . . .

Choosing a scroll at random, Araevin gently pulled it closer and began to read.

❂ ❂ ❂ ❂ ❂

The setting sun glowered in the west, sinking into the distant forest amid the acrid smoke of dozens of great fires. The day had been hot, and in the sweltering heat and fumes it seemed that Myth Drannor was burning again. But these were the fires of industry, the spewing plumes of soot and ash from new foundries Sarya's best craftsmen were raising amid the wreckage of Myth Drannor's outlying districts. The air rang with the sound of hammers beating against hot metal as her fey'ri worked to restore one by one the war machines and battle-constructs they had brought with them from Myth Glaurach.

The sound pleased Sarya well. She lingered on the balcony for a time, simply enjoying the open air and the sounds of victory being forged in the ensorcelled foundries of her folk. Then she turned away reluctantly and descended into the great hall of Castle Cormanthor, descending in a single graceful leap, her wings snapping open only at the last moment to arrest her descent.

Her captains bowed deeply, until Sarya took her seat.

"You may rise," she told them.

As they straightened and folded their wings again, she glanced to the side of the dais. There Malkizid stood, a pale swordsman dressed in black robes, his wounded forehead showing only a thin line of dark blood that evening. The devil prince smiled sardonically and inclined his head to her. In the presence of Sarya's underlings he was careful to remain subservient, advising only when asked, never instructing or issuing orders, not even in her name. She believed she was an ally that Malkizid did not want to discard for a long, long time, but only a fool would trust an archdevil, even an exiled one.

She reclined in her throne, and considered her fey'ri lords: Mardeiym Reithel, the brilliant general, resplendent in his dragon-blazoned armor of black mithral; Jasrya Aelorothi, the fierce champion, the match of any bladesinger she had ever seen; Teryani Ealoeth, back from her work among the Sembians with Borstag Duncastle's eyes in a small silk pouch at her belt. They were the tools with which she would raise her new Siluvanede, and her heart glowed with dark pride as she considered her cadre of captains.

"I have tidings from my son," she began. "This afternoon Xhalph broke the Red Plumes on the Moonsea Ride. Maalthiir's army is falling back on Hillsfar in disarray. Meanwhile the Sembian army is vanishing like the snows of last winter. Whole companies of mercenaries have abandoned their standard entirely." Sarya smiled on Teryani Ealoeth. "Lady Teryani, you have done well."

She smiled at the fierce glow of pride that sprang up in Teryani's eyes then returned her attention to the rest.

"Seiveril Miritar and the army of Evermeet are fleeing for their lives. The Zhentarim have been shown to be less than nothing. Everywhere we look, our enemies are in retreat. We are literally the masters of all we survey. No army within a thousand miles dares take the field against us. Cormanthor is ours now, the realm we have waited five thousand years to rule. We are the true heirs of Aryvandaar, and this is our ancient home. No one will deny us our birthright again."

"Command us, Lady Sarya," said Mardeiym Reithel. "We await your bidding."

The other fey'ri lords bowed, and voiced their assent.

Sarya looked down on the fey'ri. Not long ago their faith in her had wavered in the wake of their defeat in the High Forest, but they were hers once again, mind, heart, and soul. She need only stretch out her hand, and they would die to do her bidding. She felt Malkizid's eyes upon her, and she met his avid gaze with a dark smile of her own. Archdevil or not, she was the one who ruled in Myth Drannor.

"A month ago, we did not have the strength to challenge Miritar on the open field," she said. "But we have grown stronger while Evermeet's army has bled in Shadowdale and Mistledale. The time has come to smite Seiveril Miritar and break Evermeet's power, once and for all. We will fall on our ancient enemies like a hurricane of fire, and we will utterly destroy them."

☙ ☙ ☙ ☙ ☙

The blackness in the hall brightened, and Morthil's Door became sharply visible. It started to revolve again, a ghostly image made of white light, and Araevin stepped through. He felt strange, light of step and clear of mind, as if his encounter with Saelethil had served to hammer out of him the last bit of dross that weighed down his heart. His mind reeled with the things he'd survived and seen in the last few hours, and he longed to do nothing more than sit silently for a tenday and simply sort out what he had learned. But he had things to do.

He opened his hand, and let the Nightstar fall to the stone floor. It was dull and gray, its diamond-hard facets starred with countless cracks. He ground the device to powder with his foot, until a single white shard remained, bright and undamaged. He carefully picked up the smaller gemstone and slipped it into his pouch. The spells of Aryvandaar remained within, but nothing else. Then he whispered a minor spell to disperse the gem dust left on the floor.

Good-bye, Saelethil, he thought, and the corners of his mouth turned up in a small, hard smile.

"Araevin! You have returned!" Ilsevele ran up to embrace him, but when he looked up to greet her, she gasped and came to an awkward halt. She stared at him, her face open with amazement. "What . . . what happened in there?" she finally managed.

"I found Morthil's tome, just as I had seen it in my vision, and I performed the *telmiirkara neshyrr*," he said. "After that, I had a word with Saelethil Dlardrageth in the Nightstar. Do not concern yourself with the Nightstar any longer, Ilsevele. Saelethil's sentience in the loregem has been destroyed."

Maresa dropped down from the top of the great hall, alighting near Araevin. "I don't think that is what Ilsevele meant," the genasi said. Her face was tight and concerned, with little of her customary sarcasm in her voice. "Have you looked at yourself, Araevin?"

"Looked at myself?" Araevin glanced down at his clothes, and saw nothing out of the ordinary. But a faint golden glow clung to him, an aura of magic that flowed through him with the smallest motion, as if he swam in a pool of light. It was not bright, but it must have been noticeable, or his friends would not have remarked on it.

A temporary effect of the rite? he wondered. Or something more permanent?

Ilsevele looked at Maresa and said, "I don't expect he would be able to see it. Do you have a mirror?"

"Oh. Of course." Maresa hurried over to kneel by her pack, rooting through her gear for a moment. Then she returned with a hand-sized mirror, and without a word she handed it to Araevin.

Araevin felt his companions watching him, and with a little trepidation he raised the mirror to his face. He saw the cause of their consternation at once, and almost dropped the mirror in surprise.

His eyes were blank, shining orbs of pearly silver without a hint of iris or pupil. Faint streaks of emerald, rose, and sapphire danced within, slowly changing as he watched. And his face was *young,* even more so than might be expected of any elf. He looked as he had when he was twenty-five or thirty, in the first bloom of an adulthood that would last for centuries. Light, promise, and vitality had left his face free of the small marks and habitual expressions he'd accumulated over his long life.

What did the eladrin's kiss do to me? he wondered.

"Araevin . . ." Maresa said quietly. "You're not . . . dead, are you?"

"No," he answered. "No, I'm not. I am not entirely sure what has befallen me, but I know I am not dead." He looked back to Ilsevele. "How long was I inside Morthil's sanctum?"

"It's hard to judge time here," Ilsevele replied, gesturing at the lightless hall pressing in on the small company. "But I would guess twelve hours, perhaps more. We have repelled the nilshai or their monsters several times since you left."

"Did you find what you were seeking?" asked Donnor. "Can you defeat the daemonfey with the lore you've mastered?"

"Yes, I found what I was seeking. As for the daemonfey, we will have to see."

Araevin closed his eyes, thinking back to what he had seen when he stood in the Burial Glen of the ancient city and looked on its mythal's secrets. The wards were old and treacherous, much damaged by the city's fall and the centuries that had passed. Burning wheels of magic turned in his mind, sweeping arcs and crackling fonts that geysered from the ground. He found that he could set names to things he had not known before, and understand more of things he had previously glimpsed only in part.

With a sudden shock, he perceived the true peril that was rising in the heart of Cormanthor. *Doors,* he thought. *A thousand doors. And they are open wide.*

He shook himself free of Ilsevele and stared toward the west, or what would be the west if nilshai-poisoned Sildëyuir were a place where such things mattered, trying to peer through the deadly gloom of Mooncrescent Tower to distant Myth Drannor.

"Aillesel Seldarie," he breathed. "It cannot be!"

"What, Araevin?" Ilsevele demanded. "What is it? What do you see?"

"We must return at once," Araevin said. He looked around at his friends, his eyes glowing like fire opals, luminous and alive. He saw their confusion and fatigue, but he pressed on. "There is a graver threat at hand than the daemonfey, a threat to all Faerûn. We must destroy the Last Mythal of Aryvandaar, or everything is lost. Everything."

EPILOGUE

It was a peaceful spot, a grassy sward high on a hillside, with the cool waters of Lake Sember glinting through the trees a short distance below. The wind sighed in the treetops, and the forest creaked, rustled, and breathed around Fflar, warm and alive with the summer. Insects buzzed and chirped in the noontime sun, and lances of golden daylight splashed the forest floor through hidden gaps in the canopy overhead.

At his feet a smooth stone marker showed the place where Sorenna's spirit had been burned free of its mortal frame, five hundred years ago. She had outlived him by a century and a half, it seemed, there in the restful forests of Semberholme. Still, that was too young, was it not? She would have been a little more than two hundred years in age, with centuries ahead of her still.

Someone might have known her here, he thought. A few of the older moon elves who lingered in Cormanthor after the Elven Court Retreated. I hope it was a peaceful life. So much strife befell our city in the last decades, so much horror in the years of war. It would please me to think that she passed the rest of her days in peace. If I bought her a hundred years of life in Semberholme by spending my last days fighting on without hope, I would count it a bargain.

Fflar's eyes strayed to the marker beside Sorenna's stone, and he felt his heart break for the hundredth time that day. It was not his son. That would have been hard, but he would have been content that his child had lived with his wife even for a short time in Semberholme. But there was nothing there for Arafel, and he could only guess that their son had gone on to live out his days in some other place. He hoped so, anyway.

The second marker in the glade was the stone for Sorenna's husband, Ildrethor. He laughed softly at himself, even as tears gathered in his eyes.

"I would have told her not to mourn me," he said to the clearing. "I would not have wanted her to be alone for the rest of her days. But now I see that I wouldn't have meant it."

The strange thing was, he could almost remember a glimpse of Arvandor in his heart. He had been with her there, hadn't he? And he had not known jealousy, or resentment, or anything other than love in the eternal glades of the Elvenhome . . . or had he?

He looked up into the daylight streaming down through the trees, and his tears ran freely.

"Is that why I came back?" he asked. "Is this the thing I am supposed to make right, Corellon? I am a warrior. That is all. Why have you done this to me?"

He stood there for a long time, trying to make sense out of something so strange, so bittersweet and sorrowful that he could not begin to fold it within his heart. But after a time his heart did not ache so much, and the sunlight on his face felt warm and good.

He looked down at the stone markers again, and he understood that his former life was no more. He had been given a new one, and he could not use it to live the old, could he? Not after six hundred years.

With a sigh, Fflar turned his back on the silent stones. The Crusade, battered and bloodied but still intact, was encamped not far off, and he would be missed before much longer. He picked up Keryvian and slung it over his shoulder, and he left Sorenna's glade forever.

Dramatis Personae

Creatures of the Lower Planes

Demons
   (tanar'ri), a race of malevolent supernatural beings from the Abyss.

Devils
   (baatezu), a race of malevolent supernatural beings from the Nine Hells.

Yugoloths
   A race of malevolent supernatural creatures from the other lower planes.

Mezzoloth
   A type of yugoloth.

Nycaloth
   A powerful type of yugoloth.

Vrock
   A winged vulture-demon.

Glabrezu
   A huge, four-armed demon with deadly magical powers.

Hezrou
   A hulking, froglike demon.

Osyluth
   (bone devil), a lean, skeletal devil with a deadly sting.

Gelugon
   (ice devil), a bipedal, insectoid devil with terrible cold powers.

Elvish Phrases

Aillesel seldarie
(ale-LEH-sell sell-DAHR-ee) An ancient prayer translated as "may the Seldarine save us."

Seneirril Tathyr
(seh-NAYR-rill tah-THEER) The Mooncrescent Order.

kileaarna reithirghir
(kih-lee-ARE-nah rye-THIRR-gur) The Unjoining.

telmiirkara neshyrr
(tel-MIRR-kar-ah neh-SHEER) The rite of transformation.

mythaalniir darach
(mih-THALL-neer dah-RACK) The spell of mythal shaping.

Ancient Folk

Fflar Starbrow Melruth
A captain of Myth Drannor.

Elkhazel Miritar
An officer of Myth Drannor.

Olortynnal
(oh-LORE-tin-nall), Arms-Major of Myth Drannor.

Selorn
Arms-Captain of Myth Drannor.

Demron
A mage of Myth Drannor.

Ithraides
Grand Mage of Arcorar.

Kaeledhin
(kay-LEH-thln), an ally of Ithraides.

Morthil
A star elf and ally of Ithraides.

Sanathar
An ally of Ithraides.

Sorenna
Fflar's wife.

Saelethil Dlardrageth
(say-LEH-thill dlar-DRAY-geth), an evil daemonfey high mage of Arcorar.

Folk of Evermeet

Philaerin
(fi-LAY-rin), Eldest of the Circle of Reilloch Domayr, deceased.

Aeramma Durothil
(ay-RAHM-mah), a high mage of Reilloch Domayr, deceased.

Kileontheal
(kil-ee-AWN-thee-all), sun elf, a high mage of Reilloch Domayr.

Isilfarrel
(IS-ill-FAHR-rell), moon elf diviner and high mage.

Haldreithen
(hah-DRAY-ith-en), sun elf lorekeeper and high mage.

Anfalen
(ann-FAH-lenn), moon elf high mage.

Amlaruil Moonflower
(AHM-lah-ruil), Queen of Evermeet.

Quastarte
(kwah-STAR-teh), a loremaster of Reilloch Domayr.

Zaltarish
Ancient sun elf scribe and advisor to Queen Amlaruil

Keryth Blackhelm
A moon elf warrior, commander of Evermeet's defenses.

Selsharra Durothil
A sun elf matron of house Durothil.

Breithel Olithir
(bray-THELL), Grand Mage of Evermeet, sun elf.

Meraera Silden
(meh-RAY-rah), a moon elf merchant, Speaker of Leuthilspar.

Ammisyll Veldann
(AHM-miss-ill), sun elf, Lady of Nimlith.

Emardin Elsydar
(eh-MARR-din) sun elf, High Admiral of the fleet.

Nera Muirreste
Widow of Elvath Muirreste.

Folk of Aglarond and Sildëyuir

Jorin Kell Harthan
A half-elf ranger of the Yuirwood.

Phaeldara
(fail-DAH-rah), apprentice to the Simbul and regent over Aglarond in her absence.

Nesterin Deirr
(neh-STER-in deh-EER), a star elf bard.

Tessaernil Deirr
(teh-SARE-nil deh-EER), a star elf lord.

Jaressyr
A gate captain of Tower Deirr.

Leissera Aerilpé
(ley-SER-ah air-ill-PAY), a cousin of Nesterin.

Ilthor
Captain of *Windsinger*.

Araevin's Companions

Maresa Rost
A genasi.

Brant
An aspirant in the Order of the Aster, deceased.

Grayth Holmfast
A Dawnlord in the Order of the Aster, deceased.

Donnor Kerth
Dawnmaster of the Temple of Lathander.

Daemonfey and Fey'ri

Sarya Dlardrageth
  (SAR-ya dlar-DRAY-geth), queen of the daemonfey.

Xhalph Dlardrageth
  (zalf dlar-DRAY-geth), a prince of the daemonfey.

Vesryn Aelorothi
  (vez-RIN ale-oh-ROTH-ee), spymaster for Sarya.

Nurthel Floshin
  A fey'ri lord, deceased.

Teryani Ealoeth
  (ter-YAH-nee eel-OH-eth), a highborn fey'ri spy and assassin.

Mardeiym Floshin
  (mar-DIME FLO-shin), a high captain of the fey'ri.

Jasrya Aelorothi
  (jazz-REE-ah ale-oh-ROTH-ee), a high lady of the fey'ri.

Alysir Ursequarra
  (AL-ee-sirr ur-seh-KWAR-ah), a high lady of the fey'ri.

Senda Dereth
  A disguise for Sarya.

Terian
  A disguise for Teryani.

Alphon
  A disguise for Xhalph.

Deities and Powers

Malkizid
  A fallen solar and exiled archdevil.

Akadi
  The elemental deity of the air.

Sehanine Moonbow
  Elf deity of the moon.

Corellon Larethian
  Lord of the elven pantheon.

Labelas Enoreth
  Elf deity of time.

Seiveril's Crusade

Seiveril Miritar
  (say-VERR-ill), sun elf Lord of Elion and a high priest of Corellon Larethian.

Lord Elvath Muirreste
  A knight in Seiveril's service, deceased.

Thilesil
  A priestess of Corellon and Seiveril's aide-de-camp.

Jorildyn
  (joe-RIL-dihn), a half-elf mage of Tower Reilloch.

Vesilde Gaerth
  (veh-SILL-deh Gayrth), Knight-Commander in Corellon's temple.

Jerreda Starcloak
  (jeh-REH-dah), a leader of the wood elves in Seiveril's Crusade.

Ferryl Nimersyl
(FER-rill nih-MER-sill), captain of the Moon Knights and a leader in the Crusade.

Adresin
(ah-DREY-sin), a knight of the Golden Star and Seiveril's guard captain.

Edraele Muirreste
(eh-DRAY-leh mur-REST-eh), captain of the Silver Guard and a leader in the Crusade.

Daeron Sunlance
(DAY-ron), captain of the Eagle Knights.

Rhaellen Darthammel
(RAIL-len dar-THAM-mell), Blade-Major of Evereska.

Keldith Oericel
(KELL-dith OAR-ih-sell), a high captain in the Crusade.

Felael Springleap
(feh-LAYL), a wood elf captain.

Folk of Cormanthor and the Dales

Theremen Ulath
Lord of Deepingdale.

Ilmeth
Lord of Battledale.

Storm Silverhand
Bard of Shadowdale, Chosen of Mystra.

Mourngrym Amcathra
Lord of Shadowdale.

Maalthiir
   First Lord of Hillsfar.

Hardil Gearas
   High Warden of Hillsfar.

Borstag Duncastle
   A merchant-lord of Sembia.

Scyllua Darkhope
   Castellan and captain of Zhentil Keep.

Fzoul Chembryl
   Tyrant of Zhentil Keep.

Perestrom
   A Zhentarim wizard and leader of the Lords of the Black Wyrm adventuring company.

Curnil
   A Rider of Mistledale.

Ingra
   A Rider of Mistledale.

Rethold
   A Rider of Mistledale.

Dessaer
   Half-elf Lord of Elventree.

Haresk Malorn
   High Councilor of Mistledale.

Miklos Selkirk
   Leader of the Silver Ravens and son of Overmaster Kendrick Selkirk of Sembia.

FORGOTTEN REALMS®

NEW TALES FROM FORGOTTEN REALMS CREATOR
ED GREENWOOD

THE BEST OF THE REALMS
Book II

This new anthology of short stories by Ed Greenwood, creator of the FORGOTTEN REALMS Campaign Setting, features many old and well-loved classics as well as three brand new stories of high-spirited adventure.

CITY OF SPLENDORS
A Waterdeep Novel

ED GREENWOOD AND ELAINE CUNNINGHAM

In the streets of Waterdeep, conspiracies run like water through the gutters, bubbling beneath the seeming calm of the city's life. As a band of young, foppish lords discovers there is a dark side to the city they all love, a sinister mage and his son seek to create perverted creatures to further their twisted ends. And across it all sprawls the great city itself: brawling, drinking, laughing, living life to the fullest. Even in the face of death.

SILVERFALL
Stories of the Seven Sisters

This paperback edition of *Silverfall: Stories of the Seven Sisters*, by the creator of the FORGOTTEN REALMS Campaign Setting, features seven stories of seven sisters illustrated by seven beautiful pages of interior art by John Foster.

ELMINSTER'S DAUGHTER
The Elminster Series

All her life, Narnra of Waterdeep has wondered who her father is. Now she has discovered that it is no less a person than Elminster of Shadowdale, mightiest mage in all Faerûn. And her anger is as boundless as his power.

www.wizards.com

FORGOTTEN REALMS and its logo are trademarks of Wizards of the Coast, Inc. in the U.S.A. and other countries. ©2005 Wizards.

FORGOTTEN REALMS®

THOMAS M. REID

The author of *Insurrection* and The Scions of Arrabar Trilogy rescues Aliisza and Kaanyr Vhok from the tattered remnants of their assault on Menzoberranzan, and sends them off on a quest across the multiverse that will leave FORGOTTEN REALMS® fans reeling!

THE EMPYREAN ODYSSEY

BOOK I
THE GOSSAMER PLAIN

Kaanyr Vhok, fresh from his defeat against the drow, turns to hated Sundabar for the victory his demonic forces demand, but there's more to his ambitions than just one human city. In his quest for arcane power, he sends the alu-fiend Aliisza on a mission that will challenge her in ways she never dreamed of.

BOOK II
THE FRACTURED SKY

A demon surrounded by angels in a universe of righteousness? How did that become Aliisza's life?

November 2008

BOOK III
THE CRYSTAL MOUNTAIN

What Aliisza has witnessed has changed her forever, but that's nothing compared to what has happened to the multiverse itself. The startling climax will change the nature of the cosmos forever.

Mid-2009

"Reid is proving himself to be one of the best up and coming authors in the FORGOTTEN REALMS universe."
—fantasy-fan.org

FORGOTTEN REALMS, WIZARDS OF THE COAST, and their respective logos are trademarks of Wizards of the Coast, Inc. in the U.S.A. and other countries. ©2007 Wizards.

FORGOTTEN REALMS®

PAUL S. KEMP

"I would rank Kemp among WotC's most talented authors, past and present, such as R. A. Salvatore, Elaine Cunningham, and Troy Denning."
—Fantasy Hotlist

The New York Times best-selling author of *Resurrection* and The Erevis Cale Trilogy plunges ever deeper into the shadows that surround the FORGOTTEN REALMS® world in this Realms-shaking new trilogy.

THE TWILIGHT WAR

BOOK I
SHADOWBRED
It takes a shade to know a shade, but will take more than a shade to stand against the Twelve Princes of Shade Enclave. All of the realm of Sembia may not be enough.

BOOK II
SHADOWSTORM
Civil war rends Sembia, and the ancient archwizards of Shade offer to help. But with friends like these...

September 2007

BOOK III
SHADOWREALM
No longer content to stay within the bounds of their magnificent floating city, the Shadovar promise a new era, and a new empire, for the future of Faerûn.

May 2008

Anthology
REALMS OF WAR
A collection of all new stories by your favorite FORGOTTEN REALMS authors digs deep into the bloody history of Faerûn.

January 2008

FORGOTTEN REALMS, WIZARDS OF THE COAST, and their respective logos are trademarks of Wizards of the Coast, Inc. in the U.S.A. and other countries.
©2007 Wizards.

FORGOTTEN REALMS®

PHILIP ATHANS

The New York Times best-selling author of *Annihilation* and *Baldur's Gate* tells an epic tale of vision and heartbreak, of madness and ambition, that could change the map of Faerûn forever.

THE WATERCOURSE TRILOGY

BOOK I
WHISPER OF WAVES

The city-state of Innarlith sits on one edge of the Lake of Steam, just waiting for someone to drag it forward from obscurity. Will that someone be a Red Wizard of Thay, a street urchin who grew up to be the richest man in Innarlith, or a strange outsider who cares nothing for power but has grand ambitions all his own?

BOOK II
LIES OF LIGHT

A beautiful girl is haunted by spirits with dark intentions, an ambitious senator sells more than just his votes, and all the while construction proceeds on a canal that will alter the flow of trade in Faerûn.

BOOK III
SCREAM OF STONE

As the canal nears completion, scores will be settled, power will be bought and stolen, souls will be crushed and redeemed, and the power of one man's vision will be the only constant in a city-state gone mad.

"Once again it is Philip Athans moving the FORGOTTEN REALMS to new ground and new vibrancy."
—R.A. Salvatore

FORGOTTEN REALMS, WIZARDS OF THE COAST, and their respective logos are trademarks of Wizards of the Coast, Inc. in the U.S.A. and other countries.
©2007 Wizards.

FORGOTTEN REALMS

THE KNIGHTS OF MYTH DRANNOR

A brand new trilogy by master storyteller

ED GREENWOOD

Join the creator of the FORGOTTEN REALMS® world as he explores the early adventures of his original and most celebrated characters from the moment they earn the name "Swords of Eveningstar" to the day they prove themselves worthy of it.

BOOK I
SWORDS OF EVENINGSTAR

Florin Falconhand has always dreamed of adventure. When he saves the life of the king of Cormyr, his dream comes true and he earns an adventuring charter for himself and his friends. Unfortunately for Florin, he has also earned the enmity of several nobles and the attention of some of Cormyr's most dangerous denizens.
Now available in paperback!

BOOK II
SWORDS OF DRAGONFIRE

Victory never comes without sacrifice. Florin Falconhand and the Swords of Eveningstar have lost friends in their adventures, but in true heroic fashion, they press on. Unfortunately, there are those who would see the Swords of Eveningstar pay for lives lost and damage wrecked, regardless of where the true blame lies.

August 2007

BOOK III
THE SWORD NEVER SLEEPS

Fame has found the Swords of Eveningstar, but with fame comes danger. Nefarious forces have dark designs on these adventurers who seem to overturn the most clever of plots. And if the Swords will not be made into their tools, they will be destroyed.

August 2008

FORGOTTEN REALMS, WIZARDS OF THE COAST, and their respective logos are trademarks of Wizards of the Coast, Inc. in the U.S.A. and other countries.
©2007 Wizards.

FORGOTTEN REALMS®

R.A. SALVATORE
The New York Times best-selling author and one of fantasy's most powerful voices.

DRIZZT DO'URDEN
The renegade dark elf who's captured the imagination of a generation.

THE LEGEND OF DRIZZT
Updated editions of the FORGOTTEN REALMS® classics finally in their proper chronological order.

BOOK I
HOMELAND
Now available in paperback!

BOOK II
EXILE
Now available in paperback!

BOOK III
SOJOURN
Now available in paperback!

BOOK IV
THE CRYSTAL SHARD
Now available in paperback!

BOOK V
STREAMS OF SILVER
Now available in paperback!

BOOK VI
THE HALFLING'S GEM
Coming in paperback, August 2007

BOOK VII
THE LEGACY
Coming in paperback, April 2008

BOOK VIII
STARLESS NIGHT
Now available in deluxe hardcover edition!

BOOK IX
SIEGE OF DARKNESS
Now available in deluxe hardcover edition!

BOOK X
PASSAGE TO DAWN
Now available in deluxe hardcover edition!

BOOK XI
THE SILENT BLADE
Now available in deluxe hardcover edition!

BOOK XII
THE SPINE OF THE WORLD
Deluxe hardcover, December 2007

BOOK XIII
SEA OF SWORDS
Deluxe hardcover, March 2008

FORGOTTEN REALMS, WIZARDS OF THE COAST, and their respective logos are trademarks of Wizards of the Coast, Inc. in the U.S.A. and other countries. ©2007 Wizards.

FORGOTTEN REALMS

You cannot escape them, you cannot conquer them,
you can only hope to survive...

THE DUNGEONS

DEPTHS OF MADNESS
Erik Scott de Bie
Twilight awakes in the dungeon of a deranged wizard surrounded by strangers as lost as she is. Twisted magic and deadly traps stand between her and escape, and threaten to drive Twilight mad—if she lives long enough....

THE HOWLING DELVE
Jaleigh Johnson
Meisha returns to find her former master insane, and sealed in his dungeon home by Shadow Thieves. She must escape, but her survival isn't enough: she must also rescue the mentor she left behind.

STARDEEP
Bruce R. Cordell
The seals that imprison an eldritch wizard within his prison are breaking down, and the elves scramble to find the reason before the wizard's nightmarish revolution begins.

November 2007

CRYPT OF THE MOANING DIAMOND
Rosemary Jones
When an avalanche of stone traps siegebreakers undermining the walls of a captured city, their only hope lies deep within the tunnels. With water rising around them, and an occupying army waiting above them, will they be able to escape alive?

December 2007

FORGOTTEN REALMS, WIZARDS OF THE COAST, and their respective logos are trademarks of Wizards of the Coast, Inc. in the U.S.A. and other countries.
©2007 Wizards.